DATE DUE

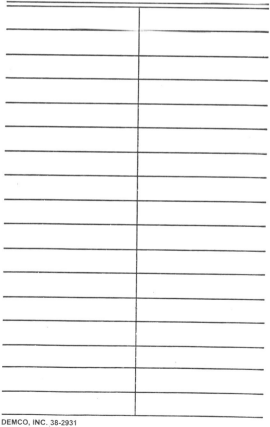

(GALAXY BLUES)

NOVELS BY ALLEN STEELE

NEAR-SPACE SERIES
Orbital Decay
Clarke County, Space
Lunar Descent
Labyrinth of Night
A King of Infinite Space

The Jericho Iteration
The Tranquillity Alternative
OceanSpace
ChronoSpace

COYOTE TRILOGY
Coyote
Coyote Rising
Coyote Frontier

COYOTE UNIVERSE
Spindrift
Galaxy Blues

COLLECTIONS BY ALLEN STEELE

Rude Astronauts
All-American Alien Boy
Sex and Violence in Zero-G: The Complete "Near Space" Stories
American Beauty

NONFICTION BY ALLEN STEELE

Primary Ignition: Essays 1997–2001

(GALAXY) BLUES

ALLEN STEELE

ACE BOOKS, NEW YORK

THE BERKLEY PUBLISHING GROUP
Published by the Penguin Group
Penguin Group (USA) Inc.
375 Hudson Street, New York, New York 10014, USA
Penguin Group (Canada), 90 Eglinton Avenue East, Suite 700, Toronto, Ontario M4P 2Y3, Canada
(a division of Pearson Penguin Canada Inc.)
Penguin Books Ltd., 80 Strand, London WC2R 0RL, England
Penguin Group Ireland, 25 St. Stephen's Green, Dublin 2, Ireland (a division of Penguin Books Ltd.)
Penguin Group (Australia), 250 Camberwell Road, Camberwell, Victoria 3124, Australia
(a division of Pearson Australia Group Pty. Ltd.)
Penguin Books India Pvt. Ltd., 11 Community Centre, Panchsheel Park, New Delhi—110 017, India
Penguin Group (NZ), 67 Apollo Drive, Rosedale, North Shore 0632, New Zealand
(a division of Pearson New Zealand Ltd.)
Penguin Books (South Africa) (Pty.) Ltd., 24 Sturdee Avenue, Rosebank, Johannesburg 2196, South Africa

Penguin Books Ltd., Registered Offices: 80 Strand, London WC2R 0RL, England

This is an original publication of The Berkley Publishing Group.

This is a work of fiction. Names, characters, places, and incidents either are the product of the author's imagination or are used fictitiously, and any resemblance to actual persons, living or dead, business establishments, events, or locales is entirely coincidental. The publisher does not have any control over and does not assume any responsibility for author or third-party websites or their content.

Copyright © 2007 by Allen Steele.
Published in serial form in *Asimov's Science Fiction*.
Illustration by Rob Caswell and Allen Steele.
Text design by Laura K. Corless.

First edition: April 2008

Library of Congress Cataloging-in-Publication Data

Steele, Allen M.
  Galaxy blues / Allen Steele.—1st ed.
    p. cm.
  ISBN 978-0-441-01564-1
  1. Interplanetary voyages—Fiction. 2. Outer space—Exploration—Fiction. 3. Space colonies—Fiction. I. Title.

  PS3569.T338425G36   2008
  813'.54—dc22   2007052054

PRINTED IN THE UNITED STATES OF AMERICA

10 9 8 7 6 5 4 3 2 1

For Linda . . .
Wife. Lover. Ambulance driver.

(CONTENTS)

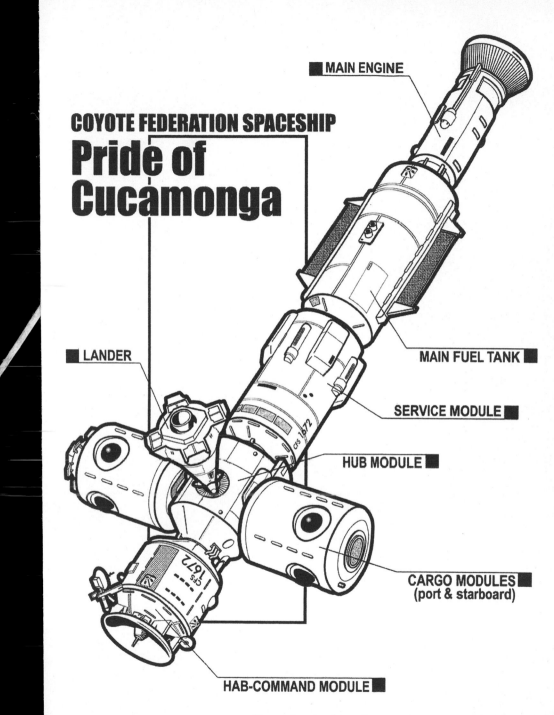

MAIN ENGINE

COYOTE FEDERATION SPACESHIP
Pride of
Cucamonga

MAIN FUEL TANK

LANDER

SERVICE MODULE

HUB MODULE

CARGO MODULES
(port & starboard)

HAB-COMMAND MODULE

Illustration by Rob Caswell. Design by Allen Steele.

(PART 1)

Down and Out on Coyote

(ONE)

The narrative begins . . .

our protagonist leaves Earth, in a rather illicit manner . . .

subterfuge and the art of baseball . . .

fashion tips for stowaways . . .

suspicious minds.

I

My name is Jules Truffaut, and this is the story of how I redeemed the human race.

It pretty much happened by accident. At the very least, it wasn't something I intended to do. But life is that way sometimes. We make our own luck, really, even when we don't mean to.

II

Perhaps it's best that we start at the beginning, the day I came aboard the CFSS *Robert E. Lee*. Not as a crew member, despite the fact that I was qualified to serve as a junior officer, nor as a passenger, although I'd gone to the considerable trouble and expense of acquiring a first-class ticket. Instead, circumstances forced me to become a stowaway . . . but we'll get to that later.

Hitching a ride aboard a starship isn't easy. Takes a lot of advance preparation. I'd been on Highgate for nearly ten months, working as a longshoreman, before I managed to get myself assigned to the section of Alpha Dock where ships bound for Coyote were berthed. I'd taken the job under a false identity, just the same way I'd got on the station in the first place. According to my phony ID, purchased on the black market back home in the Western Hemisphere Union, my name was Lucius Guthrie, and I was just one more guy who'd left Earth in hopes of getting a decent job in space. So I schlepped freight for six months before the foreman—with whom I'd spent a lot of time in the bar, with yours truly picking up the tab—determined that I was capable of operating one of the pods that loaded cargo containers aboard ships bound for Mars and the Jovian moons. I did my job well enough that, two months later, he reassigned me to take care of the *Lee* when it returned from 47 Ursae Majoris.

Which was exactly what I wanted, but even then I was careful not to make my move before I was good and ready. I only had one shot at this. If I screwed up, my true identity would doubtless be revealed and I would be deported to the WHU, after which I'd spend the rest of my life in a lunar penal colony. I couldn't let that happen, so my next step was to cultivate a friendship with a member of the *Lee*'s crew while he was on shore leave. Like my boss, I plied him with drinks and massaged his ego until he agreed to satisfy my curiosity by sneaking me aboard for an unauthorized tour. Pretending to be nothing more than a wide-eyed yokel—*gee, this ain't nuthin' like one of 'em Mars ships!*—I memorized every detail of its interior, comparing what I saw against what I'd gleaned from engineering docs.

Two days later, the *Robert E. Lee* left port, heading out once more for Coyote. Two weeks after that, it returned again, right on schedule. Another two weeks went by, and then it was ready to make the trip again. That was when I put my plan into motion.

So there I was, seated within the cockpit of a cargo pod, gloved hands wrapped around the joysticks of its forward manipulators. I couldn't see much through the wraparound portholes—my view was restricted by the massive container I was loading aboard the *Lee*—yet my radar and side-mounted cams told me that the vessel lay directly below me, its cargo hold yawning open like a small canyon. All I had to do was slide this last container into place, and . . .

"X-Ray Juliet Two-Four, how are we looking?" The voice of Alpha Dock's traffic controller came through my headset. *"Launch in T minus twenty-two and counting. You got a problem there?"*

Nag, nag, nag. That's all traffic controllers ever did. Sure, they had their own schedule to keep, but still . . . well, one of the things I liked the most about my scheme was that it gave me a chance to use their insufferableness against them. A bit of revenge for ten months of henpecking.

"Negatory, Trafco. Putting the last container to bed now." I tapped the sole of my right boot ever so slightly against the starboard RCS pedal. This caused the reaction-control system to roll the pod a few degrees to the left. "Aw, hell," I said, even as I compensated by nudging the left pedal. "Damn thing's getting flaky on me again."

The thrusters worked fine, but no one would know it until the maintenance crew took them apart. I'd been playing this game for the last couple of hours, though, complaining that something was wrong with the pod, thereby establishing an alibi for the precious few moments I would need.

"Bring it in when your shift's over." The traffic controller was impatient. *"Just load the can and get out of there. Lee's on final countdown."*

"Roger that." The truth of the matter was that I had perfect control of my craft. Handling a cargo pod was child's play for someone who'd been trained by the Union Astronautica to fly Athena-class shuttles. But in my role as Lucius Guthrie, I had to make this job seem more difficult than it actually was. "I'm on it. Tell *Lee* not to hold the count for me."

A short pause. The controller was doubtless on another channel, discussing the situation with *Lee*'s bridge crew. *Just a small problem with one of our pods. Pilot says he's getting it worked out.* Meanwhile, I continued to descend slowly toward the starship. A few seconds later, I heard Trafco again. *"We copy, X-Ray Juliet Two-Four. Don't stop for a coffee break."*

"Wilco." I smiled. Fly ball to center, outfielder caught napping. All I had to do was make it to first base.

I carefully guided the container into *Lee*'s hold, where it would join the nine others already aboard. Keeping an eye on the comp, I took a quick look around. As I expected, the hold was deserted. The two other pods that had assisted me earlier were gone, and with the countdown this close to zero, the crew member assigned to overseeing the load-in—who just happened to be the fellow who'd shown me around the ship—would have already cycled through the airlock so that he could get out of his suit before the captain sounded general quarters. Just as he'd told me he usually did.

So I was alone. My suit was sealed, the cockpit depressurized. I felt a slight bump as latches on either side of the hold seized the container and locked it into place. A double beep from my console confirmed this. Safe on first, and the ball still in the outfield.

"All right, it's in." I reached forward, typed a command into the navigation subsystem. "Gimme a sec, and I'm outta here."

I grabbed the horseshoe bar of my chest restraint, pushed it upward. A stab of the thumb against the buckle of my waist strap released me from my seat. Floating free within the cockpit, my own private countdown under way. *Four . . . three . . . two . . . one . . .*

Obeying the preset program I'd surreptitiously entered into the comp, the pod's manipulators released the canister. A moment later, the RCS fired a brief burst lasting only a second. Through the forward porthole, I saw the canister slowly receding as the pod moved away.

"Roger that, X-Ray Juliet Two-Four," Trafco said. *"You're looking good."*

No doubt I was. A camera within the forward bulkhead monitored everything I was doing, its image relayed to both the traffic controller and a junior officer aboard *Lee's* flight deck. Everyone was ready to relax; the last container was loaded, and once my pod was clear of the hold, the crew would shut the hatch.

"Copy, Trafco," I replied. "I'm . . . aw, damn!"

Right on the dot, the pesky starboard RCS thruster misfired again, once more rolling the pod around. This time, though, the accident caused my pod to pitch forward so that the bottom of its hull faced the camera.

And that was when I popped the canopy hatch and bailed out.

III

I love baseball. It's a game that seems relaxed, almost effortless, yet as with any great performance art, timing is everything. When a player steals second, for instance, he has to pick that moment when the pitcher is looking the other way. Sometimes that occurs in the split second after the ball has left the mound. That's when the guy on first makes his move.

Although I'd worked over this part of my plan to the last detail, a dress rehearsal had been impossible. So my heart was pumping as I pulled myself free of the cockpit. Grabbing hold of a fuselage rung,

I twisted myself around until I was able to slam the hatch shut with my free hand.

"X-Ray Juliet! What's going on out there?"

I kept my mouth shut, and a moment later I heard my own voice through the headset. *"Hang on, it's just that damn thing again. I'm . . . okay, here it goes . . ."*

That was my cue. I kicked myself away from the pod, careful to keep it between me and the camera. Perhaps there would be a minor, telltale perturbation caused by my kickoff, but I was counting on it being corrected by the pod's thrusters. I didn't look back to check as I sailed toward the containers neatly arranged in triple-stacked rows just below me. They were less than twenty-five feet away, yet I knew that I was exposed, if only for a few seconds. With any luck, though, anyone watching the screens would be too distracted by the runaway pod to notice what was going on in the background.

I just managed to insert myself into a four-foot gap between two of the topmost containers when I heard Trafco again. *"All right, roger that, Two-Four. Get out of there and bring it home. We'll have someone . . ."*

"Thanks. Sorry about that." My prerecorded voice cut off the controller before he was finished. *"Need to take a breather here. X-Ray Juliet Two-Four out."*

I let out my breath. From my hiding place between the containers, I looked up to see the pod rising from the hold. The autopilot would safely guide it back to its port within Alpha Dock; in the meantime, any further queries from Trafco would be met with my own voice, saying noncommittal things like *we copy* or *roger that*. The pod's polarized windows wouldn't reveal that its cockpit was vacant, and if Lady Fortune continued to stay on my side, no one in the maintenance crew would check out XRJ-24 for at least ten or fifteen minutes after it docked. Even then, it was a safe bet that it would be a while before anyone put two and two together as to why Lucius Guthrie was AWOL. At least not until they checked the bar where I hung out, and that might take some time. The foreman was a nice guy, but he wasn't all that swift.

Wedging myself between the containers, I used my wrist unit to access the primary com channel. For the next couple of minutes, I eavesdropped on the chatter between the *Lee* and Highgate controllers. No sign that my trick had been detected. Cool beans. I was safe on second.

Exactly two minutes after I made my escape, I felt a vibration against my back and the soles of my boots. Looking up through my helmet faceplate, I watched the enormous doors slowly lower into place. The moment they shut, the interior floodlights shut down, and the hold was plunged into darkness.

I was still wary of the camera, though, so I didn't switch on the suit lights. Instead, I opened a pocket on my left thigh and pulled out a small UV penlight. Lowering my helmet visor, I activated its ultraviolet filter, then used the light to guide myself, hand over hand, between the containers until I reached the airlock in the forward bulkhead.

The airlock was already depressurized, just as I expected. Climbing into the tiny compartment, I shut the hatch behind me. A glance at the heads-up display on my faceplate: less than twenty seconds to spare. Grasping elastic loops on the walls and tucking the toes of my boots within the foot restraint, I braced myself for MCFA.

I couldn't hear the warning bells, but the Millis-Clement field activated on schedule. Gravity returned as an abrupt sensation of weight, welcome after two and a half hours of zero g. Even as my boots settled against the floor, though, I detected a faint rumble through the deck plates. The *Lee* was being released from its berth; in another moment, tugs would begin hauling the starship through the mammoth sphere of Alpha Dock, guiding it toward the giant hangar doors that had confined the vessel until then.

Time to make a run for third. Unsnapping a shoulder pocket, I pulled out a miniature tool kit. Within it was a small flat-head screwdriver that I used to pry open the service panel beneath the airlock controls. Part of my preparation included learning how to circumvent the internal sensors; it took less than a minute to locate the proper wire, which I cut with a penknife. That done, I'd be able to pressurize the airlock without anyone on the bridge taking notice.

The tugs had detached their cables and peeled away from the *Lee* when a green lamp on the airlock panel lit, telling me that the compartment was fully pressurized. I released my suit's collar latch and pulled off my helmet, then went about removing the rest of my suit. Beneath it were ordinary clothes: dress shirt and cravat, travel jacket, trousers, and a thick pair of socks. All woven from cotton microfiber, they provided almost as much warmth as the single-piece undergarment I normally wore inside my suit, albeit without the luxury of internal waste-removal systems; for that, I'd taken the precaution of not eating or drinking for two hours before I went on duty.

From the thigh pocket of my discarded suit, I pulled out a pair of faux-leather boots. I put them on, then stood erect and checked my appearance in the glass window of the inner hatch. What I saw pleased me: a young guy in his early twenties, well dressed and obviously wealthy, but otherwise inconspicuous. Not an immigrant or a tradesman, but rather the sort of person who'd have enough money to spend on a vacation to the new world. No one would guess that I was a former Union Astronautica officer desperate enough to escape from Earth to stow away aboard a starship with little more than the clothes on my back.

Yet I was more than what I wore. Once again, I patted the inside pocket of my jacket. The documents I'd need to prove my identity were there, along with L2,000 that I had converted into colonial dollars—C1,200 at the current rate of exchange—at the Banque-Americano branch on Highgate just two days ago. These things would come in handy once I reached my destination.

At the moment, I was a stowaway. Very soon, though, I'd play the role of a passenger . . . and once I set foot on Coyote, I'd become a defector.

IV

Four bells through the loudspeaker, followed sixty seconds later by a vibration passing through the floor, told me that the *Lee* had activated its differential drive. The ship was now on the way to rendezvous with Starbridge Earth.

A quick glance through the hatch window to make sure I was alone, then I turned the wheel counterclockwise. Beyond the airlock lay an EVA ready room, its walls lined with suit lockers. I found one that was empty and shoved my suit inside, then eased open the door and peered out.

I was on Deck One, the ship's lowest level, about one-third of the way back from the bow. The central passageway was deserted, yet I knew that it was only a matter of minutes before the captain called an end to GQ and the crew would be able to move about freely. Closing the hatch behind me, I moved quickly down the narrow corridor, heading toward the bow.

From either side of me, I heard voices from behind the closed doors of various compartments. If an encounter was unavoidable, I was prepared to play stupid: *whoops, silly me . . . you mean this isn't the way to the lounge?* Yet I didn't run into any crew members before I found the ladder leading to Deck Two. A quick jog up the steps, and from there it was a short walk down another passageway until I reached the hatch to the passenger section.

I peeked through the window. No one in sight. I took a moment to straighten my cravat and run my fingers through my hair, then I grasped the wheel. The hatch opened with a faint sigh as I stepped out into the narrow alcove leading to the restrooms. The signs above the doors showed that they were all unoccupied. I quietly opened the door of the nearest one, shut it just loudly enough to be heard, and then commenced down the center aisle.

Before it was seized by the Coyote Federation during Parson's Rebellion—an incident that was something of a coda to the Revolution—the *Robert E. Lee* belonged to the European Alliance, where it'd been known as the EASS *Francis Drake*. Once it was rechristened and became the flagship of Coyote's fledgling navy, the vessel had undergone a major refit that allowed it to serve as the principal means of transportation from Earth to the new world. Although most of Earth's major governments had signed trade and immigration agreements with the Coyote Federation, the easiest way to get to 47 Ursae Majoris was to buy passage aboard the *Lee*. Tickets were cheaper, tariffs were lower, and—provided that one possessed the proper credentials—the customs hassles were fewer.

When I arrived on Highgate ten months ago, I didn't have a ticket, nor did I possess a tourist visa. Circumstances made it impossible for me to obtain either one, or at least not by legal means. Over the course of the last ten months, though, I'd scraped up enough money to buy first-class passage aboard the *Lee*, and the same sources who'd provided me with Lucius Guthrie's identity were happy to do the same again, this time with fake documents proving that I was a gent by name of Geoffrey Carr. The real Geoffrey Carr was a naïve young lad from England who had become stranded on Highgate after failing to make a living as a nightclub comedian. As luck would have it, he'd run into Lucius Guthrie, who'd been willing to provide him with a ticket home in return for a little subterfuge on his part, no questions asked.

So it was Geoffrey Carr who had a private cabin reserved for him aboard the *Lee*, along with the visa that would allow him to pass through customs once he reached Coyote. All he had to do was show up at the right gate at the right time, present his credentials and ticket . . . and once they were scanned, disappear into the loo just before the passengers were allowed to board ship. If Geoff did all that, he'd find a third-class ticket back to Earth waiting for him in my abandoned quarters, along with forged documents that he'd use to establish his identity as Lucius Guthrie.

This was the only part of my plan that depended upon me trusting someone else. I was confident that Geoff wouldn't let me down—in his own way, he was just as desperate as I was— nonetheless, I couldn't help but feel a certain twinge of anxiety as I strolled through the second-class cabin. I distracted myself by sizing up my fellow travelers. Seated four abreast on either side of the aisle, some were immigrants heading for a new life on an-other world; mothers and fathers held their childrens' hands as they gazed through the portholes, taking one last look at the planet they'd once called home. A pair of clergymen in black suits, both wearing the helix-backed crucifixes of Dominionist missionaries. A couple of rich tourists, dressed in expensive clothes, speaking to each other in German. Businesspeople in business suits, studying business notes for business meetings in hopes of making business deals on the new world. And dozens of others, of all nationalities—except, of course, citizens of the Western Hemisphere Union, who were forbidden under law to use space transportation not chartered by the WHU—about whose reasons for being aboard I could only speculate.

I'd almost reached the front of the cabin when a uniformed steward stepped out of the galley. Surprised to see a passenger up and about, her eyes widened when she spotted me. "Sir, what are you doing out of your seat?"

"Very sorry. I had to use the . . . um, facilities." I feigned embarrassment. "Just a little nauseous, I'm afraid," I added, clutching my stomach. "Shouldn't have eaten before coming aboard."

A sympathetic nod, yet her eyes remained suspicious. A quick glance past my shoulder told her that all the second-class seats were occupied. "Where are you supposed to be?"

"That way." I nodded toward the bow. "Cabin . . ."

All of a sudden, I realized that I'd forgotten its number. After everything I'd just been through, that one small detail had slipped my mind. "Sorry, can't recall," I mumbled. "But it's just over here . . ."

I started to step around her, but the steward moved to block my way. "Let me help you. May I see your ticket, please?"

"Of course." I reached into my jacket, pulled out the plastic wafer. There was a scanner attached to her belt. If she used it to examine my ticket, she'd see that, although Geoffrey Carr had passed through the passenger gate, for some reason his ticket hadn't been processed before he entered the pressurized gangway leading to the ship. If that happened, I'd have to hope that my only possible excuse—*someone at the gate neglected to process my ticket; why, is that a problem?*—would be enough to convince her.

Yet the steward didn't unclip her scanner. Instead, she glanced at the name and number printed on the card. "Cabin 4, Mr. Carr," she murmured, then glanced up at me. "Wonder why I didn't see you earlier."

"My mistake." I assayed a weak smile. "Haven't been to my cabin yet. Went straight to the head as soon as I came aboard." I hesitated, then moved a little closer. "You may want to have the other passengers avoid using it for a while. I switched on the fan, but still . . ."

"Yes, right." The steward hastily turned toward the passageway leading to the first-class cabins. "This way, please . . ."

My accommodations were no larger than the airlock I'd cycled through, with barely enough room for two persons. Two seats facing each other across a small table, all of which could be collapsed into the bulkheads to make room for a pair of fold-down bunks. It's questionable whether being able to stretch out and sleep during the sixteen-hour voyage was worth two months' salary as a longshoreman, but the added measure of privacy was priceless. However remote the possibility that I would encounter someone who'd met either (the fake) Lucius Guthrie or (the real) Geoffrey Carr, that was a risk I didn't want to take. Hence the private cabin.

The steward showed me how everything worked, then inquired whether I would like anything from the galley. My throat was dry, so I asked for orange juice. She left, returning a few minutes later with my drink. Another admonishment for not being where I should've been during launch, but this time it was only a mild rebuke, like that given to a mischievous child. I accepted the scolding with good grace, and then she left me in peace, sliding the door shut behind her.

Alone again, I settled back in the forward-facing seat, sipping my OJ as I watched the Moon drift past the starboard window. Too bad I wasn't seated on the other side of the ship; if so, I could have bid Earth a fond farewell. Perhaps it was just as well, though, and maybe even appropriate. I'd turned my back on home a long time ago . . .

Considering this, I couldn't help but chuckle under my breath. No, that wasn't quite right. I had covered the bases. It was about time to steal home.

V

It took nearly six hours for the *Lee* to reach Starbridge Earth. I passed the time by playing solitaire on the table comp, now and then glancing up at the small wallscreen on the bulkhead. It displayed the ship's trajectory as it traveled from Highgate toward the starbridge, with occasional departure-angle views of Earth and the Moon. The steward stopped by to offer the lunch menu. I ordered Swedish meatballs with spinach pasta, and after I ate, I switched on the DO NOT DISTURB light, put my legs up, and took a nap.

A birdlike chirp woke me. I opened my eyes just as a woman's voice came through the wallscreen speaker. *"This is Commodore Tereshkova from the flight deck. We're now on primary approach to the starbridge, with final approach to hyperspace insertion in about ten minutes . . ."*

Realizing who was speaking, I sat up a little straighter. I wondered how many of my fellow travelers recognized the captain's name. Anastasia Tereshkova, former commanding officer of the *Drake* and, before that, the EASS *Columbus*, the first European starship to reach 47 Ursae Majoris. After she'd led the *Drake*'s crew in mutiny against the European Alliance, Captain Tereshkova had defected to the Coyote Federation, where President Gunther had subsequently appointed her commodore of its navy. To be sure, her fleet consisted of one starship and a small collection of shuttles and skiffs, but nonetheless I was surprised that she was still on active duty. Apparently the commodore wasn't ready to hang up her astronaut wings just quite yet.

"As a necessary part of our maneuvers, we will soon deactivate both the main drive and the Millis-Clement field," Tereshkova continued. *"This means that we will lose artificial gravity within the ship. For your safety and comfort, we ask that you return immediately to your seats. Put away all loose items, then fasten your seat straps and make sure that they are secure . . ."*

I located my waist and shoulder straps and buckled them into place. Outside the door, I could hear stewards moving past my cabin.

"Once we enter the starbridge, the transition through hyperspace will take only a few seconds. The entire event will be displayed on your screens. However, if you are prone to vertigo or motion sickness, we strongly recommend that you switch off your screens, lean back in your seats, and close your eyes. Stewards will provide you with eyeshades if you so desire . . ."

The last thing I wanted to miss was going through hyperspace. Yet I could already imagine some of the passengers making sure that vomit bags were within reach, while perhaps regretting that they'd ordered lunch only a few hours ago.

"Once we're through the starbridge, our flight to Coyote will take another ten hours, at which point you will board shuttles for transfer to the New Brighton spaceport. In the unlikely event of an emergency, please be reminded that this ship is also equipped with lifeboats, which may be boarded from Deck One below you. Stewards will escort you to those lifeboats, which in turn will be operated by a crew member . . ."

I couldn't help but snort at this. Although the *Lee* could still serve as a military vessel in a pinch, insurance underwriters on Earth had insisted that, once it was refitted as a civilian transport, certain accommodations had to be provided to ensure the safety of her passengers just in case there was a catastrophic accident. I doubted that the life-boats had been jettisoned since their test flights.

"We will have engine shutdown in four minutes, and commence final approach to the starbridge five minutes after that. For now, though, just relax and enjoy the rest of the ride. Thank you very much."

Tereshkova's voice was replaced by classic jazz—Miles Davis's "Sketches of Spain"—and the image on the screen changed to a forward view: the starbridge, seen as a small silver ring illuminated by moonlight, with red and blue beacons flashing along its outer rim. It had grown to twice its original size when there was a knock on the door.

Before I had a chance to respond, it slid open. Instead of the steward, though, a man about my own age stepped in. He wore the dark blue uniform of a Coyote Federation spacer, the insignia on his shoulder boards telling me that he was the chief petty officer.

"Mr. Carr?" he asked. "Mr. Geoffrey Carr?"

"Yes?" Pretending nonchalance, I gazed back at him. "May I help you?"

"Just want to make sure that you're secure." His gaze flitted about the cabin, as if he was searching for something. "Your belongings all stowed away?"

"Yes, of course." I forced a smile. "Thank you. The service has been excellent."

"Glad to hear it, sir." Another quick glance around the compartment, then he gave me a perfunctory nod. "Be seeing you."

I waited until he shut the door, then I unsnapped my harness and stood up. Moving to the door, I rested an ear against the panel. I heard a voice just outside—the petty officer, speaking to someone else—but the constant thrum of the engines rendered his words unintelligible.

I returned to my seat, fastened my harness again. Perhaps it was only a courtesy call by a senior crew member to a first-class passenger, but I didn't think so. The way he'd studied my cabin . . .

Laying my head against the back of my seat, I stared out the porthole. Safe on third . . . but the catcher had become wise to the play.

Stealing home might be trickier than I thought.

(TWO)

Forty-six light-years in five seconds . . .

trouble comes knocking . . .

a chat with the Commodore . . .

truth and consequences.

VI

I watched through my cabin porthole as Starbridge Earth grew steadily larger, its gatehouse passing by so quickly that I caught little more than a glimpse of the small station that controlled access to the ring. I wasn't able to eavesdrop on communications between the gatehouse and the *Lee*'s bridge, but I knew that, at the five-minute mark, our AI would be slaved to the one aboard the station, ensuring that the *Lee* wouldn't enter the ring until, at T minus sixty seconds, the wormhole was formed.

Once again, I wondered if many of the passengers appreciated the delicate yet infinitely complex ballet of quantum physics that made this miracle possible, or just how much their lives depended upon split-second calculations that only a pair of AIs could make. If everything worked right, the *Lee* would be transported across forty-six light-years in little more than the blink of an eye . . . well, fifteen blinks of an eye, if you really want to nitpick. If anything went wrong, the ship and everyone aboard would be sucked into a singularity and reduced to a stream of subatomic particles . . . at which point, the notion of using lifeboats would be too absurd to even deserve a laugh.

I tried not to think about this, and instead sought solace in the fact that no ship had yet suffered such a fate. Even if I was in the command center—which is the place where I really belonged, not sitting in first-class—there would have been little that I could've done. So I grasped my chair armrests and took slow, deep breaths as I continued to watch the monitor.

The chronometer at the bottom of the screen had just reached the sixty-second mark when, from within the center of the ring, there was a brilliant flash of defocused light. I winced and involuntarily raised a hand to my eyes, but not before I had a retinal afterimage of every color of the visible spectrum, swirling around each other as if caught in the cosmic whirlpool of the wormhole's event horizon.

And then the remorseless hand of gravity shoved me back in my seat, and the *Robert E. Lee* plunged into the maelstrom.

VII

The transition through hyperspace was as violent as it was swift. I tried to keep my eyes open. Really. I wanted to see what it was like, to be shot through a wormhole like a bullet down the barrel of God's own gun, but maybe there are some things that the Great Spirit just doesn't want us to see. In any event, my eyes squeezed shut as, for the next few seconds, reality itself seemed to twist inside out. The ship shook so hard, I thought I'd lose a molar or two, and when it turned upside down, I opened my mouth to scream only to find myself unable to breathe. Only the pulse hammering in my ears told me that

I was still alive. So I clutched the armrests and gritted my teeth, and then . . .

It was over. As suddenly as it had begun, the violence ceased.

I opened my eyes, let out my breath. On the screen, all I saw at first were stars, yet even then I noticed that their patterns weren't the same as those I'd seen only a few seconds earlier. I had an urge to retch, but managed to fight it down. Sure, I knew how to keep from throwing up, yet despite years of training and hundreds of flight hours, hyperspace was the most grueling experience I'd ever endured.

The screen changed a few seconds later, this time to depict a schematic diagram of the *Lee* moving away from a different star-bridge. Tereshkova's voice came over the speaker: *"We've successfully made hyperspace transition. Many apologies for any discomfort you may have experienced. We will soon restore internal gravity, and then we'll reactivate the main drive and commence the final leg of our journey. If you require assistance, please alert the nearest steward and they will help you as soon as . . ."*

I ignored the rest. Unfastening my harness, I pushed myself out of my seat and, grabbing hold of a ceiling rung, pulled myself closer to the porthole. The hell with what was on the screen. This was something I had to see for myself.

For a minute or so, I saw nothing but stars, with a white sun shining just beyond my range of vision. Then the *Lee* rolled to port and an immense planet hove into view. Swathed by wide bands of pale blue, violet, and purple upon which nearby moons cast small black shadows, the gas giant was encircled by silver-blue rings, so close that it almost seemed as if I could reach out and touch them.

47 Ursae Majoris-B, the superjovian locally known as Bear. And nearby, illuminated by the sunlight reflected from its outer atmosphere, its inner system of satellites. Dog was the closest, shepherding the rings. Hawk was a little farther out; Eagle was on the other side

of the planet, so I couldn't see it. Yet in the far distance, little more than a small green orb, lay the fourth and most significant of Bear's companions.

Coyote.

Something moist touched the corners of my eyes. I tried to tell myself that they weren't tears, but when I blinked and rubbed at my eyelids, tiny bubbles rose from my face. Yeah, okay, so I'm a big wuss at heart. Perhaps tears were appropriate at that moment, though, just as they'd been for the first person who'd laid eyes upon the new world.

I was there. After all that I'd gone through, all that I'd sacrificed . . . I was *there*.

The ship's bell rang four times, signaling the reactivation of the Millis–Clement field. I grasped the brass rail above the porthole and tucked the toes of my boots within the foot restraint. A minute later, there was a brief sensation of falling as weight returned, then my feet gently settled against the carpeted floor. I released the bar but remained by the window.

If my identity had been discovered, as I suspected, then it wouldn't be long before I knew for sure.

I was right. A few minutes later, there was knock at the door.

VIII

My first impulse was to open it. But that's something Jules Truffaut would've done. Geoffrey Carr, on the other hand, was a spoiled young turk with little zero-g experience; I had to pretend to be him, if only for a little while longer.

"Just a sec!" Pushing myself back to my seat, I buckled the lap strap, then took hold of the shoulder straps and gave them a quick twist and pull that tangled them together around my chest. A few loud obscenities for good effect, then I called out again. "Come on in!"

The door slid open, and I wasn't surprised to see the chief petty officer who'd visited me earlier. "Thank heavens you're here!" I exclaimed, making a show of fighting with the straps. "Why these damn things couldn't have been designed better, I have no idea. Could you please . . . ?"

He coldly regarded me for a moment, then silently nodded to someone in the passageway. Another crewman appeared; my heart sank when I saw that it was the same one whom I'd befriended on Highgate a few weeks earlier. He gazed at me, and I watched as his expression changed from astonishment to anger.

"That's him, Mr. Heflin," he said quietly. "Same guy."

"Thank you, Mr. Marcuse. If you'll wait outside, please." Mr. Heflin stepped into the cabin. "I think you know how to release your harness, Mr. Guthrie. Please don't embarrass yourself by pretending you don't."

I can't tell you how relieved I was to hear this. Not that I wasn't dismayed that I'd been caught—I knew that was coming—but that Mr. Heflin had addressed me by my alias. My *other* alias, that is. This meant that no one had yet matched Lucius Guthrie's biometric profile to that of Jules Truffaut . . . and that meant there was hope for me yet.

"Certainly. Of course." I deftly unsnarled the shoulder harness, then unbuckled the lap strap. "Yes?" I asked, looking back at him again. "May I help you?"

"Commodore wants to see you." He cocked his head toward the door. "Let's go."

I could have made a fuss about this—I'd purchased a ticket, after all, so I was technically a first-class passenger—but I had little doubt that the chief petty officer could've called in a couple more crewmen and had me frog-marched to the bridge. And just then, I wanted to show that I was willing to cooperate. So I stood up and left the cabin without protest. The steward stood in her alcove, her face set in prim disapproval; past her, I caught a glimpse of second-class passengers craning their necks to see what the commotion was all about. Mr. Marcuse had the sullen expression of someone who'd been betrayed; I gave him an apologetic shrug, but he just looked away. I felt sorry for him; it would be a long time before he'd trust anyone during shore leave again.

I was heading down the passageway, with Mr. Heflin behind me and a warrant officer waiting at the hatch, when I spotted another passenger standing in the open door of his cabin. A short, middle-aged man, with a shaved scalp and sharp eyes. He studied me as I walked past, and I was about to dismiss him as another curious by-stander when he favored me with a sly wink. Almost as if he knew something that I didn't.

This was the wrong place and time to strike up a conversation, though, and the warrant officer wasn't interested in letting me make new friends. An unnecessary shove against my shoulder, and I ducked my head slightly to exit the hatch leading from the first-class section. Now I was back in the utilitarian confines of the rest of the ship. Mr. Heflin slammed the hatch shut behind us, then the warrant officer beckoned toward an access shaft. As I began to climb the stairs, I noticed that they went downward as well, leading to Deck One.

A useful bit of knowledge. I tried to keep it in mind.

IX

The bridge was located on Deck Three, within the superstructure that rose above the ship's bow. Although I'd seen photos of the command center during UA intelligence briefings, nonetheless I was surprised by just how small it actually was. A narrow compartment, with major flight stations on either side of a long aisle: very tight, without an inch of wasted space. Nothing like those of the Western Hemisphere Union starships that once journeyed to Coyote at sublight speeds . . . but then again, the Union Astronautica weren't building them anymore, were they?

The captain's chair was located at the opposite end of the bridge, overlooking a split-level subdeck where the helm and navigation stations were located. Commodore Tereshkova was waiting for me; when she stood up, I almost had an urge to ask for an autograph. Or even a date. Sure, she was almost old enough to be my mother, but no command-rank officer in the Union Astronautica ever wore a uniform so well.

Then she turned glacial eyes upon me, and my sophomoric fantasies were forgotten. "Is this our stowaway, Mr. Heflin?"

Before he could respond, I cleared my throat. "Pardon me, but . . ."

"When I want to hear from you, I'll let you know." She looked at her chief petty officer. "Mr. Heflin?"

"Yes, ma'am. Cabin 4, first-class section, just where the passenger manifest said he would be." He paused. "He came quietly, without any resistance."

"And you have no idea how he got aboard?"

"No, ma'am. When Ms. Fawcett double-checked the manifest, she discovered that his ticket hadn't been scanned at the gangway. It was processed at the gate, but not . . ."

"Let me save you a little time," I said. "I slipped aboard through the cargo airlock, right after I ejected from the pod I was driving. If you send a man down to check, he'll find my suit in the ready room. Second locker from the left, if I—"

"We already know you're a longshoreman." Perturbed by the interruption, Tereshkova glared at me. "That we learned when we matched your biometric profile against Highgate's employment records. In fact, we had you pegged as a stowaway even before we went through the starbridge." She returned to Mr. Heflin. "Have someone go down to Airlock Five and see if he's telling the truth."

The chief petty officer nodded, then touched his headset mike and murmured something. "Excuse me, ma'am," I said, "but if you knew I was a stowaway, then . . . ?"

"It took some time." A faint smile. "Your steward became suspicious after she noticed that there were no carry-on bags in your cabin. This was, of course, after she found you wandering around the passenger section. She checked the cargo records, and when she discovered that you hadn't checked any baggage, she alerted the chief petty officer. The two of them accessed the passenger database, and that's when they realized that you weren't the same person who'd checked in at Highgate. So Mr. Heflin pulled up the IDs of everyone who works at the station, and when your face came up, he put it on the crew data screens. Mr. Marcuse recognized you as someone he'd met while on shore leave, and that was when Mr. Heflin decided to pay you a visit."

"But by then," I said, "the ship was already on final approach to the starbridge. Too late to turn back then, right?" She blinked but said nothing. "Well, at least I got that far . . ."

"Too far, so far as I'm concerned. We'll have to review our security procedures." Tereshkova sighed, then resumed her seat. "Good work, Mr. Heflin," she said as she picked up a datapad. "Please extend my compliments to Ms. Fawcett and Mr. Marcuse as well. Now, if you'll summon the warrant officer back to the bridge, I think Mr. Guthrie would like to see his new quarters."

"And you don't want to know why I'd go through so much trouble?" I tried to remain calm, even as I heard Heflin mutter something else into his headset. "After all, I purchased a ticket. That means I'm not a . . ."

"Without bona fide ID or a valid visa, you're whatever I say you are." Tereshkova was quickly losing interest in me. So far as she was concerned, I was little more than a nuisance. "Hope you enjoyed our first-class accommodations. I regret to say that the brig isn't nearly as comfortable."

"My name isn't Lucius Guthrie." Straightening my shoulders, I stood at attention. "I'm Ensign First Class Jules Truffaut, formerly of the Union Astronautica, Western Hemisphere Union. I hereby request political asylum from the Coyote Federation."

Tereshkova's gaze rose from her pad, and the navigator and helmsman darted curious glances at me from over their shoulders. I couldn't see Mr. Heflin, but I could feel his presence as he took a step closer. All at once, the bridge had gone silent, save for the random boops and beeps of the instrument panels.

"Come again?" Heflin asked.

I didn't look back at him. "As I said, sir . . . my name is Jules Truffaut, and I'm a former ensign in the Union Astronautica. My reason for being aboard your ship is that I wish to defect from the Western Hemisphere Union to the . . ."

"Is this true?" Tereshkova's eyes bored into my own. "If you're lying, so help me, I'll put you out the nearest airlock."

"Yes, ma'am. I can prove it." Raising my right hand as slowly as possible, I reached into the inside pocket of my jacket, pulled out my papers. "Copies of my birth certificate, citizen's ID, Union Astronautica service record . . . all here, Commodore." I handed them to her, and went on. "If you check my . . . excuse me, Lucius Guthrie's . . . biometric profile against whatever recent intelligence you have on the Union Astronautica, you'll find that it matches that of Jules Truffaut, who was expelled from the corps a little more than eleven months ago." An ironic smile came to me before I could stop myself. "I prefer to think of it as a forced resignation. Didn't have much choice."

"Uh-huh." Tereshkova unfolded my papers, gave them a brief inspection. "And what led you to make that decision, Mr. Guthrie?"

"Not Guthrie, ma'am . . . Jules Truffaut, as I told you." I hesitated. "It's a long story. I would prefer not to get into details just now."

"I'm sure you would." She studied me with cool skepticism, her hands refolding my papers. "Of course, you realize that your allegation will take some time to investigate. Until then, we'll have to hold you in custody."

"Aboard ship?"

"Of course." A shrug that was almost patronizing. "It's an extraordinary . . . well, an unusual . . . claim you've made, and naturally we will have to look into it further. So until then . . ."

"So you're not willing to take me to Coyote." A chill ran down my back. "Commodore, please . . ."

"I'm sure my government would be willing to consider a petition for amnesty pending a thorough investigation. Until then, you're a stowaway and will be treated as such." She glanced at her chief petty officer. "If you will . . ."

Mr. Heflin grasped my arm. Looking around, I saw that the warrant officer had returned, his right hand resting upon a stunner holstered in his belt. No doubt about it, my next stop was the brig.

There was nothing more to be said. I turned to meekly allow myself to be taken below.

X

So there it was. I'd managed to cover the bases, but when I tried to steal home, the catcher tagged me before I could cross the plate. No sympathy from the ump. It was off to the showers for the rookie.

As Mr. Heflin and the warrant officer escorted me from the bridge, I contemplated my prospects. They didn't look promising. These two men would take me below and lock me in the brig, and there I'd remain for the next couple of weeks, until the *Lee* made the trip back through hyperspace to Earth. If I was lucky, my cell would have a porthole . . . well, no, maybe that wouldn't be so lucky after all. Because the most that I'd see of Coyote would be the distant view of a place that I'd never visit.

I had little doubt of what would happen next. Once we returned to Highgate, the Western Hemisphere Union would be informed that a stowaway had been caught aboard a Coyote Federation starship, and that this person claimed to be a former Union Astronautica officer. A Patriarch would quickly verify this, and make a formal claim of extradition. Under the articles of the UN treaty the Coyote Federation had signed with the WHU, there would be no way for this to be legally contested, because although I'd been nabbed aboard a Coyote vessel, I hadn't yet set foot upon Coyote itself.

That small fact made all the difference in the world. The Coyote Federation was considered to be a sovereign nation, true, but one can only defect to another country if you're already there. And although the *Lee* was under the flag of the Coyote Federation, it wasn't Coyote soil. At least not for someone who wasn't a citizen.

Nor had I given anyone aboard good and sufficient reason to break an international treaty. Like it or not, I was little more than an illegal immigrant who'd managed to con my way aboard the *Lee*, my former rank as a UA officer notwithstanding. If I'd been carrying top-secret documents, the situation might have been different; Tereshkova might have been willing to go to bat for me. But I had nothing but the clothes on my back and a sunny smile, and neither of them cut much ice with her. Nor could I blame her. She had rules by which she had to play, and I was just some schmuck lucky enough to get to third base on a bunt.

But this was just the end of an inning. The game wasn't over yet.

We left the bridge and started down the ladder to the lower decks, Mr. Heflin in front of me and the warrant officer bringing up the rear. The steps were narrow; Heflin had his right hand on the railing, and I was willing to bet that the warrant officer was doing the same. And both of them were relaxed. After all, I'd been a perfect gentleman about this whole thing, giving no one any trouble at all.

I waited until we were about three steps from Deck Two, then I quickened my pace just a little bit. Not enough to alarm the warrant officer, but enough to put me within range of Mr. Heflin. Hearing me come closer, he started to turn to see what I was doing . . . and then I gripped the rail with my right hand and shoved my right foot against the ankle of his left foot.

Heflin tripped and sprawled forward, falling the rest of the way down the ladder. He hadn't yet hit the deck when, still holding the rail tight with my right hand, I threw my left elbow back as hard as I could.

Just as I hoped, I caught the warrant officer square in the chest. He grunted and doubled over, and I twisted around, grabbed hold of his collar, and slammed him against the railing hard enough to knock the wind from his lungs. Gasping for air, he started to fall against me. I let him go and jumped forward, landing on the deck next to Heflin.

By then, the chief petty officer realized what was happening. Raising himself on one elbow, he started to make a grab for me. I hated to do it—he seemed like a pretty decent chap, really—but I kicked him in the head, and down he went.

The warrant officer was beginning to recover. Still on the ladder, he clutched the rail as he sought to regain his feet. I snatched the stunner from his holster before he could get to it, though, and there was the awful look of someone who'd just screwed up when I shot him with his own weapon. He tumbled the rest of the way down the steps, landing almost on top of Heflin.

Hearing a gasp behind me, I looked around to see Ms. Fawcett standing in the hatch leading to the passenger section. For some reason, I didn't have the heart to shoot her even though she posed a threat to my getaway.

"Thanks for the drinks," I said, and then I dove down the ladder to Deck One.

Just as I figured, the lifeboat bays were located directly beneath the passenger section, where they would be easily accessible in case of an emergency. The hatches were on either side of a narrow passageway, tilted downward at a forty-five-degree angle. I was halfway to the nearest one when someone—Ms. Fawcett, no doubt—hit the panic button.

Red lights along the ceiling began to flash as a loud *barrrruuggah-barrrruuggah* came over the speakers. A crewman darted through a hatch at the opposite end of the corridor. He saw me, and his mouth dropped open, but by then I'd grabbed the panel above the lifeboat hatch, wrenched it open, tossed it aside, and found the lock-lever within. A quick yank to the left, and the hatch opened with a hiss of escaping pressure. I jumped into the boat, then turned around and shut the hatch behind me.

No time for the niceties of strapping myself down or making sure that all systems were active. Any second now, either Ms. Fawcett or the crewman who'd seen me would be telling the bridge that their stowaway had made his way to the lifeboats. If I was going to make a clean escape, I'd have to do it before someone in the command center locked them down.

Hauling myself over to the control panel, I jabbed the red JET. button with my thumb, then grabbed a ceiling rail and held on for dear life. A loud whoosh of escaping pressure, the hollow clang of clamps being released, the solid thump of pyros being ignited. Through the round window of the hatch, I saw the cone-shaped cowling of the lifeboat port fall away amid a fine spray of crystallized oxygen and small debris.

A moment later, I caught a last glimpse of the lower hull of the *Robert E. Lee*. Then I began to fall to Coyote.

(THREE)

Aboard the good ship Lou Brock . . .

no coffee for the wicked . . .

coming in on a heat shield and a prayer . . .

wherever it is you think you are, you're not there.

XI

Forget everything you think you know about lifeboats; whatever it is, it's probably wrong. The one I stole from the *Lee* didn't have wings or landing gear, nor did it have particle-beam lasers for fending off space pirates; the first kind is rare, and the latter exists only in fantasy fics. Mine was a gumdrop-shaped capsule, about twenty feet in diameter at its heat shield, that bore a faint resemblance to the moonships of historic times. All it was meant to do was carry six passengers to a more or less safe touchdown on a planetary surface, preferably one that had an atmosphere. Other than that, it was useless.

But it *was* a spacecraft, with a liquid-fuel engine and four sets of maneuvering thrusters, which meant I had nominal control over its guidance and trajectory. And although the *Lee* was still eighty thousand miles from Coyote when I took my unauthorized departure, the boat also had a life-support system sufficient to sustain a half dozen people for up to twelve hours. Therefore, I had enough air, water, heat, and food to keep me alive for three or four days.

So as soon as I was sure that I'd made my getaway, I grabbed hold of the hand rungs upon the ceiling and pulled myself across the cabin. The lifeboat was tumbling end over end by then, but so long as I was careful not to look through the portholes, there was no real sense of vertigo. I reached the pilot's seat and pulled it down from the bulkhead. It was little more than a well-padded hammock suspended within a titanium-alloy frame, but it had a harness and a headrest, and once I strapped myself in, it was much as if I were in a simulator back at the Academy.

The next step was to gain control of my craft. I unfolded the flat-panel console and activated it. The board lit up just as it was supposed to, and I spent the next couple of minutes assessing the status of my vehicle. Once I was sure it was fit to fly, I pulled down the yoke and went about firing reaction-control thrusters, manually adjusting the pitch, roll, and yaw until the lifeboat was no longer in a tumble. The lidar array helped me get a firm fix on Coyote, and the navigation subsystem gave me a precise estimate of where it would be x-times-y-times-z divided by t minus so many hours later. Once I had all that lined up, I entered the data into the autopilot, then pushed a little green button marked EXECUTE.

A hard thump against my back as the main engine ignited. Gazing at the porthole above my head, I watched the starscape swerve to the left. Coyote, still little more than a green orb capped with white blotches at either end, drifted past my range of vision until it finally disappeared altogether. I wasn't heading toward where it was at the time, though, but where it would be. That is, if I hadn't screwed up in programming the comp. And if the comp was in error, then I would be taking a tour of the 47 Ursae Majoris system that would last until the air ran out.

The engine fired for four and a half minutes, giving me a brief taste of gravity, then shut down, causing my body to rise within my harness. I checked the fuel reserves, and muttered a curse under my breath. That maneuver had cost me 42 percent of what was in the tanks; I'd have enough for braking, final course corrections, and atmospheric entry, but practically zero for fudge factor. Like I said, the lifeboat was little more than an uprated version of the cargo pod I'd flown on Highgate. Even the training craft I had piloted at the *Academia del Espacio* was more sophisticated.

In the bottom of the ninth, I'd earned myself another chance at bat. Yet there was no room for strikeouts, and my next foul ball would be my last.

I let out my breath, closed my eyes for a second. Eighteen hours until I reached Coyote. Might as well offer my apologies to the home team. Groping beneath the couch, I found a small packet. I ripped it open and pulled out a cheap headset. Slipping it on, I inserted the prong into the left side of the console, then activated the com system.

"Hello?" I said, tapping the mike wand with my thumb. "Anyone there? Yoo-hoo, do you read?"

Several long moments passed in which I heard nothing, then a male voice came over: *"CFSS* Robert E. Lee *to CFL-101, we acknowledge. Do you copy?"*

"Loud and clear, *Lee*. This is"—I thought about it for a moment—"the *Lou Brock*. We copy."

A few seconds went by. I imagined bridge officers glancing at each other in bewilderment. Then a more familiar voice came online. *"CFL-101, this is Commodore Tereshkova. Please use the appropriate call sign."*

"I *am* using an appropriate call sign." I couldn't help but smile. "Lou Brock. Outfielder for the St. Louis Cardinals. One of the great base-stealers of all time."

While she was trying to figure that one out, I checked the radar. The *Lee* was near the edge of my screen, about eight hundred miles away. So far as I could tell, it was keeping pace with me; I had little doubt that, if Tereshkova ordered her helmsman to do so, the ship could intercept my lifeboat within minutes.

"All right, so you're a baseball fan." When Tereshkova's voice returned, it was a little less formal. *"You're very clever, Mr. Truffaut. I'll give you that. If you'll heave to and allow yourself to be boarded, I'll see what I can do about getting you tickets to a game."*

I shook my head, even though she couldn't see me. "Thanks for the date, Commodore, but I'm going to have to take a rain check. Maybe next time you're in town?"

For a moment, I thought I heard laughter in the background. In the meantime, I was sizing up my fuel situation. If the *Lee* started to close in, I could always fire the main engine again. But I needed to conserve as much fuel as possible for retrofire and atmospheric entry; as things stood, I had barely enough in reserve to do that. The *Lou Brock* was no shuttle, and my margin for error was thin as a razor.

"Ensign, you know as well as I do that this is pointless." The commodore no longer sounded quite so affable. *"My ship is . . ."*

"Faster, sure. No question about it." I switched back to manual override, then raised a forefinger and let it hover above the engine ignition switch. "And *you* know as well as I do that there's no way in hell you can board me if I don't want you to do so. Allow me to demonstrate."

I touched the red button, held it down. A quick surge as the engine fired. I counted to three, barely enough time for the lifeboat's velocity to rise a quarter g, then I released the button. On the screen, the *Lee* had drifted a few millimeters farther away. "See what I mean? Get too close, and I'll do that again."

No answer. If she had any remaining doubts whether I was an experienced spacer, that little display settled them. The *Lee* was capable of overtaking my lifeboat, sure, but her ship didn't have the equipment necessary to latch on to a craft whose pilot was willing to alter delta-V at whim. Not unless she wanted to position her craft directly in front of mine . . . but even if she was foolish enough to do so, my lifeboat would collide with her vessel like a coupe ramming a maglev train.

I'd never do anything like that. For one thing, it would be suicidal; I would die a quick but horrible death. For another, there were also passengers aboard, and the last thing I wanted to do was put their lives in danger. But Commodore Tereshkova didn't know I was bluffing; perhaps she'd realized that I'd just trimmed my fuel reserves by three-quarters of a percent, but there was no guarantee that I wouldn't pull silly crap like that again. And no one but a fool would play chicken with a madman.

The comlink went silent, doubtless while she talked it over with her bridge team and tried to determine if I was the lunatic I seemed to be. While they did that, I took the opportunity to get a new flight profile from the nav subsystem and feed the updated info into autopilot. To my relief, I discovered that all I'd done was shave twenty minutes from my ETA. I'd just let out my breath when Tereshkova's voice returned.

"*All right, ensign. Have it your way, if you must.*" There was an undercurrent of resignation in her voice. "*You may proceed with your present course.*"

"Thank you, Commodore. Glad you see it my way." Another thought came to me. "I meant it when I said that all I want is amnesty. You'll communicate this to your people, won't you?"

"*I'll . . .*" A brief pause. "*I'll ask them to take this into consideration. Lee over.*"

"Thank you, ma'am. *Lou Brock*, over." I waited for another moment, but when I heard nothing more, I switched off the comlink.

All right, then. For better or for worse, I was on my own.

XII

The *Robert E. Lee* remained on my scope for another hour or so, but gradually it veered away, its course taking it farther from my lifeboat. Although I had little doubt that its crew continued to track me, the fact remained that it was a faster ship, and it had its own schedule to keep. Through my porthole, I caught a brief glimpse of its formation lights as it peeled away, its passengers probably enjoying dinner and drinks as they chatted about the minor incident that had occurred shortly after the ship had come out of hyperspace. *Sweetheart, did you hear about the man in Cabin 4 who lost his mind? Don't worry, I'm sure he's been properly dealt with . . . oh, steward? Another glass of wine, please?*

It took another eighteen hours for me to reach Coyote. I didn't have table service; my sustenance was the ration bars I found in the emergency locker, which tasted like stale peanut butter, and tepid water that I sipped from a squeezebulb. I caught catnaps now and then, only to wake up an hour or so later to find my hands floating in front of my face.

Little sleep, then, and no coffee. Not much in the way of entertainment, either, save for a brief skim of the emergency tutorials on the comp, which told me little that I hadn't known before. I sang songs to myself, mentally revisited great ball games and tried to figure out where critical errors had been made—the World Series of '44 between Havana and Seoul was one that I studied more than once—and reviewed my life history in case I ever wanted to write my memoirs.

The rest of the time, I stared out the window, watching Coyote as it gradually came back into view, growing larger with each passing hour. My flight was long enough that I witnessed most of a complete day as it rotated on its axis; what I saw was a planet-size moon a little larger than Mars, lacking oceans but instead crisscrossed by complex patterns of channels, rivers, estuaries, and streams, with a broad river circumscribing its equator. By the time I was scratching at my face and wishing that the emergency kit contained a shaver, I was able to make out geographic features: mountain ranges, volcanoes, tropical savannahs, and rain forests, scattered across subcontinents and islands of all shapes and sizes.

A beautiful world, as close to Earth as anything yet discovered in our little corner of the galaxy. Worth the effort to get there . . . provided, of course, that I didn't end my trip as a trail of vaporized ash following the slipstream of a man-made meteor.

When the lifeboat was about three hundred nautical miles away, the autopilot buzzed, telling me that the time had come for me to take over. By then I was strapped into my couch again. I took a deep breath, murmured the Astronaut's Prayer—"Lord, please don't let me screw up"—then I switched off the autopilot, grasped the yoke, and did my best to put my little craft safely on the ground.

While I was earning my wings in the *Academia del Espacio*, I logged over two hundred hours in simulators and four hundred more in training skiffs. Before I was thrown out of the UA, I'd also flown Athena shuttles, including one landing on Mars. But those were all winged spacecraft, complete with all sorts of stuff like elevators and flaps and vertical stabilizers. As I said, though, the *Lou Brock* was only a lifeboat, and for this sort of thing I'd completed only as much training as I needed to graduate from cadet to ensign: four hours in a simulator, and my flight instructor had forgiven me for a crash landing that would have killed everyone aboard.

I was getting a second chance to show that I'd learned something from that part of my education that few spacers thought they'd ever use in real life. Watching through the windows, I carefully adjusted the lifeboat's attitude until it assumed a trajectory that would bring it over Coyote's northern hemisphere. I'd studied maps of the world, so I had a pretty good idea of what was where. Once I determined that I was somewhere above Great Dakota, I initiated entry sequence.

Keeping an eye on the eight ball, I maneuvered the RCS thrusters until the lifeboat made a 180-degree turn, then I ignited the main engine. My body was pushed against the straps as the engine burned most of what remained of my fuel reserves. This lasted several minutes, and once my instruments told me that I'd shed most of my velocity, I shut down the engine and fired the thrusters again, delicately coaxing the lifeboat until it had assumed the proper attitude for atmospheric entry. Then I revved up the main once more, this time to make sure that I didn't hit the troposphere too fast. When everything looked copacetic, I goosed the yaw and pitch a bit, fine-tuning my angle of attack.

This went on for about fifteen or twenty minutes, during which I barely had time to look out the porthole, let alone give the lidar more than a passing glance. Since I was coming in backward, I didn't have the luxury of selecting a precise landing site. At that point, though, all I wanted to do was make it through the upper atmosphere in one piece. So by the time a white-hot corona began to form around the heat shield, I couldn't tell where the hell I was going. Except down.

Gravity took over like a baby elephant that had decided to sit on my chest. Gasping for air, I struggled to remain conscious . . . and when my vision began to blur and I thought I was about to lose it, I hit the button that would activate the automatic landing sequence. It was a good thing that I did so, because I wasn't totally myself when the *Lou Brock* entered Coyote's stratosphere.

I was jerked out my daze by the sudden snap of the drogue chutes being released. The altimeter told me that I was twenty-seven thousand feet above the ground. Through the porthole, I could see dark blue sky above a cotton-gauze layer of clouds. So far, so good, but I was still falling fast . . . but then there was another jolt as the drogues were released, and one more as the three main chutes were deployed. I sucked in a lungful of air. All right, so I wasn't going to become toast. Thank you, St. Buzz, and all other patron saints of dumb-luck spacers.

But that didn't mean that I was out of danger yet. Although the fuel gauge told me that I still had .03 percent in reserves, that was practically worthless so far as controlling my angle of descent. Firing thrusters now might cause the parachute lines to tangle, and then I'd be dead meat. So my fate was cast to the wind. Although I'd done my best to pick my landing site, so far as I knew I might splash down in a channel. Or descend into the caldera of an active volcano. Or land on top of the Wicked Witch of the East and be greeted by the Lollipop Guild.

In any event, I had no vote in the outcome. So I simply hung on tight and clenched my teeth as I watched the altimeter roll back. At one thousand feet, there was the thump of the heat shield being jettisoned, followed by the loud whoosh of the landing bags inflating.

By then my rate of descent was thirty-two feet per second, according to the altimeter. I began a mental countdown from the half minute mark. *Thirty . . . twenty-nine . . . twenty-eight . . . twenty-seven . . .* At the count of twenty, I decided that this was pointless, and simply waited.

Touchdown was hard, but not so violent that I did anything foolish like bite my tongue. To my relief, I didn't come down in water; there was no rocking back and forth that would have indicated that I'd landed in a channel or a river, just the tooth-rattling *whomp* of hitting solid ground. A few seconds later, there was the prolonged hiss of the airbags deflating; when I felt the bottom of the lifeboat settle beneath me, I knew that I was safe.

Welcome to Coyote. Now where the hell was I?

XIII

I waited until the bags collapsed, then unbuckled the harness and rose from my couch. After eighteen hours of zero g, my legs felt like warm rubber, but otherwise I had no trouble getting on my feet. The deck seemed stable enough; nonetheless, the first thing I did was look out the window to make sure that the lifeboat hadn't come down in a treetop. Nothing but what appeared to be a vast savannah of tall grass.

I already knew the air was breathable, so I went to the side hatch, removed the panel covering the lock-lever, and twisted it clockwise. The hatch opened with a faint gasp of overpressurized air. A moment later my ears popped. Coyote's atmosphere was thinner than Earth's, so I swallowed a couple of times to equalize the pressure in my inner ear, then I climbed through the hatch and dropped to the ground, landing on top of one of the deflated bags.

It was early afternoon, wherever it was that I'd landed, the alien sun just past zenith in a pale blue sky streaked here and there with thin clouds. Although the air was a little cooler than I had expected, nonetheless the day was warm; it was midsummer on Coyote, if I correctly recalled recent reports of this world, which meant that it wouldn't get cold until after Uma went down. About two or three miles away, beyond the edge of the field, was a line of trees; when I stepped away from the lifeboat and turned to look the other way, I saw more forest, with low mountains rising in the far distance.

The lifeboat had a survival kit; I'd already found it during my long trip here. Yet although it included a map of Coyote and a magnetic compass, a fat lot of good they'd do me now. The mountains represented no landmark that I recognized from ground level, and although the compass would help me tell north from south and east from west, a sense of direction was all but useless when I was ignorant of exactly where I had landed. So far as I knew, I was on the outskirts of Munchkinland, about a hundred miles from the Emerald City.

But the kit also included food sticks, six liters of water, a fire-starter, a survival knife, and a satphone. I could always use the sat-phone to call for help . . . but only as a last resort. I'd arrived aboard a stolen lifeboat, after having made a somewhat violent escape from a Coyote Federation starship. Therefore, it made little sense to yell for help when it was all but certain that my rescuers would take me to the nearest jail. And although my two feet were safely planted on Coyote soil, these weren't exactly the right circumstances to beg for political asylum.

So . . . first things first. Gather as much stuff as I could carry, pick a direction, and slog it out of there, with the hope that I wasn't too far away from civilization. I climbed back into the *Lou Brock* and used the survival knife to cut away the lining of my seat, with the intent of using it as a makeshift pack for everything I'd take with me, and perhaps also as a bedroll. Once I had a nice, long strip of fabric, I laid it flat on the deck, then placed within it water bottles and food sticks. Once I wrapped the strip tightly around my belongings and lashed it across my chest and back, it made an acceptable sling. The satphone and firestarter went into my jacket pocket along with the map and compass, and the knife was attached to my belt. As an afterthought, I removed my cravat and tied it around my forehead as a sweatband.

So now I was good to go. Ready to tackle the Coyote wilderness, wherever it might lead me. Despite my trepidation, I found myself eager to discover whatever lay out there. This was why I'd joined the Union Astronautica in the first place: to explore new worlds, to go places where no one had ever gone before. Well, I'd finally have my chance . . .

One last look to see if I'd forgotten anything, then once again I dropped out of the lifeboat. Farewell, *Lou Brock*. You've stolen one more base, and this time slid home farther than you ever have before. Making sure that my sling was tightly knotted, I began to walk away from the lifeboat . . .

And straight into the muzzle of a Union Guard carbine, pointed at me from less than six feet away.

"Stop right there!" The kid holding the gun wore a blue vest over a short-sleeve uniform of the same color and looked barely old enough to shave. "Don't move!"

"Not moving." Nonetheless, I started to raise my hands. The customary gesture of surrender wasn't appreciated, because the kid's trigger finger twitched ever so slightly. "Easy, soldier," I added, making like a statue. "Harmless. Unarmed. See?"

"Keep it that way." Still keeping his hands on his weapon, the boy spoke into his headset mike. "Charlie two, this is Bravo leader. We've got him. Repeat, we've got him."

We? Keeping my hands half-raised, I turned my head as much as I dared. To my left, another trooper was emerging from the high grass only a few yards away. I looked to my right, and caught a glimpse of a third soldier coming into view from behind the lifeboat. Like the squad leader, both carried Union Guard rifles, probably leftovers from the Revolution. Unless my guess was wrong, they belonged to the Colonial Militia, second-generation members of the Rigil Kent Brigade that had kicked the Western Hemisphere Union off Coyote nearly twenty-five years ago. These were the descendents of guerrilla fighters, and therefore wouldn't care much for the son of the son of their enemy.

I might have been surprised to find them, but they sure as hell weren't surprised to find me. Within minutes, a gyro roared down out of the sky, its twin-prop rotors flattening the grass around us as it touched down only thirty feet away. By then Bravo Company had forced me to my knees, ripped my sling from my shoulders, patted me down, and removed everything from my pockets, then used a plastic strap to tie my hands behind my back. They marched me to the gyro at gunpoint and offered little assistance as I struggled aboard.

And that's how I came to Coyote.

(FOUR)

Busted on Coyote . . .

the discreet charm of the Colonial Militia . . .

weird incident in the stockade . . .

a business proposition from Mr. Morgan Goldstein.

XIV

A couple of hours later, I was in a jail cell in Liberty. We will now have a brief pause to relish the irony of that statement.

As it turned out, my lifeboat landed in a savannah on the southern half of Midland, a large subcontinent just across the East Channel from New Florida. Indeed, if the *Lee* hadn't tracked the *Lou Brock* on its way down and informed the Colonial Militia of its touchdown point, I could have hiked east to Goat Kill River, then followed it north to Defiance, a settlement near the mountains I'd seen from my landing site. If I'd headed south, I would have found a fishing village called—so help me, I'm not lying—Carlos's Pizza, located on the banks of the Great Equatorial River. And if I'd gone west, I would have eventually reached the East Channel, where one of any number of pirogues, catamarans, tugboats, or yachts that plied the river could have picked me up.

In any case, I was never more than a day or two away from civilization. All the same, though, perhaps it was just as fortunate that the Colonial Militia found me when they did. Although I was close enough to a couple of towns to reach them on foot, the grasslands were rife with boids . . . and considering that I was unarmed save for my survival knife, an encounter with one of those man-eating avians would have been fatal. But the blueshirts got to me before that could happen, and so . . .

Well, to make a long story short, I wound up in what was colloquially referred to as the stockade, even though it was an adobe structure larger than some of the homes in town. Liberty, of course, was the first colony on Coyote, established almost a half century ago by the original colonists from the URSS *Alabama*. It had since grown into what might pass as a city if you squinted hard enough. I didn't get to see much of it, though; once the gyro landed just outside the stockade, the blueshirts marched me straight in.

The crime rate on Coyote must be really low, because the six cells on the ground floor were unoccupied save for a drunk passed out in the first one. The blueshirts handed me over to a proctor, a not-unkindly old guy they called Chief Levin. He walked me down to the end of the cell block, where he unsnapped my handcuffs before sliding open the iron-bar door. Dinner would be at sundown, the Chief told me, and my arraignment was scheduled for the next morning. If I needed anything before then, just yell. Then he slammed the door shut and walked off. I heard him return a little while later to rouse the drunk and usher him out, and after that I was pretty much left alone.

My cell was primitive but comfortable, or at least as much as these things go. A foam pad on a wrought-iron frame, complete with a blanket woven from some coarse fabric that I'd later learn was called shagswool. A pitcher of water and a ceramic cup. A commode that didn't flush, but instead was . . . well, call it a porcelain throne above a foul-smelling netherworld eight feet below; one whiff, and I resolved to keep the lid shut. Baked-clay walls upon which previous guests had scratched their initials, along with some fairly interesting, if sometimes rude, graffiti. A ceiling light panel that looked as if it had been recently installed, evidence that modern technology had lately been imported from Earth.

It was the window that I enjoyed the most. Ribbed with four iron bars sunk deep within the adobe, with hinged wooden shutters on the exterior, it wasn't glazed, but instead was open to the air outside. As I sat on the cot, back propped against the wall and legs dangling over the side, I savored the warm breeze of a late-summer afternoon. Sure, I was a prisoner, and it was very possible that I would soon be aboard the *Robert E. Lee* again, this time as a deportee bound for whatever punishment the Patriarchs and Matriarchs of the Union Astronautica had in store for me. But for a short while, I'd get a chance to . . .

Something itched at my mind.

There's no other way to describe it. Imagine a mosquito bite, perhaps at your ankle. Annoying, but not painful. But when a mosquito tags you, it's just a flesh wound; you can scratch it until it goes away.

What I felt was a little like that, but instead deep within my head. Like something had crawled into my cerebrum and given me a tiny yet distracting little sting. Sitting up on my bunk, I reached up to rub the back of my neck. For a moment, the sensation went away, and I breathed a sigh of relief. Evening was closing in, with light fading through the window. I hoped that someone would close the outside shutters before it got too cold. And perhaps bring me something to eat, too. I hadn't . . .

Then I glanced at the window and saw someone standing just outside.

In the waning light of day, it was difficult to make out his features. I stood up, stepped closer to the window. "Hey there," I said. "Who are you?"

He said nothing, but continued to stare in at me. He wore a dark brown robe, its hood pulled up around his face. A fairly young man, a little older than me, or at least that was my first impression.

Again, there was the itch in my mind . . . and suddenly, I tasted chicken. Roast chicken, warm, perfectly seasoned with just the right amount of paprika, garlic, saffron, sea salt, and black pepper. The chicken of the gods. Chicken the way Mama used to make it, back when I was . . .

Then my mind fell open.

Again, I have no other way to describe it. Imagine that there's a little trapdoor at the back of your skull, one that's been closed for so long, you've forgotten that it even exists. Then, one day, someone who has the key inserts it within the lock, turns it . . . and *whomp*, everything that is you rushes out. All your memories, all your knowledge, all your fantasies, all your little loves and hates, everything that comprises what you might call your soul gushes out as a stream of viscous black sludge.

As swiftly as it had opened, the door of my mind slammed shut. And as it did, the taste of chicken faded from my palate. Staggering away from the window, I managed to make it to the bunk before I keeled over.

I slept for only a little while before I woke up. Feeling strangely hungover, I stumbled back to the window. Twilight was fading, and the stranger was nowhere to be seen. Once again, I was alone.

Something within my mind insisted that this was an illusion—*you dozed off,* a small voice said, *and had a vivid dream*—yet I couldn't quite believe this. I'd just received a visitor. Of that, I had little doubt.

XV

Dinner arrived about an hour later, on a tray carried in by Chief Levin, who slipped it through a rectangular opening in the door. By coincidence, it was roast chicken. Nowhere near as tasty as the mental impression I'd received just a little while earlier, but I was in no position to complain. Besides, I was starving. So I wolfed it down, cleaning the plate of the green beans and sweet potatoes that came with it. A small surprise to find that I'd been given a knife and fork; apparently no one seriously believed that I might try to make use of them as weapons. But the Chief wasn't dumb; when he came for my tray, he made sure that the utensils were in plain sight before he took it back from me.

Once again, I wondered why I hadn't yet seen the magistrates, let alone been charged with anything. I'd arrived late in the day, of course, but surely the legal system must have some means of processing those who've just been arrested. Perhaps the magistrates were trying to find a lawyer who would represent me pro bono. Come to think of it, did they even have lawyers on Coyote? A few days ago, I would've hoped not—at least not by the standards of the Western Hemisphere Union, where one is guilty until proven innocent—but cooling my heels in a jail cell, I found myself praying for someone who had a better grasp of colonial law than I did.

I was still trying to figure out whether or not to plead guilty to whatever I would be charged with when I heard the cell-block door swing open. Two pairs of footsteps came down the corridor, and I sat up on my bunk. Okay, this would be my solicitor. I hoped that his sheepskin hadn't been mail-ordered from Earth.

Then the Chief stopped in front of my cell, and with him was a short, rather pudgy middle-aged man with a shaved head. He looked familiar, yet I couldn't quite place him.

51

"Here he is, Mr. Goldstein." Chief Levin nodded in my direction. "Sorry, but I can't let you in. Rules . . ."

"Quite all right, Chris. So long as we can talk." Goldstein looked around. "Of course, if I could have a place to sit . . ."

He cast a look at the Chief, and Levin turned and walked away. Goldstein waited patiently, the fingers of his left hand absently playing with the crease of his tailored trousers. Wearing a tan linen suit, a red silk scarf hanging loose around his thick neck, he was easily the best-dressed man I had yet seen on Coyote. Which wasn't saying much, because everyone I'd met so far was a blueshirt or a proctor. Nonetheless, this person practically smelled like money. Had to be a lawyer . . . and yet, I couldn't shake the feeling that I had seen him before.

Chief Levin returned with a straight-backed wood chair that he'd found somewhere. "You're too kind," Goldstein said, as the proctor placed it in front of my cell. "That will be all for now, thanks." He raised his right hand to the proctor, and I caught a brief glimpse of green paper neatly folded within his middle and ring fingers. The Chief shook Goldstein's hand, deftly causing the colonial to disappear, then he vanished as well.

Goldstein waited until the cell-block door slammed shut, then he turned to look at me. "Ensign Truffaut," he said, favoring me with a broad smile. "So good to see you again."

"I'm sorry, but . . ."

"Of course we have." Smoothing the back of his trousers with his hand, he sat down in the chair the Chief had brought him. "Can't blame you if you don't remember me, being rather preoccupied at the time. Mr. Heflin is very efficient in his duties, don't you think?" A sly grin. "But perhaps that lump you delivered to the back of his head will teach him not to mistake efficiency for attention to detail."

It was then that I recognized him. The passenger who'd emerged from his first-class cabin aboard the *Lee* just in time to see the chief petty officer escort me to the bridge. Goldstein nodded, his grin growing wider as I gaped at him.

"Ah, so . . . now you know." Goldstein reached into a pocket of his jacket, produced a pair of thick brown cigars. He offered one to me; when I shook my head, he shrugged and put it away. "If you hadn't been exposed," he continued, "I might have come over to ask if you wanted a poker game to pass the time." He used a pocket guillotine to clip the end of his stogie. "Then again, if I'd done that, I might have taken your cover story at face value . . . that you were a gentleman by the name of Geoffrey Carr, and nothing more interesting than that."

"Sorry to disappoint you."

"Disappoint me?" An eyebrow was raised as a gold-plated lighter was produced. "Far from it. In fact, you may be the answer to a problem I have. And I may be the answer to yours."

XVI

I didn't know quite what to say to that, so I simply waited as he flicked his lighter and used it to gently char the end of his cigar. Blue-grey fumes rose toward the ceiling; I don't smoke, but it was fragrant enough that I almost regretted not accepting the one he'd offered me.

"Name's Goldstein. Morgan Goldstein." He settled back and stretched out his legs, so self-assured that you could have sworn that he owned the stockade. "Ever heard of me?"

"No, I . . ." Then I stopped myself. "There's a Morgan Goldstein who's in charge of Janus, but . . ."

"But what?" He rolled his cigar between his fingertips, not quite looking at me. "Please. Speak your mind."

What was on my mind was the improbability of a billionaire sitting in a cell block, having a smoke and a chat with someone about to be convicted on felony charges. Sure, I knew who Morgan Goldstein was. Founder and CEO of Janus, Ltd., the largest private space firm in the solar system. Earth's, that is, or at least until just a few years ago, when he abruptly uprooted his corporation from the Western Hemisphere Union and relocated it to Coyote, where he reestablished it as the richest company in the new world, with himself as its wealthiest citizen. Although most of Janus's shipping interests still remained forty-six light-years away, the corporate headquarters were now located in Albion, not far from the New Brighton spaceport where, if things had worked out better, Geoffrey Carr would have peacefully disembarked.

"Yeah . . . sure, you're that same guy." I waved my hand back and forth to clear the air in front of my face. "And I'm Dorothy Gale from Kansas."

His face darkened for a moment, as if nonplussed to find someone who wouldn't instantly take him at his word. Then he relaxed and tilted back his head to exhale smoke at the ceiling. "Then I'd have to ask where you left your little dog and why you couldn't have found a better place to park your farmhouse." He shook his head. "I'm not normally accustomed to proving my identity, but if you insist . . ."

Reaching into a coat pocket, he produced a datapad. I couldn't help but notice that it was a SonAp Executive: state-of-the-art, top-of-the-line, in what appeared to be a platinum casing. He pressed his thumb against the ID plate, then raised the pad to his face so that the retinal scanner could check his eyes. A soft *click*, and the pad opened. He tapped a couple of commands into the keypad, waited a moment, entered yet another set, then leaned forward to pass the unit through the cell bars.

"I'd prefer that you keep this information to yourself," he said quietly. "I'd rather not have it become common knowledge."

I took the pad from him, then read the screen. Displayed at the top was the logo of Lloyd's of London. Beneath it was an account statement for Mr. Morgan Goldstein, along with a routing number that had been carefully blacked out. And under it was a figure in euros that stretched into ten digits. Ten *high* digits.

"That's my net holdings in this one particular establishment," Goldstein said, his voice low. "At least of as yesterday morning, the last time I was able to update my portfolio via hyperlink. Sorry, but I'd rather not reveal my holdings in Zurich or the Bank of Coyote. They're considerably larger."

The datapad trembled in my hand. I wasn't completely convinced, though, so I used my fingertip to move the cursor to the BIO tab within the menu bar. Goldstein waited patiently while the screen changed again . . . and suddenly, I saw a portrait photo of the man seated on the other side of the bars. About ten years younger, with nearly as many hairs remaining on top of his head, but unmistakably the same individual.

"It's okay to breathe," Goldstein said after a moment. "I do it all the time. Good for the lungs."

I managed to give the pad back to him without dropping it. He was grinning like a fox as he closed it. "Now then, Dorothy . . . or may I call you Ensign Truffaut?"

"Ensign Truffaut is fine." I swallowed, tried to get us back to the informal level. "Jules is good, too."

"Jules, then . . . and you may call me Mr. Goldstein." The grin faded as he slipped the pad back in his pocket. "So you know who I am and what I represent. Now I'll tell you why I need you, and what I can do for you in return." Another languid drag from his cigar. "You've heard of the *hjadd*, of course."

Who hadn't? An alien race, their homeworld located in the Rho Coronae Borealis system, they'd made contact with humankind about three years ago, when they permitted the survivors of the EASS *Galileo* to return to Coyote after their ship was destroyed fifty-three years earlier. The *Galileo* had been sent out from Earth to investigate a deep-space object called Spindrift; a foolish mistake by the captain led to a lethal encounter with a *hjadd* starship, but the three surviving members of the expedition managed to convince the aliens that our race meant them no harm. This in turn led to the *hjadd* dispatching an emissary to Coyote, with a small delegation sent not long thereafter.

First contact, in other words. "Sure," I said. "I was hoping I'd get a chance to see one of them while I was here."

"Yes, well . . . you and me both, kid." Goldstein knocked an ash to the floor. "They've had an embassy here nearly a year, by local reckoning. A compound on the other side of town, not far from the Colonial University. But it's off-limits to everyone except a few people who they've accepted as go-betweens, and only rarely do any of them come out . . . and only then in environment suits so that we can't see them."

"But we know what they look like." I'd seen the same photos everyone else on Earth had: creatures that looked sort of like giant tortoises, only without shells, who stood upright on stubby legs and wore togalike garments that seemed to shimmer with a light of their own. "Pretty weird, but . . ."

"Ah, yes . . . and it's the 'but' that's the crux of the matter, isn't it?" Goldstein studied the glowing end of his cigar. "A year on this world, and we still know little more about them than we did before they arrived. Although they know a lot about us . . . even Anglo, which their emissaries speak with the assistance of translation devices . . .

they're very protective of what we learn about them. Believe me, I've had my people working at this for some time now. The best insight that I've been given is that they're probably descended from a 'prey species' . . . a lesser form of life on their native world . . . that was subject to attack by predators until they learned how to compete. So they're cautious by nature, not given to opening up to others."

"So you're afraid of them?"

Goldstein gave me a cold look. "No. Not at all. The Dominion-ists consider them a threat to their doctrine, but me . . . ?" He shook his head. "If I really wanted, I could have their embassy nuked from orbit."

"I think someone tried that already." I remembered what had happened to the *Galileo*.

"True, and I have no desire to repeat that mistake. Besides, it would be contrary to my interests." He took another drag from his cigar. "The *hjadd* want to pursue trade relations with humankind. Not with Earth, mind you . . . they don't trust that place, not after what happened with the *Galileo* . . . but with us, here, on Coyote. We have something they want, and they're willing to bargain for it."

"And that is . . . ?"

"Patience. We'll get to that." I shut up, and he went on. "I'm not a diplomat, nor am I a scientist." Dropping his voice, Goldstein gave me a conspiratorial wink. "Fact is, I'm not that much of a spacer even though I own a fleet of commercial spacecraft. The reason why I was aboard your ship in the first place was because I had to tend to busi-ness interests back on Earth, and the accommodations aboard the *Lee* are more comfortable than the ones aboard my own vessels."

"I was wondering about that."

"Keep it to yourself." Another puff from his cigar. "At any rate . . . I'm an entrepreneur, Jules. A businessman, and a damn good one if I may say so myself. Started out by buying a secondhand lunar freighter that was about to be decommissioned and went from there." He patted the coat pocket in which he'd put his pad. "The trick to striking it rich is spotting opportunities when they come up and seizing them before anyone else does. And the *hjadd* . . ."

"Are an opportunity."

"Kid, I'm beginning to like you even more. Yes, the *hjadd* are an opportunity. Better yet, they're an opportunity no one else . . . particularly not my competitors . . . has managed to get their hands on. If Janus can reliably deliver what they want, then I stand to gain a monopoly upon whatever they have to trade in return. Not only that, but I'll have access to any other races with whom they have contact. When that happens, my company will become the sole freight carrier between us and the rest of the galaxy."

"Uh-huh. And what does the Coyote government have to say about that?"

"Oh, don't worry." Goldstein grinned. "They're in on it, too. The Federation Navy only has one ship big enough to handle that amount of cargo, and the *Lee* is already committed to the Earth run. After that, they have nothing but shuttles. And since I have the ships they need, they're just as willing to subcontract my company . . . for a generous share of the profits, of course."

"Sounds like you've got everything lined up."

"I've been working on this deal for the last six months, Coyote time. If all goes well, within the next two or three weeks we'll be sending the first commercial freighter to Hjarr . . . their homeworld, that is. There's just one last detail that needs to be taken care of . . . and that's where you come in."

Goldstein glanced at the cell-block door, making sure that we were alone, then he shifted forward in his chair, leaning closer until his face was only a few inches from the bars. "One problem I had with this is putting together a crew," he went on, his voice lowered once more. "I've got a lot of good people, but I know damn well that some of them are spies for my competitors . . . just as I've placed my own informants within their outfits. That's the way business is. Everyone wants to know what the other guy is doing and tries to use that info to their advantage. But with something like this . . . well, the fewer risks I have to accept, the happier I'll be."

He toyed with the cigar in his hand. "So instead of bringing in a crew from Earth or Mars, I've decided to build a new team from scratch." He stopped himself. "Well, almost entirely a new team. Out of necessity, my chief engineer comes with his ship. But he's been working for me for a long time now, and I trust him like I would my own brother. For all other positions, though, I've had to recruit local talent."

I could see where this was leading . . . and even then, I couldn't quite believe it. "You want me?" I asked, and he nodded. "Why?"

"Because you impressed me." Goldstein exhaled a mouthful of smoke, then looked me straight in the eye. "It took a lot of guts to steal that lifeboat the way you did, and it took even more to bring it safely to the ground. I know those lifeboats, kid . . . I've got the same type installed on my own ships . . . and they're a bitch to handle. And you managed to land one on your own, with no help from either the *Lee* or local traffic control. Like I said, I am impressed."

"Thank you." Yet I remained skeptical. "How do you know I'm not just lucky, though?"

"Once I found out who you were, I had my people check you out. You're a rather interesting fellow, Jules. Graduated fourth in your class at the *Academia del Espacio*. Served as a junior officer aboard the . . . what was the name of that ship?"

"The WHSS *Victory of Social Collectivism on Mars*."

"Oh, yes. Right." He rolled his eyes in distaste. "Never could understand the Union Astronautica's penchant for propagandizing ship names." He frowned. "You might have eventually earned your captain's bars if it hadn't been for that business with your brother." A pause. "You realize, of course, you could've saved your career if . . ."

"You're not saying anything I haven't heard before." I didn't like to talk about Jim, particularly not with strangers. And so far as I was concerned, Morgan Goldstein was still little more than a rich guy who'd come to visit me in jail. "So what is it you want me to do? Be your commanding officer?"

Goldstein stared at me for a couple of seconds, then laughed out loud. "You certainly do have balls, don't you?" Leaning back in his chair, he shook his head in obvious amusement. "I already have a CO, son, along with a capable first officer. What I need now is someone qualified to fly a shuttle, or just about any other small craft we may have aboard." His smile reappeared. "I had one or two other people in mind, but when I saw that you'd worked as a longshoreman on Highgate . . . well, I knew I had my man."

If he meant to knock me down a peg or two, he did a good job of doing so. So I wasn't being recruited for the big chair, nor even for the little one, but for a task that notoriously falls to Academy wash-outs, with my former employment as a pod jockey being the final selling point. If this was a job interview, I might have been tempted to walk out of the room . . . if I'd been able to, that is.

"Thanks for considering me," I murmured, trying to keep my temper in check. "So happy to hear that I'm suitable for your needs."

"More than suitable. You're the very man I've been looking for." Goldstein became more somber. "That is, of course, unless you want to go home. Then all I have to do is leave and let my friends among the magistrates know that you're not interested. In that case, they'll call you in first thing tomorrow morning. The legal system here on Coyote may not be very merciful, but it is quick. You'll get a fair and speedy trial, and I have little doubt that you'll be deported. After that . . ." He shrugged.

"And if I sign up with you?"

"Then I put in a good word for you with the maggies, informing them I'm willing to post bail for you if you plead *nolo contendere.* You get one year probation, the government takes into consideration your petition for political amnesty, and in the meantime you go to work for me." Another smile. "I'll even throw in a salary commensurate with that of a first-class spacer . . . nonunion, of course . . . and see what I can do about finding you a room at an inn here in town. So what do you say?"

As if I had a choice? Besides, I had to admit, what he was offering was tempting under any circumstances. In the Union Astronautica, I might have eventually risen to the rank of captain . . . in which case I would have commanded a Mars cycleship, or even a Jovian freighter, and spent my life shuffling back and forth across the solar system.

At one time, that sort of thing had been my highest ambition. But now I was being given the chance to travel to the stars, to see things no one else in my class had ever dreamed of seeing. Sure, maybe it wasn't going to be from the vantage point of the captain's chair . . . but better this than a lifetime of sleeping on a prison cot.

"Yes," I said. "I'd like that very much."

"Excellent. Pleased to hear it." Standing up, Goldstein dropped his cigar on the floor. "I'll have a chat with my friends," he said as he ground the stogie beneath the heel of his shoe, "and send someone by to pick you up tomorrow morning." He paused to look me over.

"If you have a chance, write down your clothing sizes. That's a fine outfit you're wearing, but totally unsuitable for life here."

"I will. Thank you." All this and a trip to the tailor, too. It suddenly felt as if I'd hit the jackpot.

But not quite. Goldstein started to walk away when another thought occurred to me. "By the way . . . you didn't say what sort of cargo we're taking to the *hjadd*."

He stopped. For a second, I thought he was going to turn around, but instead he merely glanced over his shoulder. "Oh, did I forget that? Sorry."

And then he disappeared. The cell-block door creaked as it was opened from the outside, then it slammed shut once more. Leaving me to wonder if I'd just talked my way out of jail or negotiated a deal with the devil.

(FIVE)

Good-bye, Your Honor . . .

take me out to the ball game . . .

where the aliens are . . .

o, Captain! my Captain! . . .

a cold Rain.

XVII

Morgan Goldstein was true to his word.

Early next morning, not long after Chief Levin brought in breakfast—which I didn't mind skipping; if the eggs had been any runnier and the bacon a little less fatty, I could have raced them against each other around my plate—another proctor showed up to take me to court. I straightened my clothes as best as I could, hoped that I didn't smell too ripe, then let him put the cuffs on me and lead me from my cell.

Two more proctors were waiting outside the stockade, along with a wagon drawn by an animal that looked like a cross between a water buffalo and a giant anteater. At least there was one creature on Coyote who stank worse than me. The shag farted at least twice on the way across town, and I seemed to be the only one who noticed; my guard and the driver had enough sense to pull scarves up around their noses.

I got a good look at Liberty along the way. Clapboard houses and log cabins lined packed-dirt streets; men and women in homespun clothes walked to work on wooden sidewalks raised a half foot above storm gutters. We passed a schoolyard in which a crowd of children were at play, and from somewhere far off I heard a bell-tower clock strike eight times. Here and there, I spotted indications of advanced technology—sat dishes on rooftops, a hovercoupe parked in an alley, comps on display in a shop window—but otherwise the town looked as if had been transported across time and space from nineteenth-century America. Despite the opening of the starbridges, Coyote remained a frontier where the inhabitants had learned how to make do with what they could build with their own hands. I wasn't sure whether I liked this or not.

We finally arrived at Government House. The wagon trundled around the statue of Captain R. E. Lee, commanding officer of the URSS *Alabama* and founder of the colony, and came to a halt at a side door of the two-story wood-frame building. The proctors helped me climb down from the wagon; the shag passed gas one last time as a fare-thee-well, then I was marched inside.

A quick walk down a short corridor, and then I was escorted into a small courtroom. On the other side of a low rail, two men were seated at a long, wooden table. One of them stood up as I walked in, and introduced himself as my court-appointed attorney. Rail-thin and affable, with curly hair that seemed to stand on end, he seemed more like someone you'd find throwing darts in the nearest pub. Better to have him on my side, though, than the other barrister, who barely nodded in my direction before returning sour eyes to his pad; I wondered if being a prosecutor was his way of compensating for going bald before he was thirty.

My lawyer had just finished telling me, in a low whisper, not to speak unless I was spoken to, and only then to say just what was necessary—*play dumb, and let me do the talking*—when another door opened and the magistrates walked in. Two men and a woman, each wearing long, black robes, all of whom looked as if they'd had lemons for breakfast. Everyone rose as they strode to the bench, and we took our seats again when they did. The Chief Magistrate picked up her gavel, gave it a perfunctory smack on the table, and called court to order, and then we were off and running.

And I do mean running, because we were in and out of there in less than twenty minutes. The head maggie asked the prosecuting attorney if he was ready and willing to press charges against the accused, identified as Jules Truffaut. He responded that he was indeed: two counts of identity theft, possession of forged documents, stowing away aboard an interstellar vessel registered to the Coyote Federation, two counts of assault against Federation Navy officers, theft of a spacecraft registered to the Federation, unauthorized intrusion into Federation airspace, and unauthorized landing upon territory in possession of a Federation colony.

I didn't need to be familiar with Colony Law to know that I was seriously up a creek, and not just one found on this planet. Forget deportation. Considering that there was no question that I'd committed every single offense, I would be lucky if I spent the rest of my days in the stockade . . . if they didn't first ship my criminal ass back to Earth.

When the Chief Magistrate asked how I would plead, though, my attorney calmly rose to tell her that I was pleading *nolo contendere* to all charges, on the grounds that, as a citizen of the Western Hemisphere Union who had grievances with his government, I had been forced to defect to Coyote with the intent of requesting political asylum. The magistrates took a few minutes to study their pads and murmur to one another, and then Her Honor summoned both attorneys to the bench. They spoke for five or ten minutes, their voices too low for me to hear. The lawyers returned to their seats, and my attorney barely smiled when the Chief Magistrate announced that my case would be remanded to a future date, as yet to be determined by the court. Until then I was free on bail, which had already been posted by a third party.

Another bang of the gavel, and it was over and done. My attorney shook my hand, wished me good luck, then turned and walked away. The last I saw of him, he and the prosecutor were ambling together from the courtroom, chuckling over some small joke I didn't catch. The magistrates had already disappeared; a brief glimpse of black robes gliding through the anteroom door, and they were gone. Even the proctors who'd brought me took a powder after one of them came forward to release my handcuffs; he clapped me on the shoulder, told me to stay out of trouble, and followed his pal out of the room.

All at once, I was alone. Nowhere to go, with nothing to my name save for the clothes on my back and a few bucks in my pocket. I stood there for a moment, wondering what the hell had just happened . . .

And then someone who'd been sitting quietly in the gallery all this time rose to his feet and came forward. A big guy, about a head taller than me and twice my size, with long blond hair and a thick beard to match. In a surprisingly mild voice, he informed me that his name was Mike Kennedy, and that he worked for Mr. Goldstein. Would I come with him, please?

XVIII

A hoverlimo was parked out in front of Government House, only the second ground vehicle I'd seen on Coyote that didn't have an animal hitched to it. Kennedy opened the rear door for me, and I wasn't surprised to find Goldstein seated inside.

"Mr. Truffaut, good morning." In hemp jeans and a light cotton sweater, Goldstein was more casually dressed than when I'd seen him the night before. "I trust your arraignment went well."

"Yes, sir, it did." I climbed into the back of the limo. "No small thanks to you, I assume."

"Think nothing of it. I try to . . ." His voice trailed off, and there was no mistaking the look on his face as he caught a good whiff of me. I tried to sit as far from him as possible, but even so he pushed a button that half opened a window on his side of the car. "I endeavor to accommodate my employees," he finished, his voice little more than a choke, then he leaned toward the glass partition between the passenger and driver seats. "Could you turn on the exhaust fan, please, Mike?"

Without a word, Kennedy switched on the vents. Cool air wafted through the back of the limo. "Sorry," I murmured. "Three days without a bath . . ."

"No need to apologize. Can't be helped." Goldstein tapped on the glass. The limo rose from its skirts and glided away from Government House. "I'm afraid I'm still a little overcivilized. There are still settlements where people take baths only two or three times a week . . . that's a Coyote week, nine days . . . and then in outdoor tubs just large enough to sit in." He paused, then added, "I've had to do it myself, from time to time."

"Of course." He'd made it sound as if going without a bath for more than a day or two was an act of barbarism. For him, perhaps it was. "At any rate, thank you. I appreciate your acting on my behalf."

"Think nothing of it," he replied, waving it off. "You're working for me now . . . and you wouldn't do me any good if your residence were the stockade, now would you?" He smiled. "Soon enough, I'll have you at an inn here in town. Nice place . . . hot running water, two meals a day . . . and there are clothes in your room that Mike has bought for you. You didn't have a chance to give me your sizes, so we had to guess a bit, but . . ."

"I'm sure they'll be fine. Thank you, sir." I was gazing out the window beside me. This part of Liberty had apparently been built more recently than the neighborhood around the stockade and Government House. I caught a brief glimpse of shops, open-air markets, tidy parks surrounded by redbrick bungalows. Very few vehicles, although I spotted a teenager seated on a hoverbike, chatting with a couple of young ladies. More often than not, though, I saw hitching posts to which both horses and shags had been tied up.

"Look over here," Goldstein said, and I craned my neck to gaze past him. A collection of adobe and wood-frame buildings arranged around a quadrangle. "The Colonial University. Established a few years after the Revolution by some of the original colonists. It's grown lately, thanks to endowments from Janus."

"I'm sure they appreciate it." My new boss never seemed to let a chance to brag about his munificence slip by. Not that I could blame him; if I owned what was probably the only hoverlimo on a world where most people rode horses, I'd probably do the same. I was about to ask whether any schools had been named after him when something in a field across the road from the campus caught my eye.

The moment I saw it, I knew exactly what it was.

"Stop the car!" I snapped. Kennedy hit the brakes, and before Goldstein could stop me, I opened my door and hopped out. For a few moments I stared at the field, utterly surprised by what I'd found.

Four bases, with white powder lines running between them, a

small mound within the center. Bleachers behind the first and third bases, and a tall chain-link fence forming an open-sided cage just behind home plate. Small wooden sheds on either side of the cage, with wood benches inside each one. And from the top of the cage, a blue-and-gold pennant that rippled in the morning breeze:

Beak 'Em, Boids!

"Well, I'll be damned," I murmured. A baseball diamond. Of all the things I'd least expected to see on Coyote . . .

"Oh, that?" Goldstein had followed me from the limo. "Belongs to the university team. The Battling Boids." A disinterested shrug. "Next week they go up against the Swampers, or whatever they're called . . ."

"The Fighting Swampers." Mike Kennedy gazed at us from the open window of the limo. "From Petsloc U." He pronounced it as *pets-lock.*

"The People's Enlightenment Through the Spirit of Social Collectivism University." Goldstein shook his head. "Not much of a school, really. More like a small liberal arts college set up by some unreformed social collectivists. But they've got a pretty good ball team . . ."

"Are you kidding?" Kennedy laughed out loud. "Boss, they stink. Half the time, they're arguing over who's most politically correct to play shortstop . . ."

"Never mind." Goldstein was obviously amused by my reaction to something as trivial to him as a baseball diamond. "If I'd known you were such a sports fan, Jules, I would've mentioned this earlier."

I bit my lip at his condescension, but said nothing. Although I'd read as much as I could about Coyote before making the decision to defect, I hadn't a clue that baseball was played there. And for those of us who truly love the game, it isn't just a sport; it's a fixation nearly as consuming as sex, drugs, or religion, albeit with none of the unpleasant side effects. When I left Earth, I had thought baseball one thing I would be leaving behind. In hindsight, I should have known better. Humankind always carries its culture with it, and no place is truly habitable unless it has baseball.

"I think . . ." I let out my breath. "I think I'm going to like this place."

"Hmm . . . well, so long as we're here, there's something else I'd like to show you." Goldstein touched my elbow. "Take a walk with me?"

It didn't sound like a request, but after two days floating around in a lifeboat and another cooped up in a jail, any chance to stretch my legs sounded like a fine idea. I nodded, and Goldstein turned to begin walking toward the university. As we crossed the road again, he raised a hand to Kennedy, gesturing for him to remain behind.

He said nothing as we cut across campus. The Colonial University was a little larger than it appeared from the road. Some of the buildings were taller than others, and someone had obviously devoted some time and effort to landscaping. Shade trees lined gravel walkways, with benches and abstract sculptures placed here and there; students strolled between buildings, chatting among themselves, or sat alone beneath trees, engrossed in their books and pads. We sauntered past a kidney-shaped pond, where an elderly woman was holding an open-air seminar with a dozen or so pupils. None appeared much younger than me, and I felt a twinge of envy. Before things had gone sour for me, I could have been one of them. An academic life, shielded from the realities of the larger and sometimes very harsh world.

We'd reached the far side of the campus and had walked up a

small hill overlooking the pond, when Goldstein came to a halt near a tree-shaded bench. "Over there," he said, pointing away from the university. "See it?"

Just beyond a small glade, only a few hundred yards away, lay what I first took to be a fortress. A ring-shaped structure, built of what seemed to be solid rock, its outer walls sloping inward to surround a cylindrical inner keep that vaguely resembled an enormous pillbox of the sort that had once been built by German soldiers during one of the world wars back on Earth. Narrow, slotlike windows were set deep within the keep's round walls, while wiry antennae jutted from its flat roof. There were no openings of any sort visible in the outer walls, although an indentation of some sort gave the impression of a gate that I couldn't make out through the trees.

"The *hjadd* embassy." Goldstein's voice was subdued, almost as if he expected to be overheard. "The original structure was built by us, on land President Gunther ceded to them as sovereign territory. That was shortly after the *Galileo* crew returned from Rho Coronae Borealis, with the Prime Emissary aboard. Once heshe determined that hisher people would be safe here, though, heshe summoned a ship from home. A few days later, two of their shuttles touched down over there, and then . . ." He paused. "They created that place in four days."

"Yeah, okay, but . . ." Then what he'd just said struck home. "Did you say four *days*?"

"Uh-huh." Goldstein nodded toward the bench. "They wouldn't allow any of us to come near, but when I heard what was happening, I got someone to let me join the faculty members who were observing everything from here." There was an expression of wonder on his face as his gaze returned to the distant compound. "It was like seeing a flower blossom in the early morning. At first, it didn't seem as if anything was happening. But after a while, we saw that something was growing . . .”

“Being built, you mean.”

“No. I mean it *grew*. No scaffolds, no heavy equipment . . . not even construction crews. It just rose from the ground, little by little, so slowly that you didn’t think anything was happening. Then you’d go away for coffee or to have a smoke, and when you came back you’d see that the outer walls were just a little taller than the last time you’d looked. And all of it solid . . . perfect, like it was a stone plant of some sort.”

“Nanotech?”

“That’s our best guess, yeah . . . but far more advanced than anything we’ve ever developed. Spectrographic imaging reveals that the walls are comprised of minerals found in the native soil, but that’s as much as we know. It resists everything else we throw at it. Thermographs, sonar, radar, lidar . . . totally airtight. Even the windows are reflective. Nothing gets in and nothing gets out.”

“So what have you . . . I mean, what have our people found out? About what goes on in there, I mean?”

“So far, the *hjadd* have allowed only three people inside. Carlos Montero, the former president, in his role as official liaison. He doesn’t say much to anyone, but that’s to be expected. A Dominionist missionary who . . . well, he’s not talking to anyone either, but from what I’ve heard, he’s had a crisis of faith.” He paused. “And I’m the third person.”

“You?”

“Only so far as an anteroom, where I spoke with them through a glass window. That’s the farthest they’ve allowed anyone, or so I’ve been told.” Goldstein tucked his hands in his trouser pockets. “I wanted you to see this, to give you an idea of what we’re going after.

It's not just establishing trade relations with another race . . . it's getting our hands on technology of such magnitude that something like that is little more than a trinket."

Before I could answer, he turned his back to the compound. "Come on," he said as he began to walk down the hill. "Let's get you cleaned up. Then I'll introduce you to the rest of the crew."

XIX

Goldstein had made a reservation for me at a small B&B called the Soldier's Joy, in the old part of Liberty, not far from the grange hall that had been the meetinghouse of the original colonists. Before he dropped me off, Goldstein pointed to a tavern just down the road from the inn and told me that he'd meet me there in three hours. Then the limo glided away, leaving me alone again in a strange town.

My room was on the second floor, and, while it wasn't the presidential suite, at least it had its own bath, which was all that I cared about just then. So I took a long, hot shower that rinsed away the last of my travel sweat, then wrapped myself in a robe I found hanging on the bathroom door and lay down on a feather-stuffed bed that felt nothing like a jail cot. I hadn't slept well in the stockade, and I figured I had time for a midday siesta.

The afternoon sun was shining through the windows when I woke up. Opening the dresser and closet, I discovered three changes of clothes, along with a shagswool jacket and a sturdy pair of boots stitched from what I'd later learn was creek cat hide. There were even toiletries in the bathroom, including a sonic toothbrush and shaver. I got rid of my whiskers and brushed my teeth, then tried on a pair of hemp trousers, a cotton shirt, and a shagswool vest. Everything fit me better than I had expected, even the boots; either Goldstein had an amazingly accurate sense for clothing sizes, or his people had found my specs during their research. I didn't know which prospect unnerved me more.

In any case, I arrived at the tavern a little less than three hours after promising Goldstein that I would meet him there. I was on schedule, but my new boss wasn't. Or at least his hoverlimo was nowhere in sight. And the tavern itself was rather run-down. With a weather-beaten signboard above the front door proclaiming its name to be Lew's Cantina, it was little more than a log cabin with a thatch roof and fieldstone chimney to one side. Just a shack that someone had neglected to tear down.

I hesitated outside for a few moments, wondering whether I'd misunderstood Goldstein and gone to the wrong place. But there was nothing else in the neighborhood that looked even remotely like a bar or restaurant, and he'd told me that he'd buy me a drink once I got there. So I walked across a wood plank and pushed open a door that creaked on its hinges.

Inside, Lew's Cantina was little more inviting than its exterior. A low ceiling with oil lamps suspended from the rafters. An unfinished floor upon which wood shavings soaked up spilled ale. Faded blankets hanging from log walls. Battered tables and wicker chairs, some of which looked as if they'd been repaired several times. A stone hearth with a couple of half-burned logs. The bar was no more than a board nailed across the top of a row of beer kegs; behind it stood an old lady, thin and frail, who scowled at me as she wiped a chipped ceramic mug with a rag that probably played host to three or four dozen different strains of bacteria.

Yeah, this was definitely the wrong address. Yet just as I started to turn toward the door, someone in the back of the room called out.

"Hey! Your name Truffaut?"

I looked around, saw three people seated around a table next to an open window. Two men and a woman, with a pitcher of ale between them. I nodded, and the guy seated on the other side of the table beckoned to me. "You're looking for us. C'mon over."

As I walked across the room, the fellow who'd spoken rose from his chair. "Ted Harker," he said, offering his hand. "Commanding officer of the . . ." His voice trailed off, as if unsure how to finish. "Well, anyway, just call me Ted. We don't stand much on formality. Have a seat. We've been waiting for you."

Ted Harker? The name sounded familiar, although for the moment I was unable to place it. A young guy in his late thirties, with long black hair tied back behind his neck and a trim beard just beginning to show the first hint of grey. "Thanks," I said, shaking his hand, "but I thought I was supposed to meet someone else here . . ."

"Morgan?" This from the woman seated next to him. A little younger than Ted, with short blond hair and the most steady gaze I'd ever seen. Like Harker, she had a British accent. "Yes, well . . . figures he'd put you on the spot like this."

"Typical." The second man at the table, same age as Ted, with an olive complexion and a Middle Eastern lilt to his tongue. "Bastard has his own agenda."

"C'mon, now. Speak no evil of the man who signs our paychecks." Ted motioned to an empty chair, then turned toward the bar. "Carrie? Another round for the table, please, and a mug for Mr. Truffaut here."

"Jules. My friends call me Jules."

"Pleased to meet you, Jules." The woman smiled at me as I sat down. "I'm Emily. First mate." She didn't mention her last name, but neither did she have to; when she lifted her beer mug, I noticed the gold band on her ring finger. First mate in more ways than one.

"Ali Youssef. Helmsman and navigator." The other man extended his hand as well. "I take it you're our new shuttle pilot."

"That's what Mr. Goldstein . . . Morgan . . . hired me to do." I looked at the three of them. "So this is it? The entire crew?"

Ted shook his head. "We've got two more. One of them is using the facilities just now . . . she'll be back in a minute . . . and the other is arriving with the ship. And we'll have two passengers as well . . ."

"More than two," Ali interrupted. "I spoke with Morgan earlier today, and he told me he's bringing someone else."

"What?" Ted stared at him in disbelief. "Well, that's bloody wonderful. So when was he going to tell the captain, pray tell?"

"Don't look at me." Ali shrugged as he took a sip from a glass of ice tea; he was the only person at the table not drinking ale. "I just happened to see him on the street, and he told me . . ."

"Morgan's going along?" That was news to me; he hadn't mentioned it during our previous conversations.

"He has to. After all, he's the one who's trying to make a deal." Emily let out her breath. "At least we don't have to deal with Jared again."

"No. He backed out at the last minute. Said one trip to Hjarr was enough for him." A wry smile from Ted. "Just as well. I had enough of him on Spindrift."

Spindrift. As soon as he said that, everything clicked. "Oh, good grief," I said, feeling my face go warm. "So you're . . . I'm sorry, but I didn't recognize you. You were on the *Galileo*." Before he could answer, I looked at his wife. "And that would make you . . ."

"Morgan didn't tell you?" Emily glanced at her husband. "Nerve of that guy."

Theodore Harker. Emily Collins. First officer and shuttle pilot respectively, they were two of the three surviving members of the

76

Galileo expedition. Like everyone else on Earth, I'd heard about their encounter with Spindrift, the rogue planet that turned out to be a starship carrying the remains of an alien race called the *taaraq*. Along with a third member of the expedition—it took me a moment to recall his name; Jared Ramirez, the astrobiologist—they had landed on Coyote fifty-three years after the *Galileo*'s disappearance, bringing with them the *hjadd* Prime Emissary. And they were in the same room, seated across the table from me . . . and I hadn't even heard that they'd gotten married.

Ted looked as if he was ready to blow a mouthful of beer through his nose. He swallowed with difficulty, then looked at Emily. "Morgan certainly enjoys his little games," he grumbled, then returned his attention to me. "Yes, you've found us out. Not that we were trying to keep it from you, but—"

"Keep what from whom?" a voice said from behind me, and I looked around to see a girl about four or five years younger than me. Shoulder-length hair the color of cinnamon, a narrow but pleasant face, nicely curved everywhere that mattered. Incredible eyes, the shade of green you find at twilight on a midsummer day.

And then she looked at me and said, "Who the hell is this?" Like I was a bug she'd happened to find.

"Ensign . . . sorry, I mean Jules Truffaut," Ted said. "He's our shuttle pilot."

"Yeah. Okay." She started to sit down but waited while the bartender hobbled over to the table with a fresh pitcher of ale. Carrie placed a mug in front of me, then quietly pulled back a chair for the girl. "Thanks, Carrie," she said, giving the old lady a sweet smile. "Oh, by the way . . ." She crooked a finger, and Carrie bent closer while the younger woman murmured something in her ear. She nodded, then stood erect and shuffled back to the bar.

"What was that about?" I asked once she was gone.

"No more paper in the outhouse. Thought she should know." She shook her head, then glanced at the pitcher with distaste. "You guys already on another round? For the love of—"

"You can have mine." I picked up my mug, offered it to her. "Too early for me."

"Don't drink." Ignoring me, she looked at Ted. "So who's keeping what from whom?"

"Never mind." Ted picked up the pitcher and reached for his mug. "Jules, allow me to introduce you to Rain Thompson. Our quartermaster and cargo officer."

"Happy to meet you. I—"

"Likewise." Rain barely glanced my way. "Skipper, I just saw Morgan's limo pull up. Looks like he's brought someone with him . . . besides his bodyguard, I mean."

"If you mean Mike Kennedy, I believe he prefers to be regarded as a valet." Ted frowned. "Probably our other passenger. Anyone you recognize?"

"Nope. Thought it might be this guy here"—meaning me—"but now that I know better . . ." She shrugged.

I was still trying to figure out what it was about me that put her off so much, or if she was naturally rude to people whom she'd just met, when the door opened and there was Goldstein. He hesitated just inside the door, looking back for a moment as if to see if someone was following him, then walked into the tavern. I noticed that he left the door open behind him . . . not by accident, but deliberately, as if to give someone lingering just outside a chance to make up his or her mind whether to come in.

"Gentlemen, ladies . . . good to see you again." He stopped just behind my chair, placed his hand on my shoulder. "You found your way here, Jules. Excellent. And I trust you've introduced yourself to everyone?"

"Yes, sir, I have. Thank you, Mr. Goldstein." From the corner of my eye, I caught a sour look on Ted's face. Perhaps I was coming off as being just a little too deferential to a boss whom no one seemed to respect very much. No one likes a brownnose, especially when he's the new kid in town. "I didn't have any trouble finding my way here," I added. "All I had to do was follow the cockroaches."

No one laughed. There was a cold silence as everyone stared at me. "If there are any cockroaches here," Rain said quietly, "they're probably just the ones you brought with you."

Emily coughed politely behind her hand, and Ali murmured something in Arabic. Yet Goldstein simply nodded as he pulled back an empty chair. "Perhaps I should have told you about this place before I directed you here," he said. "The cantina was erected by the original *Alabama* colonists, back in c.y. 01. They built it from materials left over from the construction of their houses, and it's older than even the grange hall. During their first winter on this world, they'd gather around the fireplace, keeping each other company on those long, cold nights when they were unsure of whether they'd survive until spring."

He glanced over at Carrie, who continued to putter around behind the bar. "Carrie's one of those colonists," he went on, lowering his voice. "She and her husband kept this establishment going on little more than barter and trade credit until the Union occupation. After the Revolution they came back, repaired the place, and opened it for business again. Lew died a few years ago, but she continues to brew her own ale and fix her own food. So show a little respect, please. You're on hallowed ground."

There was something in my mouth that tasted like my own foot. "Sorry," I mumbled. "Didn't know."

"Don't worry about it," Ted said. "Thought much the same thing when I first came here. Tip well, and we'll call it even." Then he turned to Goldstein. "Right. So we've got our shuttle jockey. So where's our ship?"

"Your ship is on the way, Captain Harker. Ganymede-class freighter with only three Jupiter runs logged to her name." Ted opened his mouth, but Goldstein raised a hand before he could object. "I know you wanted a new vessel, but this is the best I could arrange on short notice. The next boat in its class is still in the shipyard, two Earth-years away from completion."

"Boat?" Emily scowled at him. "We want a spacecraft, not a tub."

"Believe me, it's a good ship." Goldstein leaned back in his chair with the same air of confidence I'd seen when I was in the stockade. The man with all the answers, and the money to buy them. "Besides, you'll have an experienced chief engineer to go with it . . . someone who knows his ship backward and forward."

"All right. I'll take your word for it." Ted picked up his mug, took a sip. "So who are our passengers?"

"Well . . ." Goldstein took a deep breath. "As you know, one of them is the Prime Emissary, Mahamatasja Jas Sa-Fhadda."

That caused me to sit up straight. That one of our party would be a *hjadd* was news to me. One more detail about this voyage that Goldstein had neglected to reveal. Or at least to me; no one else seemed to be surprised. "One of the reasons why the ship has been delayed," Goldstein continued, "is because we've had to retrofit one of its passenger decks as suitable quarters for it . . . himher, I mean."

"All right. I can understand that." Ted folded his arms across his chest. "What about our other passenger?" He nodded toward Ali. "He tells me that you told him that you were bringing someone else, too."

Goldstein glanced toward the door. He hesitated, and for a moment it seemed as if he was waiting to hear someone say something. "A consultant," he said at last. "Someone who we'll need for this voyage, strictly in an advisory capacity."

Again, he gazed toward the door. A few seconds passed, and then a figure slowly appeared. A form draped in a dark cloak, hood pulled up around his face. He lingered for just a moment, then vanished again, without ever setting foot inside the cantina.

"That's Mr. Ash," Goldstein said. "He's rather shy, and I hope that you'll respect his privacy."

Rain stared after him. "Weird . . ."

Yes, he was. Just the same as when I'd first seen him, peering in through the barred window of my jail cell.

(PART 2)

The *Pride of Cucamonga*

(SIX)

Downtime . . .

the nightlife on Coyote . . .

the mysterious tenant . . .

a tense breakfast during which various matters are discussed.

I

We hung around Liberty for another week, local time, more out of necessity than anything else. Our ship had recently undergone refit at Janus's shipyard in Earth orbit, and we were told that it wouldn't be delivered to Coyote until the chief engineer was satisfied that all the new work was up to spec. So we had little to do until then but wait for our ride to arrive.

Before I left Lew's Cantina, Ted handed me a data fiche for a Zeus-class shuttle. It was a different sort of boat than the ones I'd trained to fly—a single-stage-to-orbit heavy lifter—yet I had little doubt that I could handle it. The next day, I wandered around town until I found the comp store I'd spotted while Morgan was driving me to the inn and used a good chunk of the money I'd brought with me to buy a new pad, complete with hologram heads-up. Once I loaded the fiche, I was able to pull up a 3-D simulation of the flight controls, which I used to familiarize myself with what I'd find once I climbed into the cockpit.

I used most of the remaining cash to buy other stuff. Goldstein had given me new clothes, sure, but he hadn't anticipated everything that a well-dressed spacer might need. It took a while, but I finally managed to locate a shop that catered to pros like me. I picked up a pair of stickshoes for zero-g work, a pilot's watch—electronic analogue, with three programmable time zones, a radiation counter, and a bevel—and a pair of sunglasses, along with a utility vest and a miniature tool kit to go with it. The sort of stuff I'd carried when I belonged to the Union Astronautica but which I'd been forced to give back when I was kicked out of the service.

So I shopped, and I studied, and otherwise looked for ways to kill time until my ship came in. That turned out to be harder than I expected. Liberty was the largest colony on Coyote, but that didn't exactly make it a hoppin' party town. Most people there possessed a puritanical work ethic—get up in the morning, have breakfast, go off to work, come home in the evening, have dinner, go to bed—that they had inherited from the original settlers. Once the sun went down, the streets were just about dead. Oh, there was a theatre ensemble—one evening I caught a performance of a play written by a local author, a comedy packed with topical references that might have been side-splitting if I'd known what they were about—and I eventually found a bar on the other side of town that had a half-decent folk trio, if you like music played so slow and soft that you could fall asleep between songs. But even then, everything closed down long before midnight, leaving me to walk home as Bear ascended into the night sky, its silver rings illuminating deserted sidewalks and houses where the lights were going out one by one.

A couple of other things got my interest. One was baseball. Late in the afternoon, once I got through my daily routine of memorizing the layout of the shuttle cockpit and practicing the tutorials, I would mosey over to the Colonial University and watch the Boids practice. For a bunch of kids who'd never set foot on Doubleday Field, they weren't bad. Not great, by any means, but they had their hearts in the right place. I sat in the right-field bleachers and watched the team while they divided into two squads and played off against each other. At first, I winced while these boys and girls committed errors that would have put a Little League team to shame, until I gradually realized that these were third-generation colonists who'd inherited the game from their fathers and grandfathers. Once I came to accept this, I stopped cursing the pitcher every time he walked a batter. Even so, I found myself wishing I could be out there, if only to show these guys how baseball was really played.

My other distraction was Rain.

Most of the crew had other places to live besides the inn. Goldstein flew back to Albion, where I was told he had an estate just outside New Brighton. Ted and Emily had a house in town, and Ali lived in an apartment above a cheesemaker's shop; I'd run into them from time to time, usually while I was out doing errands. Ash had a room at the inn, too, just down the hall from mine, but I rarely saw him, and then only late at night, when he'd lurch back to the Soldier's Joy from Lew's Cantina. He never spoke to me, and from what I could tell, he seemed to be perpetually drunk. On occasion I'd hear a guitar being played in his room, but that was about it. Altogether, everything about him was ominous—there's nothing worse than having a jughead aboard ship—but since he was Morgan's passenger, there was little I could do about it.

Rain had been put up at the inn as well, something I didn't know until the morning of my third day there, when I spotted her in the dining room. She'd arrived before I did, though, and it was clear that she wasn't thrilled to see me. Before I could go over to ask if I could join her for breakfast, she hastily stood up, dropped a few colonials on the table, and scurried out the garden door. When the innkeeper's wife came by to take my order, I asked if the young lady who had just left was another guest. She told me, yes, she was indeed . . . and pointedly added that Rain's room was on the ground floor, just across the hall from the apartment where she and her husband lived. Just in case, I suppose, I might be a little *too* interested.

Which I wasn't. The last thing I wanted to do was waste my time pursuing a girl who acted as if I had spinach stuck between my teeth. Yet Rain Thompson wasn't just another girl. She was also a shipmate, which meant that we'd have to work together for the duration of our voyage. It wouldn't do either of us any good if she refused to talk to me. One way or another, I'd have to make peace with her.

That turned out to be difficult. Over the course of the next few days, I'd see her every so often, but always from a distance . . . a distance that she'd seemed determined to keep between us. Several times while walking through town, I saw her coming from the other direction, but when I quickened my pace to catch up with her, she'd either cross the street to avoid me or duck down an alley and disappear. Once while watching the Boids work out, I caught a glimpse of her strolling across the university campus, yet she vanished by the time I came down from the bleachers. On another occasion, I spotted her through a shop window . . . but that time I held back, not wanting her to feel like she was being cornered.

Yet even as she and I played this little cat and mouse game, I found myself becoming intrigued by her. I'd seen plenty of women who were more beautiful—and to be honest, I'd even slept with a few of them—but there was something about her that fascinated me. I liked the way she moved, the way she dressed, the way she let her hair fall around her shoulders. The only thing I couldn't stand was the coldness in her eyes whenever she looked my way . . . but even then, that was just one more part of the mystery that was Rain Thompson.

On my eighth day in Liberty, I resolved to solve this enigma once and for all. She got up early in the morning. Well, so would I. That night, I set my watch alarm for 5:00 A.M., laid out my clothes so that I could get dressed as quickly as possible, and went to bed early. By sunrise, I was seated in the ground-floor parlor, casually reading yesterday's edition of the *Liberty Post*, when I heard a door open and shut just down the hall.

Keeping the newspaper open in front of my face, I waited until I heard her walk into the parlor. The dining room wasn't open yet, though, and her footsteps stopped in front of the door. She hesitated, turned around . . . and that was when I lowered the newspaper.

"Good morning," I said.

Rain's eyes went wide, and for a second I thought she'd leap a foot into the air. "Oh my god!" she snapped. "Don't do that!"

"Sorry. Didn't mean to surprise you." Sure, I did, but there was no point in letting her know that. "Coming in for breakfast? So am I."

"Well, I . . . I . . ."

"Nothing else open at this hour, so far as I know. Unless you'd like to take a walk."

Her eyes darted toward the front door. "As a matter of fact, I . . ."

"Good. I'll go with you." I put aside the paper and stood up. "A little constitutional first thing in the morning is good for the heart, don't you think?" She was still trying to figure out how to answer this when the dining-room door clicked from the inside, and the innkeeper's wife pushed it open. "Or maybe some breakfast first," I added. "Shouldn't exercise on an empty stomach, you know."

Rain looked first at the dining room, then at the front door, and finally at me. Unless she wanted to flee back to her room, she was trapped, and she knew it. "Well . . . all right," she said, her expression lapsing into sour resignation. "If you insist."

"Breakfast? Or a walk first?" She shrugged, as if the choice mattered little to her. "Breakfast, then." I raised two fingers to the landlady. "Table for two, please . . . and yes, we'd like coffee."

II

Rain wore a calf-length hemp skirt and a thin wool sweater. When I pulled back the chair for her, I noticed the silver ankle bracelet above her left foot and the turquoise pin with which she'd pulled back her hair that morning. As always, she wore her clothes with elegant simplicity. I'd known women back on Earth who spent hours primping before a mirror to achieve the look she managed to capture with casual ease.

She let me seat her, but said nothing while we glanced at our menus. The Soldier's Joy offered the same breakfast every morning, so the choice wasn't difficult to make: I took two scrambled eggs, a rasher of bacon, toast, and a glass of tomato juice, while she ordered a poached egg, toast, and water. A pot of black coffee was already on the table; once the landlady disappeared into the kitchen, I picked it up and poured a cup for myself.

"You were waiting for me, weren't you?" she asked.

My first thought was to pretend that this was nothing but a coincidence, but she was too sharp for that kind of nonsense. "Uh-huh," I said. "Got up early. Waited until you showed up." A yawn rose from my chest as I put down the coffeepot, and I raised my hand to my face. "Pardon . . . a little early for me."

"Why?"

"Well . . ." I picked up my cup, took a sip. "First off, you and I are going to have to work together, and my experience has been that it's best to make friends with your shipmates . . . or at least get to know them a little better." The coffee was strong that morning; I added a splash of goat's milk to tone it down. "Second, I'm wondering why you keep trying to avoid me, when . . . so far as I know, at least . . . I've done nothing to offend you."

"Is that a fact?" She sat back in her chair, arms folded across her chest.

"That's a fact." I took another sip. "Your turn."

She regarded me for a few moments, as if sizing me up. "Very well, then," she said at last. "The fact of the matter is that I don't trust you."

Of all the things she could have said, that was the one that I least expected. At least she could have waited until I didn't have a drink in my hand. Hot coffee sloshed over the rim of the cup and scalded the web of my thumb, causing me to wince. "Damn," I muttered, hastily putting down the cup and picking up a napkin. "Don't mince words, do you?"

An offhand shrug. "You asked."

"So what makes you think I can't be . . . ?" A thought occurred to me. "Oh, right. You mean the way I got here. Look, it's a long story, but if you'll let me explain . . ."

"Don't bother. I know all about that already." Rain poured coffee for herself; she took it black, ignoring both the milk and sugar on the table. "The fact that you're a stowaway only confirms my suspicions . . . although, I have to admit, the way you pulled it off was pretty clever."

"Right up until I got caught, sure." She said nothing as I folded a corner of the napkin, dipped it into the water glass, and used it to nurse my burned hand. "But why do you say that confirms your suspicions of me?"

91

Rain absently toyed with a fork, running a finger along its handle. "When Morgan became interested in you, he got someone who works for him to check you out . . ."

"He told me that. I assume one of his people managed to access my service record."

"Morgan has his resources." She picked up her coffee. "There's more to you than meets the eye."

I had to smile at this. "How kind of you to say so."

She wasn't amused. "Your brother, Jim, probably thought so, too. Right after you betrayed him."

Suddenly, this conversation was no longer as charming as it might have been. I stared at her from across the table, trying to decide how much of a gentleman I wanted to be. "That's"—I took a deep breath—"none of your business."

"It isn't?" Rain stared back at me. "You said it yourself . . . people should get to know one another if they're going work together on a ship." She shook her head. "And what I found out about what you did to your brother . . ."

"You don't know squat about—"

The landlady chose that moment to come through the kitchen door with our plates in each hand. She must have noticed the tension between us, because she hesitated for a moment before she approached our table and, without a word, put the plates in front of us. Neither Rain nor I spoke until she'd vanished once more. I'd lost my appetite by then, but at least the interruption gave me a moment to get my temper back under control.

"Did it ever occur to you," I said, trying hard to remain calm, "that what's in my files may not be the truth? Or at least not all of it?"

"Why wouldn't it be?" Rain picked up her fork, used it to pierce the yolk of her poached egg. "There's no reason for anyone to lie."

"Oh, yes, there is. Especially when it has to do with the *Academia del Espacio*." I let out my breath. "Look, let me tell you about what happened to Jim . . ."

III

Jim Truffaut was my younger brother, born a couple of years after our mother brought me into the world. She and my father had already decided that they wanted to have two sons, so genengineering assured them that I didn't have a sister instead. Since our folks were also fans of classic cinema, they decided to take advantage of our family name to christen us after one of their favorite French films. You can look it up if you don't catch the allusion; reference TRUFFAUT, FRANÇOIS, DIRECTOR, and go from there.

Skip forward eighteen years. Since my lifelong dream had been to become a spacer, once I graduated from high school I applied to the Union Astronautica. In the Western Hemisphere Union, this was the only way to get into space. My grades were good, and with my father's assistance—which included a nice bribe to the local Matriarch for whom he'd done a few favors as a loyal Party member—I was accepted into the *Academia del Espacio*, the UA's training school for its astronaut corps.

Jim didn't necessarily want to go to the stars, but neither did he want to live in Kansas for the rest of his life. The same Matriarch wrote a recommendation for him, and Jim entered the Academy as a plebe just as I was entering my senior year. But while I sailed through the program without much of a hitch, Jim had problems from the moment he set foot in the Academy. And let's face it: although social collectivism dictates that all men are created equal, the fact of the matter is that some of us are more equal than others. I had stardust in my blood, but Jim had to struggle every waking moment just to get through his classes.

I tried to help him as much as I could, and as an upperclassman I was able to do so. But the day finally came when I graduated from the Academy, with the attendant rank of Ensign First Class, and I had to leave my brother behind. Jim's poor grades had already caused him to fall back a semester; he'd been put on probation and was in danger of washing out by the time I was assigned to a Mars cycleship. My future was bright, but his lay in shadow.

I'd promised him, though, that I'd try to help him as much as I could, and see that he'd get posted on my ship once he graduated. Jules and Jim, off to conquer the universe. That was a promise I'd live to regret, because I'd just finished my first tour on the *Victory* when I received a coded communiqué from Jim. His finals were coming up in two weeks, and he was having problems remembering vital equations he needed to know in order to pass. Could I help him in any way? Hint, hint.

I knew the written part of the exams like the back of my hand. I'd also learned, from idle small talk with fellow junior officers aboard the *Victory*, that the questions hadn't changed in at least five or six years. So, using a bypass that would circumvent Academy mail filters, I sneaked those questions to Jim, along with the appropriate answers.

Sure, I was helping Jim cheat. And I didn't feel much guilt about doing it, either. All that stuff I'd been forced to memorize was already loaded into every pad and comp I'd used aboard ship; the Academy only wanted its cadets to know them in the unlikely event of a system crash. So sliding him the answers to a redundant part of a written exam . . . where was the harm, in the most practical sense?

The harm was that it *was* cheating, plain and simple. The instructors who examined Jim's test didn't notice any discrepancies; however, as a matter of routine, the test was fed to a comp, which matched its answers against those given by other cadets in previous years. The comp immediately saw that two questions I'd gotten wrong during my finals were identical to those Jim failed to answer correctly during his. Given our relationship, this caused a red flag to be raised. And when the board of inquiry came to me . . .

My eggs had gone cold by then, my bacon as brittle as a lie. The only thing on my plate that was still worth eating was the toast; I daubed some jelly on it only because it gave my hands something to do.

"I didn't have a choice," I said, reluctant to look Rain straight in the eye. "Even being suspected of cheating on an exam is enough to sink a cadet."

"And so you sold out your own brother." Her gaze was remorseless. "To save your career."

"That's what you were told?" I looked up at her. "That I finked on him?"

"Yes. And—"

"Get it straight . . . *I denied everything!*"

She blinked. "But I thought—"

"Forget what you've heard. Do you honestly believe that I'd burn my own brother just to save my skin?" Before she could answer, I went on. "When I was called before the board, I stood before six Patriarchs and Matriarchs and told them that I'd never passed any information to Jim."

"Then how did they find out?"

"Because Jim had already confessed. He was so scared, he told his advisor about what he'd done even before the board called him up. But they kept us from seeing each other, and so when I walked into the room, all I knew was that my brother was under suspicion." I sighed, shook my head. "I figured that, if both of us denied everything, all they'd have was statistical probability, and that wouldn't be enough to prove anything. What I didn't count on was Jim fessing up."

"So you lied to save your brother."

"Uh-huh . . . and my own ass, to tell the truth." I picked up my coffee. It had gone lukewarm by then, but I slugged it down anyway. "Didn't work. With Jim's confession on record, they had both of us nailed. So they expelled him from the Academy and tossed me out of the service."

"The Union Astronautica would do that?" She stared at me. "Kick out one of its own just because . . . ?"

"Yes, it would." She clearly didn't understand. "Look," I went on, leaning forward to rest my elbows on the table, "in a system like the one I grew up in, the rights of the individual matter less than the rights of society. Not much grey area in between. You're either right or wrong, with us or against us." I raised a fist in a mock Union salute. "All hail the glory of social collectivism, and all that happy crap."

"I can't believe that," she murmured, her gaze falling to her plate. I noticed that she hadn't touched her food either.

"Well . . . sorry, but there is it. I've told you the truth, the whole truth, and nothing but the truth." Even though my breakfast had gone cold, I wasn't about to let it go to waste. I picked up a piece of bacon and nibbled on it. "You can believe me, or you can believe a UA file you've managed to hack. Doesn't matter either way. Morgan hired me, and that's what counts."

Something I said rekindled her anger, because her eyes flared when she looked up at me again. "All that tells me is that you can't be counted on. Maybe you tried to save your brother, but you lied to people who trusted you to do so . . ."

"Aw, c'mon . . . !"

"And then you went further. You faked your identity . . . twice, if I understand it right . . . in order to stow away aboard a Coyote starship, when you could have simply purchased a ticket . . ."

"I did buy a ticket. Under another name, sure . . . but I wasn't a freeloader." She looked confused, and I went on. "When I was thrown out of the service, the government revoked my passport. The last thing they wanted was to have a former UA officer leave the country and take their secrets with him . . . that's happened before, until they clamped down on it. That's why I had to sneak aboard the *Lee* . . . there was too much of a chance of having red flags go up if I'd tried to ship out any other way."

"Uh-huh." She remained skeptical. "And when you got caught, you hijacked a lifeboat and . . ."

"Oh, for the love of . . ." Angry again, I tossed the rest of the bacon on the plate. "What kind of dreamworld do you live in? I'd hit rock bottom. At least Jim was able to return to Salina and get his life back . . . he hadn't really wanted to go into space, so all he lost was a job he hadn't been cut out for in the first place."

"Sounds like you've got a bone to pick with him."

"We're not on speaking terms anymore, if that's what you're asking." I didn't add that Jim had never bothered to apologize for ratting me out to the board, or that he'd told our folks that it had been my idea to pass the test answers to him. "After what happened, I had nothing left. I couldn't get hired by anyone else because, in the WHU, there *is* nothing else. You want to be a spacer, you join the UA. Or . . . well, that's it. Nothing else. Unless you decide to play dirty."

"Play dirty?"

"Sure. You scrounge up what little cash you can, buy a phony ID and passport on the black market, and leave the continent on whatever suborbital freighter you can find. Then you land somewhere in

Europe, hitchhike your way across another continent until you reach a spaceport where you can bribe your way aboard a ship bound for Highgate. Then . . ."

This was quickly turning into a rant. I pulled myself up short. "Anyway, please don't tell me about the virtues of a clean and honest life unless you've lost everything you once had, or had a brother who's a worthless piece of . . ."

"Don't you talk about my brother!"

That came as an angry shout, one that would have silenced the entire room if anyone else had been there. Rain's face had gone red; it was her turn to be pissed off. Past her shoulder, I caught a glimpse of the kitchen door easing open a crack as the landlady peered out at us. I looked back at her and shook my head ever so slightly; satisfied that the guests weren't about to start throwing furniture at each other, she eased the door shut once more.

"My apologies," I said, keeping my voice as low as possible. "Didn't mean to offend you."

Realizing that I hadn't meant any harm, she closed her eyes as she sought to regain control of her emotions. "Sorry," she whispered. "I don't know what . . . I mean, you couldn't know about . . ." A deep sigh, then she straightened her shoulders. "Look, maybe we got off on the wrong foot there."

"I think so, yeah." Finding nothing else to say, I looked around the table. "More coffee?" I asked, picking up the pot. "It might still be . . ."

"No . . . none for me, thanks." Rain's hands trembled as they found the napkin in her lap, brought it to her face. I was surprised to see that the corners of her eyes had become moist. "I just . . . sorry, but something you said . . ."

"I . . ."

"Forget it." She snuffled back tears. "Didn't mean to bark at you like that. I just . . ."

Whatever she intended to say to me, I didn't get a chance to hear it, for at that moment the dining-room door opened, and I looked around to see Ted come in. The captain spotted Rain and me, and quickly walked over to our table.

"Good. You're both up." He glanced at our plates. "Sorry to interrupt. Just started?"

"Yeah, but . . ." I glanced at Rain; to my relief, she'd dried her tears and put away the napkin. "I don't think either of us is very hungry. Why, what's going on?"

"Just got a call from Morgan." Ted pulled back an empty chair, sat down. "Our ship's here. Came through the starbridge about an hour ago, and it'll be in orbit later today. We're to pack up and grab the noon gyrobus to New Brighton."

"We're shipping out? Just like that?"

"Just like that." Ted picked up a piece of toast from my plate and munched on it. "Hope you're ready to pilot that shuttle, because you're about to get your chance."

"Yeah, sure." After all the hours I'd put in on the tutorials, I could fly it blindfolded if I had to. "But what's the rush? I mean, don't we have to load the cargo and . . . ?"

"Cargo's already at the spaceport, ready to go aboard the shuttle once it lands." Ted looked over at Rain. "Ready for this, sweetie?"

"No problem here, skipper." I was amazed by how quickly she'd recovered. No clue on her face that, only a few minutes ago, she'd been on the verge of tears. Or, just before that, ready to belt me across the room. "Just get me to New Brighton. I'll handle the rest."

"That's my girl." Ted gave her a fond smile, then checked his watch. "Gyro leaves in a few hours. Go upstairs and pack your gear.

I'll check you out of your rooms and call a cab." He looked around. "Anyone seen Ash this morning?"

I was about to say that I never saw him before sundown when Rain supplied the answer for me. "Still in his room, I think." She hesitated, than quietly added, "I doubt he's in much condition to fly."

Oh, so she'd also noticed the inebriated state in which our mystery passenger constantly resided. Yet there was something in the way she and Ted looked at each other that gave me reason to think that they knew more about Ash than anyone had divulged to me. "I'll wake him up," Ted said, standing up again. "He's coming with us, whether he wants to or not."

I reached into my pocket, pulled out a couple of colonials, and put them on the table. If no one was going to tell me about Ash, I'd just have to live with it. Yet there was something else I deserved to know.

"Pardon me, Captain," I said as I pushed back my chair, "but just one little thing . . ."

"Yes?"

"The name of our ship . . . what is it?"

Ted didn't reply at once. Then he pulled back his shoulders, hitched his thumbs within his belt, and looked me straight in the eye.

"Mr. Truffaut," he said, "the name of our ship is the *Pride of Cucamonga.*"

I almost laughed out loud. "What kind of a name is that for a . . . ?"

"We're getting whatever Mr. Goldstein has decided to give us." He shrugged. "Our job is to fly it."

(SEVEN)

Shipping out . . .

Loose Lucy *and her motley crew . . .*

caution: weird load . . .

and an even weirder passenger to go with it . . .

shake, rattle, and roll.

IV

The New Brighton spaceport was more sophisticated than I expected. I'm not sure what I'd anticipated—an overgrown meadow, perhaps, with goats grazing among rusted-out fuel tanks and some old codger sitting on the front porch of a log cabin ("A-yuh, we have spaceships land here now and then")—but what I found instead were several square miles of steel-reinforced concrete, with service vehicles moving among gantries that looked as if they'd been built the day before. At one end of the field was a sleek new passenger terminal; next to it rose the slender pylon of a control tower, its roof bristling with antennae and sat dishes. Even Port Olympus on Mars didn't look so good.

The gyrobus touched down on the commercial side of the spaceport, not far from a row of hangars where several shuttles were parked. Everyone aboard the afternoon flight from Liberty was a pro spacer, with most of them working for the Federation Navy; before we'd boarded the gyro, Ted had quietly told us to say nothing to them and refrain from talking about our mission. So we kept to ourselves, drawing curious glances from the Federation guys but little more. We waited until they disembarked before we picked up our bags and filed out of the aircraft, walking down the steps into the warmth of the equatorial sun.

We'd been told that someone would be there to meet us, but apparently they hadn't gotten the message. While Ted got on the phone to make a hurry-up call, I took a good look at the people whom I'd be flying with. No wonder the Feds had given us the fish-eye; none of us looked as if we'd ever set foot aboard a spacecraft, let alone served as its flight crew. No one wore a uniform of any sort. Rain had changed out of her skirt into a long-sleeve tunic and a pair of drawstring trousers, while Ted wore an old *Galileo* ball cap; Ali carried a rolled-up prayer mat under his arm, and Emily had brought along a knitting bag. Ash was obviously hungover; sitting on his duffel bag, his shoulders slumped forward and the hood of his dark brown robe pulled up over his head, he stared at the ground as if he was about to throw up any minute. I noticed a battered guitar case among his belongings and wondered if he had a bottle of booze stashed in there.

After a while, an open-air hovercart showed up, driven by a kid barely old enough to peer over the steering wheel. With mumbled apologies for being late, he helped us load our belongings into the rear, then climbed behind the wheel. The cart did a one-eighty and purred off across the field, the driver dodging cargo loaders and fuel trucks as we passed the hangars. From the other side of the spaceport, there was a roar as a passenger shuttle lifted off, no doubt headed for orbital rendezvous with the *Robert E. Lee*. We'd just heard the loud *boom* of it going supersonic when I caught my first look at my new craft.

The CFS *Loose Lucy* was eighty feet tall from the pads of its landing gear to the blunt cone of its nose fairing, forty feet abeam where the nozzle of its nuclear engine protruded from the oblate plate of its stern. Judging from the dents, scratches, and scorch marks along the sides of its bell-shaped hull, it was apparent that *Lucy* had more than a few flight hours on her. Not a very promising sign.

I glanced at Ted and Emily, saw the dubious expressions on their faces. Ted looked back at me and shrugged. "No one promised us a new boat," he said quietly, trying to make the best of it. "And I've been told it's flightworthy. Think you'll have any trouble?"

"Nope . . . if it doesn't fall apart during takeoff." Behind me, Ali was whispering something in Arabic that sounded vaguely like a prayer.

A gantry tower had been rolled up beside the shuttle, with a gangway leading to the passenger hatch at the top of the craft. *Lucy's* middeck cargo hatch was open; the shuttle's freight elevator had been extended upon its T-bar crane, its cage lowered to the ground. A cargo loader was parked next to the craft, and, as the cart coasted to a halt, a familiar figure detached himself from a group of pad rats and walked over to greet us.

"Glad to see you made it," Goldstein said, as if we had any choice in the matter. "Sorry this was on such short notice, but I didn't know exactly when the ship was supposed to arrive until early this morning."

"Not a problem, boss." Ted shook his hand, then stepped back to gaze up at the shuttle. "It . . . well, looks like it's been quite well broken in."

"And put back together again," I muttered.

Emily scowled at me, and Ted chose to ignore my comment, but Morgan's expression darkened. "Sorry, Mr. Truffaut," he said, cupping an ear. "I didn't quite hear that."

"I said, she looks solidly put together, sir." *For something that looks like it came straight from the salvage yard,* I silently added.

"Don't let looks fool you. She's had long and dependable service. I went for nothing but the best." The rest of us looked askance at one another, but no one said anything as Goldstein went on. "We've almost finished loading the cargo. Rain, you may want to take a look at the manifest, make sure that everything is . . ."

"Pardon me," I said, "but would someone finally tell me what we're going to be hauling?" I was looking at the cargo loader. Stacked on its flatbed were enormous rolls, tightly wrapped in white nylon and lashed together with coils of rope. They somewhat resembled the bales of winter hay one might see in a cow pasture back on Earth, but I couldn't imagine hay being exported to Rho Coronae Borealis.

"Hemp," Morgan replied.

"Hemp?" I raised an eyebrow. "You can't be . . ."

"Well, not exactly." He hesitated. "Female *cannabis sativa*, dried and cured, to be more precise . . ."

"Marijuana," Rain said.

I stared at her. "You've got to be kidding."

She calmly looked back at me. "No, I'm not kidding. Five thousand pounds of marijuana, from hemp plantations just south of Shuttlefield."

"What the . . . ?" I was having a hard time keeping my jaw from hitting the ground. "What the hell do the *hjadd* want with two and a half tons of marijuana?"

Ted let out his breath. "It's a long story, but . . . to make it short, when the *hjadd* rescued Emily and me from Spindrift, one of the things they found aboard our shuttle was a few grams of marijuana our companion happened to be carrying for his own consumption. The *hjadd* discovered that it was an edible herb they could use in their own food."

"They *eat* marijuana?"

"Think of it as tea, or perhaps chocolate." Goldstein smiled as he led the way over to the loader. Its operator was using the crane to lift one of the bales from the flatbed and place it on the freight elevator. "The *hjadd* are vegetarian by nature, so they consider it to be a rare delicacy. Fortunately, the sample Dr. Ramirez had with him was the seedless variety, so they've been unable to cultivate it on their own world. Therefore, if they want more, they need to come to us."

He reached up to pat one of the bales. "As luck would have it, the colonists have been growing hemp for years, for use in clothing, paper, natural oils, whatever. The female plants are necessary for cultivation, of course, but they're usually discarded during processing. After all, no one smokes the stuff anymore, except for the occasional eccentric like Ramirez. So . . ."

"So Coyote has tons of the stuff, and the *hjadd* are willing to trade for it."

"You're catching on." Morgan grinned. "We've already given them fifty pounds . . . a free sample, to whet their appetites . . . but this is the first large shipment. If all goes well, it'll become a major export item, with more to follow . . ."

"Sure." I shrugged. "And who knows? After this, we can introduce them to tobacco. Maybe even opium."

Morgan glared at me, then turned to Ted. "Captain Lesh is over there. If you'll follow me, I'll introduce you so you can make the change of command."

"Thanks." Ted looked at Emily. "Emcee, once Rain checks the manifest, take everyone upstairs and get them settled in." He glanced at me. "You know your job, right?"

"Prep the boat for launch. Right." Once again, I gazed up at *Loose Lucy.* "When do you want to go?"

"Soon as possible," Morgan said, before Ted could respond. "And Mr. Truffaut . . . I'd appreciate it if you'd refrain from unkind remarks about my business. That last one was uncalled for."

I suppose I should have apologized, but I didn't. Instead, I just shrugged. Morgan gave me one last look, then turned to lead Ted away. Emily watched them go, then stepped closer to me.

"Word of advice," she said quietly. "Don't push it with Morgan. He could land you back in jail anytime he wants."

I was tempted to ask where he'd find another shuttle pilot. Emily meant well, though, and there was no reason to piss her off. Besides, she was right. As affable as Morgan Goldstein might appear, there was little doubt that he was a cunning businessman. People like that don't let anyone get between them and their money.

"I'll keep that in mind," I replied, "but if . . ."

Suddenly, I forgot what I was about to say, for at that moment I looked past her to see a figure approaching us. And that was when I caught my first sight of Mahamatasja Jas Sa-Fhadda.

V

The moment I laid eyes on the Prime Emissary, I immediately knew who he . . . or rather, heshe . . . was. Even though heshe was dressed head to toe in a grey environment suit whose opaque faceplate rendered hisher features invisible, everyone on Earth had seen pictures of the *hjadd* chief delegate to Coyote. And I'd already been told, of course, that heshe was going to be another passenger on this voyage. Nonetheless, I was stunned to see himher walking toward us, escorted by two blueshirts.

Nor was I the only person in our group to be surprised. Ali took an involuntary step back, almost as if frightened by a creature that was

a head shorter than any of us. Rain had been talking to a longshoreman; when she spotted the Prime Emissary, she quickly ended the
conversation and hurried over to join us. And for the first time since
our arrival at New Brighton, Ash seemed to take notice of what was
going on.

"Hello, Jas." Emily raised her left hand, palm out and fingers
spread apart. "Good to see you again."

"It is good to see you again as well." The voice that came from
the grille beneath the faceplate was deep-throated yet oddly androgynous, almost as if an opera singer was concealed inside the suit. That
notion was forgotten the moment the *hjadd* raised hisher own left
hand; six webbed fingers, blunt but taloned, spread apart in an identical greeting. "Is this another member of your crew?"

Heshe meant me. "Umm . . . yes, I am," I replied, instinctively offering my hand. "Glad to meet you, Mr. Sa-Fhadda. My name is Jules
Truffaut. I'm . . ."

A froglike croak from the grille as the *hjadd* recoiled from me,
hisher hand dropping to hisher side. I suddenly realized that I'd made
a mistake. Before I could say anything, though, a voice spoke from
behind my left shoulder.

"The Prime Emissary is offended," Ash murmured, standing close
beside me. "*Hjadd* don't like to be touched by strangers unless they
invite such contact. Also, Sa-Fhadda isn't hisher last name, but hisher
caste and social status. Apologize at once."

I didn't know which was more surprising: the fact that a handshake could be offensive or that Ash had finally spoken. "Sorry," I said,
lowering my hand . . . and then, on sudden afterthought, hastily raising my left hand, in imitation of Emily's gesture. "I didn't know the
correct form of address. Please forgive me."

A short hiss that might have come from an angry cat, then the helmeted head weaved back and forth on its long neck. "You are for-given, Mr. Truffaut," heshe said. "You did not know better. And you may call me Jas."

Jas formally extended hisher own hand. I hesitated, then carefully grasped it. Even through the thin plastic of Jas's glove, I could feel the warmth of hisher touch, offset by the hardness of hisher talons as they briefly stroked the inside of my palm. The last thing I'd expected to do this morning when I woke up was to shake hands with an alien; definitely a moment for my memoirs.

"Good," Ash said, still whispering to me. "Your apology has been accepted, and heshe has accepted you. Now release hisher hand, back away, and shut up."

I did as I was told, without another word. As Jas turned toward Emily, I glanced back at Ash. "Thanks. I . . ."

"Be quiet." His eyes flickered toward me from within his hood.

So much for gratitude. I looked back at Emily and Jas; the two of them had already walked away, involved in a quiet conversation. Ash slipped past me, his robe whisking across the concrete as he fell in behind them. Again, I was left to speculate what his role in all this was. Liaison? Interpreter? How did he know what . . . ?

"Nice going there." Rain came up beside me. "Maybe you should leave diplomacy to the pros."

"Is that what Ash is? A diplomat?"

A moment of hesitation, then a sly smile stole across her lips. "You could say that. If I were you, though, I'd steer clear of him. He could make life hell for you if he really wanted to."

I remembered how I'd seen him standing outside my jail window, and the strange mental episode that I'd experienced a few moments later. I'd pretty much written off the incident as . . . well, I didn't know what it was, only that it was something that I'd felt compelled not to explore. Before I could ask, though, Rain pushed a pad into my hands.

"Here's the manifest. I've checked it out, and everything looks okay. All you need to do is sign it, and we're good to go." I found the blank space marked PILOT and used my fingertip to scrawl my signature across the bottom of the screen. "Thanks," she said, taking it back from me. "Now let's see if you can get through the rest of the day without screwing up again."

"Hey, now wait a minute." I thought I'd made my peace with her, but there she was, busting my chops again. It was really getting on my nerves. "I'd appreciate a little respect, if it's not too much to ask."

"Respect is earned, not given." There was enough frost in her voice to turn a warm summer afternoon into a cold day in hell . . . which apparently was when she'd have anything kind to say to me. "Get us into orbit without killing everyone aboard, and I'll take it into consideration."

Then she walked off, leaving me to wonder once again whether this job might be more trouble than it was worth.

VI

Loose Lucy was aptly named. The cockpit looked as if it had been retrofitted at least twice since the shuttle rolled off the assembly line, with new control panels installed beside ones that probably had been in use when I was in high school. The first thing I did was to check the control panels; the layout was slightly different from the one I'd learned to use in the tutorial, but otherwise it was nothing that I couldn't handle. The pilot's couch creaked noticeably as I sat down, though, and the left armrest was wrapped with frayed duct tape. I'd been in flight simulators that were in better shape.

As pilot and copilot, Ted and I were the first to climb aboard, with the rest of the crew following us through the hatch to take seats on the couches arranged around the passenger compartment. There were eight in all, with one remaining vacant; that would belong to the chief engineer, who was waiting for us aboard the *Pride*. I noted that one of the couches was different from the rest; on closer examination, I saw that it had been designed to fit a *hjadd*. As I watched, Jas settled into it, hisher short legs and long torso comfortably finding room in a space that would have been painful for a human.

From his seat beside me, Ted quietly watched while I went through the prelaunch checklist. Satisfied that I knew what I was doing, he turned to make sure that everyone was strapped in. Rain was the last aboard; she had waited on the ground until she was certain that our freight was safely stowed away before closing the cargo hatch and climbing the ladder up to the flight deck.

As soon as she was in her seat, I ordered the passenger hatch to be sealed. Once *Lucy* was airtight, I pressurized the compartment, then got on the comlink and requested gantry rollback. Bright sunlight streamed through the cockpit windows as the shuttle emerged from beneath the tower's shadow; through my headset, I could hear the crosstalk among the ground crew as they cleared the pad. A few minutes later, traffic control informed me that airspace was clear and I had permission to launch.

One last check of all systems, with Ted making sure that I hadn't forgotten anything, then I entered the flight program into the nav system and initiated the final launch sequence. At this point, I could have just as easily switched to autopilot, but I didn't do this. *Loose Lucy* was new to me, and I didn't know how much I trusted her. Besides, I wanted to show my new captain that I wasn't some rookie who'd leave everything to the comps.

So I cranked my seat back into reclining position, pulled the lap-board closer to my chest, and grasped the yoke with my left hand and the throttle bar with my right. When I had green lights across my console, I flipped open a candy-striped panel and pushed the big red button beneath it.

Loose Lucy might be an old bird, but she was no turkey. She rose from the pad quickly and smoothly, g-force pushing us back in our seats. The hull shook and rattled a bit as the shuttle began its ascent, but the noise quickly subsided as I shoved the stick all the way forward, replaced by a loud roar as the main engine went full throttle. The clouds above us leapt toward us, then the shuttle punched through them.

The sky gradually grew darker, blue fading to black, until stars began to appear. And then we were in space, on our way to orbit. I throttled back the engine, then fired the RCS thrusters to roll the craft to starboard.

Through the forward windows, Coyote hove into view, a vast hemisphere of white-flecked green, the Great Equatorial River visible as a broad blue band that stretched to the distant horizon. Beyond the limb of the moon, Bear rose as an enormous crescent, its rings jutting out into space. A hell of a sight; I found myself wishing that I wasn't a pilot, so that I could simply sit back and take it all in.

I didn't have that luxury, though. Using the nav system to get a precise fix on our target, I found the *Pride of Cucamonga* right where it was supposed to be, parked in stationary orbit several thousand miles above the equator. I could have shut down the engine and simply allowed *Lucy* to coast the rest of the way to her mother ship, but that would have meant that we'd have to orbit Coyote a few times, adding six to eight hours to our trip. The gauge told me that we had more than enough fuel for a direct ascent, so I kept the engines throttled up one-quarter percent, and programmed the comp for a trajectory that would get us there in just a couple of hours.

Once I was satisfied that everything was copacetic, I switched to autopilot, then returned my seat to upright position. "Everyone okay back there?" I asked, glancing over my shoulder. "Wasn't too rough, I hope."

A mumble from Rain that might have been a complaint, but I couldn't quite make out her words. "Gordon passed out," Emily said, "but otherwise he's all right."

"Gordon? Who's Gordon?"

"She means Ash. That's his first name." Ted cranked his own seat to horizontal position. "Good flying, kid. You can keep your job." He looked back at our passengers. "Mr. Goldstein? Jas? How are you doing?"

"Fine. Just fine." Judging from Morgan's tone of voice, I didn't have to see his face to know that it was probably a pale shade of green. "Jas is . . ."

"I am comfortable." If there was any emotion in hisher voice, the translation device of hisher suit masked it. "Thank you, Mr. Truffaut. I compliment your skills as a pilot."

I liked that. If the Prime Emissary didn't have any complaints, then Rain was in no position to argue. As usual, Ali remained stoical, although I wouldn't have expected otherwise. Pilots respect each other when they're behind the stick; if he had any criticism to offer, he'd tell me once we were out of the cockpit.

"Thank you, Jas. I appreciate it." I checked the comp again. "ETA in about two hours, thirty-six minutes, folks. So just sit back and enjoy the ride."

VII

Two and a half hours later, we rendezvoused with the *Pride of Cucamonga*.

Perhaps I was spoiled. The *Robert E. Lee*, after all, was a streamlined beauty to behold, and even cycleships like the *Victory* possessed a certain elegant symmetry. By comparison, the *Pride* was as ugly as a crowbar. About four hundred feet in length, the freighter was comprised of cylindrical subsections arranged in tandem, with the hab module at the bow and its massive fusion engine at the stern. Two enormous cargo modules, each resembling a giant drum, protruded at perpendicular angles from either side of the hub just aft of the hab module, giving the ship a cruciform appearance. The service module at the midsection was jammed with maneuvering thrusters, auxiliary tanks, and radiators, while the deflector array stuck out from the prow like an immense wok.

As we drew closer, it became clear that the *Pride* was a spacecraft with more than a few billion miles to its logbook. In places along its hull, I spotted plates that were of a slightly different color than the ones surrounding them, an indication that the ship had recently undergone a major refit. There were blackened scorch marks beneath the thrusters, and the telemetry dish appeared to be a replacement.

I wasn't the only one who noticed these things. Ted studied the ship as I matched course with it, then looked back at Morgan. "Tell me again why we didn't rate a new ship."

"For its class, it's the best one currently available." Morgan unclasped his harness and pushed himself out of his couch. "Everything else in the Janus fleet is currently committed to other contracts. Besides, my engineers told me that it would be easier to refit an older vessel than build a new one."

"Refit . . . you mean repair, don't you?" I didn't look away from my controls.

"No, I mean refit. There were certain modifications that needed to be made for this mission . . . particularly to the navigation system." Taking hold of the back of my couch, Morgan pulled himself closer to the windows, inserting himself between Ted and me. "Once we show a profit, the company will have the capital to construct a new ship specifically designed for . . ."

"Mr. Goldstein, please . . ." Ted reached up to gently push the boss away. "Give us a little breathing room, okay?" He glanced at me. "How are you doing there?"

"So far, so good." Keeping one eye on the lidar and the other on the comp screen, I fired the pitch and yaw thrusters to put *Lucy* on a direct line with the main docking port, located on the hub between the two cargo containers. Once I was holding station about five hundred feet from the ship, I touched my headset wand. "*Pride of Cucamonga*, this is *Loose Lucy*. Do you copy?"

A moment passed, then a gruff male voice came through. "*Affirmative, Lucy. Have you in sight, and you're clear to dock.*"

That had to be the chief engineer. I guessed that he was on the bridge. Obviously a man of few words. "Roger that, *Pride*," I replied. "Thank you."

"Need any help?" Ted asked quietly.

"No, thanks. Got it covered." To tell the truth, I was nervous as hell. Everything about both *Lucy* and the *Pride* gave me the uncertain feeling that neither craft was one hundred percent dependable, regardless of whatever Morgan had to say. Too late to chicken out now, though, so I opened the nose fairing to expose the docking collar, and once I had the *Pride*'s hub port lined up within the crosshairs of the forward radar, I fired aft thrusters and gently moved in.

I shouldn't have worried so much. *Lucy* was a good girl; she behaved herself as I coaxed her toward the docking port. Even so, I didn't breathe easy until the forward probe slid home and I felt the telltale thump of the flanges being engaged. An enunciator buzzed, confirming that we'd made a solid connection.

"Nice job," Emily said. "Couldn't have done better myself."

"Thank you." I safed the engines, then reached up to pressurize the forward airlock. "We're here, ladies and gentlemen . . . um, no offense, Prime Emissary."

"None taken." Again, the short, catlike hiss that I'd learned to recognize as the *hjadd* equivalent of a chuckle. "My kind answers to both."

That earned a couple of laughs from everyone except Rain and Ash. I didn't have to look back to know that she continued to be unimpressed with me. As for Ash . . . well, he probably either needed to throw up or have a drink, whichever came first.

"All right, we're here." Ted unbuckled his harness, then pushed himself out of his seat. "So let's go aboard and see what this tub is made of."

(EIGHT)

Doc at the airlock . . .

Rain in space . . .

a definition of the blues . . .

great minds think alike.

VIII

The *Pride of Cucamonga* looked a lot better inside than it did on the outside. For a freighter that had put in plenty of time on the Jovian run, it was in pretty good shape. Nonetheless, with the chipped iron grey paint of its bulkheads and exposed conduits running across low ceilings, no one could have mistaken it for a passenger liner. The *Pride* was a workhorse, plain and simple.

One of the luxuries it didn't have was artificial gravity. Since the ship wasn't equipped with diametric drive, it also lacked a Millis-Clement field generator. And although the hub could be rotated to provide centrifugal force to the cargo modules, since we weren't carrying livestock, the modules would be locked down for the duration of the journey. I was glad that I'd brought along a new pair of stickshoes; all the ones aboard had been used by the previous crew, and their insoles looked like fungal colonies.

The chief engineer met us at the airlock: Doc Schachner, a stocky gent in his midsixties who'd lost the hair on top of his head but made up for it with a thick white beard that went halfway down his chest. Doc knew Goldstein and called him by his first name, something that Morgan seemed to tolerate only barely; I'd later learn that Doc had a history of disagreements with his boss that might have gotten him canned a long time ago were it not for the fact that the chief was almost always right.

And for good reason. I eventually learned that Edward J. Schachner had earned his nickname along with the doctorate in astronautical engineering he'd picked up at the University of Edinburgh. After spending a decade designing spacecraft for Janus, he'd eventually decided that he'd rather fly spaceships than a drafting board. The *Pride* was one of the ships he'd built, and there probably wasn't a wire or rivet aboard that he didn't know like the back of his hand.

Doc wasn't one for small talk. A brief self-introduction was all we got before he escorted us from the airlock to the central access shaft that led through the ship's core. As he led us from the hub into the hab module, Doc paused every now and then to open pressure hatches leading from one deck to the next. As the last person in line, I quickly learned what it was like to be on the receiving end of his temper; when I neglected to close a hatch behind us, he made me go back and dog it tight, and after that made sure that each hatch was shut before we moved on. Ted might be the captain, but the *Pride* was clearly Doc's ship, and he didn't leave anything to chance.

Deck Two contained the crew quarters, but before we got there, Doc stopped at Deck Three. Opening the hatch, he asked Jas to accompany him; during the *Pride*'s refit, a separate cabin specifically designed for *hjadd* passengers had been added. So we waited in the shaft while Doc showed the Prime Emissary to his stateroom; when he returned a few minutes later, he took us the rest of the way to Deck Two.

Our quarters were located along a ring-shaped corridor that wound its way around the inside of the hab module. They were larger than the first-class cabins aboard the *Lee*, but not much; instead of bunks, we had sleep-sacks that could be strung up to form hammocks, and lockers instead of closets and shelves. No furniture, of course—a chair was unnecessary in zero g, a desk worse than useless—but at least I had my own privy, even if the toilet had vacuum hoses and the bath stall was equipped with hot and cold running sponges. As luck would have it, my cabin was located next to Ash's; noting that the walls weren't very thick and that there was a vent between our rooms, I hoped that he didn't snore.

I didn't get much of a chance to make myself at home. I'd just swapped my boots for my stickshoes when Rain knocked on my door. Time to unload *Loose Lucy*, and she needed me to fly the cargo pod. So off I went to earn my paycheck.

And that's when my troubles began.

IX

Never take a job if you know you're going to be working for someone who has less experience than you do.

Although the *Pride* was a civilian ship, nonetheless there's a certain hierarchy aboard merchanteers that's quasi-military in nature. In this instance, the quartermaster outranks the shuttle pilot when it comes to taking care of the payload. Therefore, Rain was my boss for this particular chore. Under any other circumstances, that wouldn't have been a problem, but from the moment we suited up for EVA, I knew working with her would be difficult.

The *Pride*'s secondary airlock was located on the opposite side of the hub from where *Lucy* was docked. Before you cycled through it, you entered the ready room where the EVA gear was stowed. Prepping for a spacewalk isn't for the modest; it entails stripping down to your birthday suit in order to put on the one-piece undergarment that, among other things, collects your sweat and urine to be distilled and recycled as coolant water and oxygen for the life-support system. If nudity is a problem, then you can always keep your back turned . . . but nonetheless, in a compartment little larger than a closet, it's hard to keep from bumping into the other guy.

Rain wasn't willing to trust me, despite my promises that I'd keep my hands to myself and not sneak a peek. Can't say that I blamed her; in zero g, it can be hard to be gallant, especially since you're having to use both hands to pull on the overgarment while attaching all the necessary lines and hoses. But she'd have nothing of it, so I had to wait outside while she suited up. That was my first indication that she had precious little experience, because nearly an hour went by before she let me in . . . and then, as soon as I saw her, I noticed that she'd missed a couple of steps, not the least of which was neglecting to close the zipper on her left wrist, something that might have caused a blowout.

Rain didn't like it very much when I pointed this out to her, nor was she appreciative when I properly attached the electrical line from her backpack to her chest unit. In fact, she squawked as if I was trying to grope her, until she realized what I was trying to do and why. Then she insisted on waiting for me in the airlock while I suited up . . . a violation of safety protocols, since the buddy system calls for no one to enter an airlock alone.

Prude. I took my time getting into my gear, meaning that I was ready to go in twenty minutes. A final check-out of each other's suits, followed by a comlink test, then we put on our helmets, pressurized our suits, and voided the airlock.

The cargo pod was docked on the hub's outer hull. It was almost identical to the one I'd operated on Highgate, so nothing about it was unfamiliar. Nonetheless, I waited until Rain attached her safety line to a hook just outside the airlock, then made her way hand over hand along the outside of the hub until she reached *Loose Lucy*, before I climbed into the cockpit. She spacewalked well enough, but nonetheless I couldn't help but notice a certain clumsiness in the way she moved. It was obvious that she hadn't spent a lot of time in EVA.

Rain was . . . how old? Nineteen, maybe twenty? I had time to think about this while I waited for her to find her way to the shuttle. How much previous experience could she have had before Morgan hired her? Probably not very much . . . especially not since the Federation Navy only consisted of a handful of small ships, plus the *Lee*. So how come someone so young got the job of quartermaster aboard a freighter, particularly one vested with such an important mission?

A bad sign, indeed. And it only got worse.

The way we were supposed to work was that, once Rain opened *Lucy*'s cargo deck and climbed inside, she'd untie each bale and, one at a time, push them to the hatch. I would then use the pod to transfer the bales to the cargo modules, alternating between Cargo One and Cargo Two, so that the mass would be evenly distributed on either side of the ship. Once the bales were aboard, Rain and I would enter the modules and tie them down, making sure that they were securely lashed to the inside decks before we closed the hatches.

It should have been a simple operation, one that would've taken a few hours at most. If I'd been working with a seasoned grunt, that is. But Rain seemed to have little idea what she was doing. She struggled to untie lines, tumbled the bales toward the hatch and swore at me when I had trouble catching them with the pod's manipulators, and frequently forgot the order in which we were supposed to reload them aboard the modules. Three times, I returned to the shuttle only to discover that she'd already pitched out another bale; on one occasion, I had to chase after a bale that had floated away from *Lucy*, barely managing to retrieve it before it drifted too far to be rescued.

None of these problems were her fault. They were always the result of my incompetence and stupidity. I was an oaf, an idiot, a doofus, an amateur, a complete zero, and God only knew how she'd been saddled with the likes of me. Even after Ted, overhearing her more unkind remarks over the comlink, told her to calm down and cooperate with me, she continued to insist upon doing things her way.

It wasn't until Emily suited up and came down to give us a hand that we finally managed to get the shuttle unloaded. I docked the pod, but instead of helping them secure the bales, I went straight to the bridge. Didn't bother to take off my suit; simply shelved the helmet, plugged the backpack into its recharger unit, took off my gloves, then hauled myself up the access shaft to Deck One.

The command center was a circular compartment ringed by rectangular portholes, with a pentagonal control console dominating the center of the room. A hologram image of the *Pride* floated above the table, with close-up views of the ship displayed on flatscreens suspended from the low ceiling. Ted was at the engineering station, peering over Doc's shoulder as they ran through a systems check; on the other side of the table, Ali was seated at the helm. Everyone looked up as I entered through the floor hatch. The women's voices were coming through the ceiling speakers, so no doubt they'd heard everything that had gone on between Rain and me.

"Something on your mind, Jules?" Ted turned to me as I used a ceiling rail to make my way across the compartment.

"Damn right." I was trying hard to keep my temper in check, but I wasn't succeeding. "I can't work with her, skipper. She's insane."

"Hmm . . . yes, I think I see your point." He thoughtfully stroked his chin as if pondering a solution to the problem. "Well, I'd hate to lose you, but I suppose Emcee can do double duty as shuttle pilot." He reached to his earpiece. "I'll put in a call to New Brighton, have someone bring up a skiff to take you home."

"Whoa, wait a minute! That's not what I . . ."

"You just accused one of your crewmates of insanity. Since I picked Rain myself, I suppose that means that you lack respect for my judgment. And if you're unable to work with either of us . . ."

"Just a second! I . . ."

"I'll give you"—Ted glanced at his watch—"sixty seconds. But that's all. We're rather busy just now."

He wasn't joking. Ted Harker might be an easygoing chap, but no one questioned his authority on the bridge of his ship and got away with it. I took a deep breath, started over again. "Sir, I have total respect for your judgment. And . . . all right, maybe she isn't insane. But you heard what happened out there . . ."

"I did, indeed. All of us did. That's why my wife went down below." His eyes narrowed. "Which is where you should be right now. Why aren't you?"

"Because . . . Captain, how much experience does Rain have with this sort of thing? Seriously?"

"Very little. In fact, this is only her third time in space . . . and her first assignment as quartermaster."

I stared at him. "Her first . . . what did she do before then?"

"She worked groundside at New Brighton for eight months before signing on with Janus. After that, two orbital sorties aboard cargo shuttles, unloading freight from the *Lee*. True, she hasn't logged as many hours as you have, but she takes her job seriously, and I have complete confidence in her. I'm sorry that you have problems working for someone younger than you, but . . ."

"No, sir, that's not it. It's just that . . . look, she's been on my case ever since I met her. I've been trying to get along with her, but it's gotten to the point where . . ." Again, I hesitated. "If you really want me to leave the ship, then I will. But I can't work with someone who carries a chip on her shoulder all the time."

Ted didn't say anything for a moment, and I wondered if I'd just talked myself out of a job. Behind him, Doc was quietly shaking his head. An old pro, he knew how petty feuds among crew members could escalate if left unresolved.

"Very well," Ted said at last. "I'll have a few words with Rain once she gets off duty, ask her to calm down. If she continues to harass you, I want you to let me know. As for now . . . since you're here, I have a small errand for you." He glanced over his shoulder at Doc. "Can you get along without me for a minute?" The chief nodded, and Ted unstuck his shoes from the deck. Grabbing hold of a ceiling rail, he pulled himself around the console. "Come along, please."

I followed Ted to the other side of the bridge, where we stopped beside a locker recessed in the bulkhead behind his chair. "One thing you should know about Rain," he said quietly once we were away from the others. "She comes from a rather powerful family on Coyote, and they have a lot of pull with Janus."

"So Morgan insisted that you hire her?" I was no stranger to cronyism—the Western Hemisphere Union is rife with it—but this was something I didn't expect.

"Pretty much so, yes . . . although I meant what I said about having confidence in her." He produced a key ring from his vest and began sorting through it. "But the Thompson Wood Company is a major investor in Morgan's company, and if Molly Thompson wants her great-niece to have a job . . ."

"I see."

"Yes, well . . ." Ted inserted a key into the locker. "Off the record, I think she's rather nervous about all this, so she's taking it out on you. Once you get to know her, you may find that she's actually quite nice. But she's had a tough time lately, though, what with her brother and . . ." He stopped himself. "Sorry. Think I said too much. And it's none of our business, besides."

That was the second time I'd heard about Rain's brother. The captain had clearly overstepped the boundaries, though, and I wasn't about to press the issue, not when I'd come so close to getting fired. So I said nothing as he opened the locker and reached inside.

He withdrew a ceramic jug, its neck sealed with a cork stopper. Since I'd spent some time in Liberty's taverns, I immediately recognized it for what it was: a quart of corn liquor, known on Coyote as bearshine.

"I've trusted you with one secret already," Ted murmured as he handed it to me. "Now I'm going to trust you with another. I want you to take this to Ash and be quiet about it."

"Yeah. Okay." I tucked the jug under my left arm; Ted added an empty squeezebulb, which I stuck in a thigh pocket of my suit. "He's an alcoholic, isn't he?"

"I suppose. But again, he's here because Morgan insists, so what he does in his cabin isn't our concern." Ted closed the locker. "I'm keeping him on a short leash, though, and that means keeping his liquor supply under lock and key. This should be enough to get him to where we're supposed to go . . . after that, he'll have to work for the rest."

"And what is his job, exactly?"

"He . . . ah, perhaps we should call him an interpreter, and leave it at that." He nodded toward the floor hatch. "Now off with you. Change out of your suit, then pay a visit to Mr. Ash. I'll have a word with Ms. Thompson. Fair enough?"

"Yes, sir," I murmured. "Thank you." Ted nodded, then began to make his way back across the bridge.

I stared at the jug of bearshine in the crook of my arm. A brat and a wetbrain. This mission was getting stranger by the minute.

X

I heard Ash's guitar as soon as I opened the hatch to Deck Two, melancholy chords that drifted down the corridor. Whatever he was playing, it had no clear rhyme or pattern, but nonetheless spoke of loneliness and regret. Like finding a bouquet of dying roses in the heart of a machine.

I lingered just inside the deck hatch for a few moments before I remembered why I was there. Grasping the ceiling rail with my free hand, I pulled myself down the corridor toward Ash's cabin. I was trying to be as quiet as possible, not wanting to disturb him, yet the moment before I raised my hand to knock on his door, the music suddenly stopped.

"Come in," he called out. "It's not locked."

How did he know I was there? Perhaps he'd heard the deck hatch open, but still . . . trying to shake off the willies, I slid open the door.

Ash floated in midair, cross-legged and upside-down, one foot hooked over a ceiling rail, guitar nestled within his arms. Fashioned of fine-grained brown spruce, with silver strings running along a black fingerboard, it was as beautiful as the sounds it produced. It was the first time I'd seen him without his robe; he wore a tan cotton tunic and matching trousers, loose-fitting and almost monkish in appearance. Ash himself was older than I originally thought: lean and bony, with a mop of brown hair growing grey at the temples. His eyes were surrounded by dark rings, as if he hadn't slept well in years.

"Hi, Gordon," I began. "Captain sent me down here to . . ."

"Bring me a bottle. Yes, I can see." He idly strummed at his guitar. "You can put it over there," he added, nodding toward a net for personal items that dangled from the bulkhead next to his sleep-sack. "I'll get to it later."

Apparently he wasn't a social drinker. Well, that made sense; I'd met a few drunks, and the hard-core boozehounds usually preferred to drink alone. Twisting around so that I could attach my shoes to the floor, I stepped into the cabin. "Nice guitar. Heard it down the hall."

"Thanks." He didn't look up at me. "And by the way, I prefer to be called Ash. No one calls me by my first name."

"Sure . . . sorry." I stuck the jug into the net, then pulled the squeezebulb out of my pocket. "Ever use one of these before? You need to unscrew the top, see, like this"—I demonstrated by removing the cap—"then fit it over the . . ."

"I can manage." Irritation crossed his face. "Incidentally, just so that you know . . . I'm not an alcoholic." His fingers plucked out sharp, discordant notes as he spoke, as if to accentuate his words. "Or a drunk, or a wetbrain, or whatever else you've decided to label me."

That brought me up short. I stared at him, trying to figure out what I'd said or done to lead him to believe what I thought of him. "I didn't . . ."

"Of course you didn't. You're being polite. But I can . . ." A brief glare, then he looked away again. "Never mind. Just in a mood, that's all."

"Sure. No problem." He was making me nervous, so I screwed the cap back on the squeezebulb and stuck it in the net beside the jug. "Well, look, if you need anything else, I'm right next door."

Ash didn't respond. Seeing that my presence wasn't wanted, I turned to leave. I was halfway to the door when he suddenly spoke up.

" 'Galaxy Blues,' " he said.

I stopped, looked back at him again. "Excuse me?"

"The song I was playing . . . it's called 'Galaxy Blues.' " His hands returned to the strings, and once again I heard the same progression I'd caught while I was in the corridor. "Been working on it for a while," he went on, his eyes still avoiding mine. "Kind of weird, I know, but . . . well, I'm getting there."

"Sounds nice." I hesitated. "Got any words for it?"

"Nope. No lyrics." Ash glanced up at me, and I was surprised to see a sly smile on his face, as if he was sharing a private joke. "That's what I like about music. You don't need words to get a point across. Just screws things up, really, when all you really should have is . . ."

His right hand abruptly shifted farther up the neck of his guitar, and he produced a quick succession of warbling, high-pitched notes. "That's you . . . trying hard to rationalize something that doesn't really need to make sense."

I felt my face grow warm, but before I could say anything, his smile became a knowing grin, and the progression drifted into a lower, more solemn bass sound. "And that's what happens when you find that nothing really fits into your safe and conservative worldview. But believe me, out here in the great beyond"—a snakelike ramble of notes—"everything is strange. The sooner you get used to that, the better off you'll be."

He was beginning to piss me off. "What are you, some kind of . . . ?"

Something cold crept down my back as I suddenly recalled the first time I'd seen him, peering in through the window of my jail cell. As incredible—let's face it, as impossible—as it seemed, nonetheless it was the only explanation that made sense.

"Mind reader?" Ash chuckled as he pushed aside his guitar. Uncoiling himself from his lotus position, he pushed himself off the ceiling. "You could say that," he said as he glided over to where I'd left the jug. "Or maybe I'm just an astute observer."

Perhaps he was only that . . . but all the same, his hands trembled as he uncorked the jug, and he swore under his breath as a few globular droplets of bearshine floated away before he managed to fit the squeezebulb around the neck. Ash finally managed to fill the bulb and close the jug again without wasting any more booze; he looked almost infantile as he put the bulb's nipple to his lips and took a slug that would have choked anyone else.

"You can go now," he rasped, as he pinched the bulb shut. "Come back again when you've got more of this."

A brisk wave of his hand as he dismissed me. No doubt he'd spend the rest of the day getting bombed. Once again, I turned toward the door . . . but not before he had some parting words for me.

"She really does like you, y'know," he murmured. "Just as much as you're attracted to her. Too bad neither of you will admit it to yourselves."

I almost asked how he could possibly be aware of these things . . . but I already knew the answer to that, didn't I? And just then, I only wanted to put a wall between us. Hoping that a bulkhead was enough to separate my mind from his, I hurried from his cabin, shutting the door behind me.

And found Morgan Goldstein waiting for me in the corridor.

"What are you doing in there?" It wasn't a polite question, and there was no mistaking the anger in his eyes.

"Captain Harker told me to bring him a jug of bearshine." I pretended innocence, even though it was clear that he'd been eavesdropping all the while. "Just stopped to have a chat. Anything wrong with that?"

"Yes." Morgan kept his voice low. "For now on, you're to leave him alone. If anyone asks you to bring him anything, you come to me first. I'll . . ."

"Pardon me, sir, but if the skipper gives me an order, it's my duty to carry it out. I'm under no obligation to ask your permission to do that." I would have turned away from him, but he was blocking the way to my cabin. "Now, if you'll excuse me . . ."

"Of course . . . you're right." His manner softened. "My apologies, Mr. Truffaut. I forgot that you were only following orders." Morgan moved aside to let me pass. "But in the future, I'd appreciate it if you'd . . . minimize your contact with Ash. He's quite sensitive and needs all the privacy he can get."

"I'll try to keep that in mind." Unsticking my shoes from the floor, I started to push myself down the passageway. But then . . .

"Just one question, though," I said, grabbing the ceiling rail and turning back to him again. "Does he drink so much to keep from hearing everyone else's thoughts?"

Morgan's face went pale. His mouth fell open, but for a moment he couldn't respond. Maybe he was having trouble coming up with an adequate lie. Whatever the reason, I realized that my guess was right on target.

"He just drinks too much," he said at last, his voice little more than a whisper. "If I were you, though, I'd keep my distance." Then he twisted himself around and headed toward the deck hatch.

I went to my cabin, but even after I closed the door, I was aware of Ash's presence. Through the wall vent, I heard the sound of his guitar. After a little while, though, it stopped, and all I could hear was his voice.

I couldn't tell, though, whether he was laughing or weeping.

(NINE)

Off to see the lizard . . .

peace with Rain . . .

the Order of the Eye.

XI

We remained in orbit overnight, Coyote time, and next morning after breakfast the *Pride of Cucamonga* headed out for Rho Coronae Borealis.

As customary, all hands assembled in the command center for final countdown. As shuttle pilot, there was little for me to do; once I verified that *Loose Lucy* was ready to serve as a lifeboat in the unlikely event that we'd have to abandon ship, my only job was to take a seat and watch while everyone else went about getting the *Pride* under way. Yet Emily was nowhere to be seen until fifteen minutes before launch; when she finally showed up, Mahamatasja Jas Sa-Fhadda was with her.

This was the first time since coming aboard that I'd seen the Prime Emissary. Jas had remained in hisher quarters while the crew made preparations for the journey, and I'd expected himher to stay there until the *Pride* arrived at its destination. So I was surprised when the *hjadd* followed Emily through the manhole into the command center.

Everyone stopped what they were doing as the first officer led Jas onto the bridge. As always, the Prime Emissary wore hisher environment suit; I would've thought that heshe would be encumbered by it, yet heshe was surprisingly nimble. Reaching up to grasp a ceiling rail with a six-fingered hand, Jas lingered near the floor hatch for a few moments, the opaque faceplate of hisher helmet turning first one way, then the other, as heshe gazed around the deck.

"Guess heshe decided to come up and join us," I murmured to Rain. We were seated off to one side of the control console, near the life-support station; like me, she had little to do just then. "Must have gotten curious about how we do things up here."

Rain gave me a patronizing look, but if she had any insults in mind, she refrained from giving voice to them. "More than curiosity," she whispered. "Without himher, we're not going anywhere."

This was the first time she'd spoken to me since our altercation the day before. When I'd seen her a couple of hours earlier, during breakfast in the wardroom on Deck Two, she had avoided me as much as possible. Ted must have had a few words with her. Well, if she was willing to bury the hatchet, so was I.

"How do you figure that?" I asked.

"You don't know?" She darted a look at me, and I shook my head. "Watch and learn," she added. "This is where it gets interesting."

Ted unbuckled his harness and rose from his seat. "Prime Emissary, welcome," he said, raising his left hand in the *hjadd* gesture of greeting. "The *Pride of Cucamonga* is ready to depart. If we may have your permission . . . ?"

"You have my permission." As before, an androgynous voice emanated from the mouth grille of hisher helmet. "Please direct me to the navigation system."

"It would be my honor." Careful to avoid touching the Prime Emissary, he extended a hand toward the helm. "This way, please."

Jas followed Ted across the command center. As they approached the helm, Ali turned around in his seat. I couldn't help but notice his sour expression and wondered whether our pilot harbored a secret revulsion for the *hjadd*. I wasn't the only one who saw it. On the other side of the deck, Ash was seated next to Morgan Goldstein. Although he once again wore his robe, I caught a glimpse of the sickened look on his face. Goldstein must have observed Ali, too, because he leaned closer to Ash and whispered something. Ash didn't respond, but instead nodded ever so slightly. Ash had picked up on something . . . that is, if I was right, and he was a telepath of some sort.

Ted stopped beside Ali's console. "Mr. Youssef, if you will . . ."

Ali said nothing but instead typed a few commands into his keyboard before shrinking away from Jas. If the Prime Emissary noticed the pilot's reaction, heshe said nothing. Instead, heshe reached into a pocket of hisher environment suit, then pulled out a small object about the size and shape of a data fiche.

"That's the bridge key," Rain said quietly. "Until Jas uses it, we're not going anywhere."

Then I understood. One of the things the *Galileo* survivors had learned was that the *hjadd* belonged to something called the Talus, a loose coalition of alien races that had developed the technology to build starbridges in order to travel to other worlds. The main purpose of the Talus was to provide trade and cultural exchange, but it also made sure that the galaxy remained at peace. To prevent one race from attacking or invading another, each member of the Talus protected the starbridges of its home system by means of hyperlink transceivers, each of which was accessed by its own individually coded signal. Unless one race provided another with a key containing that signal, its starbridges would remain closed, and navigation through hyperspace would be impossible.

One of the conditions the *hjadd* had made upon establishing contact with humankind was that we would be unable to travel to Rho Coronae Borealis without their express permission. That could only be granted if they transmitted a coded signal via hyperlink to their own starbridge. This was the reason that no human ship had visited Hjarr since the return of the *Galileo* survivors; until the *Pride*, only *hjadd* vessels were equipped with the proper navigation equipment.

"So Jas is carrying the *hjadd* key with him," I whispered. "Guess they're not quite ready to trust us."

Rain nodded. We watched as Jas moved toward a rectangular box that had been installed in the center of the nav station. Featureless save for a narrow slot at its top and a reflective black surface beneath it, the box remained inert until the Prime Emissary slid the key into the slot. The panel glowed to life, emitting a blue-green luminescence. Jas removed the glove of hisher left hand, and I caught a glimpse of mottled brown flesh, leathery and reptilian, as heshe laid hisher palm against the panel.

Its surface became bright orange, and vertical bars of alien script that vaguely resembled Farsi scrolled down it. A small drawer slid open from the bottom of the box, revealing a narrow row of buttons. Extending the middle finger of hisher hand, Jas delicately pushed the buttons in what appeared to be a predetermined sequence. The script changed, the panel became purple, and the drawer slid shut once more.

"The code has been entered, Captain Harker," Jas said, hisher voice a low purr. "You may proceed."

133

"Thank you, Prime Emissary." Ted turned to Emily. "Contact the gatehouse, Emcee, and inform them we're on our way." Then he tapped Ali on the shoulder. "Proceed with final countdown for main engine ignition."

Ali nodded. He waited until Jas moved away from the helm, then swiveled his chair back toward the console and began entering commands into his keyboard. At her station on the other side of the table, Emily was murmuring into her headset, telling Starbridge Coyote that we were about to launch. Ted watched as Jas put hisher glove back on. "We'll be ready to go in about five minutes. If you'd like to stay here, we can . . ."

"Thank you, Captain, but I would prefer to return to my quarters." Turning away from him, Jas almost seemed to disregard Ted. "Would you please have a member of your crew take me back?"

"Certainly." Ted looked around the command center. Emily was busy, and both Doc and Ali were needed on the bridge just then. On the other side of the deck, Goldstein was already unfastening his harness. Then Ted's gaze fell upon me. "Jules, if you'll please . . . ?"

Goldstein's eyes widened, and there was no missing the scowl on his face. Before he could protest, though, I snapped open my harness. "I'd be glad to, sir," I said, pushing myself out of my chair. "If it's all right with the Prime Emissary, that is."

Ted looked at Jas. Hisher head moved back and forth upon hisher long neck; at first I thought heshe was objecting, until I remembered that this was the *hjadd* equivalent of a nod. Then Rain spoke up. "Skipper, may I join them? With the Prime Emissary's permission, of course."

Ted looked dubious. "I don't know why we need to send two . . ."

"You are curious?" Jas's helmet turned toward her, and Rain nod-

134

ded. "Very well. I would be delighted to have guests . . . if your captain approves."

Ted hesitated. "Very well . . . but don't overstay your welcome, either of you."

"Thank you, sir." Rain unbuckled her harness, then rose from her seat. "After you," she said to me, gesturing toward the access shaft.

I'd be lying if I said that I was pleased to have Rain tag along. Perhaps we were getting along a little better, but I didn't want to have her henpecking me all the way down to Deck Three. Besides, I wanted Jas all to myself. Call it selfish, but how often in life does one get the chance to have private time with an alien?

Nothing I could do about it, though, so I pushed myself over to the hatch and pulled it open. From the corner of my eye, I saw the jealous scowl on Morgan's face, yet I couldn't help but notice that Ash was grinning broadly, as if he was enjoying his own private joke . . . or, perhaps, savoring his patron's irritation.

Then I ducked down the manhole and—with Jas close behind me and Rain bringing up the rear—began to make my way down the access shaft.

XII

None of us said anything until we reached Deck Three, but three bells rang just as we entered the passageway, warning us that the main engine ignition was imminent.

I had just enough time to brace my hands against the corridor walls and rest my feet on the floor before a prolonged shudder passed through the ship. I glanced over my shoulder to make sure that the others were all right; Jas's broad feet had found the carpet as well, and although Rain had been caught off guard, she quickly recovered by grabbing hold of the ceiling rail and planting the soles of her stickshoes against the carpet. For the next fifteen minutes or so, we would enjoy one-third gravity while the *Pride* accelerated to cruise velocity.

"Well, we're off," I said, stating the obvious if only for the sake of conversation. Lowering my hands, I stepped aside to make way for Jas. "Prime Emissary, if you'd like to lead the way . . . ?"

"Thank you." As the *hjadd* moved past me, I caught my reflection in hisher faceplate. "There is no need to be so formal, Mr. Truffaut," heshe added. "You may call me Jas."

"Uh, sure . . . right." I'd forgotten that heshe'd told me so before. Behind us, Rain was closing the deck hatch. I waited until she'd dogged it shut, then followed Jas down the corridor. "Thank you for letting me . . . I mean, both of us . . . see your quarters."

A sibilant hiss from hisher mouthpiece. "The courtesy is long overdue," Jas said as heshe led us past the medical bay. "We have allowed only a few of your kind to enter our compound on Coyote. Perhaps the time has come for us to be less jealous of our privacy. Very soon we will be arriving at *Talus qua'spah*. A little cultural acclimation is desirable."

"*Talus pah-squa . . . ?*" I stumbled over the words. "I'm sorry, but what . . . ?"

"*Talus qua'spah.* In your language, the House of the Talus." Jas came to a halt beside an unmarked hatch. A black plate had been set within it; once again, heshe removed hisher left glove, then placed hisher palm against it. "That is only an approximate translation of what it really means, but it will suffice."

The panel turned purple, then the hatch slid open, revealing a small antechamber that I assumed was an internal airlock. Jas stepped into it, then turned to look back at us. "Please remain here until I summon you. I must prepare myself for visitors." Then heshe touched a button beside the door, and the hatch closed once more.

That left Rain and me alone in the corridor. An uncomfortable silence settled between us. With nothing to say or do, I gazed at the bulkhead, idly speculating how much effort it must have taken Janus's engineers to retrofit this part of the ship to *hjadd* specifications. I was beginning to count the rivets when Rain quietly cleared her throat.

"I just want to . . ." She paused, started again. "Look, I'm sorry about yesterday. I mean, about what happened during load-in."

"Don't worry about it." I continued to study the bulkhead.

"No, really . . . I mean it." Putting herself between me and the wall so that I couldn't ignore her, she looked me straight in the eye. "You knew what you were doing out there . . . better than I did, to tell the truth . . . and I was just trying to see if I could piss you off."

"Yeah, well, you succeeded."

"Uh-uh. I've been told I have a talent for that." A crooked smile that quickly faded. "Ted told me that you almost quit."

That wasn't *quite* what had happened, but I wasn't about to correct her if it made her feel guilty. "Believe me," she went on, "that's not what I want. I just . . . look, can we still be friends? I promise that I won't snap at you anymore."

I could tell that she was making a sincere effort to make up. I was still a little angry about the things she'd said to me, but if she was willing to apologize, it would have been churlish of me to refuse. "Yeah, all right," I said, and as an afterthought offered my hand. "Case closed."

"Okay. Case closed." Rain grinned as she took my hand. I was surprised by how soft her touch was, and was almost reluctant to let go. "Glad to put that behind us."

"Yeah, well . . . so am I."

Another silence fell between us. Perhaps we'd ceased fire, but there were still old wounds that hadn't healed. The hatch remained shut, and I wondered what Jas was doing in there. But there was something else that roused my curiosity . . .

"Pardon me, but may I ask a personal question?"

"I don't know." She frowned. "Depends how personal it is."

I hesitated. Too late to back down, though, so I forged ahead. "Yesterday, when we were at breakfast and talking about my brother, I happened to mention yours, and that set you off." There was a spark within her eyes, and I quickly raised my hand. "Hey, I'm not trying to pick another fight. I'd just like to know . . . what was it that I said about him that got you so riled?"

"You didn't know?" Rain stared at me. "No one told you?"

"I'm new around here, remember? I couldn't find my way to the outhouse without a map."

That brought another smile to her face. "At least you admit that," she said with a slight laugh before becoming somber again. "It's not something I like to talk about, but . . . well, you're not the only one with a black sheep in the family." She looked down at the floor. "My brother killed my father."

Of all the things she could have said to me, nothing could have been more unexpected. It was my turn to be apologetic. "I . . . I'm sorry, I didn't . . ."

"No, of course not. Like you said, there's no reason why you should've known." Rain shook her head. "I guess I've become so used to having people talk about him behind my back, it's like I have it tattooed on my forehead."

She let out her breath as a tired sigh. "My brother, Hawk . . . who's about your age, by the way . . . murdered my father. *Our* father, I mean. There's a lot of people who say he had it coming . . .

my father was a mean drunk, and even my mother says he was a bastard, which was why they were separated . . . but all the same, Hawk
shouldn't have . . ."

She broke off when the hatch abruptly slid open, a silent invitation for us to enter. "Guess that means we can come in," I said, making a courtly bow. "Ladies first . . ."

"Thank you." Rain seemed happy to be interrupted. Not that I
could blame her, but Jas couldn't have picked a worse moment. Yet I
let the subject drop as we stepped into the antechamber.

XIII

The airlock was a small foyer just large enough for the two of us,
with an identical hatch on the opposite side. Once the outer hatch
closed behind us, the ceiling lit with a pale yellow luminescence.

"*Welcome*," said Jas, hisher voice coming from a speaker beside a
small control panel. "*Before I repressurize the room you are in, you will
need to put on breathing masks. You will find them in the compartment to
your right.*"

Rain turned around, located a small candy-striped panel recessed
within the wall; inside were two full-face air masks. We slipped them
on, and I helped Rain activate the miniature oxygen-nitrogen cylinders on either side of the lower jaw. Jas must have been observing
us, because as soon as we were ready, there was a faint buzz and the
airlock began to repressurize.

We could've breathed the air within Jas's quarters, but not for
very long. Watching the digital gauge on the control panel, I saw
the atmospheric pressure drop 250 millibars while the nitrogen content increased by 20 percent. Without air masks, we would have suc-
cumbed to anoxia and fainted from lack of oxygen. The change-out

took about five minutes; when it was done, there was another buzz, then the inner hatch revolved open.

We walked into what had once been the ship's lounge before it was converted into a cabin suitable for *hjadd* passengers: a large suite divided into three rooms, two of them serving as private sleeping quarters and the third as a sitting room. At least heshe had furniture, even if it was designed to accommodate hisher shorter legs and longer torso; I noticed that the couch and chair were equipped with safety harnesses. There was even what appeared to be a small galley, no doubt stocked with vegetarian food palatable to the *hjadd*. If there was a privy, I didn't see it. Yet other than a porthole, the cabin was spartan, the ceiling rails lending it the same utilitarian appearance as the rest of the ship.

But the surroundings didn't catch my attention so much as Jas himherself. Since the Prime Emissary no longer needed to wear hisher environment suit, heshe had changed into a long, togalike robe that looked like silk yet seemed to shimmer with red and purple radiance. Hisher head, resembling that of a turtle only with a short fin on the back of hisher skull, rose from the high collar of hisher robe, while the hands I'd glimpsed earlier were folded together within bell sleeves embroidered with intricate designs.

"Please, come in," heshe said. "Make yourselves comfortable." A six-fingered hand, its talons white against the dark brown of hisher skin, emerged from a sleeve in the gesture of welcome. "I'm afraid I cannot offer refreshment, but I doubt you would enjoy anything that I eat or drink anyway."

When Jas spoke, I heard two voices: the familiar one that addressed us in Anglo, which came from the grille of a small device that heshe wore around hisher neck, and the low-pitched series of hisses, croaks, and whistles that matched the movements of hisher mouth.

The Prime Emissary didn't know our language; heshe merely possessed the means to have it translated for himher. The device heshe wore around hisher neck apparently did the trick; a slender prong was suspended in front of hisher lipless mouth, while thin wires led to small caps that covered the membranes on either side of hisher head.

"No need to apologize." Rain recovered more quickly than I did; I was getting over my first sight of Jas without hisher environment suit. "Once we reach your world, maybe we will have a chance to sample your cuisine."

"Uh . . . yeah," I stuttered. "I'd like that a lot, too." I was at a loss for what else to say. "Umm . . . nice place you have here."

Lame, but Extraterrestrial Diplomacy 101 wasn't a course I'd taken at the Academy. Whatever I said, though, was apparently enough to tickle hisher funny bone—where that was located, I hadn't a clue—because it was received by a short, high-pitched hiss. Jas's heavy-lidded eyes, which bulged from the front of hisher skull, closed slightly.

"Your people have done well to accommodate us," heshe replied. "Perhaps we will be able satisfy your curiosity about our food, once we have arrived at *Talus qua'spah*."

I was still getting over the spooky way hisher eyes moved on their own when Jas stepped a little closer. "However," heshe continued, "our time is short, and you will soon need to return to your duties. Therefore, I will ask the question that I would like to have answered, if you may."

"Question?" That startled me. "Ah . . . yeah, sure, whatever you . . ."

Rain's cough was muffled by her air mask, but I heard it nonetheless. "Of course, Prime Emissary," she said, interrupting me, "although you'll have to forgive us if we're not very helpful. After all, we're ixnay on the alktay."

I caught her meaning and dummied up, hoping that Jas's translator wasn't as efficient as it seemed. Apparently it wasn't up to pig latin, because Jas went quiet for a moment, the fin on hisher head rising ever so slightly. "Yes, certainly," heshe responded after a second. "I understand. But nonetheless, I'd like to know . . . are there members of the Order of the Eye aboard this ship?"

I didn't have to pretend ignorance. "Sorry. Don't know what you're talking about." I glanced at Rain. "You?"

"Neither do I." She shook her head, but something in her expression told me otherwise. "Is that something you've heard about on Coyote?"

Jas's fin rose a little more, hisher eyes twitching back and forth. "A rumor, perhaps little more," heshe responded, "yet enough to rouse our interest." A short pause. "One of your passengers . . . Gordon Ash . . . we have reason to believe belongs to this group. Do you know anything of this?"

"Nope. Nothing at all." I shrugged, hoping that my lie was convincing. "Just that he drinks a lot, that's all."

"Drinks?" The *hjadd's* left eye rotated toward me.

"He means alcohol. An affliction among my kind." Rain was about to continue when, from outside the room, we heard four bells, giving us the one-minute warning that the main engine was about to shut down. "We should go," she said, glancing at her watch. "Many thanks for your hospitality, Prime Emissary."

"The pleasure has been mine." Jas folded hisher hands together and bowed from the waist. "Feel free to visit me again."

Neither of us said much to the other as we cycled back through the airlock. The main engine cut off while Rain and I were still inside; we grasped handrails along the walls, and once the atmosphere returned to normal, we removed our air masks and placed them in their compartment. But as soon as we'd left the airlock and moved far enough down the passageway that I was sure Jas couldn't hear us, I pulled her aside.

"All right, now," I said, keeping my voice low. "How about telling me what's going on?"

"What do you mean?" Her expression remained neutral.

"C'mon . . . you know exactly what I'm talking about." I nodded in the direction of Jas's cabin. "This business with the Order of the Eye. You know something I don't."

"I don't know what you're—"

"Ash reads minds." Her face went pale as I said this, and I went on. "I don't know how he does it, but . . . well, it's there, and don't try to pretend that I'm wrong."

Rain glanced both ways, as if to make sure that we were alone. "Okay, you're right," she replied, her voice little more than a whisper. "Ash is a telepath . . . or at least strongly empathic. That's why Morgan brought him along . . . to verify whatever the *hjadd* have to say to us, since we still don't know their language even though they're able to interpret ours. We've tried to keep this from the *hjadd*, but apparently they've already figured it out."

Despite the fact that she'd confirmed what I had already suspected, I couldn't help but feel a chill. "How did Ash learn how to do that? This is . . . I mean, I've never met anyone who . . ."

"Not on Earth, no. But lately, a few people on Coyote have developed the ability to read minds . . . or at least pick up emotions." She hesitated. "Rumor has it that it comes from long-term exposure to pseudowasps. Supposedly they belong to a cult that calls itself the Order of the Eye."

I knew about pseudowasps: a flying insect native to Coyote, its sting contained a venom that produced low-level hallucinations among humans. There were even people who ingested the venom as a recreational drug; some of it had found its way to Earth, where it was sold on the black market. This was the first time that I'd ever heard of its producing telepathic abilities, though. If it hadn't been for my earlier encounter with Ash, I would have discounted it as hearsay.

"And Ash belongs to them?" I asked.

"I've heard that the Order got started by someone who used to work for Morgan. That's how Ash was able to hook up with him . . . Morgan has been bankrolling them on the sly." Rain shrugged. "It's only when Ash is drunk that he can't hear what's going on inside other people's heads. That's why Morgan had Ted bring along a couple of jugs of bearshine."

I'd figured that out already. If Ash was loaded most of the time, he wouldn't be able to hear the thoughts of everyone else aboard. Even Goldstein wouldn't want that, except when he wished Ash to do so . . . say, when he had to negotiate with the *hjadd*, and therefore wanted to have a level playing field.

"So Ash is Morgan's ringer," I said, and Rain nodded. "Sounds like Jas got wind of it, though. Are you going to tell him?"

Rain shook her head. "Not if I don't have to," she said, pushing herself toward the deck hatch. "None of my business, and I'd just as soon not have anything to do with Ash if I can help it." She looked back at me. "And neither should you. The Order is . . . well, if they really do exist, then they're not something you'd want to mess with."

That sounded like good advice. "Okay," I said as I followed her toward the hatch. "I'll take your word for it. Thanks for being straight with me. I appreciate it."

Rain paused just before entering the access shaft. "You're welcome," she said, then favored me with a smile. "What are friends for, right?"

(TEN)

A matter of trust . . .

transit to Rho Coronae Borealis . . .

Talus qua'spah . . .

an indelicate request.

XIV

It took about ten hours for the *Pride* to reach Starbridge Coyote. Time enough for both lunch and dinner in the wardroom, plus a long nap in between. Ted could have cut it in half if he'd ordered the engines to remain at full thrust, but that would have meant spending fuel we might need later. The only person impatient to reach Hjarr was Goldstein, and Ted made it plain that, although Morgan might be the ship's owner, it was the captain who called the shots.

That gave us nearly half a day to kill. Since the *Pride* was on autopilot, there was little reason for Ali to remain at the helm. Regulations called for a flight-certified crewman to be on duty in the command center at all times, though, and Ted, Emily, and Doc all wanted to be relieved. So Ali sat me down at his station and gave me the quick-and-dirty on how to drive the ship. The helm wasn't much different than that aboard the *Victory*: although the controls were a bit more complex, the thrusters controlling yaw, pitch, and roll were operated by the same sort of trackball I'd learned to use in the Academy.

Ali had already laid in the course for rendezvous with the starbridge; he told me that Morgan had assured him that, once we were through hyperspace, the *hjadd* would transmit a signal that would interface with the newly installed nav system and automatically dock the *Pride* with *Talus qua'spah*. Even so, Ali had taken the precaution of programming an emergency override into the *Pride*'s AI; two finger-strokes on the keyboard, and he could resume control of the helm at any time.

"I don't care what Morgan says," Ali said. "I'm not quite ready to trust the *hjadd*."

I remembered the way he'd recoiled from Jas when heshe had inserted the key. "With the ship, or anything else?"

A wry smile crept across his face. "Let's just say I prefer to err on the side of caution, especially when dealing with a race that looks like it might possibly eat its young."

I considered reminding him that the *hjadd* were vegetarians, but decided against it. Nonetheless, I wondered how someone so xenophobic had come to be hired as command pilot for this particular mission. Perhaps the same reason why Goldstein recruited me; pickings were slim on Coyote when it came to experienced freelance spacers, and Morgan had to settle for what he could find.

Once Ali was confident that I knew what I was doing, he left the bridge to grab some lunch and observe his midday prayers. For the first time since we'd departed Coyote, I found myself alone on the deck; everyone else had gone below. Through the starboard windows, I could see 47 Ursae Majoris-B as an immense blue-and-purple disc, its silver-yellow rings casting a broad shadow across its cloud bands.

Hard to believe that, little more than ten days ago, I'd been in the same place, only aboard a stolen lifeboat. Fate had dealt me an odd hand, to be sure.

I was still gazing at Bear when the deck hatch opened. Looking around, I saw Doc pull himself up through the manhole. Seeing me seated at the helm, he nodded with satisfaction.

"Good man . . . you're at your station." A perfunctory nod, then he reached to his utility belt and unhooked a squeezebulb. "Here's your reward . . . catch!"

He tossed the bulb across the deck. I reached up to snag it from midair. Hot coffee, just what I needed just then. "Thanks," I said. "Why, did you think I wouldn't be here?"

"Not really, but you never know." Doc closed the hatch, then turned a somersault that put him upside down to me. "One time, when we were going through the Belt on the way from Jupiter, the skipper put a rookie on watch during graveyard shift." He tucked the toes of his shoes within the ceiling rail. "I came up here to get something and found him catching z's, with an asteroid only eight hundred klicks off port bow. Stupid kid had turned off the collision alert so that it wouldn't interrupt his siesta. Never turned my back on a new guy since."

"If I'd done that in the Union Astronautica, my old captain would've put me out the airlock."

"That kid was Union Astronautica, too." Doc unhooked another squeezebulb from his belt and opened its nipple. "So am I, for that matter."

I'd gathered as much; his accent was *Norte Americano*, from somewhere out West. Which wasn't surprising; I was hardly the first UA spacer to have defected. "Morgan recruited me from the European Space Agency," he went on. "He'd just expanded his company and needed people to build ships for him. After a while he let me leave the desk and do what I really wanted to do."

"Why the name? This ship, I mean."

"*Pride of Cucamonga*? After my hometown . . . Cucamonga, California. And before you ask, *Loose Lucy* was named after my ex." Doc shook his head. "Word of advice . . . never christen your ship in honor of your wife. Not unless you intend to stay married, that is."

"I take it that's why it's called *Loose Lucy*," I said, and he gave me a rare smile. "Well, I have to hand to you . . . the *Pride* doesn't look like much, but she flies just fine."

"Looks aren't important. It's how they're built that counts. Only thing I don't like is having to add equipment that I don't know how to operate." Doc scowled as he gazed past me at the black box on the console. "It came to us just as you see it. A few cables in the back, with instructions on how to hardwire them to the console. Soon as we turned it on, though, it interfaced with the main AI bus. But we can't open it, and there's no way for us to change its settings or anything. Only Jas can do that."

I hesitated, wondering whether I should let him in on Ali's secret. Doc was the chief engineer, though, so it was his job to know what was going on with his ship. "Ali told me he rigged a manual override. Says he can . . ."

"Did he now?" A sip of coffee, then he reattached his bulb to a vest loop and twisted himself until he was right side up. "Actually, that's my doing. Ali's just taking credit for it . . . and don't worry, Ted and Emily know about it, too. Just don't let on to Morgan . . . he'd throw a fit if he thought we didn't trust the *hjadd*."

This was beginning to sound like a familiar refrain. "I take it you don't?"

"Oh, I trust 'em, all right . . . just not with my ship." Another

148

smile that quickly vanished. "Like with you. I have no problem with having a wet-behind-the-ears ensign standing watch, so long as I know you're not going to take a snooze."

"Yeah, well . . ." I shrugged. "Trust seems to be in short supply on this ship."

Doc didn't reply at once. Instead, he regarded me with what seemed to be sympathy. "Son, this isn't the Academy," he said at last. "They do everything by the book, and that way they minimize the risks. Out here, though, the book doesn't apply. We're pretty much making it up as we go along. Especially on this flight."

As he spoke, Doc pushed himself over to one of the starboard windows. "With any luck, this'll be pretty routine," he said, gazing out at Bear. "We deliver cargo, we pick up cargo, we go home. But I'm not going to count on it, and neither should you. So if we don't completely trust the Prime Emissary . . . well, it's because there's a first time for everything, and trust is something you earn only from experience." He reached up to fondly pat the ceiling. "But if you put your faith in this ship, and the people you're working with, then you'll get through this just fine."

If I'd heard that from anyone else, I would've considered it to be hopelessly saccharine. Yet sweetness and light clearly weren't part of Doc's character; he was a pragmatic old spacer who'd been doing this for a very long time. "Thanks. I'll keep that in mind."

"Uh-huh . . . well, that's all I have to say about that." Turning away from the window, Doc pulled himself back across the command center. "Okay, kid, the conn is yours. Don't wreck my ship, or I'll kick your ass."

He opened the deck hatch and floated headfirst down the access tunnel. The hatch closed behind him, and once more I was alone on the bridge. Yet I found myself remembering something Ash had said to me:

Out here in the great beyond, everything is strange. The sooner you get used to that, the better off you'll be.

XV

Six hours later, we were on primary approach to the starbridge. By then Ali had relieved me at the helm, and everyone had returned to the command center—including Jas, whom Goldstein had escorted up from Deck Three. Doc had installed a specially made couch for the Prime Emissary, into which heshe strapped himherself; I noticed that, although Jas tried stay away from Ash as much as possible, Morgan traded chairs with his "interpreter" so that Ash was seated next to the *hjadd*. Funny how even the smallest of coincidences gained significance, once I knew what was going on.

If Ted was aware of all this intrigue, he paid no attention. "Emcee, open a channel to the gatehouse," he said, keeping an eye on the screens above the control console. Once Emily told him that she'd made contact, he touched his headset mike. "Starbridge Coyote, this is CFS *Pride of Cucamonga*, requesting permission for hyperspace transition to Rho Coronae Borealis."

A moment passed, then a voice came over the loudspeaker. *"Roger that,* Pride. *Standing by to receive destination code."*

"We copy, gatehouse." Ted glanced over his shoulder at his wife. "Send the key, please."

Ali typed in a command that relayed the key code to Emily's station; she transmitted the signal to the gatehouse, which in turn sent it via hyperlink to Rho Coronae Borealis. A minute went by, then we heard from the gatehouse again: *"Code received at destination and confirmed. You have permission to commence final approach."*

"Roger that, gatehouse. Thank you." Ted let out his breath.

"Right, then . . . Ali, interface AI with the gatehouse, then fire main engine on my mark."

Ali tapped at his keyboard, studied his comp for a moment, then looked back at him. "Interface completed, skipper. Ready when you are."

"Mark."

A brief surge as the engine ignited. Looking up at the nearest screen, I saw Starbridge Coyote grow in size. Above the console, a holographic miniature of the *Pride* moved toward a three-dimensional funnel that grew from the ring. Remembering the turbulence I'd experienced a few days earlier, I cinched my harness a little tighter, then glanced over at Rain.

"Hang on," I whispered. "This could be rough." She nodded and gave her own harness a quick yank. Although she said nothing, the perspiration on her face showed just how nervous she was. I remembered then that she was the only person aboard who hadn't made a hyperspace jump; everyone else had gone through this at least once before, if only from Earth to Coyote. "Don't worry," I added. "It'll all be over in just . . ."

"I know, I know." Her voice was tight. "Don't remind me."

She didn't want to be babied, so I left her alone. Ali had taken his hands from the console; with the *Pride*'s guidance system slaved to the gatehouse AI, there was nothing for him to do. Yet Doc continued to study his board, alert for any signs of trouble, while Ted and Emily watched the comp displays at their stations.

The engine cut off a few seconds later. Another glance at a screen told me that the *Pride* was only a few miles from the starbridge. Any moment now, we'd be entering the event horizon . . .

A sudden flash from within the ring, and then it felt as if we were being pulled into the wormhole. I was about to close my eyes when someone grasped the back of my wrist. Looking down, I was sur-prised to find that Rain had grabbed hold of me.

"Don't watch," I said quietly, taking her hand. "Just shut your eyes. You'll be . . ."

I didn't get a chance to finish, for at that moment we entered the starbridge.

This time, I saw what happened. Bright light in every color of the visible spectrum streamed through the windows as the com-mand center turned upside down, becoming a barrel that some malicious giant had decided to kick down a slope. For an instant, it seemed as if everything stretched, like matter itself had become little more than warm taffy. The holo flickered and went dead. From the other side of the bridge, I heard someone scream—Ash, perhaps, or maybe it was Morgan—and Rain's grip became so hard that I almost yelped.

And then, as suddenly as it had begun, it ended. The light faded, the spinning stopped, everything resumed its normal proportions. We were through the starbridge.

Rain let out her breath, slowly opened her eyes. "Oh, god, that was . . ." Then she realized that she was still clutching my hand. "Sorry," she muttered, and quickly released it. "Didn't mean to . . ."

"That's okay." I couldn't help but grin. "Anytime."

Her face had been pale; then it became red, and she looked away in embarrassment. Hearing the sound of someone retching, I turned to see Ash blowing his cookies into a bag while Goldstein regarded him with disgust. Everyone else was shaken and sweaty, save perhaps for Jas, whose turtlelike visage remained invisible behind the opaque mirror of hisher suit helmet.

"Well, now . . . that wasn't so bad, was it?" Ted glanced around the deck. "Everyone all right? No casualties, I hope?" Satisfied that we were all in one piece, if perhaps a little worse for wear, he looked over at his wife. "Send a message back home. Tell them we've arrived in one piece."

Emily pushed a damp lock of hair from her face as she opened a hyperlink channel to Starbridge Coyote. Ted turned back toward the helm. "A fix on our position, Ali, if you will."

Our pilot seemed to shake himself awake, then hunched over the console. It took a minute for him to reactivate the holo and match it against the charts in the comp's stellar catalog. "We're in the HD 143761 system. Approximately one and a half AU's from the primary, one thousand miles from . . ."

His voice trailed off as he slowly raised his eyes to the nearest window. "Allah's blessings," he muttered. "Will you look at that?"

I followed his gaze. Through the window, we could see a nearby planet, oddly Earth-like but with oceans larger than those of our own world. Hjarr, apparently, but this wasn't what got our attention. In orbit above the planet was something that appeared at first to be a small constellation, yet obviously wasn't of natural origin.

"Is that what I think it is?" Rain stared at it in astonishment. "I mean, I'd heard that it was big, but . . ."

Emily put a 3-D image up on the holo, and we could see the object more clearly: a vast, snowflake-shaped structure, perhaps two hundred miles or more in diameter, like an elaborate toy cobbled together by some infant god. It slowly rotated upon a central axis, catching the light of a distant sun; all around it moved tiny specks that, I suddenly realized, were starships larger than the *Pride* itself.

A space colony, but much, much bigger than any built by humans. Even Highgate would have been dwarfed by this thing. I'd heard of it, of course, yet in real life it was more awesome than anything I'd imagined.

"There it is . . . *Talus qua'spah*." Ted looked over at Jas. "Welcome home, Prime Emissary."

"Thank you, Captain." The *hjadd* had already unfastened hisher harness and was floating free of hisher couch. "First Officer, will you please open a channel? The proper frequency has already been programmed into your system."

"Sure." Emily reached to her keyboard. "But what do you want me to . . . ?"

"There is no need for you to speak. I will communicate for you." Jas pushed himherself over to the console. "If you will . . . ?"

"Skipper?" Ali continued to stare at the holo. "What do you want me to do?"

"Move us away from the starbridge, then hold position." Ted watched as Emily entered commands into her keyboard. "Just wait."

Emily raised an eyebrow, then looked up at Jas. Apparently the Prime Emissary had switched off hisher translator and activated an internal mike, for when heshe spoke again, it wasn't in Anglo but rather the unpronounceable rush of hisses, clicks, and croaks that I'd heard in hisher quarters. A few seconds passed, then from the speakers we heard a response in the same tongue. Jas gave a short reply, then turned toward Ted.

"Our arrival has been acknowledged, and we have been welcomed," heshe said. "If you will kindly relinquish control of your ship, our traffic control system will guide it to the appropriate docking port."

From across the compartment, I saw Ali trade a wary glance with Ted. The captain gave him a wordless nod, and Ali entered a command into his console. "Helm control free," he said, not at all happy about it. "But I don't know how . . ."

A second later, there was an abrupt sensation of lateral movement as the maneuvering thrusters fired on their own, bringing the *Pride* around a few degrees to starboard. "Do not worry," Jas said as heshe returned to hisher couch. "Your ship is quite safe, so long as you do not interfere. All you need do is complete final docking procedures."

"Thank you." Ted looked over at Rain and me. "Right, then . . . you know the drill. Go below and prepare for arrival. We'll be using the primary docking port on Cargo Two."

I unbuckled my harness and pushed myself out of my seat. "Do you want us to open the port hatch?"

Ted shook his head. "Not until we get there. Just pressurize the module and wait for us."

"Wilco." Grabbing hold of the ceiling rail, Rain pulled herself toward the deck hatch. "Let us know when you're about to come down."

"Sure." Ted was no longer paying attention to us. Once again, he was gazing out the windows, watching *Talus qua'spah* as it steadily grew larger. One last glance behind us, then I followed Rain from the command center. She waited in the access shaft while I shut the hatch behind us.

"Is it just me," I said once we were alone, "or does that thing scare the hell out of you, too?"

Rain thought about it for a moment. "No," she said quietly as she pushed herself in the direction of the hub. "It's not just you."

XVI

Although we were supposed to pressurize Cargo Two, standard operating procedure called for us to suit up first. So our first stop was the ready room.

Rain and I had made our peace, but she still wasn't inclined to share the compartment while she put on her hardsuit. I wasn't about to press the issue, so I let her have her privacy and instead pushed myself across the hub to Cargo Two and initiated pressurization. She didn't take as long to suit up as she had the day before, so by the time she was done and I traded places with her in the ready room to put on my own gear, Cargo Two was fully pressurized and we were ready to enter it without having to cycle through its airlock. We kept our helmet faceplates open, though, and left our pressure switches on standby.

Cargo Two was divided into four decks, with the marijuana bales securely lashed to gridlike floors. We floated past them as we made our way down the center shaft to the docking port, located at the far end of the module between the cargo hatches. We'd just reached the port hatch when Emily's voice came through the comlink.

"Jas tells us we're about to enter a gravity field," she said. *"You're going to need to find something to hang on to."*

"We copy." There were hand-rungs on either side of the hatch. I grabbed a pair on one side, and Rain held on to two more on the other side. "All right, we're ready."

"Very good." A pause. *"On final approach now. We'll be docking in a couple of minutes."*

I was about to respond when Rain gasped. "Holy . . . get a load of that!"

She was peering through the small porthole in the center of the hatch. Moving beside her, I gazed out the window, and felt my breath catch. Past the flanges of the docking collar, several hundred yards away and getting closer with each passing second, we could see a giant, saucerlike construct, just one of the countless subsections that made up *Talus qua'spah*. As the *Pride* drew near, a dome at the bottom of the saucer opened like a clamshell. Beyond it lay an enormous bay, so vast that the *Robert E. Lee* could have been hangared inside.

"I think we're expected," I murmured. An obvious remark, yet Rain's face was grim as she silently nodded. She was just as intimidated as I was.

Coasting in on little more than its thrusters, the *Pride* slowly entered the bay. Through the porthole, Rain and I watched as the ship glided into the center of a latticelike cradle, its arms swinging aside to make room for our vessel. There was a hard thump as the freighter came to rest, then a tubular arm telescoped forward to mate with the port hatch.

It had just connected with the docking collar when we felt the abrupt tug of gravity, and the airlock suddenly went vertical. Rain and I both swore as we scrambled to find footholds. Fortunately, there was a narrow ledge running around the inside of the hatch that we were able to stand upon.

"All right, we're here," Emily said. *"How are you guys doing down there?"*

Behind us, I could heard the bales shifting against their restraints; now they hung from the decks, which had become bulkheads. "We're okay," Rain said, "but I hope they're able to fine-tune their gravity field. Otherwise, unloading is going to be a bitch."

A short pause, then Emily's voice returned. *"Jas assures us this won't be a problem. All they have to do is shut down the field for the hangar. How's the pressure on your end?"*

I turned my head so that I could read the panel next to the hatch. All the lights were green. "Copacetic," I replied, then I glanced through the porthole. An empty tunnel lay before us, an enclosed gangway illuminated by the *Pride's* external lights. "Waiting for you."

Another pause, then Ted came over the comlink. *"It's going to take us a bit to get things settled here. Go ahead and pop the hatch. We'll be down in a few minutes."*

157

"Roger that." The lockwheel was located on my side of the hatch. Hanging on with my left hand, I twisted the wheel clockwise, then put my shoulder against the hatch. There was a faint hiss as it swung open, and I looked at Rain. "Ladies first."

"Oh, no." She shook her head within her helmet. "I insist . . ."

I tried not to laugh. If the *hjadd* had a death ray waiting for us, we would've known already. But I wasn't about to make fun of her for being nervous, so I ducked my head and climbed through the hatch.

The tunnel was octagonal, with each surface capable of serving as a floor. For a few seconds, all I could clearly see was the first dozen feet or so . . . then the walls glowed to life with a soft radiance of their own, and I saw that the gangway extended about forty yards until it ended at a circular door.

"Now what?" Rain entered the tunnel behind me. "Keep going, or wait for the others?"

"We wait." There was no need for my helmet, and I felt foolish wearing it, so I took a moment to remove it, careful to keep my headset in place. "Always let the captain . . ."

Before I could finish, though, the door at the end of the tunnel split in half and slid open. Warm light spilled out into the passageway.

"On the other hand . . ." I murmured.

Rain had removed her own helmet. "You just said we should wait," she said, regarding the door with suspicion. "Now you're saying . . ."

"Hold on a sec." I prodded my headset. "Ted, are you there?"

"Copy. What's going on?"

"We've left the *Pride*, and now we're in some sort of gangway. Look like it leads to the station, and a door at the far end just opened. I think someone want us to come aboard." I paused. "Do we stay, or do we go?"

Several seconds passed, then Morgan's voice came over the comlink. *"Jas says that you should continue. An invitation has been made, and it would be considered rude if you declined."*

Ted's voice returned. *"I concur. We're still in the command center. Go ahead, both of you. We'll catch up."*

"Roger that." I looked at Rain; she'd heard everything over her own headset. "Well, there it is. Ready to meet the neighbors?"

She still didn't look happy about the thought of doing this alone. We hadn't been given much choice in the matter, though, so we tucked our helmets beneath our arms and headed down the tunnel. I deliberately walked slowly, in order to give Ted and the others more time to join us; nonetheless, it didn't take long for us to reach the end of the gangway.

We entered a circular room about twenty feet in diameter, with another round door on the other side. Its walls were featureless save for a set of floor-to-ceiling glass panels that emitted a dull blue glow. Above us was a transparent dome; through it, we could see the *Pride*, resting in a vertical position within its docking cradle. We were still gazing up at our ship when, very quietly, the door slid shut behind us.

"Oh, hell," Rain muttered. "I don't like the looks of . . ."

At that instant, the wall panels lit up, each displaying a different image. A north polar projection of the Milky Way galaxy, overlaid with a halo grid upon which a star near the center of the Orion Arm was circled: Rho Coronae Borealis, if my guess was right. A schematic view of *Talus qua'spah*, with a tiny saucer near its outer edge highlighted; *hjadd* script appeared next to it, apparently meaning YOU ARE HERE. A wide-angle shot of the *Pride*, looking like a bug snared within a spiderweb. Vertical bars of *hjadd* script slowly scrolled upward, significant in some way yet meaningless to our eyes.

I was still gazing at those panels when Rain tapped my shoulder.

Turning around, I saw another panel, this one showing a *hjadd*. Although heshe looked a little like Jas, I noticed that hisher face had a different skin pattern and a slightly larger fin. Heshe opened hisher mouth and addressed us in a series of hisses and clicks.

A pause, then the *hjadd* vanished, to be replaced by something that looked like a hermit crab, only lacking a shell and with smaller claws. It chirped for a few seconds, stopped and waited for a moment, then disappeared. The next creature was a tall, skinny biped, with backward-jointed legs, arms that nearly reached the floor, and a head that vaguely resembled that of a horse; when it spoke, it gurgled like someone with a mouthful of water trying to tell a dirty joke. Another pause, then it went away, and then we saw something that could have been the Abominable Snowman were it not for enormous bug eyes and a tongue that slipped obscenely in and out of its furry mouth.

"I think . . ." Rain studied the panel, her anxiety replaced by fascination. "Maybe this is some sort of reception area."

"You might be right, but I haven't the foggiest what we're supposed to . . ."

The panel suddenly went dark. A moment passed, then a human who looked a little like Ted, except with a shaved head and plucked eyebrows, appeared on it. *"Greetings, and welcome to the House of the Talus,"* he said, speaking Anglo in a voice that didn't belong to our captain. *"You have been identified as human. Please continue to visitor processing."*

A tinkling sound like wind chimes, then I felt a warm draft at the back of my neck. Looking around, I saw that the second door had slid open.

"Bad manners or not," Rain said quietly, "I really think we should have waited."

"Too late now. We're committed." Besides, I was curious. Rain glared at me, but followed me into the next room.

It was almost identical to the first, except that the ceiling was covered with translucent panels. Low, benchlike tables were scattered around; cabinets were recessed within the reflective glass walls. The air was considerably warmer as well; about seventy degrees, comfortable without being too humid.

The door closed as soon as we were inside, and once again the not-quite-Ted appeared on a wall panel.

"This is the decontamination facility," he said. *"To begin this procedure, please remove all your clothes."*

(PART 3)

The Fool's Errand

(ELEVEN)

The etiquette of decontamination . . .
a visit to the library . . .
Fah, otherwise known as Haha . . .
Ash gets strange(r).

I

Rain's scream was still reverberating from the walls when a *hjadd* materialized.

Heshe appeared so suddenly, my first thought was that heshe was some sort of extraterrestrial djinn, fresh from the lamp and ready to grant me three wishes (the first of which would've been to be any-place but here). It took a moment for me to realize that heshe was a hologram, albeit so lifelike that I could've sworn heshe was solid. Heshe regarded us with reptilian solemnity, hisher fin raised to full height from the back of hisher head.

"*Pardon me,*" heshe said, hisher voice nearly the same as Jas's, "*but what does the expression 'hell, no' mean?*"

I forced a cough to keep from cracking up. "It . . . uh, means that she's . . . ah . . ."

"It means there's no way I'm getting naked." Rain's face was

165

livid. "Not here, not now, and especially not with"—she pointed at me—"him."

The *hjadd's* left eye twitched toward her. *"Decontamination is required for all races visiting* Talus qua'spah. *I assure you that it is painless and noninvasive, and will only take a few minutes to perform. However, it is necessary for one to be bare of all accoutrements in order for the procedure to be completely effective."*

Rain opened her mouth to protest, but I cut her off. "I understand that, sure. But in our culture, nudity is considered . . . um, taboo." The *hjadd's* head cocked slightly at this unfamiliar word. "Socially unacceptable," I added. "Particularly between sexes . . . genders, that is."

"Meaning, I'm not about to . . ." Rain glared at me, and shook her head. "No. Out of the question."

The *hjadd* was quiet for a moment. I had the sense that heshe was listening to someone else whom we couldn't see. *"It is strange for a dioecious species to be so reluctant about revealing their bodies,"* heshe said at last, hisher eyes twitching back and forth between us. *"How is it possible for you to mate without exposing your reproductive organs?"*

It was my turn to become red-faced. "We're . . . um, not mates. Just friends, that's all."

The *hjadd's* fin lowered, and hisher head moved back and forth upon hisher long neck. *"I now comprehend. However, the rules of the Talus remain. You may not pass this point without undergoing decontamination, and this procedure cannot begin until you have removed all your clothing."*

I was about to respond when I heard a click in my right ear. Ted's voice came through my headset. *"Jules, do you copy? Is there a problem over there?"*

I prodded my mike. "Roger that, Captain . . . and, yeah, we've got a holdup."

The *hjadd* waited patiently while I briefly explained the situation;

166

Rain tapped into the comlink, but didn't say anything until I finished. When I was done, there was a short pause, then Ted came back online. *"Look, I understand this is uncomfortable for both of you, but Jas says that if you don't undergo decontamination, none of us will be allowed on board. No two ways about it. Sorry."*

Rain's mouth fell open. "Skipper, I can't . . ."

"Rain, stop being such a prude. The rest of us are in the next room. If you don't want to be alone with Jules, you can wait until we join you, and then we can all get naked together. Or you can trust Mr. Truffaut to be a gentleman and keep his back to you. Either way, though, you're just going to . . ."

"Okay, all right. I get the point. Over and out." Rain clicked off, then turned to give me a cold stare. "I swear to God, if you so much as . . ."

"Don't worry." I'd already turned away from her, setting my helmet down on the nearest bench. "I won't so much as peek. I promise."

Rain hesitated, then I heard her place her own helmet on the other bench. A few moments later, there was the soft sound of a zipper sliding open. From the corner of my eye, I saw that the *hjadd* had already vanished; apparently heshe realized that our primitive notions of privacy extended to himher as well.

A man of my word, I kept my promise to Rain. Not that it made much difference. The wall panels were just reflective enough that, even though I looked straight ahead, I was still able to see what was going on behind my back. I tried to distract myself by glancing down at my feet, but nonetheless it was hard to ignore the fact that a lovely young woman was peeling out of her undergarment just a few feet away.

And Rain was beautiful. No question about it. As much as I tried to ignore her reflection, she had a body that I could easily fantasize curling up against. I bit my lower lip and tried to think about baseball . . . but when I looked up again, I saw that her gaze was fastened on the wall in front of her, and that she was studying my reflection as well.

Our eyes indirectly met for a moment, and for a second I thought I was a dead man. Yet my execution was delayed by the *hjadd's* voice, coming from some invisible source: *"Please close your eyes and extend your arms."*

I did as I was told, raising my arms straight out from my sides. A low hum surrounded us; although my eyelids were closed, I could tell that the ceiling was gradually becoming brighter. For the next several minutes, we were bathed in ultraviolet radiation, followed by a hot, dry wind that whisked away dandruff and dead skin cells.

The humming ceased, the ceiling darkened, and the air became still once more. But just as I was about to open my eyes, I heard a whispered *thufft!* from somewhere behind me. An instant later, a white-hot needle jabbed me in the ass.

Rain yelped at the same moment I did, and I looked around to see her grabbing at her derriere. "What the hell was . . . ?"

"Many apologies," the *hjadd* said, still unseen to us. *"Those were darts containing mild antibiotics. They are harmless to you and will soon dissolve, but they help ensure that you're not carrying any microorganisms harmful to our kind."*

"Great." She massaged her buttock where the dart had penetrated her skin. "I thought you said this would be painless and noninvasive."

"Heshe lied," I muttered. Made sense, though; if heshe had told us what was coming, we might have refused. And it was only a little sting, after all; the pain was already going away, leaving behind little more than a tiny bruise.

"Yeah, well . . . heshe's not the only one." She glared at me. "You said you wouldn't peek."

"How did you know I did?"

"Because . . ." Her voice trailed off and she blushed, then quickly wrapped her arms across her chest and turned away from me. "So now what? Do we put on our suits again?"

"That will not be necessary. Temporary garments are available to you." As the *hjadd* spoke, a wall panel slid open, revealing a small closet. *"Please put them on. They conform to your dimensions and will keep you comfortable until your own clothes can be brought over from your ship."*

Hanging within the closet were several long shirtlike robes resembling dashikis, each embroidered with intricate patterns much like those on Jas's robes. I removed two, tossed one over to Rain, then pulled on the other. At the bottom of the closet were several socklike boots that could be put on either foot; I slipped on two of them and gave a pair to Rain. Once we were dressed and I had stored our suits in the closet, the *hjadd* spoke again. *"You may now proceed to your guest quarters. Transportation is waiting to take you there."*

The door on the other side of the room opened. Rain and I gave each other uncertain looks, and I gazed at the ceiling. "Just a second. I need to check with my people." The *hjadd* said nothing as I walked over to the bench where I'd left my headset. "Captain, are you there?"

"We're here. What's taking so long?"

"Just finished decontamination. You're gonna love it." Rain rolled her eyes, and I went on. "Look, the *hjadd* want us to go somewhere . . . to our quarters, or so they tell us. That means we're probably going to be separated, at least for a while. Should we . . . ?"

"Go ahead," Ted replied. *"I'm sure you'll be all right. We'll meet up with you there."*

"Roger that." I clicked off, then slipped the headset around my neck. Rain was waiting for a response; I gave her a nod and she shrugged, then we padded across the room toward the open door.

On the other side lay another tunnel, this one much shorter, ending at a sealed hatch only a dozen feet away. Resting upon a recessed track was a long, pill-shaped vehicle, its transparent canopy open at one end to expose six couchlike seats arranged in tandem. Obviously a tram of some sort. When I climbed into the front seat, with Rain taking the one directly behind me, the couches changed shape to conform to our bodies, with padded bars folding across us. The canopy slid shut; a prolonged wheeze as the compartment was depressurized, then the hatch spiraled open, and we shot down the tunnel . . .

And out into space.

II

Or so it seemed, for it appeared as if there was nothing on the other side of the canopy except cold, unglimmering stars.

Grabbing at the safety bar, I gasped in horror. For a moment, I thought we'd been jettisoned into the vacuum . . . then the cab passed through a ring, and I realized that the tram was a pneumatic tube running along the side of a thick cable.

We'd left the saucer where the *Pride* was docked, and were being hurled through the *Talus qua'spah*. On either side of us, stretching out as far as we could see, floated a seemingly endless array of spheres, cylinders, discs, and wheels, all connected to one another by an intricate network of cables upon which other trams sprinted back and forth. Lights like a million votive candles gleamed from countless windows while, far above us, spacecraft of every conceivable shape and size moved in stately promenade.

"Oh . . ." That was all Rain could say; I didn't have to look back

to know that she was awestruck. I seconded the motion, adding another *oh* for good measure. The *Talus qua'spah* was more than a habitat; it was a vast city of space, stunning in its beauty, humbling in its
complexity.

We didn't get much of a chance to admire the view, though,
because a few seconds later the cab took an abrupt left turn at a
Y-shaped intersection and hurtled toward a large sphere. Just as it
seemed that collision was unavoidable, a circular hatch opened at its
equator; the safety bars held us within our couches as the cab deceler-
ated and then entered the sphere.

We found ourselves in another station much like the one in the
saucer. The cab glided to a halt with little more than a slight bump;
another long wheeze, and the canopy slid open. I waited until my
couch released me from its grasp, then stood up on legs that felt as
if they'd become rubber. Rain was just as unsteady; her hand shook
when I took it to help her out of the cab.

"That was fun," I said. "Let's do it again."

"Sure. Anytime." She let go of my hand, then looked around. "All
right, so where are we now?"

As if in response, a door behind us peeled open; beyond it lay a
short corridor, its hexagonal walls lined with burnished copper panels. "Um . . . we're here," I replied. "Wherever that is."

The door shut behind us as soon as we entered the passageway.
Too late to turn back now, and nowhere to go but forward. So we
slowly walked toward the door at the other end. It split down the
middle as soon as we approached it, and . . .

"Holy . . . !" Rain whispered.

She was getting pretty good at taking the words right out of my
mouth. All I could do was stare.

A library, much like one might find in a nineteenth-century

manor somewhere in England. Beneath a vaulted ceiling from which crystal chandeliers were suspended, we saw mahogany-paneled walls lined with brass-caged bookcases, their shelves filled with leather-bound volumes. Antique armchairs and sofas stood here and there upon a thick Persian carpet, with brass reading lamps resting on oak tables and lithographs of country scenes framed upon the walls. A spiral staircase led to an upper gallery, and a mellow fire crackled gently within a marble hearth at the far end of the room.

It was comfortable, and luxurious, and lovely, and totally unexpected. My first thought was that this place was nothing more than a clever illusion, perhaps another hologram. Yet the carpet was soft beneath my feet, and when I laid my hand upon the back of an armchair, I felt supple brown leather. No, it was really . . . real.

"What in the world?" Rain gazed around the room, her eyes wide. "How could they . . . I mean . . . ?"

"*It is very simple to explain,*" a familiar voice replied, and I nearly jumped a foot in the air when the *hjadd* we'd met in the reception area materialized beside me. Heshe regarded me with hisher usual stoicism, yet hisher fin rose slightly. "*I apologize. Did I startle you?*"

"Yes . . . yes, you did." My heart hammered against my chest, and I took a deep breath. "A little warning next time, please, um . . . what did you say your name was?"

"*I did not say.*" A short hiss of amusement. "*Since you have asked, though, I am Hahatahja Fah Tas-Saatja. I have been delegated to be your liaison while you are here.*"

"Hahatafahjasat . . ." It was a mouthful of a name; when I stumbled over the syllables, sacs on either side of hisher throat puffed outward. "Sorry. No offense . . . is it Fah for short? Or Haha?"

"*Fah. Please do not attempt to pronounce the rest . . . it would only be an insult.*" The throat sacs deflated, and heshe raised a hand before I could go on. *"Your names, of course, are known. Jas Sa-Fhadda has already relayed that information to us."*

"Yeah, sure." Maybe heshe preferred to be addressed as Fah, but I couldn't help but think of himher as Haha; heshe was definitely one for practical jokes. "We met aboard our ship. Nice guy."

"Jas said the same about you." Fah's head rose upon hisher neck, as if to inspect me more closely. *"In fact, heshe said you expressed an interest in our cuisine. Perhaps you will have that opportunity next evening, before the reception we plan to hold in your honor."*

Reception? This was news to me. I wondered if Ted knew about it yet. "We would be delighted," I replied, trying my hand at diplomacy. "And I'm sure . . ."

"Excuse me," Rain said, interrupting us, "but you still haven't answered my question." She waved a hand at the room in which we stood. "How did you know what . . . I mean, how did you build all this?"

"Ah, yes . . ." Fah's eyes rotated to take in the library. *"It is a replica of the crew lounge of the* Galileo. *We duplicated it from images we found in the data banks of the* Maria Celeste *after we recovered it from Spindrift, and used it to help the surviving members of the expedition acclimate themselves once they were revived from biostasis. Since then, we have expanded it to serve as living quarters for human visitors."* Heshe pointed to the gallery. *"Your bedrooms are located up there, along with hygiene facilities. I hope the accommodations are suitable for your needs."*

"It's . . . very nice, thank you." Rain's voice was low; I could tell she was still trying to wrap her head around finding a Victorian library in an alien space colony. "I'm sure the others will . . . um, find it interesting."

As they spoke, I wandered over toward the hearth. As I suspected, the fire was just another holo; it cast no warmth, and the logs remained unconsumed. I picked up a book from a side table, only to discover that I was unable to open its cover. Stage props, nothing more. I hoped that the bathroom toilets were functional, or otherwise we'd be in big trouble.

"I'm pleased that you're satisfied with the arrangements." Fah cocked hisher head to one side, listened for a moment, then went on. *"Your companions are on the way. They will be joining you shortly. If there is nothing else I can do for you . . ."*

Before either of us could say anything, heshe vanished, winking out of existence as suddenly as heshe had appeared.

III

Rain stared at the place where Fah had stood, then let out her breath. "Just for once, I'd like to see himher use the door." An irate scowl. "And you're a big help . . . can't you learn to say their names correctly?"

"Sure, I can. Fah. Jas. Can't wait till we meet the one named Duh."

"Hush. They might be listening." Self-conscious, she wrapped her arms around herself. "Come to think of it," she added, glancing up at the ceiling, "we'd better watch what we say."

"Yeah. Easily offended, aren't they?" I sauntered over to the nearest bookcase and opened its cage but wasn't able to remove any of the books upon its shelves. More props. "Next time we come here, we'll have to bring our own . . ."

The door leading to the tram opened just then, and we turned to see Ted walk in. "Ah, there you are," he said, giving us a wry grin. "Serves you right for getting ahead of us."

"Your idea, skipper." Rain smiled back at him. "You just missed our host. He was here a second ago."

"Fah? Met him while we were going through decontamination."
The captain gazed around the library, apparently unsurprised by our
surroundings. "Yeah, same place," he murmured. "Looks like they've
fixed it up a little, though."

"Maybe they finally got some real books." Emily followed him
through the door, followed by Ali, Goldstein, and Ash. The others
were as startled by our surroundings as Rain and I had been, but
Emily accepted it as a place where she'd been once before. Seeing the
two of us, she chuckled. "Nice pajamas."

"Thanks." I couldn't help but notice that they were all wearing
their own clothes. Well, that made sense; they hadn't had to put on
EVA gear before leaving the ship. "They're comfortable enough, but
I wouldn't mind going back to fetch my stuff. Think they'll let me
do that?"

"I don't see why not if you don't mind taking the roller-coaster
ride again." Emily sat down on a nearby sofa. "Doc's still on the
Pride. We decided that we should follow protocol and leave someone
aboard."

"Where's Jas?"

"Left us as soon as we came down the gangway. Guess his pals
don't think he poses any sort of contamination threat." Ted sat down
next to his wife. "All right, we're here," he said to Morgan. "So now
what?"

Goldstein was still staring at the library. Hearing Ted, he glanced
back at the captain. "Tomorrow we'll unload the cargo, and I'll begin
trade negotiations . . . with Mr. Ash, of course. For now, though, we
should make ourselves at home."

Ash had walked over to the hearth; he quietly gazed at the fake
fire, trying to ignore the rest of us. No telling how long it had been
since he'd last had a drink. Once again, I had to wonder what it

must be like, to be able to hear everyone else's thoughts whether you wanted to or not. Nor was he the only one ill at ease; Ali kept glancing at the door, as if wishing that he, too, had remained aboard ship.

"Sounds like good advice." Ted yawned, stretched out his legs. "Been a long day. Going to be a long one tomorrow, too." He looked at Emily. "Should've brought some food over from the ship. I could use dinner."

"Fah said that a reception is going to be held for us tomorrow." I ran a fingertip across the back of an armchair. The upholstery wasn't real leather, but whatever it was, it felt like cowhide all the same. "We should get a good meal then."

"I wouldn't recommend it." Morgan peered up at a chandelier, almost as if speculating about how much it was worth. "I've tried *hjadd* food. Rather disgusting."

"I'm with you," Emily said. "Besides, our systems may not be able to digest whatever they give us. I'll head back to the ship later, gather some provisions. Won't be much . . . sandwiches and coffee . . . but it'll get us through."

"Thank you." Ted stifled another yawn, then stood up. "Right. So let's rest up and get ready to go to work tomorrow."

He headed for the stairs, apparently interested in checking out the guest quarters. Ali followed him, while Rain went over to Emily and quietly conferred with her. Morgan continued to stroll around the room, inspecting every artifact in the library with a trader's curiosity.

That left me with Ash. I walked over to join him at the fireplace. "So . . . penny for your thoughts?" He didn't respond, nor did he look away from the holoprojected flames. Apparently he wasn't in a talkative mood. "Well, look," I went on, "I'm going back to the ship in a little bit to fetch my clothes. If you'd like me to bring anything to you . . ."

"My bottle, you mean." It wasn't a question; he and I both knew better. Ash glanced over his shoulder at Morgan, who was out of earshot and not paying any attention to us. "It's in my cabin, in the locker," he added, keeping his voice low. "Morgan wants to keep me dry, but if you can get it for me . . ."

"Sure." I had little doubt that he'd relax a bit if he could shut out everyone, if only for a little while. "And your . . . ?"

"My guitar, too, yes. Please." He favored me with a conspiratorial smile. "You're all right, Jules. You're easy to be around."

"Thanks . . . I guess."

"I meant that as a compliment. You should take it as such." Ash sighed, his gaze traveling to the fox-hunting scene above the mantel. "God, this is hard. My people should've never let Morgan talk them into sending me."

"Your people." I hesitated. "The Order of the Eye?"

Looking away from the lithograph, he stared straight at me. Once again, I felt a door open within my mind. "So . . . Jas knows," he whispered. "Heshe is aware of why I'm here."

All of a sudden, I found myself wishing that I'd kept my mouth shut. "I . . . yeah, I think so. Heshe asked if you belonged to . . ."

"I understand." Ash shook his head. "Don't worry. You're not involved in this . . . but I advise you to keep your distance. Things might get . . . strange."

"Aren't you the one who told me I should get used to strangeness?"

The smile returned. "Yes, I did, didn't I?" Then his face became solemn. "But there are degrees of strangeness, and just now"—a moment of hesitation—"I don't know what to believe."

And then he turned and walked away, leaving me to wonder what he'd meant by that.

(TWELVE)

Raw deal . . .

Ash talks back . . .

what do you do with two thousand paperweights? . . .

getting the pink slip.

IV

Next morning, Rain and I returned to the *Pride of Cucamonga* to unload the cargo. There were no quarrels this time around; in fact, you could've almost sworn we'd been working together for years. Of course, things were made easier by the fact that we had an unexpected bit of help.

Since the last time I'd visited the *Pride*, a second gangway had been extended from the saucer, this one leading to the primary airlock. Made it a little easier for us to get back aboard. Once Rain and I suited up and exited the ship through the docking port, we discovered a half dozen things that resembled bowling balls with two arms waiting just outside. Doc informed us that, according to Jas, these were Talus 'bots tasked to carry away the cargo. A small, sledlike craft hovered nearby, piloted by a *hjadd* who never spoke to us but instead waited patiently while we opened the cargo modules. I suppose heshe was the one named Duh, although I was careful not to say as much over the comlink.

The gravity field within the saucer was temporarily switched off; since I didn't need to operate the pod, I helped Rain untie the bales and move them to the lateral hatches, where the 'bots captured them and, in turn, carried the massive rolls over to the sled. Once its bed was full, the sled would glide away, disappearing through a hatch on the other side of the hangar and returning a few minutes later to take on another load.

It didn't take long for us to get used to working with the 'bots, and although Duh remained quiet the entire time, heshe seemed to understand exactly what we were doing. At one point, though, while waiting for the sled to return, I happened to notice four figures—two humans, along with a pair of *hjadds* in environment suits—watching us from a cupola overlooking the bay. I had little doubt who they were: Morgan, Jas, and Fah, with Ash quietly standing nearby, making sure that all the merchandise had arrived safely.

It took about four hours for us to empty both modules. Once Rain and I were done, Duh disappeared without so much as a thank-you, the 'bots trailing hisher sled as it returned to its hatch. Rain and I cycled back through the airlock. Much to my surprise, Rain allowed me to share the ready room with her, so long as I promised to keep my back turned. Even so, we ended up helping each other remove our gear; she blushed a few times, but otherwise didn't object to my presence. One more sign that she was getting used to working with me.

After we put on our civvies, we went back to the saucer. At least we didn't have to endure decontamination again. Just as well; we were bone-tired, and all we wanted was to get a bite to eat and perhaps a nap.

Ted, Emily, and Ali were waiting for us in the library. While Rain and I were busting our humps, they'd had little to do except listen in on the comlink, but Emily had made lunch for us from the provisions she'd brought over from the ship. The five of us were working our way through a plate of turkey and cheese sandwiches when the door opened, and Morgan stormed in, trailed by Ash.

"We've been robbed." His face was dark with anger, and beneath his left arm he carried a small, oblong object wrapped in silky white fabric.

"Come again?" Ted stared at him, then glanced at Rain and me. "Was anything missing?"

"No, damn it," Morgan snarled. "I didn't mean it that way. Everything's accounted for, down to the last pound. It's just that . . ." Inarticulate with rage, he jabbed a finger at Ash. "A fat lot of good you were! I was looking for an inside lead, and all you could do was . . ."

"Don't blame me." Beneath his robe's hood, Ash's expression was neutral. "I've told you what I can do and what I can't, and I can't—"

"Like hell! I've seen you do it dozens of times." Morgan glared at him. "So help me, if you've been drinking . . ."

"No, but after putting up with you all morning, I need a stiff one." Ash headed for the stairs leading to the gallery, no doubt to retrieve the jug of bearshine from his bedroom. I hoped that no one would wonder how it had made its way from the *Pride* to our quarters.

Morgan started to go after him, then seemed to think better of it. Instead, he placed the cloth-wrapped object on the lunch table, then slumped in an armchair. Putting his face in his hands, he let out a long, depressed sigh. "I'm ruined," he muttered. "God, I'm ruined . . ."

"Calm down." Emily poured a cup of coffee and carried it over to him. "Just tell us what happened. Did the negotiations go bad?"

"Hell, yes, they went bad! You think I'm happy about this?" Raising his head, he regarded her as if she was an idiot. "Worst goddamn

180

deal I ever made! We were screwed the minute we walked in there, all because that alcoholic son of a . . ."

"It's not my fault!" Ash's voice came as an angry shout from the gallery above us. Looking up, we saw him standing at the railing. He'd pulled back his hood, and there was an uncorked jug in his hand. "I did the best I could, but I can't . . ."

"Back off, both of you." Ted rose to his feet. "Mr. Goldstein, get a grip. And you"—he glared at Ash—"put that thing away, or so help me I'll put it under lock and key and you'll be dry until we get back home."

Ash stared back at the captain. Apparently realizing this wasn't an empty threat, he reluctantly jammed the cork back in the jug. "That's better," Ted said, then turned to Morgan. "Right . . . now how about telling us what happened, without any accusations."

Morgan let out his breath. Before he could begin, though, my curiosity got the better of me. "What's this thing?" I asked, reaching across the table toward the wrapped object he'd brought in with him.

"Don't touch that!" Morgan snatched it away from me, then seemed to reconsider. With a resigned shrug, he put it back on the table. "Aw, what's the point? Go ahead, open it up. Doesn't matter . . . you'll be seeing plenty more like it soon enough."

I picked up the object. For something little more than twelve inches tall, it was fairly heavy. Carefully unwrapping the cloth, I found myself holding what appeared to be a small black obelisk. Carved from opaque, unreflective stone and attached to a matching square base, it resembled a rectangular pylon that had been given a ninety-degree twist at its center.

"What is this?" Vaguely amused, I hefted it in my hand. About ten pounds or so, I reckoned. "Some sort of paperweight?"

"It's called a *gnosh*." Morgan studied me. "Do you like it?"

"Well . . . yeah, I guess so." Actually, I did like it. A lot. The *gnosh* fit smoothly within my palm, its surface warm to the touch. A small thrill raced down my back that was pleasant, almost sexual. "Can I have it?"

Morgan shook his head. "That's my sample. I've give you one later . . . Lord knows I'll have plenty to spare." Another sigh of dejection. "Two thousand, to be exact."

"Two thousand of . . ." Ali stared at the *gnosh*. "These things? In exchange for . . . ?"

"That's right." Morgan picked up the cloth in which the *gnosh* had been wrapped. "This is what we're getting in trade for our cargo." Carefully draping the cloth over his hand, he reached for the obelisk. "Jules, if you'll please . . . ?"

I found myself reluctant to give it up. Morgan was insistent, though, so I surrendered the *gnosh* to him. The moment it left my hand, the ecstasy I'd felt left me. "Wow," I mumbled. "That was interesting."

"What in the world are you talking about?" Rain looked first at me, then at the *gnosh*. "Let me see that."

"Oh, no you don't." Ted shook his head, then turned to Morgan. "What is this thing? What does it do?"

"So far as I can tell, it's an emotion enhancer." Morgan swaddled the *gnosh* within the cloth, then placed it on the table. "Touch it, and it gives you pleasure . . . or at least if you're in a neutral frame of mind, as Mr. Truffaut was. Since I'm rather pissed off just now, I'm being cautious about handling it. Otherwise, I might be tempted to strangle Drunko the Clown up there."

"Keep it up, and I'll show you my next trick." Ash was making his way down the stairs. At least he'd put away the jug, but not before he'd sneaked one last slug of bearshine; I noticed that he carefully held the banister as he descended.

"Steady, gents." Ted bent down to study the *gnosh*. Although it was safely wrapped again, he was prudent enough not to touch it. "So what else has Fah offered us?"

"What else?" A short, humorless laugh. "That's it! Two thousand of these stupid things." Again, Morgan shook his head. "Oh, did I get screwed . . ."

"What did you expect?" Ali picked up the *gnosh*, gave it a casual inspection. "We just brought them two and a half tons of weed, for heaven's sake. What did you think you were going to get for them? The key to the galaxy?"

"Yup . . . that's exactly what he thought." Ash was visibly sway-ing as he reached the bottom of the stairs. He shuffled toward us, his breath reeking of booze. "Morgan believed that he could get something for nothing . . . faster-than-light drive, advanced nano-tech, some other kind of miracle technology, all for just a few bales of hemp." He grinned and shook his head. "Manhattan for a hand-ful of beads and trinkets . . . but this time, the injuns outfoxed the white men."

"Ash . . ." Morgan's eyes were cold. "I'm warning you, don't . . ."

"Don't what? Disclose the details of your sleazy little deal?" Ash reached beneath his robe, pulled out the squeezebulb I'd given him. It was half-full of bearshine; apparently he'd filled it before leaving the jug in his room. "Give up already," he went on as he unsealed the nipple. "There's nothing you can do about it now."

He took a drink, then turned to look at me. "Get this," he said, as if none of the others were around. "Morgan brought me aboard . . . brought me along, that is . . . 'cause he thought I might give him an inside edge. I mean, what could be better than to have a telepath at your side when you're doing business? That way, you can tell what the other guy is thinking when you're trying to drive a bargain. Great idea, really . . . except there's just one catch." A pause. "C'mon, Jules, you're a smart lad . . . what do you think it is?"

He was clearly waiting for an answer. I thought about it for a moment. "Umm . . . you don't know *hjadd*?"

"Bingo!" Ash almost tripped over the hem of his robe as he wheeled away from me. "I can read their minds, all right . . . but it doesn't mean a goddamn thing if I don't know *what* they're thinking!"

"That's not what you told me." Morgan's face was red. "You said you could . . ."

"No. I told you that I could pick up their emotions. No problem there." Snickering beneath his breath, he sauntered over to Rain and flung an arm around her shoulders. "In fact, you wanna know how they feel about your boss?" Ash confided to her in a stage whisper. "They think . . . well, not think exactly, but y'know what I mean . . . he's a fool for even trying to pull something like this."

"Look who's talking." Rain irritably peeled his arm from her.

Ash didn't seem to notice. He sailed away once more, taking another mighty swig of corn liquor. "But what they actually *think* . . . well, damn if I know! They don't know Anglo, really . . . they just use those . . . those whatchamacallits . . . to translate our language into their own, and vice versa. Their coga . . . congi . . . cognitive processes are in their own tongue. And believe me, Fah and Jas were real careful not to even think about any of the few words of our language that they actually understand."

"So you couldn't read their minds." Ted had raised a hand to his face, and he was trying to hide his smile behind it.

"You got it, Cap'n." Ash propped himself up against the back of a chair. "Y'know, just between you and me . . . I think they've dealt with telepaths before. 'Cause as soon as Fah saw me comin', he . . .

heshe, I mean . . . put up a mental wall, and the only thing I could make out was the vague impression that heshe needed to pee."

"The Order of the Eye." I hadn't meant to blurt that out, but at that moment it seemed pointless to keep it a secret any longer.

Morgan stared at me. "How did you know about that?"

"Jas asked me if Ash belonged to them. When I visited himher in hisher quarters." I hesitated, realizing that I'd said more than I should. "They knew about him already. How, I don't . . ."

"So why didn't you . . . ?" Morgan stopped himself and shook his head. "Never mind. Doesn't matter anyway." He picked up the *gnosh* from where Ali had left it on the table, turned it over in his hands. "Two thousand tchotchkes," he said quietly. "Well, maybe it's not a total loss. If I sell them wholesale at two hundred colonials per unit, perhaps I can recoup the overhead costs."

"We'll get paid, won't we?" Emily asked.

"Rest assured, I'll abide by the terms of my contract. No commission, though, I'm afraid." Then he looked at Ash. "As for you . . ."

"What?" Ash tipped back his head and held the squeezebulb above his mouth. He crushed it within his fist until the last drop of bearshine was gone, then tossed the empty bulb aside. "You're going to fire me? You know better."

I wondered what he meant by that, but before I could say anything, Ted let out his breath. "Well, there it is. We'll load up the . . . paperweights, or whatever . . . and go home. Maybe next time we'll get a better deal, but for now . . ." He shrugged. "At least it's a start."

The start of what, he didn't say. No one else was willing to speculate, either. All I knew was that not even feeling up a *gnosh* could have made anyone feel better just then.

V

I went upstairs and lay down, intending to take a nap. But I had just dozed off when Ted knocked on my door. Fah had appeared again, this time to inform him that the shipment of *gnoshes* was packed and ready to be put aboard the *Pride*. Since the captain wanted to return home as soon as politely possible—we still had the reception to attend that evening, but he'd scheduled our departure from *Talus qua'spah* for 0900 in the morning—he needed Rain and me to load the cargo that afternoon.

No problem, so far as I was concerned. Rain didn't voice any objections either, so we headed back to the saucer. As we were leaving the guest quarters, though, Ali asked if he could join us; he was bored, and wanted to watch the load-in from the ship. Couldn't blame him very much. Ash had passed out on the downstairs couch, and from behind the closed door of Morgan's bedroom I could hear him discussing something with Ted and Emily—the details of the deal he'd made with the *hjadd*, I assumed. So there was nothing for our pilot to do. At least Rain and I were keeping busy.

Once we returned to the *Pride* and suited up again, we found Duh and hisher minions waiting for us in the hangar. The sled was loaded with square metal crates, each four feet wide on a side. I opened one before we put it aboard and found that it contained fifty *gnoshes*, each individually sealed in plastic, stacked and separated from one another by removable dividers. Either the *hjadd* had packed the crates in a hurry, or else they'd decided what they wanted to give us in exchange for our cannabis long before we got there. I wondered if Morgan was aware of this.

So Rain and I spent the next four and a half hours loading the crates aboard the *Pride*; there were forty in all, and once again we alternated between Cargo One and Cargo Two, making sure that the mass was evenly distributed on either side of the ship. The *hjadd* 'bots did much of the work for us, carrying the crates from the sled to the cargo hatches, where either Rain or I would take possession of them and push them over to the inside decks to be lashed down. Once this was done, she and I carefully counted the crates, using light pens and datapads to maintain inventory control. Unless the *hjadd* had decided to put rocks inside some of those boxes, we had exactly two thousand *gnoshes* to take home. I hoped Morgan was as shrewd of a business-man as he claimed he was, or otherwise he'd be stuck with a whole lot of paperweights.

Rain and I cycled through the airlock for what we hoped was the last time, but when we left the ready room, we discovered Doc Schachner waiting for us at the airlock. Apparently Ali had decided that he'd had enough of extraterrestrial hospitality; with Ted's permis-sion, he'd elected to remain aboard the *Pride* for the remainder of the trip, taking over for Doc as watchman. Which was fine with our chief engineer; he wanted to see *Talus qua'spah* for himself. So we escorted him down the tunnel to the decontamination facility and waited for him while he endured the strip-and-jab procedure.

Another tram ride, which by then had become almost dull, and we were back at the library. Ash was still crashed out on the couch, although someone had rolled him over so that he wouldn't snore so much. The door to Ted and Emily's room was shut, so I figured they were spending some quality time together. I was thinking about taking a siesta when Morgan appeared at the gallery railing. Would I please come up for a private meeting? It didn't sound like I had much choice, so I went upstairs to his room.

For a race with limited exposure to human needs, the *hjadd* had furnished our rooms well. A bed, a desk, an armchair, and a private bath complete with toilet, sink, and shower: nothing fancy, but comfortable all the same. Morgan had turned his quarters into a temporary office; a comp was open on his desk, with papers spread out on either side of it. He closed the door behind us, then took a seat on the only chair in the room.

"Did the load-in go well?" he asked.

"Sure. No problem." I shrugged. "Forty crates, fifty items per crate. Two thousand paperweights in all."

He frowned. "I'd just as soon that you not refer to them as paperweights. Once Janus puts them on the market, they'll be sold as alien artifacts . . . mood enhancers, most likely. What our customers do with them is their own business, of course, but 'paperweights' makes them sound trivial."

"Sure. Whatever." So far as I was concerned, he could call them Ol' Doc Morgan's Magic Elixir and pitch them as rheumatism cures. "Anyway, they're aboard, safe and sound."

"Uh-huh. Good." He didn't say anything else for a moment, but instead simply regarded me with what might have been a forlorn expression if it had extended to his eyes. But there was something in his gaze that was cold and ruthless, and I began to realize that whatever he wanted to discuss with me, it wasn't good.

"Jules," he said, after letting me stand there for a little while, "you've disappointed me. When I interceded on your behalf, it was because I thought you'd be a major asset. Indeed, I believed you'd be a good employee. But now . . ."

Morgan sighed, running a hand across the top of his shaved head as he glanced up at the ceiling. "What you've done . . . your conduct the last couple of days . . . has been nothing short of a betrayal of my confidence. At the very least, it was unprofessional. At worst, it undermined everything I was trying to achieve."

"Huh?" I blinked. "What are you . . . ?"

"I asked you to stay away from Mr. Ash, and not approach him without my permission. I explained to you that his . . . well, his talent . . . makes him sensitive, and that your dealings with him should be minimal. But instead, you chose to ignore my request, and . . ."

"So I spoke to him. Big deal."

"No." He scowled at me. "It's worse than that, and you know it. You brought him bearshine from the ship, just when I needed his judgment to be unimpaired. And that . . ."

"Oh, no you don't!" I snapped. "You're not sticking this on me. I saw Ash this morning before he went into that meeting with you and Fah, and he was cold sober."

"No, he wasn't. He was hungover."

"Maybe so . . . but that doesn't mean he was drunk." I shook my head. "Either way, it didn't matter. Ash couldn't read Fah's mind because he didn't know hisher language. All he could get were vague impressions. He told you that himself."

"Yes, he did. But you also kept from me the fact that Jas knows that Ash belongs to the Order of the Eye. This is something you should have reported to me at once."

"Sorry, but I was under the impression that you wanted me to mind my own business."

"When it comes to something like this, your business is my business."

"In that case, Mr. Goldstein, you should pay closer attention to your business." I couldn't help but smile. "Funny thing about all those paperweights"—his left eyelid ticked as I spoke—"for something you bought just a few hours ago, they looked as if they'd already been packed for a while. Either the *hjadd* are really, really efficient, or they'd decided upon the terms long before we got here. If that's the case, nothing Ash could've told you would have made any difference."

An icy stare. "Don't tell me how to negotiate a deal, son. I was making my first million when you were still in diapers."

"Then maybe you shouldn't rely on telepaths." Something occurred to me just then, a thought that had eluded me until that moment. "Ash is a good guy," I went on, "but as a reliable source, he's got a lot to be desired. Did you know, when you got him to read my mind while I was in jail, that he got the facts mixed up? I didn't betray my brother . . . he betrayed me. But that's not what he told you, was it?"

"How did you . . . ?" He stopped. "You talked to Rain, didn't you?"

"She told me a little, yeah . . . but I didn't figure out the rest until just a second ago. I thought your people had somehow managed to access my Academy files, but that wasn't how you found out about my past, was it? Instead, you sent Ash to see me in jail."

He shrugged. "So?"

"So, what does his little mistake tell you about his reliability? Sure, he may be able to dig into people's brains . . . but for him to stay sane, he has to drink. And you should know better than to trust whatever a drunk tells you."

"Yes, well . . . I'll be having some words with Mr. Ash once he wakes up. For now, my primary concern is with you." Morgan paused. "I'm afraid I've had to reconsider the terms of our arrangement, Mr. Truffaut. Once our business here is concluded, I won't be needing you any longer."

"You mean, I'm fired."

"Consider it a termination of contract, effective once we've returned to Coyote. You'll be paid for services rendered, of course . . . but you will no longer be employed by Janus, which means that you will no longer be eligible for its benefits."

It took me a second to realize what he meant by that. The fact that I'd be evicted from my room at the Soldier's Joy was the least of my problems. More important was the fact that Morgan had posted bail for me, with his lawyer seeing to it that my court case had been remanded to a future date. While I was working for him, it was doubtful that the magistrates would ever take serious legal action against me. But once I was no longer a Janus employee, I wouldn't have that protection . . . and the next time I showed up in court, the maggies would have fresh meat to barbecue.

"You son of a bitch," I murmured. "You know what that's going to do to me."

A cold smile stole across Morgan's face. "I have no idea what you're talking about," he replied, then he turned around in his chair to pick up some papers from his desk. "That's all. You may leave now."

My legs felt rubbery as I turned toward the door. "Oh, and one more thing," Morgan added. "Please remember that we've been invited to a reception this evening." He looked up at me again. "And you are expected to attend . . . I think the *hjadd* would consider it rude if any of our party were absent."

I should've said something about his own lack of manners, but this was one of those moments when your brain can't find the right words. "Please don't slam the door on the way out," Morgan said as I left the room.

Screw him. I slammed it anyway.

(THIRTEEN)

Weird food . . .

feeling kind of ethereal . . .

party with the aliens . . .

a momentary lapse of reason.

VI

I went back to my room and lay down again but this time didn't even try to take a nap. All I could do was stare at the ceiling. My mind was a blank, save for an elaborate daydream about somehow luring Morgan into the *Pride*'s airlock and giving him the heave-ho. For a revenge fantasy, it was rather satisfying, but out of the question. The Talus would probably object to us mucking up their space colony with our garbage.

After a long while, I sighed and got out of bed. Nothing I could do now except try to get along as best I could for the rest of the trip. At least I'd met the *hjadd*. It'd give me something to talk about with my fellow prison inmates once I was deported back to Earth.

When I left my room, I saw that everyone had gathered around the table where we'd been having our meals. Everyone except Morgan and Ash, that is; Goldstein's door was still closed, and I noticed that Ash was missing from the couch where he'd passed out a few hours earlier. The others gave me wary looks as I came downstairs; I didn't have to ask to know that they'd already learned that I'd been canned.

Ted confirmed this by offering an apologetic hand. "Heard about what happened," he said quietly. "I'm really sorry. Morgan shouldn't have done that to you."

"Yeah, well . . . guess he needs a scapegoat." I was glad to get whatever sympathy I could just then. "Would it be too much to ask if you could put in a good word for me?"

"I could, but"—a helpless shrug—"it wouldn't make much difference. Once he makes up his mind, he seldom changes it."

Emily walked over to join us. "Anyway, you may not be the only one who's going to be looking for another job." She cautiously glanced up at the gallery, making sure that we weren't being overheard. "When we talked to him a little while ago, he said something about putting our contracts under review. My guess is that, after this run, he's going to replace us with another crew . . . probably from Earth."

I stared at her. "What for? You guys haven't done anything."

"Like you said . . . he's looking for scapegoats." A scowl crept across her face. "So far as he's concerned, this trip has been a complete bust, and Morgan's the kind of person who blames anyone but himself. Besides, he has to tell his investors something, so . . ."

I felt a soft hand on my arm and looked around to find Rain standing beside me. She didn't say anything, nor did she have to; the look in her eyes was sufficient. For a brief instant, I was almost angry with her—despite what Emily said, Rain was the last person Morgan would fire, if only because of reasons of patronage—but it quickly passed. Rain had nothing to do with any of this; the fact that she was sympathetic at all toward me showed just how far our relationship had come in such a short time.

"Thanks," I murmured, and she forced a smile and nodded. At loss for words, I glanced over at the table. "So . . . what's going on here? Coffee break?"

"Something like that." Doc stepped aside to let me look. "Although I don't think anything here would qualify as coffee."

Spread out across the table were an assortment of platters, plates, and bowls, each containing food of some variety or another. One bowl held something that looked like blue seaweed; another was filled with a murky black porridge. Limp green vegetables that resembled overcooked bean sprouts were piled upon a platter; next to it was a plate of small brown cubes a little like rice cakes. In the middle of the table was a bottle filled with some reddish gold liquid that might have been maple syrup.

"Dinner?" I bent over the black porridge, inspected it a little more closely. It smelled vile, and the chunky stuff floating around in it didn't look very appetizing, either.

"Uh-huh." Doc picked up the bottle, experimentally tilted it back and forth. "Fah and a couple of *hjadds* delivered it while you were napping . . . along with a few other things. Heshe said that since we wouldn't be able to eat at the reception along with everyone else, we were being served dinner in advance." Twisting open the cap, he reached for a nearby glass. "Must be the local brew. Might as well try it out . . ."

"Might as well not." Ted hurried over to take the bottle away from him. "We have no idea whether any of this is edible or not. And since we don't have a physician aboard . . ."

"Oh, c'mon." Doc raised a skeptical eyebrow. "You don't seriously think they'd try to poison us, do you?"

"No, but . . ."

"He's right." Rain eyed a plate of something that looked like rancid cabbage. "I wouldn't eat this stuff if you held a gun to my head."

I picked up one of the cakes. It had a granular texture and a nice, spicy odor; I was greatly tempted to have a bite. "I dunno. If we don't at least try some of it, they might take offense . . ."

"Put it down, Jules. That's an order." Ted frowned at me. "This is your fault, you know. If you hadn't told Jas you'd like to sample their cuisine . . ."

"Hey, I was just trying to be polite." I reluctantly put the cake back on the plate. "How was I to know that heshe would take me seriously?"

"Yes, well . . . even so, the last thing we need now is to have someone come down with food poisoning." Emily sighed. "If they ask, we'll just have to tell a little white lie and say that we enjoyed it very much." She paused. "Maybe I'll dump some of it down the toilet, to make it look like we've eaten."

"That might work. As for now"—Ted pointed to the other side of the table—"we've been brought our evening clothes. Those, at least, I know we can wear . . . so long as we're careful."

Stacked upon the table were several off-white bundles; on top of each was what appeared to be a small plastic air mask. Rain picked up one of the bundles; as she unfolded it, we saw that it was a long, white robe, similar to the one Ash wore except without a hood, with intricate patterns stitched across its thick, plush fabric. "What is this, anyway?" she asked, holding it up against her. "We're supposed to put these on?"

"It's called a *sha*," Emily replied. "Ted and I were given ones just like these the first time we were here. Consider it an honor . . . apparently they have some ceremonial significance."

"Okay, but what do you mean by being careful?" So far as I could tell, they were no more menacing than the outfits Rain and I had worn after we'd gone through decontamination.

"They're sensitive to electrodermal charges from the skin . . . see?" To demonstrate, Emily took the *sha* Rain had opened and slipped it on over her clothes. Rolling back a sleeve of her work shirt, she allowed the *sha's* bell sleeve to rest against her forearm. A moment passed, then its whorl-like patterns turned a pale shade of yellow. "That means I'm calm, but if I get angry"—she closed her eyes and concentrated, and the pattern became black—"the *sha* shows that, too."

"Oh, great." Doc shook his head. "That means we have to make sure no one gets pissed off."

"It's not so bad," Emily added. "They're really quite comfortable. I've found that if you have a T-shirt and knickers on underneath, it mitigates the sensitivity a bit. So long as you keep control of your emotions, you'll be fine."

"And what if we decide to come as we are?"

"Can't do that." Ted let out his breath. "Maybe we can get away without eating the food they've offered us, but showing up without these will definitely be considered rude. Sorry, but that's the way it is." He picked up one of the air masks. "Fah told us these contain translators. You activate them by touching this little button." He pointed to a small stud recessed within one side of the mask. "No one uses it unless they have to, though, right? Just let me do the talking."

Doc regarded the mask with suspicion. "They definitely have a low tolerance for cultural differences, don't they?"

"I just don't want any misunderstandings, that's all." Ted glanced at his watch. "We're expected in about an hour or so. Everyone go change, and we'll meet back here."

"And then what?" I asked.

"Then we're off to the party." Ted grinned. "Don't worry. Remember, we're the guests of honor. What could go wrong?"

VII

Taking the *sha* and air mask under my arm, I went back up to my room and put them on. It felt like I was wearing a bathrobe, but once I tied its sash in place and hung the air mask around my neck, the *sha* was pleasantly warm, its patterns taking on a subtle yellow glow. When I experimented a little by recalling my earlier fantasy about pitching Morgan through an airlock, though, they gradually turned black. All right, then: no more nasty thoughts about the boss, or at least until I was back in my own duds.

I was the first person to return to the library. The others were still in their rooms. In hindsight, I realized that perhaps I should have taken a bath. Too late for that, though; I'd just have to wait for everyone else. So I puttered around the room, looking at the lithographs on the walls while trying to ignore the growling in my stomach. Perhaps I could make a sandwich . . .

My gaze fell upon the food the *hjadd* had brought us. Emily had left some sandwiches on the table, but hadn't yet disposed of the alien repast. The porridge still looked obscene, and I've always disliked cabbage and bean sprouts regardless of their color, but the cakes were awfully tempting. I picked one up, peered at it closely. It appeared no more sinister than a chocolate brownie, and it smelled positively delicious.

What the hell. I was hungry, and I was tired of sandwiches. I took a tentative nibble of the cake; it had a satisfying crunch, and tasted like gingerbread spiced with nutmeg, albeit with a strong herbal aftertaste. I swallowed, waited to see what would happen next. When I didn't have an urge to vomit, I glanced up at the gallery to make sure that no one was watching, then ate the rest. And then, simply because I wanted to, I helped myself to another.

I was on my third cake when a door upstairs opened and shut. I stuffed the rest of it in my mouth and chewed as fast as I could. I'd just wiped the incriminating crumbs from the corners of my mouth when Ash came downstairs. He must have slept off the booze because he didn't stumble on the way down. He stopped at the bottom of the steps, regarded me with curious eyes.

"What are you doing?"

"Nothing. Just waiting for everyone to show up." I noticed that he wasn't wearing a *sha*, but instead his own robe. "Didn't you get one of these?" I asked, plucking at the sleeve of my outfit.

"Yeah, but I'm not putting it on." He didn't bother to explain why but instead continued to study me. "You're feeling guilty about something. What is it?"

I stepped away from the table, hoping that he wouldn't subject me to a deep probe. The patterns of my robe had turned red, though; I tried to make the color go away by thinking about something else. "Don't worry about it. How did things go with Morgan?"

"Did he fire me, too, you mean?" Ash shook his head. "He's not going to do that . . . not so long as I belong to the Order. We've got too much on him." A cynical smile that quickly faded. "Sorry I got you into trouble. That wasn't my intention."

"Nah. Don't worry about it." For some reason, I wasn't as angry as I had been. Indeed, I'd come to accept my situation as inevitable. "Would've happened sooner or later, I guess."

"Hmm . . . yes, if you say so." Ash's eyes narrowed. "Are you sure you're all right?"

"Yeah. I'm great." Although I wished he hadn't interrupted me when he did. Those cakes were pretty good; I could have used another one.

He was about to say something else when another door opened and shut. A moment later, Morgan came downstairs, tying the sash of his robe around himself. When he saw Ash and me, his *sha's* patterns turned dark brown; he avoided looking at either of us, though, but instead marched over to the fireplace, where he stood with his back to us. He shouldn't have been so nervous; any animosity I'd felt toward him had disappeared, replaced instead by a vague sense of amusement. Hard to believe that I'd once respected him; in fact, I couldn't help but think that he looked like nothing more than a fat old guy in a hotel bathrobe.

It wasn't long before the rest of our group joined us. As I thought, both Rain and Emily had taken baths. Rain's hair was still a little wet, but that only seemed to add to her sensuality. For the first time, I truly realized what a sexy creature she was and how much I'd love to get beneath that robe of hers. There must have been a certain look in my eyes, for when she turned my way a blush appeared on her face that matched the color of her *sha*. Yeah, she knew what I was thinking . . . and so what? I was a red-blooded, heterosexual male, and proud of it.

Meanwhile, Emily had walked over to the table. She glanced at the platter holding the spice cakes, and I wondered whether she'd notice that two or three were missing. Perhaps she did, because she turned to Ted. Before she could say anything, though, Fah suddenly materialized.

"Are you ready?" heshe asked no one in particular.

Ted glanced at the rest of us, making sure we were all present. "Yes, we are. Where should we go?"

"The tram will transport you to the Great Hall." Fah raised a hand

toward the door, which opened on its own. *"Please board it at your earliest convenience. We are waiting for you."*

We walked down the corridor to the tram station, where we found a car parked at the platform, its canopy already open. As I climbed into a rear seat, I had a sudden urge to invite Rain to sit in my lap. No need for that, of course; there was plenty of room for all of us. So I shut my mouth and kept my horny little hands to myself, and instead pulled the safety bar into place.

I'd been aboard the tram enough times already that the trip should have been familiar, but on this occasion we didn't return to our ship but instead were transported deeper into *Talus qua'spah*. As the car shot through the tubes, taking one sharp turn after another, I found myself staring at the vast habitat as if seeing it for the first time. All those lights, their colors blurring together as if caught in a kaleidoscope, fascinated me as never before; I stared at them in amazement, feeling like a kid riding the best roller coaster in the universe. At one point I laughed out loud, an unself-conscious expression of childish delight that caused Rain to glance back at me in puzzlement.

The car took a long, spiraling turn, then hurtled straight toward an enormous sphere. A couple of thousand feet in diameter, lights gleamed from hundreds of windows along its sides, while dozens of tramways converged upon its equator. I was still gaping at it as the car began to decelerate; it entered a portal and glided to a halt at a station identical to the ones we'd visited before.

"Welcome to Talus caan-saah," a disembodied voice said as we disembarked from the tram. *"The door to your right leads to an airlock."* Right on cue, the sphincter door swirled open, revealing a small anteroom. *"At this point, you will need to put on your breathing apparatus."*

The door irised shut behind us, and we took a moment to fit the air masks over the lower parts of our faces. So far as I could tell, they didn't contain their own air supply, but instead reduced the nitrogen of the ambient atmosphere while boosting the oxygen levels and removing carbon dioxide. They were obviously designed to be idiot-proof, yet even so, I struggled to adjust the elastic straps. For some reason, my fingers felt thick and clumsy, the straps frustratingly complicated; long after everyone else had theirs in place, I was still trying to get mine to fit correctly, until Ted finally stepped over to give me a hand.

"You're in a silly way tonight," he murmured, untwisting the straps from where I'd tangled them behind my head. "What did you do, sneak off with Ash's booze?"

I didn't know how to answer that, so I simply shrugged as I suppressed the crazy giggle that wanted to rise from my throat. Ash stared at me, his expression unfathomable behind his own mask, but I couldn't have cared less what he or Ted or anyone else thought. I was having the time of my life.

Apparently someone was watching to see how we were doing, because as soon as my problem was solved, there was a prolonged hiss as the atmosphere was changed out. Another door opened, this one leading to a long corridor with another door at the opposite end.

The others were calm as they marched toward the corridor, yet for no reason at all, I became anxious. Unbidden, my mind began to concoct all sorts of horrors awaiting us beyond that door. Medieval dungeons, where we'd be stripped naked and tortured upon racks. Operating theaters filled with *hjadd* doctors waiting to dissect us alive. An underground coal mine on Hjarr where we would work as slaves until we dropped dead. Oh, sure, they'd told us that we'd be attending a reception in our honor . . . but what did they *really* have in mind?

My steps faltered, and I hesitated just before we reached the door.

"Y'know, maybe I should go back to the ship," I muttered. "Check on Ali, see how he's doing . . ."

"Jules, what the hell is wrong with you?" Ted's voice was muffled by his mask as he turned to look at me. "I swear, you've been acting weird ever since . . ."

"Sorry. Never mind." I shook my head. "Just feeling kinda ethereal, that's all."

He stared at me for another moment, as if trying to decide whether it might be a good idea to let me return to the ship. Then he sighed and turned toward the door. "Well, we're here. Let's see what . . ."

Then the door spiraled open, and we saw what.

VIII

More specifically:

A vast amphitheater, whose steep walls sloped upward to a domed ceiling supported by delicately curved arches, from which hung slender pennants inscribed in what seemed to be several different languages. Arranged in tiers along the walls were dozens of glassed-in cells resembling the box seats of a sports arena; within each one were small figures, none of which were even remotely human.

The amphitheater floor was nearly the size of a baseball field, with a long aisle leading straight down its center toward a raised dais. On either side of the aisle, separated from us by gilded ropes, was a multitude of extraterrestrials. Some I recognized from the images I'd seen on the screens of the docking saucer's reception area, but most were . . . well, alien. They regarded us with eyes slitted, multifaceted, and cyclopean, raised on stalks or recessed deep within skulls; antennae switched in our direction, and elephantine ears swiveled toward us. Fur and exoskeletons, stalklike legs and wormy tentacles,

202

mandibles and sucker mouths, pincers and claws, pads and pods and hooves . . . the denizens of a score of worlds, turning as one to study the handful of strangers who'd come among them.

The cacophony of voices—chirps, clicks, burbles, grunts, hisses, and howls—that had echoed across the enormous room fell away as we made our entrance, until we found ourselves surrounded by an eerie silence. Ted was leading us; he stopped at the end of the aisle, and it was clear that he didn't have the foggiest notion what to do next. Nor did the rest of us; we looked at each other uncertainly. Should we kneel and bow? Raise our hands to show that we'd come unarmed? Try a little bit of the old soft-shoe? Nothing had prepared us for this moment.

The crowd to our left suddenly parted, allowing two familiar figures to approach us: Jas and Fah, neither one wearing environment suits but instead dressed in ornate robes. They walked down the aisle until they stopped a few feet away; then, as one, they raised their hands in the *hjadd* gesture of welcome.

"Greetings and salutations," Jas said, hisher native tongue translated into Anglo by the device around hisher neck. "Welcome to the *Talus caan-saah* . . . the Great Hall of the Talus."

"Thank you." Ted raised his left hand; the rest of us did the same. "As captain of the Coyote Federation ship *Pride of Cucamonga*, I'm pleased to . . ."

Fah made a sharp, coughlike grunt that couldn't have been anything except a protest, as from all around us came a low resumption of the same voices we'd heard only moments before. Jas's fin rose slightly, and heshe stepped closer. "They cannot understand you unless you use your translator," heshe murmured, then heshe reached to Ted's mask and gently pressed the small button. "Now you may speak."

"Oops, sorry." As he spoke, Ted's amplified voice boomed across the enormous room, followed an instant later by its translation into dozens of extraterrestrial tongues. This time, the audience response was louder, and there was no mistaking their amusement. The first words of a human to the collective races of the Talus: *oops, sorry.*

Ted's face went as red as the patterns of his *sha.* Before he could try again, though, Morgan stepped up beside him. "Thank you, Prime Emissary Mahamatasja Jas Sa-Fhadda of the *hjadd*," he said smoothly, raising his left hand while assaying a perfunctory bow. Once more, the Great Hall fell silent. "As leader of the first trade delegation from the human world of Coyote, Morgan Goldstein humbly accepts the invitation of the Talus, in hopes that this meeting leads to peaceful and profitable relations between its worlds and our own."

Nice speech, albeit a bit presumptuous. Even as its translation echoed through the *caan-saah*, Ted gave Morgan a sharp look. Perhaps Morgan had come to the rescue, but Ted was obviously irritated at having been upstaged. Morgan just smirked; after all, he'd spent more time with the *hjadd* than anyone else, even Ted and Emily, and thus knew the proper protocols.

"We recognize you, Morgan Goldstein of Coyote, along with your companions." Fah's fin had lain down flat against hisher skull; apparently heshe was no longer miffed. "The Talus welcomes your delegation and hopes as well that this first meeting will result in a long and prosperous relationship."

From all around us, dozens of voices rose at once, as the aliens gathered within the amphitheater spoke in unison. I had no idea what they were saying, but I couldn't help but grin. Okay, everything was hunky-dory. We weren't about to be tortured or dissected or enslaved; thanks to my good and dear friend Morgan Goldstein, I was an honored guest of the Talus.

"Yippie-yo ky-yay," I muttered. "Let's party."

Rain was standing next to me. She quickly raised a finger to her mask, silently shushing me. I shrugged. My translator wasn't activated, and I hadn't spoken loud enough to be heard by anyone else. But again, from the corner of my eye, I caught the worrisome look on Ash's face.

Neither Jas nor Fah seemed to notice. "A place of honor has been reserved for you," Jas said, extending a hand toward the center of the room. "If you will be so kind, we will take you there."

"Thank you, Prime Emissary." Ted was not about to let Morgan steal the limelight again. "As captain of the Coyote Federation ship *Pride of Cucamonga*, I accept your hospitality on behalf of my crew."

As we followed Jas and Fah toward the dais, the swarm of voices resumed its former volume. Countless alien faces stared at us from either side of the aisle . . . and just beyond the ropes, something that looked like a cross between Mardi Gras and a Texas hoedown was under way. Now that they had dispensed with the necessary formalities, the members of the Talus were going back to what they'd been doing before we showed up. From various locations within the crowd, fumaroles of fragrant incense rose in the air, while shimmering white balls floated overhead, serving no purpose that I could perceive except to be pretty. A quartet of hairy arachnids pounded upon an array of drums, supplying the music to which several bipedal giraffes performed an intricate dance. A pair of blue-skinned, four-armed beings, as skinny as ballerinas but with heads like giant bananas, juggled luminescent gold batons, tossing them back and forth to each other to form complex airborne patterns. A hideous caterwaul, and I glanced around to see an enormous creature that looked like a yeti pounding its fists against its barrel chest; several white balls shot toward it, and the yeti abruptly calmed down.

"Oh, man," Doc said quietly. "Haven't seen anything like this since my nephew's bar mitzvah."

That made me laugh so hard, I doubled over, clutching at my stomach. Everyone stared at me, and even Jas turned hisher head upon hisher long neck. Rain grabbed my shoulders, pulled me upright. "What's gotten into you?" she whispered, her voice low and urgent.

Ted fell back a couple of steps. "Cut it out!" he hissed angrily. "This isn't the time or place!"

"I know, I know . . . sorry." Yet I couldn't wipe the grin off my face. Everything was so ludicrous, so surreal, that it was nearly impossible to take any of it seriously. Fifty-four light-years from home, and what did I find? The biggest party in the galaxy, with everyone wearing the damnedest costumes I'd ever seen. I took a deep breath, shook my head in an effort to clear it. Ted gave me a warning glare, then moved back to the front of the line.

We reached the end of the aisle, where six chairs had been arranged in a semicircle facing the dais, upon which stood a large, throne-like couch proportioned to nonhuman contours. Jas and Fah took up positions on either side of us; they waited patiently while we took our seats, yet I noticed that their eyes kept swiveling toward an elevated runway leading to the throne from a door off to the right. Obviously they were expecting someone.

Yet that wasn't what got my attention. Perched on the left arm-rest of my chair was a *gnosh*, identical to those I'd packed aboard the *Pride* earlier that day. Whether it was supposed to be a party favor or merely a decoration, I didn't know, but nonetheless I was delighted to find it.

I wrapped my hand around its delicately curved shaft, and ecstasy flooded through me. If I'd been in a happy frame of mind before then, once I touched the *gnosh* I was positively delirious. You could have hit me over the head with a ball-peen hammer and I would've only giggled. Pure joy, unbridled and without end, was at the center of my personal universe; so swept up in pleasure as I was, it only barely occurred to me that no one else in our group was touching their own *gnoshes*.

"Jules." Rain was sitting beside me, yet her voice sounded as if it was being transmitted from some planet many parsecs away. "Jules, snap out of it. You're . . ."

The long, loud toll of a gong, and once again everything went quiet as all eyes turned toward the runway. A door opened at the side of the amphitheater, and two dozen *hjadd*, wearing armor that vaguely resembled that of ancient Romans, entered the room. Carrying staffs from which dangled ribbonlike flags, they marched in perfect cadence until, two at a time, they took up positions on either side of the runway. Raising their staffs to shoulder height, they unfurled their flags, then stood at stiff attention.

"All rise for the *chaaz'braan*!" Jas commanded.

At a loss for what else to do, we stood up from our seats, gazed toward the door. The Great Hall had gone silent, yet from two seats to my left, I heard Morgan's quiet voice. "The *chaaz'braan*," he whispered to no one in particular. "Spiritual leader of the Talus. Sort of a holy man, if you could call him that. He's . . ."

He abruptly went quiet as the gong sounded once more, and then the *chaaz'braan* entered the room.

I don't know what I was expecting—the Pope, maybe, or perhaps the Dalai Lama—but that wasn't what I saw. What came through the door was something that looked like a bloated and incredibly ancient bullfrog. Swaddled in heavy robes of crimson and gold whose train dragged behind him, he lurched forward on thick, bipedal legs, his shoulders bowed by the weight of years. Rubbery jowls fell from either side of a broad, thick-lipped mouth, and sparse white hair hung limp from a flat, slightly ridged skull. Two deep-set eyes—one half-closed and slightly askew—gazed straight ahead in what appeared to be an expression of senile boredom.

As the *chaaz'braan* slowly approached the throne, it suddenly occurred to me that this was the funniest thing I'd ever seen. So this was the High Hoodoo of the Talus. If he'd been a bit smaller, I could have stuck him in a terrarium and fed him houseflies. Almost as if to confirm my impression, his mouth lolled open, and a long tongue spilled out for a moment before disappearing again, leaving behind a moist tendril that drooled from his lips.

Feeling an uncontrollable urge to crack up, I quickly raised a hand to my mouth. Yet I was too late to keep from laughing out loud. In the silence of the Great Hall, it sounded like someone busting a gut during a funeral . . . which made it even more ridiculous.

Rain grabbed my arm. "Shut up!" she snapped, no longer trying to be quiet. "You're going to . . . !"

But the damage was done. The *chaaz'braan* had heard me. Stopping just short of his throne, he slowly turned to regard me with a walleyed stare that was both wise and moronic at the same time. And, indeed, everyone else in the Great Hall seemed to be watching me as well. My crewmates, Jas and Fah, the *hjadd* honor guard, the hundreds of extraterrestrials gathered around us . . . all had turned to see what was going on with the impetuous young human who'd brayed in the presence of the holiest of holies.

"Sorry . . . I'm so sorry." I gazed back at the *chaaz'braan*, trying to show the proper respect yet still incapable of hiding my grin. "My apologies, your worship . . . your highness . . . your frogginess, or whatever . . ."

"Jules!"

Ignoring Rain, I stepped forward, approaching the dais with my hands outstretched. "No, really . . . I mean it. I'm just some poor goof from Earth . . . hell, two weeks ago, I was a stowaway . . . and now, here I am, face-to-face with the greatest . . . um, toad, I guess . . . in the entire galaxy."

Ted tried to grab my arm and pull me back, but I was on a roll. Slipping free of his grasp, I continued walking toward the *chaaz'braan*. "So I'm absolutely, completely, totally overwhelmed," I babbled, making my way up a short flight of steps to the dais. "This is a real honor, your . . . um, whatever they call you back in the pond . . . and I just want to say that me and my friends are happy to be here, and thanks for all the paperweights, and . . ."

By then, I'd reached the top of the dais. The *chaaz'braan* was only a few feet away; his one good eye peered at me with what seemed to be amusement, as his mouth stretched open to allow his tongue to loll forward again.

"Well," I finished, "I promise I won't eat your legs."

I was about to wrap my arms around him in what I meant to be a brotherly hug when, all of a sudden, the small airborne balls I'd seen earlier swooped down upon me. They circled me like the electrons of an enormous atom, preventing me from getting any closer to the *chaaz'braan*. Annoyed by their interruption, I raised my hands to swat them away.

One of them touched the back of my left hand, and that was it. I was out like a light.

(FOURTEEN)

The morning after . . .

the frog-god is amused . . .

truth and consequences . . .

an act of atonement.

IX

Exactly how long I was out of commission, I couldn't know. What I did know for certain is that, when I woke up on the sofa in the library, it was with the worst hangover of my life. Which isn't saying much, because I've never been a heavy drinker. If this was what Ash had to deal with every time he went on a bender, though, it was enough to make me vow then and there never to get smashed again.

But . . . I hadn't been drunk. The last thing I recalled was raving at the *chaaz'braan*; then little glowing balls swarmed in upon me. Up until that point, my behavior had been erratic, to say the least, but I could've sworn in good faith that neither grain nor grape had passed my lips. And if not, then why did my brain hurt so much and my eyes feel as if they'd been rubbed with sandpaper?

Rolling over on the sofa, I looked up to find Rain gazing down at me. The expression on her face wasn't pleasant; she'd changed out of her *sha*, but I didn't need its patterns to tell me that her mood was black.

"Umm . . . hey there," I muttered. "What happened?"

"I don't know. You tell me." Despite her anger, her voice was gentle, genuinely concerned. She reached over to a side table, picked up a glass of water. "Here. Drink this."

I managed to sit up enough to take the glass from her without spilling it. Even that, though, was sufficient to make my skull feel as if it was ready to explode. But my mouth tasted like a sandbox, and a drink of water was worth the pain. "Thanks," I gasped once I'd quenched my thirst. "Where . . . I mean, how did I get back here?"

"We carried you. Hold on a sec." Rain was wearing her headset; she tapped its lobe and murmured something I didn't quite catch. "Everyone's in bed," she continued, "but the skipper said he wanted to be awakened as soon as you came to."

"So you've been up with me all night?" She nodded, and I glanced at my watch. A quarter to seven, by the ship's clock. "Thanks. I appreciate it . . . and the lift back, too."

"Yeah, well . . ." Rain pushed my legs aside so that she could take a seat at the other end of the sofa. "You're lucky we were able to get you out of there. The *hjadd* . . . Fah in particular . . . wanted to take you into custody for what you did back there. Fortunately, Morgan interceded on your behalf, and, well . . ."

"Wait a minute." Holding up a hand, I struggled with my memory. Lots of holes there that needed to be filled. "What *did* I do back there?"

She stared at me. "You mean you don't remember?" I started to shake my head; it was too painful to do so, but she got the idea. "God, Jules . . ."

"I'm in trouble, aren't I?"

"No . . . *we're* in trouble," Ted said. "You're just the guy who got us there."

I hadn't heard the door of his room open and shut; when I looked up at the gallery, though, I saw the captain heading for the stairs, with Emily behind him. Like Rain, they were back in their own clothes. Realizing that I was still wearing my *sha*, I suddenly wanted to get out of it; the robe felt filthy, as if I'd done something embarrassing while wearing it. Which apparently was the case.

"Next time I give you an order," Ted went on as he came down the stairs, "you damn well better listen to me." He nodded toward the table where the food the *hjadd* had brought us still lay. "And that includes skipping a free meal."

Ouch. So they figured it out. But still . . . "I don't understand. Are you telling me it's something I ate?"

He and Emily stopped at the bottom of the stairs, looked at each other. "All right," Emily said, walking over to pick up the plate of spice cakes I'd sampled, "we already know you had some of these. What I don't know is how many?"

It took me a second to refresh my memory. "Two, I think . . . no, three."

"Three? You're sure about that? Not four or five?" I forced myself to nod again, and she sighed. "Three. Wow. They must be loaded to do that to someone."

"Loaded with what? I don't . . ."

"Marijuana. The same stuff we brought with us." Emily held up one of the cakes. "Jas tells us they're called *saqis*. A delicacy, intended as dessert. They're usually made with a native herb found on their own world, but it's only in recent years that the *hjadd* have learned that cannabis is a fine substitute. Apparently they decided that we'd like to find out how they cook with it."

"But if . . ." I was confused. "Look, if they knew that these things would have that kind of effect on us, then why did they . . . ?"

"That's just it. They didn't know." She dropped the *saqi* back on the plate, brushed her hands clean against her trousers. "Cannabis is no more potent to them than coffee is to us, which is why they enjoy it so much. But with humans, particularly in large concentrations . . ."

"It's not entirely your fault." Ted settled into a nearby armchair. "You didn't know what you were getting into. And I should've realized what was going on when you started behaving oddly even before we walked into the reception."

"It wasn't just those things." With my head beginning to clear, my recollection of the night was starting to come back to me. "I was just feeling a little goofy going into the hall. But when I touched the paperweight . . . the *gnosh*, I mean . . ."

"Oh, crap." He closed his eyes. "That just made it worse, didn't it?"

"Uh-huh. You could say that." The longer I was awake, the more I was able to remember . . . and none of it was good. "Did I really tell the . . . what do they call him, the *chaaz'braan*? . . . that I wanted to eat his legs?"

"Not exactly, but close enough." A wan smile from Rain. "At least you lucked out in one way . . . you didn't switch on your translator. The only ones besides ourselves who understood what you were saying were Jas and Fah. So it could've been worse."

"Oh, good . . ."

"Sorry, but you're not off the hook." Ted shook his head. "None of us are. Among the Talus, the *chaaz'braan* is revered as a spiritual leader. Almost a prophet. You don't approach someone like that without much bowing and scraping . . . and you were ready to dance an Irish jig with him."

"Actually, I think I just wanted to give him a nice, big hug . . . not that it makes much difference." I paused. "Those globes, the ones that swooped down on me . . ."

"They're called *naya'Talus*, or so Jas tells us." Emily yawned. "Automatic sentries, intended to keep everyone in line. Nonlethal, fortunately, or you wouldn't be here. In fact, it's lucky you got out of there at all. The *hjadd* honor guard were ready to tote you off to whatever they call a prison before Morgan stepped in."

"That's what Rain said, yeah." I winced with more than physical pain. "I'm so sorry. I can't . . . I mean, hell, I don't believe I . . ."

"But you did," Morgan said. "And now we're going to pay for it."

Great. Just the person I needed to make the morning complete. None of us had noticed Morgan coming down the stairs, but there he was, wrapping a dressing robe around himself. "Someone make coffee," he growled, less a request than an order. When no one hopped to it, he stared at Rain until she reluctantly rose from the sofa and wandered off to the kitchen. Morgan watched her go, then turned to me. "A fine mess you've put us in. Now I'm going to have to salvage what's left of . . ."

"With all due respect, Mr. Goldstein, it's not entirely Jules's fault." Ted folded his arms together. "If the *hjadd* hadn't brought us a dessert made with cannabis, he wouldn't have been tempted to eat it." He darted a glance in my direction. "Perhaps he should've listened to me, but still . . ."

"Captain Harker, please don't tell me how to run my business." Morgan plainly wasn't in a mood to listen. "What happened last night was inexcusable. Worse than inexcusable . . . it was a disaster. It's only fortunate that I have some pull with these people, or otherwise the lot of us could have been imprisoned on charges of heresy."

"Look . . ." I stopped myself and tried again. "I'm sorry for what I did. I was out of line, and I apologize for that. But since my translator wasn't on, no one except Jas and Fah knew what I was saying. And if that's the case, so far as the Talus is concerned, all I did was make a fool out of myself." I shrugged. "Big deal."

Morgan scowled at me. "Do you seriously believe that's all you did?" he asked, then shook his head in dismay. "Yes, of course you do . . . you're that dumb."

"Now, that's uncalled for . . ." Emily began.

Morgan ignored her. "The *chaaz'braan* isn't just a spiritual leader. Among his own people, he's considered to be a deity incarnate . . . or rather *was*, because he's the sole surviving member."

"He is?" I blinked. "How . . . ?"

"Before the destruction of their homeworld, the *askanta* made sure that the *chaaz'braan* wouldn't perish along with the rest of them." He held up a hand before any of us could ask the obvious question. "It's a long story, and I'm not sure I understand all the details. What little I know, I got yesterday from Fah, as small talk during our negotiations. Suffice it to say, though, that the *chaaz'braan* single-handedly managed to preserve that which the *askanta* valued the most . . . their religion. Since then, *Sa'Tong* has been embraced by most of the Talus, with the *chaaz'braan* himself revered as its prophet."

"Like Jesus, you mean," Emily said. "Or Mohammed."

"More like Buddha, I think, but you get the general idea." Morgan looked at me again. "So when you pulled that stunt last night, the Talus didn't need to understand what you were babbling . . . they were offended all the same."

"Then we'll offer a formal apology," Ted replied. "I think some of us did so last night, but it can't hurt to do so again."

Morgan sighed in exasperation. "Yes, we can do that . . . but I'm not sure how much it will help. One of the main objectives of this mission was to convince the Talus that humankind is mature enough to join them. If they believe we're just a bunch of heathens . . ."

He was interrupted by a bedroom door slamming shut. Everyone looked up to see Ash shuffling across the gallery, heading for the stairs. He seemed to be barely awake, and I assumed that he was hungover again, but before Morgan could continue his harangue, Ash cleared his throat.

"Doesn't matter," he said. "The fix was in from the beginning."

"Pardon?" Emily turned toward him as he walked downstairs. "What do you mean by that?"

"I don't think it was an accident that Jules got stoned." For once, Ash appeared to be clear of eye and lucid of tongue; as he came closer, I noticed that the reek of bearshine that normally surrounded him was absent. "Nor was it a coincidence that *saqis* were delivered here just before the reception. In fact, we were all supposed to eat them."

"Of course we were." Morgan gave him a patronizing smirk. "It's common courtesy of the *hjadd* to feed one's guests before a formal event, so that they won't be hungry later on. You're not telling me anything I don't already know."

"Morgan"—Ash stared straight at him—"shut up."

This came not as an insult, but as a direct command. Morgan started to say something, then abruptly went silent. Almost as if Ash had said something to him that only Morgan could hear. I recalled a comment Ash had made the day before, when he'd said Morgan wouldn't fire him because he belonged to the Order of the Eye: *we've got too much on him.* I didn't know what he'd meant by that . . . apparently Morgan did, because he . . . well, he shut up.

"There . . . that's better." As the rest of us glanced warily at one another, Ash went on. "As I was saying . . . maybe it's *hjadd* custom to send food to guests, but I doubt they were ignorant of the fact that marijuana has a strong effect upon us. Particularly when ingested in large quantities . . . more potent that way. After all, Morgan shipped quite a few pounds to them long before we came here. A sample, so to speak. So they've had plenty of time to study it."

"Well . . . yeah, that's true." Ted rubbed his chin. "But that doesn't necessarily mean they deliberately tried to . . . um, dose us." He paused. "Besides, didn't you tell us that you couldn't read their minds?"

"I can't understand what they're thinking, no . . . but I *can* sense their emotions. So I can tell you that, just as I figured out that Jules was stoned before the rest of you did, I also picked up that Fah was particularly satisfied by his behavior. Jas was appalled, to be sure, but the *chaaz'braan* was more amused than insulted . . ."

"He was?" That came as a surprise to me.

"Oh, yes." Ash favored me with a smile. "He had no idea what you were saying, of course, but it helped that you were wearing a *sha*, and that its patterns showed you to be nothing more than a harmless little chucklehead." He shrugged. "So the *chaaz'braan* just thought you were funny."

"What a relief," I said dryly.

"Nonetheless, Fah was satisfied by your performance . . . and disappointed that the rest of us weren't in the same condition." Ash turned to the others. "Again, do you think it's a coincidence that each of our chairs had a *gnosh* waiting for us? I can't be sure, but I believe that was Fah's idea as well. Sort of stacking the deck . . . trying to make sure that everyone would be good and messed up by the time the *chaaz'braan* made his appearance."

Morgan coughed loudly, and Ash glanced at him. "Yes, Morgan . . . Fah *does* have a reason to want this mission to fail. Unlike Jas, heshe doesn't like humans very much. I can't tell you why, but what I get from himher is a vague sense of distrust and fear. Heshe would rather see us go away and never return . . . and that's probably why heshe tried to set things up so that we'd embarrass ourselves in front of the entire Talus."

"But it didn't work, because no one except Jules had any *saqis*." Emily nodded. "Makes sense . . . but why didn't you warn us about Jules?"

"I thought it was just about Jules doing something stupid, that's all." Ash shook his head. "I didn't really put two and two together until we were in the Great Hall . . . and by then, it was too late to do anything about it."

"Well . . ." Ted scratched the back of his head. "Not a hell of a lot we can do about it now. What's done is done. All we can do is offer apologies, then pack up and go home."

He stood up, stretched his back, then headed for the stairs. Rain was coming down from the gallery, carrying a tray laden with mugs of hot coffee. "Thanks," he said as he took one from her. "I'll call Ali, tell him to prepare the ship for departure. Once we hear from Jas, I think we can be out of here in"—he glanced at his watch—"a couple of hours or so. That okay with the rest of you?"

That was the moment Jas chose to show up.

X

Speak of the *hjadd*, and heshe appears.

By that time, we should have become used to aliens suddenly materializing in our midst. All the same, Mahamatasja Jas Sa-Fhadda's arrival was so abrupt that Rain yelped and nearly dropped her tray. A mug toppled over the side and fell to the floor, spilling hot coffee across the carpet. None of us paid attention. If Jas was there, it could only mean trouble.

"I've come to relay a message from the High Council of the Talus," Jas said, without so much as a salutation. *"It has convened to discuss the events of last night, and has settled upon what it considers to be an appropriate decision."*

By then, Ted had recovered himself. Stepping closer to the holo, he extended his hands. "We've been talking it over ourselves. First, I'd like to offer our most sincere apologies for our conduct." He glanced at me, then went on. "Particularly that of my crewman. His behavior was uncouth, and we realize how much it must have insulted the *chaaz'braan,* along with everyone else who was present at the . . ."

"Be quiet." Jas's fin rose to its full height, a clear sign that heshe was irate. *"Captain Harker, we fully comprehend the nature of this situation. Although there is no question that Mr. Truffaut was rude, the Talus also recognizes the fact that he was not totally responsible for his actions."*

"Then you know about the *saqis?*" Despite Jas's demand that he remain quiet, Ted seemed determined to defend me. "If that's the case, then you should also be aware it has a certain narcotic effect upon our people."

"Yes, we know, just as we have come to learn that Hahatahja Fah Tas-Saatja deliberately included saqis *with your meal with the intent to subvert the reception."* Hisher fin slowly lowered itself as Jas's right eye twitched in my direction. *"Fah has been opposed to the* hjadd *negotiating a trade agreement with your race, in the belief that the Talus should not formally recognize a species that has only so recently achieved interstellar travel."*

"Yeah, well, gee," Emily murmured. "Two hundred and eighty years is such a short time."

Ted gave his wife a stern look, but Jas appeared not to have noticed her sarcasm. *"As a result, Hahatahja Fah Tas-Saatja has been re-*

moved as trade delegate to your people. Heshe will have no further contact with you, and heshe will also be punished in accordance with hjadd *law. We offer our own apologies for this unfortunate occurrence."*

Morgan coughed again. He seemed to want to say something. From the corner of my eye, I saw Ash nod once in his direction. Apparently that was enough to release Morgan from whatever psychic voodoo spell Ash had put on him, because he stepped forward. "Thank you, Prime Emissary. I hope this incident won't affect any trade agreements our races may . . ."

"Be quiet." Jas's left eye rotated toward him, and Morgan reluctantly shut up again. *"Nonetheless, a grave insult has been made, not only to the dignity of the* chaaz'braan, *but also to the Talus as a whole. Regardless of the causes, there are many within the High Council who have come to believe that humankind is not mature enough to conduct trade or cultural exchanges with other races, and that it may be in our best interests to isolate ourselves from your species."*

Morgan's face went pale. "Prime Emissary, please . . ."

Jas's throat sacs bulged, hisher eyes becoming narrow as they turned once more toward Morgan. *"Do not interrupt me. I have not finished."* Ted glared at Morgan, and he went silent. *"I have spoken on your behalf, explaining to the High Council that your party was insufficiently indoctrinated to the customs of the Talus, including proper social protocols within the Great Hall. After great deliberation, the High Council has decided to give humankind another chance . . ."*

"Thank you," Ted began. "We appreciate . . ."

". . . provided that you make amends."

Oh, crap, I thought, *here it comes.* I found myself remembering the dire fate that I'd imagined awaited me within the Great Hall. The rack, the cat-o'-nine-tails, the iron maiden . . . the *hjadd* must have some way of dealing with heretics.

"The Talus has a task we wish for you to perform," Jas continued. *"One of great importance that, if successfully completed, will be of great benefit to all the races of the galaxy."* Heshe turned toward Ted. *"Captain Harker, you are already familiar with one aspect of this assignment, from your earlier encounter with my kind. I am sure that you will remember Kasimasta . . . what you'd call the Annihilator."*

Ted's mouth dropped open. He stared at Jas in shock, stunned by what heshe had just said. "Yes, I remember. What about it?"

"We want you to rendezvous with it, with the purpose of undertaking a scientific survey. Your vessel will be provided with the proper coordinates for a hyperspace jaunt that will take you to a system Kasimasta has recently entered, along with an automatic probe that you will deploy within its estimated trajectory. Once this probe is in place . . ."

"I'm sorry, but the answer is no." Ted shook his head. "I'm sorry, Jas, but I can't do that. My ship is a freighter, not an exploration vessel, and my crew hasn't been trained for that sort of mission. The risk is much too great."

Jas peered at him. *"Captain Harker, I believe you do not fully understand your situation. If you refuse to accept this mission, the High Council will have no choice but to sever all contact between the Talus and your race. That includes diplomatic ties with the* hjadd.*"*

"I understand the situation completely . . . and the answer is still no." He hesitated. "If you wish to return to Coyote, you're more than welcome to join us. No doubt you'll want to break the news to your staff, perhaps even close down your embassy. But I'm not about to put my people in harm's way simply for the sake of atonement."

"You can't do that." Morgan's voice quivered with fury; for a moment, I thought he was going to stamp his feet on the floor. "The *Pride* belongs to me. If I tell you . . ."

"Mr. Goldstein, you may be the ship's owner, but I'm still its captain. When I say we're returning to Coyote, that's exactly where we're going to go. You're just going to have find another way to make money." Ted looked at Jas again. "My decision is final. Sorry, but that's just the way it is."

Jas didn't respond for a moment, although hisher throat sacs throbbed and hisher fin stood fully erect. *"As you will, Captain,"* heshe said at last. *"I trust that you still intend to depart* Talus qua'spah *today?"*

"As soon as possible, yes."

"Very well. We have already taken the liberty of refueling your ship and its shuttle."

"Thank you. I . . ."

"I will meet you at your ship in an hour." Without another word, Jas vanished.

"Harker . . ." Morgan began.

"Don't start." Ted held up a hand. "If you want to fire me, I understand perfectly. Perhaps you'll be able to find another captain and crew willing to undertake this mission. But I'm not risking our lives just so that you can corner the market on alien knickknacks."

Morgan was livid. Hands balled into fists, he took a menacing step toward Ted . . . and stopped when he apparently realized that Harker could paste him across the carpet. "You're making the biggest mistake of your life," he muttered instead. "Better hope you've made plans for early retirement."

"If that means I'll get in a little more fishing," Ted replied, "it beats the hell out of working for you."

Morgan started to say something, but seemed to think better of it. Or maybe he just decided that any further argument was pointless. In any case, as a cold silence fell between them, I took the opportunity to ask a burning question: "Pardon me, but would someone mind explaining what Kasimasta is?"

Ted let out his breath. "I'll tell you later . . . but believe me, it's something we don't want to mess with." He looked at the others. "Right, then. Back to your rooms and pack up your gear. I want us out of here within the hour. Less if possible."

I was about to pull myself off the sofa when a door slammed upstairs. Looking up at the gallery, we saw Doc standing at the railing, peering down at us.

" 'Scuse me"—he stifled a yawn with his hand—"did I miss something?"

XI

There wasn't much left for any of us to do except stuff our clothes into our duffel bags, so only a half hour later we were ready to go. One last look around the library to see if we'd forgotten anything, then Ted led us down the corridor to the tram station. The ride back to the saucer was made in silence; no one spoke as our car hurtled through the tubes, but I found myself regretting the way things had gone. I would've liked to see more of this place, perhaps on a return trip. But it appeared that we'd be the last humans ever to lay eyes upon *Talus qua'spah* . . . and soon, the rest of the galaxy would be closed to us as well.

And it was all my fault.

When we arrived at the gangway, we found Jas waiting for us. Once again, the Prime Emissary was wearing hisher environment suit. I'd become so used to seeing himher in the flesh, it was startling to find myself staring at an opaque faceplate. Perhaps it was just as well. Jas said little to any of us, but instead followed us down the tunnel to the *Pride*'s airlock. If heshe was disappointed or angry, it was impossible to tell.

Ali was already on the bridge. He'd been asleep in his cabin when Ted called to tell him that we were making an early departure, so he had gone up to Deck One and initiated the prelaunch countdown. After everyone was aboard, Rain and I sealed the outer hatches, and once they all stowed their belongings in their cabins, the crew and passengers gathered in the command center. Seating herself at her station, Emily opened a comlink and, in Anglo, requested permission to depart; Jas repeated the same message in hisher tongue, and a minute later we felt a slight jar as the *Pride* was released from its cradle.

Perhaps our leave-taking should have been more eventful, but it wasn't. There was only a cold and unwelcome silence from the com, as if the Talus had turned its collective back on our party: good-bye and good riddance. With Ali gently working the maneuvering thrusters, the *Pride of Cucamonga* glided backwards out of the docking bay, and soon the ship was in free space. One last glimpse of *Talus qua'spah*, then Ali performed a 180-degree turn that put us on a heading for the nearby starbridge.

Once we were under way, Jas floated over to the helm. This time, Ali made no attempt to disguise his loathing for the Prime Emissary; he backed as far away from the *hjadd* as he possibly could, and watched with disgust while Jas removed hisher glove and planted hisher left hand against the *hjadd* navigation system. Jas said nothing as heshe slipped hisher key into the slot and entered a code into its keypad; but once heshe was done, heshe turned to Ted.

"I wish to return to my quarters now, Captain," heshe said. "If you want to speak to me, you will find me there."

Ted responded with only a nod; his gaze remained fixed on his instruments. Jas hesitated, and for a moment it seemed as if heshe wanted to say something else. But instead, heshe turned away from the console and, using the ceiling rails, pulled himherself over to the floor hatch. Without another word, Jas disappeared down the manhole.

Several people breathed a quiet sigh of relief once heshe was gone. But when I looked over at Ash, I couldn't help but notice that his face was pale. Perhaps he couldn't tell what Jas was thinking, but nonetheless . . . well, he knew something was wrong, even if he was unable to say exactly what it was.

Hjarr fell away behind us as the *Pride* headed toward the *hjadd* starbridge. Once the ship was on final approach, Ali slaved the helm to the starbridge AI, then lifted his hands from the console and folded them together in his lap. Everyone cinched their seat harnesses a little tighter; Rain didn't take my hand this time, but I could tell that she was nervous. She felt it, too—a certain sense of foreboding, as if something lay ahead of us that was both unidentifiable and unavoidable.

The silver ring lit up, and the *Pride* hurtled toward it. I took a deep breath, shut my eyes, and we plunged into hyperspace.

(FIFTEEN)

Hot Jupiter fudge . . .

four and a half million miles from Hell . . .

double cross . . .

the only acceptable option.

XII

One second, we were in hyperspace. The next, we were in trouble.

I knew something had gone seriously wrong the instant the *Pride* emerged from the wormhole, because every major alarm aboard ship seemed to go off at once. Startled, I opened my eyes, only to be blinded by white-hot light that blasted through the windows.

I screamed an obscenity and clapped a hand over my face, but not before a negative afterimage was burned into my retinas. Everyone else was shouting as well, and for several seconds bedlam reigned within the command center. No one was able to make out what anyone else was saying, though, until Ted's voice rose above the confusion.

"Close the shutters! Close the goddamn shutters!"

"I can't find the . . . wait, I got 'em!" Emily managed to locate the button that operated the outside blinds. The intense glare that swept through the bridge suddenly diminished, although harsh light still seeped through cracks at the bottom of the shutters.

"Someone kill the alarms!" Ted yelled. "No, wait, I think I . . . !"

Through the brown haze that blurred within my vision, I saw him searching for the master alarm. The various bells, buzzes, and shrieks abruptly went dead, and I suddenly became aware of a frigid blast against the back of my neck. Turning around, I nearly caught a faceful of cold halon gas pouring from a ceiling vent behind me. The fire suppression system had automatically kicked in, even though I couldn't see a fire anywhere. But come to think of it, why was the bridge so damn hot . . . ?

"Cut the extinguishers!" Rain was struggling to unclasp her harness; her eyes were squinted half-shut, though, and she evidently couldn't see any better than I could. Someone managed to find the fire-control button, and the vents clamped shut, but not before everyone seated beneath them had their hair frosted. A moment later, exhaust fans activated, evacuating the remaining gas from the compartment.

"What the hell's going on here?" On the other side of the deck, Morgan's voice rose in outrage. "How . . . Captain Harker, what are you . . . ?"

"Shut up!" Ted kneaded his eyes with his fingertips, trying to clear his vision. "Doc! What's our status?"

"Working on it." Doc was bent over the engineering panel on his side of the console, peering closely at comp readouts. "Ship's okay . . . no hull breaches, all systems still online . . . but I've got outer skin temperature at two hundred four degrees Celsius and climbing." He hastily tapped a command into his keyboard. "Emergency cryonics activated. We can keep the major systems cool, but I don't know how much longer."

"Keep on it." Ted looked over at Ali. "Helm, report . . . where are we?"

"Don't have a fix yet." Either his reflexes had been a little quicker than anyone else's, or else Arabs just have thick eyelids, but apparently Ali had managed to avoid being blinded by the unexpected glare. "Wherever we are," he added, staring at his screens, "we're not where we're supposed to be."

"No kidding? Really?" Ted let out his breath, then looked up at the flatscreens above the console. All had gone dark, save for the ones displaying data from the ship's comps. "Emcee, can you get us an outside view?"

"Starboard bow cam is fried, but . . . wait a sec, I think the aft and middeck starboard cams are copacetic." Emily worked at her console, punching one button after another. "Lemme . . . oh, my god . . ."

An image appeared on the screens, and I felt my heart stop. Filling the screens was an immense sun, bright yellow and burning with all the fires of Hell itself, its surface spotted here and there with the tiny black smudges of solar storms. The cameras had been polarized to the max, but one look at this star and I knew that it wasn't 47 Ursae Majoris.

"Got something on the aft port cams." Emily punched up another image, and now we saw, only a couple of hundred thousand miles away, the bloated sphere of a gas giant. Half of it lay in darkness, with the tiny sparks of electrical storms racing across its night face, while reddish orange cloud bands slowly moved across its daylight side. Whatever the planet was, it obviously wasn't Bear or any other world in the 47 Uma system.

"Hold that picture!" Ali's hands raced across his keyboard. "I can use the background stars to get a fix on our position."

"Skin temp still rising." Doc had remained calm until then, but his voice had gained an edge. "And don't even ask about radiation levels." He glanced up at Ted. "If we don't find some shade real soon . . ."

"Wait a sec . . . okay, I got it!" Ali tapped another command into the comp, and a miniature solar system materialized within the holotank. "HD 217014 . . . 51 Pegasi, approximately seventy-five light-years from Rho Coronae Borealis, eighty-two light-years from where we should be." He nodded toward the gas giant on the screen above him. "That's its closest planet, Bellerophon, approximately point oh-five AUs from its primary . . ."

"Oh, Christ!" Emily exclaimed. "A hot jupe!"

I didn't have to ask what she meant by that. A hot Jupiter is a jovian planet whose orbit has gradually become unstable to the point that it begins to spiral inward toward its star. Because of the way they perturb the motions of their primaries, hot jupes were among the very first extrasolar planets discovered by astronomers, way back in the twentieth century. Although they are freakish in nature, the galaxy is full of them.

"How the hell did we . . . ?" Ali looked over at Ted, his face writhing in fury. "Jas. I told you we couldn't trust that turtle-faced . . ."

"Must be a mistake." Ted wiped a hand across his forehead, dislodging tiny beads of perspiration. The command center was getting warmer by the second; everyone's clothes were becoming damp with sweat. "Never mind that now. Where's the starbridge . . . the one we came through, I mean?"

"Should be . . ." Ali tapped at his console, and a tiny ring appeared within the holotank, positioned in orbit around Bellerophon. "There. About three hundred kilometers behind us." He shook his head. "Why the devil would anyone put a starbridge here . . . ?"

"I don't know, but that's not my concern just now. We need some breathing room while we figure out what's going on." Ted pointed to the jovian. "Think you can adjust course to put us in orbit around the night side, but still stay close enough to the starbridge that we don't lose it?"

"It'll be tricky, but . . . yeah, I can do it." Ali's brow furrowed as he began to plot a new trajectory. "That's providing, of course, that we can go back the way we came."

Ted didn't respond. He glanced across the console at Doc. The chief didn't say anything either, but the look on his face spoke volumes. The *Pride of Cucamonga* was a good ship, but it was old all the same, and it had never been designed to fly this close to a star. If something wasn't done soon, its instruments would begin to melt down; before then, everyone aboard would be broiled alive.

"Emily . . ." Ted began.

"I'm paging Jas." Already one step ahead of her husband, Emily clasped a hand against her headset as she murmured something into her mike. A pause, then she looked up at Ted. "I've got himher."

"Put Jas on open channel." Ted touched his headset lobe. "Prime Emissary, this is Captain Harker. We have a problem here . . ."

"Yes, Captain, I am aware of the situation." Like everyone else in the command center, I heard Jas through my headset. Hisher voice was ethereally calm, as if nothing unusual had happened. *"I have been expecting you to call me."*

Ted's eyebrows rose. "If you're aware of this, then you must also know that the ship is not where it should be. I assume that a navigation error has occurred . . ."

"No, Captain, there has not been an error. Your ship has emerged from hyperspace precisely where I programmed my key to take it . . . the star system you refer to as 51 Pegasi."

For a second, no one spoke. We all stared at each other in complete and total shock, unable to believe what we'd just heard.

Morgan was the first to react. "Damn you, Jas!" he yelled, the knuckles of his hands turning white as he gripped the armrests of his chair. "What the bloody hell . . . ?"

"I told you! I told you he couldn't be trusted!" Ali reached for the *hjadd* navigation system. "That's it! I'm overriding this damn thing, right now!"

"Stop!" Stretching against his harness, Doc swatted Ali's hands away from the helm. "Don't touch it, or we'll never get out here!"

"Stand down!" Ted wrapped a hand around his mike. "Everyone, just cool it!"

An absurd order, considering that we'd just been thrown into an oven, but no one laughed. Ted waited until he was sure no one else was about to do anything rash, then released his mike. "Jas, what are you doing?"

"I am in my quarters, praying for my soul and those of you and your crew." As before, the Prime Emissary was strangely at ease, as if resigned to our fate. *"With fortune, our demise will be quick and relatively painless."*

I swore under my breath. Rain's hand closed around my own; glancing at her, I saw only terror in her eyes. We were about to die, no question about it.

"However," Jas continued, *"there is one way this can be averted. Captain Harker, will you please meet with me in my quarters? I have to discuss our new mission with you."*

"Our new mission ..." Ted took a deep breath, slowly let it out. "The Annihilator. You're committing us to that, aren't you?"

"The choice remains your own. Please come down here to meet with me." A pause. *"Please bring Mr. Truffaut with you. This concerns him as well. No one else may come."*

My heart stopped when I heard my name. Around the bridge, everyone looked in my direction. Ted glanced at me, and I forced myself to nod.

"We'll be there soon." Ted ran a finger across his throat, signaling Emily to break the comlink. "All right, then ..." He unbuckled his harness, pushed himself out of his seat. "Ali, get us in that new orbit. Doc, Emcee, do whatever you can about holding the ship together. Jules, you're with me."

My hands were clammy with sweat as I fumbled with my harness. Suddenly, the last thing I wanted to do was pay another visit to Jas's cabin. No choice in the matter, though. One last look at Rain, then I followed the captain to the access shaft.

XIII

When Ted and I cycled through the airlock into Jas's quarters, we found the Prime Emissary waiting for us, hisher feet anchored to the floor. Although Jas still wore hisher environment suit, heshe had removed hisher helmet. It was obvious that Jas was just as agitated as we were; hisher fin stood upright, and hisher eyes twitched back and forth, nervously assessing us.

And that wasn't all. As we floated into the compartment, Jas raised hisher left arm and pointed it straight at us. Wrapped around hisher wrist was something that looked like an oversized bracelet, except that it had four narrow barrels that looked uncomfortably like those of a pistol. Obviously a *hjadd* weapon of some sort.

"Halt," Jas demanded. "Come no closer, or I will shoot you."

Ted settled the soles of his stickshoes against the floor. "This isn't a good way to open a dialogue, you know." His voice was muffled by his air mask, but I could hear the anger in it all the same. "Especially among friends."

"After what I have done, I doubt that you still consider me to be your friend." As before, the voice that emerged from Jas's translator was different from the croaks and hisses that came from hisher mouth. "There is also the fact that there are two of you."

"You asked for me to come along, didn't you?" Placing my own shoes against the floor, I raised my hands to show that I was unarmed. "See? Nothing up my sleeves."

Apparently Jas didn't get this colloquialism, because hisher head cocked sideways, giving himher the appearance of a curious tortoise that, under any other circumstances, might have been amusing. "Besides," Ted added, "what's the point of us trying to harm you? Without your help, no one gets out of here alive."

"This is true." Jas's fin lowered to half-mast. "I am pleased that you recognize your predicament, Captain Harker. If I do not reprogram my key to the proper coordinates, your ship will not be able to reenter the starbridge, and we will remain in orbit around this planet until we die."

"I understand this perfectly." Ted paused. "Just out of curiosity . . . why is there a starbridge here? So far as we can tell, this planet is uninhabitable. So's the rest of this system, for that matter."

"My race built it during the period when this world was still in the outer reaches of its solar system. We used it to gain access to one of its outer moons, which was rich with vital materials that we were able to mine, and also to establish an outpost from which our scientists could study the planet's migration. The moon has long since been destroyed, but the starbridge remains intact and operational. It has been seldom used, until now."

"I see . . . and we can't leave unless you insert your key and program it to take us home."

"Correct." Jas's eyes slowly blinked. "Once you agree to my terms and accomplish them, this ship will return to *Talus qua'spah*, where you and I will report on the outcome of our mission. Once that is done, then you will be allowed to go home."

"Sort of a roundabout way, isn't it?" I couldn't help it; at this point, sarcasm was my best response to his generous offer.

233

Hisher right eye flickered in my direction. "Mr. Truffaut, if you had not behaved in such a boorish manner, none of us would be here. Indeed, this is not my choice either. But the High Council has demanded atonement for your actions, and since I am the Prime Emissary to your race, it has fallen to me to carry out their wishes."

Ted and I glanced at each other. If Jas was telling the truth, then this wasn't hisher idea. In fact, heshe was caught in the middle, forced by hisher diplomatic position to do the bidding of hisher masters.

"Right, then," Ted said, "so let's hear it. But first"—he nodded toward Jas's weapon—"why don't you put that away? I give you my word; no one aboard will do you any harm."

Jas hesitated, hisher throat sacs inflating for a moment. Then heshe visibly relaxed, and heshe slowly lowered hisher arm. "Thank you, Captain. I apologize for any offense I may have given."

Ted didn't say anything, but instead folded his arms across his chest and waited for Jas to continue. Still keeping an eye on him, the Prime Emissary reached into a pocket of hisher environment suit and produced something that resembled a datapad.

"This is our objective." Holding it out in hisher right hand, Jas flipped open its cover and touched a stud on its side. "Kasimasta, the Annihilator . . ."

A small shaft of light twinkled into being above the pad's surface, then resolved itself into something that I first thought to be a planetary nebula: a bright yellow nimbus, resembling a dust cloud, surrounded by a reddish orange disc. Yet plasma flares above and below the nucleus told me that it was no infant star but instead something much more menacing.

"Holy crap," I murmured. "That's a black hole."

Jas's right eye swiveled toward me. "You do not know of this thing?" Again, heshe cocked hisher head as heshe looked at Ted. "Captain Harker, you have not told your crew about this?"

"No, Prime Emissary, I have not." Ted slowly let out his breath. "Most of my people are unaware of its existence. It has remained a secret, known to very few individuals within our government."

"A black hole is classified?" I looked at him askance. "What for?"

Ted shrugged. "Who knows? Most likely it's because . . . well, because governments like to keep secrets, that's all. Maybe they thought people would panic if they knew it was out there." He nodded toward the holo. "Believe me, when Emcee and I first learned about this thing, it gave us the creeps."

"Since you do not know, Mr. Truffaut, I will explain." Jas increased the magnification of the holo, and it slowly swelled in size. "Kasimasta is a rogue black hole, possibly created by the collision of two stellar clusters or dwarf galaxies billions of years ago. When the collision occurred, the intermediate-mass black holes at their centers, which were rotating in different directions, repelled each other, causing the smaller of the two to be ejected from the coalescent mass. It spun away at a velocity of four hundred miles per second, and hence began to travel through intergalactic space."

The holo image changed; we saw a miniature Milky Way, as viewed from some imaginary vantage point above galactic north. A red thread began to trace itself across the image, slowly moving toward the center of the galaxy. "At some time in the prehistoric past," Jas continued, "Kasimasta entered our own galaxy. Since then, it has traveled on a spiral course toward the galactic core, one that has taken it through the outer rim and the Perseus Arm until, several million years ago, it entered the Orion Arm."

"Damn," I whispered. "That puts it right in our neighborhood."

Ted said nothing, but only nodded as he listened to Jas. "During this time, Kasimasta has encountered several star systems. As it has done so, it has destroyed dozens of worlds. Most were uninhabited, but a few were the homes of intelligent races. The *taaraq*, whose ark Captain Harker's expedition encountered, was one. The *askanta*, of whom the *chaaz'braan* was the spiritual leader, was another. The majority, though, did not survive the encounter."

"Hold on." I raised a hand. "Look, I'm no scientist, but I know a few things about black holes, and one of them is that their singularities are actually quite small. Even if this"—I stumbled over the *hjadd* word, and settled instead for the Anglo translation—"Annihilator is moving from system to system, wouldn't it have to make direct contact with a planet in order to destroy it?"

Jas's head rose upon hisher long neck. "Under normal circumstances, this might be true. However, since Kasimasta is a rotating black hole that doesn't remain in one place, every planet, moon, and even asteroid it has consumed during its long history has contributed to its mass, with a proportionate increase of its event horizon. At the present, we estimate Kasimasta to be nearly ten thousand solar masses in size, with an event horizon more than one hundred fifteen thousand miles in circumference and over eighteen thousand miles in radius."

I let out a low whistle. A monster that big could swallow Earth without so much as a burp. Hell, even Uranus or Neptune could fit into its maw. And I didn't have to ask Jas to know that even a near miss could be deadly; the accretion disc spinning around the ergosphere of its outer event horizon could exterminate all life upon a planet, while the intense gravitational pull of the hole itself would cause massive solar flares to erupt from any star it passed. No question about it, Kasimasta was a killer.

"Please don't tell me it's on its way toward Earth," I murmured.

Heavy-lidded eyes regarded me with contempt, as if I'd asked a selfish question. "That is no concern to you," Jas replied. "The Annihilator passed your home system long before your race became civilized." I breathed a little easier, and the Prime Emissary went on. "Nonetheless, it poses a real and present danger to this part of the galaxy. Even as we speak, it is approaching another inhabited system."

Again, the holo image changed. This time we saw a schematic diagram of a star system, with a large gas giant in its outer reaches and a couple of terrestrial-size planets orbiting closer to its sun. "This is the star you know as HD 70642," Jas continued. "It is located one hundred thirty-six-point-six light-years from our present position. Its second planet, Nordash, is home to a starfaring race known as the *nord*."

As heshe spoke, a thin red line appeared within the system's outer edge, slowly moving toward the superjovian. "Kasimasta has recently entered this system," Jas continued. "In four days, its course will bring it very close to the gas giant, Aerik, where it will consume Kha-Zann, a large moon in orbit around it. Although the Annihilator will not encounter Nordash, nonetheless the *nord* are evacuating as many of their people as possible, in expectation that its passage will precipitate a planetary catastrophe."

"Smart thinking." I nodded. "I wouldn't want to . . ."

"Be quiet." Once more, the holo changed, and now we saw a close-up of Aerik's satellite system. "The Talus has decided that this event, as unfortunate as it may be, represents an opportunity for us to gather precise information about Kasimasta. For this purpose, the *hjadd* have designed and built a robotic probe that can be deployed upon a planetary surface. This probe, once activated, will relay scientific data via hyperlink until the moment of its destruction."

"Right . . ." Ted hesitated. "Let me guess. You want this probe deployed on the moon that the Annihilator will consume."

"This is correct."

"And, of course, you've found the perfect candidate for the job of putting it there."

"You have made the correct assumption."

"Uh-huh. And this probe . . . it wouldn't already be aboard, would it?"

Jas's head weaved back and forth. "It was placed within the cargo hold of your shuttle earlier today, while Mr. Youssef was still asleep." When heshe said this, I shook my head. Doc wasn't going to like that one bit. "We did so in the belief that you would undertake this mission voluntarily," Jas went on. "Unfortunately, since you refused to do so . . ."

"You didn't bother to tell us until now." I sighed. "Great. And I get to be the guy who carries it down there."

"Jules . . ." Ted shot me a look, and I clammed up. "You realize, of course, that this makes the job even more hazardous. Why can't we simply drop it to the surface from orbit?"

"Some of its instruments are intended to register and record seismic activity leading up to Kha-Zann's disintegration. Because of this, the probe is designed to be carefully placed on the surface. Otherwise, it is a very simple procedure. All Mr. Truffaut will need to do is unload the probe, carry it a short distance from his craft, and activate it. This should take only a few minutes."

Ted didn't respond. He seemed to think about it for a few seconds, then he looked at me. "Your call," he said quietly. "I can't make you do this, you know."

Of course he could. He was the captain, after all. And even though Morgan had already fired me, I was still a member of his crew. Besides, there were two other people aboard qualified to fly *Loose Lucy*; if I chickened out, either Emily or Ali could handle the assignment. So he was offering me a way out of what could well become a suicide mission.

Yet that was out of the question. I had gotten us into this mess; I had the moral obligation to get us out of it. Ted knew that, as did I . . . and so did Jas, come to think of it, because there was no other reason why heshe would've summoned me to hisher quarters in the first place.

"Sure . . . why not?" I shrugged, feigning a casualness that I didn't feel. "Sounds like fun."

"Very good." Jas switched off the pad; the holo vanished, and heshe turned to retrieve hisher helmet from where heshe had slung it in a bulkhead net. "Let us then return to the command center, so that I may set course for Nordash."

Heshe paused, then stopped to look back at us. "I am very happy that you have agreed to do this, Captain Harker. I did not wish to die in this place."

"Yeah, well . . ." Ted seemed to be at loss for words. "I'm not sure you gave us any options."

"On the contrary, I did." A stuttering hiss that sounded like a snake's laughter. "It is only that none of them were acceptable."

(PART 4)

The Great Beyond

(SIXTEEN)

Firemen in a burning house . . .
who bells the cat? . . .
the trouble with women . . .
words for the blues.

I

We came through the starbridge at HD 70642 to find ourselves in a
traffic jam.

That's the only way to describe what I saw through the portholes.
Emily had raised the shutters just before the *Pride* made the jump
from 51 Pegasi, and it was fortunate that she'd taken that precaution—
otherwise, we might have struck the nearest starship waiting to enter
the ring. As it was, the first thing we heard upon coming out of hyperspace was the shriek of the collision alarm, followed by a string of
Arabic blasphemies from Ali as he hastened to switch off the autopilot
and take control of the helm.

Jas hadn't been kidding when heshe told us that the *nord* were
evacuating their homeworld. All around us, as far as the eye could
see, was a vast swarm of what appeared to be titanic jellyfish, their
umbrella-like membranes several miles in diameter. It wasn't until the
Pride passed the one with which we'd nearly collided that we saw that

its translucent hood was, in fact, a solar sail. Tethered behind it was a streamlined cylinder a little smaller than our own ship, its hull ringed with dozens of portholes.

A high-pitched voice like that of an irate turkey gobbled at us from the speakers, its language indecipherable but the meaning nonetheless obvious: *watch where you're going, jackass!* Jas patched into the comlink and responded in hisher own tongue. Apparently the *nord* captain had his own translator, because after a brief bit of back-and-forth between them, the com went silent.

It's been said that a fireman is someone crazy enough to run into a burning house while everyone else is running out. That's what I felt like just then. As the *Pride* slowly glided between the scores of *nord* vessels waiting their turns to collapse their sails and enter the starbridge, I saw a civilization in full rout. Several hundred thousand miles away, Nordash was a blue-green marble that bore an unsettling similarity to Earth; it was all too easy to imagine multitudes of *nord*—whatever they looked like—clamoring to board the shuttles that would ferry them to starships in orbit above their doomed world. How many of their kind would be left behind, though, and where the survivors intended to go, we did not know. Nonetheless, we were witnessing an interstellar diaspora.

No one said much of anything as the *Pride* carefully picked its way through the evacuation fleet. Save for a few subdued words between Ted and Ali, a dark silence fell over the command center, and it wasn't until our ship had eased past the outermost ships of the *nord* armada that anyone was able to breathe easy again. But we were far from safe. The *nord* were leaving . . . and we'd just arrived. Like firemen in a burning house.

Ted instructed Ali to get a fix on Aerik and start plotting a trajectory, then he unfastened his harness and pushed himself out of his seat. "Right, then," he said quietly, grabbing hold of the ceiling rail. "Everyone who doesn't have business here just now is relieved . . . at least for the time being. Take a nap, get a bite to eat, whatever. We'll call you back when we need you."

Good idea. I got up from my seat, arched my back to get rid of the kinks, then looked over at Rain. She didn't seem to be in a hurry to leave the bridge; there was a pensive look on her face as she gazed out the nearest window. I hesitated, then decided to let her be. All I wanted to do was follow Ted's advice: change out of my sweaty clothes, grab a sandwich, and maybe catch a few winks in my hammock.

As I floated over toward the manhole, Ash rose to join me. Morgan didn't pay any attention to him—indeed, it seemed as if Goldstein was deliberately ignoring him—and Jas remained strapped into hisher couch. Ash didn't say anything as we entered the access shaft, but as soon as we were alone, he took hold of my arm.

"Keep an eye on Youssef," he whispered. Before I could ask why, he beat me to it. "I caught something from him just before we went into hyperspace. The only reason Jas is still alive is because Ali knows we still need himher."

"Yeah, well . . ." I was too tired to deal with it just then. "I figured that already. But Ali's not dumb enough to . . ."

"All I'm saying is, keep an eye on him. Okay?" Ash let go of my arm and pushed past me. "We have enough problems as is."

II

I went down to my cabin and put on some fresh clothes, then floated down the corridor to the wardroom. I was making a peanut butter and jelly sandwich when three bells rang, giving me just enough time to stow everything away and plant my toes within a foot restraint be-fore main engine ignition. I could tell from the way the ship trembled that it was no maneuvering burn; the *Pride* was slowly building up thrust, and it wouldn't be long before its acceleration reached one g. The captain wasn't sparing the horsies. At least we'd be able to move around the ship without having to use handrails.

Just about the time I was finishing lunch, Ted's voice came over my headset, asking me if I'd return to the bridge. So much for my nap. When I got to the command deck, I found that everyone had left except for him, Doc, and Ali. Ted's face was grim as he waved me toward Emily's seat.

"We've set course for Aerik," he began, "and Ali and I have come up with a tentative mission profile. Sorry to bother you, but we thought that you needed to be in on this stage of the planning."

"Sure. No problem." I gazed at the holotank. A model of the local system was suspended above the console, with the orbits of Nor-dash and Aerik depicted as elliptical circles surrounding HD 70642. A curved red line was traced between the two planets. "Is that our course?"

"Uh-huh." Ted entered a command in his keyboard that overlaid a three-dimensional graph upon the holo. "We're pretty lucky, actu-ally. They're presently in conjunction, with both at perihelion on the same side of the sun. So instead of being three AUs apart, their aver-age distance at almost any other time, they're only about one and a half AUs away from each other . . . approximately two and a quarter million kilometers."

I nodded. The Nordash system wasn't nearly as large as Earth's, which was fortunate for us. The *nord* would've disagreed, of course. Just then, they would have preferred that their world was at aphelion on the far side of the sun . . . or, in fact, anywhere Kasimasta wasn't.

"Anyway," Ted continued, "this means we should be able to reach Aerik before Kasimasta does . . . provided, of course, that we don't do any sightseeing along the way. I've given the order to run the main engine at its rated capacity, two hundred and fifty thousand impulses per second. Once we reach cruise velocity, that'll mean we'll be doing about twenty-five hundred kilometers per second."

My heart skipped a beat. Maybe it wasn't light-speed, but it was a sizable fraction nonetheless. "Good grief, skipper . . . do we have enough fuel for that?"

Ted glanced over at Doc. "The *Pride* has sufficient reserves for four and a quarter AUs," he said, "enough to get from Earth to Jupiter and back again. We barely put a dent in that on the way to Hjarr, thanks to the starbridges, and the *hjadd* were kind enough to top off our tank before we left."

"Not to look a gift horse in the mouth, but"—Ted grimaced—"well, we now know that they didn't exactly do this out of the kindness of their hearts. From what Jas told us, the Talus High Council never intended to take no for an answer."

"Of course," Doc continued, "we may need a tow by the time we return to *Talus qua'spah*, and I can tell you right now that Mr. Goldstein is going to have to pay for a major overhaul . . . but, yeah, I think we'll make it."

"At any rate," Ted went on, "this means that our ETA will be approximately thirty hours from now. That should give you enough time to prepare for your part of the mission." He hesitated. "And here's where things become a bit dicey."

He magnified the image within the holotank so that Aerik and its satellites increased in size. "There's Kha-Zann," he said, pointing to a large moon at the periphery of the system. "Approximately the same mass and diameter as Europa, with much the same surface gravity.

Carbon dioxide atmosphere, but not very dense . . . about a hundred and fifty millibars at the equator . . . but enough to give you some measure of protection."

"Protection?" Although I'd had experience with landing on atmospheric planets, I would have preferred to set down on an airless moon. "Against what?"

Ted took a deep breath. "By the time you get there, Kasimasta will only be about eight hundred thousand kilometers away . . ."

"Oh, hell!"

"I told you this was the dicey part." A humorless smile played across his face. "At least the atmosphere will provide you with some radiation protection while you're down there. And Kasimasta will be coming in hot . . . mainly X-rays from its accretion disc. So the less time you spend on the surface, the better. In fact, I'd recommend landing close to the daylight terminator, if at all possible."

"Uh-huh. And how long will I have to . . . ?"

"Let's not get ahead of ourselves. First things first." Ted pointed to the red thread of the *Pride*'s trajectory. "Here's the game plan. Once we're on primary approach to Aerik and the *Pride* has initiated its braking maneuver, you'll take *Lucy* away. Our trajectory will bring us within a hundred and thirty thousand kilometers of Kha-Zann, so you shouldn't have to consume much fuel getting there."

The holo image zoomed in again, this time to display *Loose Lucy*'s departure from the *Pride* and its rendezvous with Kha-Zann. "In the meantime," Ted went on, "the *Pride* will continue toward Aerik and swing around it, initiating a periapsis burn at closest approach to the far side of the planet. That'll put us on a return heading that'll bring us back toward Kha-Zann, where we'll pick you up."

"Why not go into orbit around Kha-Zann itself?"

"We thought of that," Ali said, "but when we ran a simulation, we discovered that it would take too much time to establish orbit around Kha-Zann. Not only that, but once we broke orbit, we'd have to build up enough thrust again to achieve escape velocity, and by then Kasimasta would catch up with us. This way, we use a slingshot maneuver around Aerik to keep from shedding too much velocity. Once we fire the main engine, we blow out of there before Kasimasta reaches Kha-Zann."

"If all goes well, that is," Ted added.

I didn't like the sound of that. "What could go wrong?"

"Well . . ." Doc began, then shook his head. "All this means you're going to have a very tight window. No more than an hour on the surface . . . and believe me, that's stretching it."

I stared at him. "An hour? You've got to be . . ."

"No, he's not." Ted's face was serious. "And neither am I. You land, you drop off the probe, you take off again. If everything works according to plan, you should be able to reach the rendezvous point just in time to dock with the *Pride* as we swing by again. Otherwise . . ."

His voice trailed off. Not that he had to spell it out. If I failed to reach the *Pride*, then the captain would have no choice but to leave me behind. By then, the ship would be racing just ahead of the Annihilator, with no time left to make orbit around Kha-Zann and wait for me to show up.

"Yeah. Got it." I let out my breath. "So I'm the poor mouse who gets to put the bell around the cat's neck."

"Mouse? Cat?" Ali's expression was quizzical. "What are you talking about?"

"Old fable, courtesy of Aesop," I said, and Ali shook his head. Chalk it up to cultural differences. "Never mind. Just do me a favor and download everything into *Lucy*'s comp. I'll run a simulation from the cockpit, make sure that everything . . ."

"Just one more thing." Ted looked at the others, then back at me again. "You're not going to be able to do this alone. Someone's going to have to help you unload the probe and place it on the surface, so you're going to have to take another person with you."

That hadn't occurred to me, but now that he mentioned it, I knew he was right. I'd have to use the cargo elevator to remove the probe from *Lucy's* hold and put it on the ground. I could conceivably do it by myself, but not within the short amount of time I'd have on Kha-Zann. Like it or not, someone else would have to ride down with me.

"Yeah, okay." I glanced at Doc. "You up for this, chief? I know it's a lot to ask, but . . ."

"Sorry. Not me." Doc shook his head. "I've got to stay aboard, try to keep the ship from rattling apart at the seams."

"And don't ask for Emily, either," Ted said. "I know she's qualified, but there's no way I'm putting my wife at risk." He hesitated. "Besides, we already have someone . . . Rain."

A chill ran down my back. "Skipper . . . Ted . . . please don't do this. I can't . . ."

All of a sudden, I found myself unable to finish what I wanted to say—*I can't put her life in jeopardy any more than you can put Emily's*—because that would've meant admitting more than I was willing to these men, or perhaps even to myself.

So I played stubborn instead. "Look, I can take care of this on my own. No reason to get her involved."

Ted frowned. "Are you telling me you're still not able to work with her?"

That looked like an easy way out. "Yeah, that's what I'm saying. Cap, you don't know what a pain in the ass she . . ."

"Well, that's just too bad . . . because she's already volunteered." A sly smile; Ted didn't have to be a telepath to know a lie when he heard it. "And here I thought the two of you were getting along so well."

"Nice try, though," Doc murmured.

My face grew warm, but before I could respond, Ted nodded toward the manhole. "Right, then . . . unless you have any more questions, you've got a lot of work ahead of you. All of us do."

There was nothing left to be discussed, so I headed for the access shaft. I waited until I shut the hatch behind me before, still clinging to the ladder, I threw my fist into the nearest bulkhead.

III

The rest of the day was spent preparing for the mission.

Before that, though, I tracked down Rain and gave her a piece of my mind. Not that it got me anywhere. She was having lunch with Emily when I found her in the wardroom; seeing the look on my face, the first officer quietly excused herself and gave us the room, and once the door was shut I blew up. I don't remember most of what I said—I was just venting, really—but Rain just sat there and took it, silently regarding me with solemn eyes that I couldn't quite bring myself to meet. And when I was done, she polished off the rest of her coffee, stood up from the table, and quietly suggested that we head down to the shuttle and check out the probe.

And that was it. We never had an argument because she refused to argue in the first place. Besides, she'd already received Ted's blessing, so my opinion didn't really count. That's the trouble with women: they're smarter than men, and therefore enjoy an unfair advantage. And the hell of it is that they know it, too.

The *hjadd* probe was located in *Lucy*'s cargo hold, strapped to the deck right where Jas said it would be. Hisher people had smuggled it aboard inside a crate identical to those they'd used to pack the *gnoshes*; even if I'd spotted it before we left *Talus qua'spah*, I probably would have assumed that it was a box that somehow got misplaced.

Before I could open it, though, Rain stopped me. "Perhaps we should ask Jas to do it for us," she said. "No telling what other tricks heshe has up hisher sleeve." So I got on the comlink and asked Ted to relay our request to the Prime Emissary, and a little while later Jas came down from hisher quarters.

I noticed that heshe still wore hisher weapon around the left wrist of hisher environment suit; apparently Jas wasn't quite ready to trust anyone aboard not to take revenge for hisher actions. Remembering what Ash had said to me earlier, I couldn't blame himher. Nonetheless, I didn't say anything about it. Rain saw the weapon, too, but kept her mouth shut. Like I said, a smart girl.

Jas assured us that the crate wasn't booby-trapped, and I opened it just the way I had the others. Tucked inside was a compact sphere, about three and a half feet in diameter, its burnished-silver surface lined with hexagonal panels. Arranged around its equator were rungs suitable for either *hjadd* or human hands; recessed within the topmost panel were three small studs, blue, red, and white. Once the probe was in place, Jas told us, we were to press first the blue button, then the red, and finally the white. That was it—the probe would do the rest.

"Of course," I said, "you can make sure that we get it right by coming along with us. We've got lots of room for passengers."

I was only half-joking when I said this, yet apparently I struck a nerve, for the faceplate of hisher helmet swung sharply toward me. "My suit is not meant to be worn outside an atmospheric environment," Jas replied, as if that explained everything. "The probe is designed for simplicity of operation. My assistance is not necessary."

"How interesting." Rain bent over the probe to study it closely.

"Your people build a device to study a black hole, but you make it so that it can be operated by another race." She looked up at himher. "Guess you're just lucky we happened to come along at the right time."

Jas was silent for a moment. Hisher suit concealed the mannerisms I'd learned to interpret—the attitude of hisher fin, whether or not hisher throat sacs were inflated—but nonetheless I had a sense that hisher reticence stemmed from embarrassment. "My people have others assume risks on our behalf," heshe said at last. "It's our way."

"So that's how we . . ." I began, but before I could finish, Jas turned away from us. Without another word, heshe left the hold, climbing back up the ladder toward the top hatch.

"Coward," I murmured, once heshe was gone.

"Don't blame himher," Rain said quietly. "Morgan told us about the *hjadd*, remember? They're not accustomed to taking chances."

"Yeah, well . . . why is heshe aboard, then?"

"I have a feeling that being here isn't hisher choice either." She swatted my arm. "C'mon. Back to work."

We made sure that the cargo lift was operational, then returned to the flight deck. I downloaded the mission program from the *Pride* and began to put *Lucy* through a complete diagnostics check. Rain stayed for a little while, but there wasn't much she could do, so after a bit she returned to the ship with the intent of outfitting our suits for surface work.

I remained in the shuttle for the next few hours, repeatedly running simulations of our flight plan, tweaking the variables with each iteration so that I'd have practice dealing with whatever problems we might encounter along the way. I was feeling a little more confident about the mission, but I still wasn't satisfied that I'd considered everything that might possibly go wrong. Yet I also I knew that if I didn't get some rest, my reflexes would be sluggish by the time I had to do this for real. So I put *Lucy* to sleep and returned to the *Pride.*

The ship was quiet, save for the background rumble of the main engine, and I figured that everyone had sacked out. On the other hand, I was still wide-awake; as I opened the hatch leading to Deck Two, I realized that, even if I went back to my cabin, I'd probably just stare at the ceiling. I was thinking about going up top to visit whoever was on watch—Doc, probably, or maybe Emily—when a familiar sound came to me: Ash's guitar, its melancholy chords gently reverberating off the corridor walls.

What the hell, I thought. *Might as well see what the ol' geek is up to.* Before I had a chance to knock at his door, Ash's voice came to me from the other side. "C'mon in, Jules. We've been waiting for you."

We? Ash usually kept to himself. When I slid open the door, though, I found that he wasn't alone. Ash was sitting in his hammock, his guitar cradled in his lap, and seated on the floor next him was Rain.

She smiled up at me. "Don't look so shocked. We figured you'd show up sooner or later." She patted the floor next to her. "Here. Sit."

"And while you're at it, have a drink." Ash picked up a jug of bearshine and offered it to me.

"Umm . . . no thanks." I shook my head as I squatted down next to Rain. "Better not."

"Oh, c'mon." Rain took the jug from Ash. "We still have"—a quick glance at her watch—"sixteen hours before we have to leave. Plenty of time to get properly pissed and sober up again."

With that, she pulled out the cork and, using both hands, tilted back the jug. For a woman who once told me that she didn't drink, Rain certainly knew how to swallow. A long gulp that seemed to last forever, then she gasped. "Hot damn, that's good." She wiped her lips with the back of her hand, then held out the jug. "Go ahead. Don't be shy."

The old pilot's rule is twelve hours from bottle to throttle; I had that, with a few hours to spare. So I accepted the jug from her and raised it to my mouth. I'd never had corn liquor before; it went down like molten lava, burning my throat, and I nearly choked on it. But she was right; just then, it tasted pretty damn good.

"There's the man." Ash grinned, then held out his hand. "Here, now. Time to pay the piper." Rain took the jug from me and passed it back to him. A quick, thirsty slug, then he set it on the floor between the three of us. "All right, then . . . piper's been paid. Let's see if he can entertain the rats."

His hands returned to his guitar, but instead of the random progression I'd heard before, this time his fingers produced a slow, boozy ramble, like something that might come from a roadhouse band south of the Mason-Dixon. "Been working on that song," Ash added, glancing up at me from his instrument. "Think I finally might have some words for it . . ."

Then he sang:

Ninety light-years from home,
Lord, you gotta pay your dues.
Ninety light-years from home,
I got nuthin' to lose.
My spaceship's a junker, and I'm out for a cruise,
I gotta bad ol' case of the Galaxy Blues.

All right, so maybe it wasn't Jelly Roll Morton. All the same, it gave me a reason to smile for the first time in days. "I thought you said music doesn't need words," I said, reaching for the bearshine again.

"Changed my mind," Ash muttered, then he went on:

Stars all around me,
And I got nowhere to go.
Stars are all around me,
And light moves too slow.
I got planets in my pocket and black holes in my shoes,
It's another phase of the Galaxy . . .

Wham! Something hit the door so hard that Rain and I both jumped an inch. My first thought was that there had been some catastrophic accident, such as the main fuel tank exploding, yet when it repeated a moment later—*wham! wham!*—I realized that someone was hammering at the door.

Ash was the only one who wasn't perturbed. Although he stopped singing, he continued to strum at his guitar. "Yes, Mr. Goldstein, you may come in," he said, as calm as calm could be.

The door slammed open, and there was Morgan, bleary-eyed and wearing only his robe. "All right, you punks, that's enough!" he snarled. "Some of us are trying to sleep here, and you three are keeping us . . ."

"Mr. Goldstein . . . Morgan . . ." Ash sighed, still not looking up at him. "If you don't shut up and leave, I'm going to tell my friends how you earned your first million dollars." He paused, then added, "How you *really* earned your first million dollars."

Morgan's face went pale as all the bluster and fury of his entrance suddenly dissipated. He started to open his mouth, but then Ash lifted his eyes to gaze at him, and he abruptly seemed to reconsider whatever he was going to say. The two men stared at each other for another moment . . . and then, without so much as another word, Morgan stepped out of the cabin and quietly pulled the door shut.

For a second or two, no one said anything. I finally looked at Ash. "Y'know," I murmured, "I want to be just like you when I grow up."

Rain was similarly impressed. "How did you do that?" she whispered, awestruck.

Ash only shrugged as he went on playing his guitar. "If there's one thing that scares guys like Morgan, it's having people find out the truth about them." A secretive smile. "And believe me, he's got some pretty nasty skeletons in his closet."

I remembered the last time Ash had told Morgan to shut up, back on *Talus qua'spah*. I'd thought then that it was some sort of psychic trick . . . and perhaps it was, to the extent that the Order knew things about Morgan that he'd rather not be made public. But the fact of the matter was, all Ash had to do was verbally remind Morgan that he had the boss by the short hairs.

"Oh, do tell." Rain inched a little closer. "I'd love to know what . . ."

"Sorry. My order prohibits me from talking about things like that." Ash gave her a wink. "Not that Morgan knows this, of course. Now pass me the jug, and I'll tell you about a sweet young girl from Nantucket . . ."

And it pretty much went downhill from there. In deference to anyone besides Goldstein who might be trying to sleep, we tried to keep it down . . . but nonetheless, as the jug made its way around the circle, the songs became ruder, the jokes more coarse, as the three of us laughed and sang our way long into the perpetual night.

The irony wasn't lost on me that, only this morning, I'd sworn that I'd never drink again. Nor did I have any illusions about why we were doing what we were doing. It was all too possible that, come tomorrow, we'd all die a horrible death, consumed by a monster black hole. But there was little we could do about that at the moment except celebrate what might be the last hours of our lives.

Eventually, though, there came the point when the jug was finally empty. By then, Ash's voice was nothing more than a slur, his fingers clumsy upon the strings. I was seeing double and Rain had collapsed against my shoulder; it was plain that none of us would be able to stay awake much longer. Wincing against the dull throb in my head, I stumbled to my feet, pulling Rain with me. Ash was falling asleep in his hammock as we found our way to the door.

Half-carrying Rain, I hobbled down the corridor, heading for my cabin. Rain woke up a little as I opened the door. "Uhh . . . hold it, this's where I get off," she muttered. "Gotta go thataway . . . my room."

"Sure, sure." Yet I was reluctant to let her go. Perhaps I was stinking drunk; nonetheless, I was all too aware that there was a pretty girl draped across my shoulders. "But, y'know, y'know . . . I mean, y'know . . ."

That seemed to wake her up a little more. "Oh, no," she said, gently prying herself away from me. "Don't you start. Not th' . . . this's not th' time or th' . . ."

"Place," I finished, and that gave her the giggles. "Whatever, sure, but . . ." I stopped and gazed at her. "If not now, then when . . . ?"

" 'Nuther time, maybe, but not . . ." She shook her head. This nearly caused her to lose her balance, so she grabbed my arm to steady herself. Somehow, my hands fell to her hips, and for a moment there was a look in her eyes that made it seem as if she was reconsidering my unspoken proposition. But then she pushed herself away from me again.

"Definitely not now," she finished.

Despite all the booze I'd put away, I was still sober enough to re-member the definition of the word *no*. "Yeah, s'okay . . ."

Rain leaned forward and, raising herself on tiptoes, gave me a kiss. Her mouth was soft and warm, and tasted of bearshine. "Get us through this," she whispered, "and maybe we'll see about it."

And then she wheeled away from me. I watched her go, realizing that I'd just been given another reason to live.

(SEVENTEEN)

Eye of the monster . . .

a fine time . . .

nice place to visit, but et cetera . . .

root hog or die.

IV

Fourteen hours later, Rain and I were on our way to Kha-Zann.

By then, I'd sobered up enough to climb into *Lucy*'s cockpit. Knowing that he'd have a drunk aboard his ship, Ted had made sure that the med bay was stocked with plenty of morning-after pills, eye-drops, and antioxidant patches; finally I knew why Ash had been able to recover from his binges so quickly. Two each of the former and one of the latter, along with hot coffee and a cold sponge bath, and I was ready to fly.

Rain met me in the ready room. She didn't mention the inebriated pass I'd made at her the night before, but I couldn't help but notice the way she blushed when I suggested that we save time by suiting up to-gether. She declined with the polite excuse that she wanted to double-check her gear before putting it on. I didn't argue, but instead suited up by myself. I worried that I might have damaged our friendship, but there were more important matters to deal with just then.

Over the course of the last sixteen hours, Aerik had steadily grown larger. Through the starboard portholes, the superjovian appeared as an enormous blue shield, its upper atmosphere striated by thin white cirrus clouds. By the time I'd slugged down my third or fourth cup of coffee, Kha-Zann had become visible as a reddish brown orb in trojan orbit a little less than a million miles from its primary. We couldn't make out Kasimasta just yet, though; it was still on the opposite side of Aerik from the *Pride,* and no one aboard would be able to see it until the ship initiated the maneuvers that would swing it around the planet's far side.

Yet we were all too aware that the Annihilator was coming. I had just put on my headset when Ted informed me that the sensors had picked up a slight disturbance in Aerik's gravity well, coming from an unseen source approximately twelve million miles away. That sounded too far away to worry about, until the skipper reminded me that Kasimasta was traveling at four hundred miles per second. According to Ali's calculations, the black hole would reach Kha-Zann in about eight hours . . . which meant that Rain and I had precious little time to waste.

Fortunately, we didn't have to cycle through the airlock on the way out. Doc was waiting for us at the shuttle airlock; he insisted on giving our suits a quick check-out, but I think he'd really come down from the bridge to wish us good luck. Just before I climbed through the hatch, he produced a rabbit's foot on a keychain, which he claimed had been in his family for three generations. I really didn't want the mangy thing, but Doc was adamant about me taking it along, so I let him clip it to the zipper of my left shoulder pocket. A solemn handshake for me, a kiss on the cheek for Rain, and then the chief pronounced us fit to travel.

Doc had just shut the hatch behind us when we heard the muffled clang of two bells. Ali was about to commence the rollover maneuver that would precede the deceleration burn. So Rain and I hustled into the cockpit; we'd just strapped ourselves into our seats when we felt the abrupt cessation of g-force, signaling that the main engine had been cut off. As I began to power up the shuttle, there was the swerving sensation of the *Pride* doing a one-eighty on its short axis. Emily's voice came over the comlink; a quick run-through of the checklist, and when everything came up green, we went straight into a thirty-second countdown.

Loose Lucy detached from the docking collar, and for a few moments the *Pride* seemed to hang motionless just outside the cockpit windows. Then I fired the RCS to ease us away from the ship, and our respective velocities changed; in a blink of an eye, the big freighter was gone, with little more than a last glimpse of its forward deflector array. From the seat beside me, Rain sighed; a couple of tiny bubbles that might have been tears drifted away from the open faceplate of her helmet, but I didn't say anything about them.

As soon as the *Pride* was gone, I used the pitch and yaw thrusters to turn *Lucy* around; once she was pointed in the right direction, I switched to autopilot and fired up the main engine. A muted rumble that pushed us back in our seats; a few seconds of that, then the engine cut off and we were on the road to Kha-Zann.

Rain and I had decided we'd remain on cabin pressure until just before we were ready to make touchdown, at which point we would close our helmets and void the cabin. That way we'd save a little more time by not having to cycle through the airlock once we were on the ground. We'd also been careful not to have any solid food for breakfast or lunch; our suits' recycling systems would get a good workout, but at least our diapers would remain clean. And we'd stuffed our pockets with stim tabs and caffeine pills; maybe we'd be too wired to sleep once we returned to the *Pride*, but at least we wouldn't doze off.

So she and I had thought of everything. Or at least so we believed. Even so, nothing could have prepared us for our first sight of Kasimasta.

I had just removed my helmet and was bending over to stow it beneath my seat when Rain gasped. Looking up, I noticed that she was staring past me out the windows. I turned my head, and for a moment all I saw was Aerik, which by then had swelled to almost fill the portside windows. Impressive, but . . .

Then I saw what she'd seen and felt my heart go cold. Coming into view from behind the limb of the planet was something that, at first glance, resembled an enormous eye. Red-rimmed, as if irritated by something caught in the cloudy white mass of its pupil, it wept a vast tear that seemed to fall away into space. Altogether, it resembled the baleful glare of an angry god.

So this was Kasimasta: a cyclops among the stars. Although still several million miles away, nonetheless it was awesome, and utterly terrifying. The black hole at its nucleus was invisible to us, surrounded by the ionized gas that made up its ergosphere, but we knew that it was there, just as we also knew that nothing could survive an encounter with the ring of dust and debris that swirled at sublight velocities around its outer event horizon.

As we watched, Kasimasta slowly moved toward the cockpit's center window . . . and stayed there. *Loose Lucy* was taking us straight toward the moon that lay between us and it. I had an impulse to disengage the autopilot, turn the shuttle around, and flee for . . . well, anywhere but there. An insane notion; there was no way *Lucy* could catch up with the *Pride*, just as it would be impossible to outrun the monster before it caught up with us. Like it or not, we were committed.

For a minute or so, neither of us said anything. Then we found ourselves reaching out to take hold of each other's hand. Despite the fact that I hadn't wanted her to come along, I suddenly realized that I was glad Rain was there.

Yeah. I'd picked a fine time to fall in love.

V

For a moon on the verge of destruction, Kha-Zann was strangely beautiful. As *Lucy* closed in upon it, we looked down on a world that somewhat resembled a miniature version of Mars, save for a noticeable lack of polar ice caps. A reddish brown surface, streaked here and there with dark grey veins, whose cratered terrain was split and cracked by labyrinthine networks of crevices, fissures, and canyons. Early morning sunlight reflected off a thin, low-lying haze that quickly dissipated as the day grew longer, with shadows stretching out from crater rims and bumpy hills. Probably an interesting place to explore if one had time to do so.

But we weren't there to take pictures and hunt for souvenirs. In fact, all I really wanted to do just then was drop in, drop off, and drop out. So once we were a couple of hundred miles away, I picked out what looked like a low-risk landing site near the daylight terminator—a broad, flat plain just north of the equator, away from any valleys and relatively clear of large craters—then switched off the autopilot and took control of my craft again.

By then, Rain and I had put on our helmets again; once we were breathing suit air, she vented the cabin. A final cinch of our harnesses to make sure that they were secure, then I turned the shuttle around and initiated the landing sequence. As we'd been told, Kha-Zann didn't have much in the way of an atmosphere; there was some chop as *Lucy* began to make her descent, and an orange corona grew up from around the heat shield. But it quickly faded, and after a few seconds the turbulence ended and we had a smooth ride down.

Even so, my hands were moist within my gloves as I clutched the yoke. Sure, I had plenty of experience landing on the Moon and Mars, but never had I expected to touch down on a world ninety light-years from home. Even putting down on Coyote in a stolen lifeboat wasn't as butt-clenching as this. Maybe it was because I was landing where no one—or at least no human—had ever gone before. Or maybe it was simply because I was all too aware that, if I screwed up, my life wouldn't be the only one placed in jeopardy.

In any case, my attention never left the instrument panel, and I kept a sharp eye on the aft cams and the eight ball all the way down. Rain helped by reciting the altimeter readout, but it wasn't until *Lucy* was six hundred feet above the ground and I was certain that there were no surprises waiting for us at the touchdown point that I lowered the landing gear and throttled up the engine for final descent.

We landed with little more than a hard thump, but I didn't breathe easy until I'd safed the engine and put all systems on standby. Through the windows, the dust we'd kicked up was already beginning to settle, revealing a barren landscape beneath a dark purple sky. We'd landed in the last hour of the afternoon, on the side of Kha-Zann that still faced the sun; to the east, just beyond the short horizon, Aerik was beginning to rise. Kasimasta was nowhere to be seen, yet I knew that the Annihilator would soon make its appearance.

"Okay, no time for sightseeing." I unbuckled my harness. "Let's do this and get out of here."

"*Really? No kidding.*" Rain was already out of her seat. "*I sort of thought we could look for a nice place to build a house.*"

If I'd been listening a little more carefully to what she'd just said,

I might have given her a double take. Perhaps she was only being sarcastic, but it might have been a serious proposition. The only plans I had for us were no more than a couple of hours in the future, though, so my response was nothing more than a distracted grunt as I followed her from the cockpit.

In Earth-normal gravity, the probe probably weighed about two hundred pounds; on Kha-Zann, though, it was only one-fifth of that. The case was bulky, though, so it took both of us to load it aboard the elevator. Once it was securely lashed to the pallet, I opened the cargo hatch. The doors creaked softly as they parted, and a handful of red sand, caught upon an errant breeze, drifted into the hold. I used the elevator controls to rotate the T-bar of the overhead crane into position, then I turned to Rain.

"You know how to operate this, right?" I pointed to the joystick. "Up for up, down for down, and it stops in the middle. Take it easy when you lower me, though, because I don't want to . . ."

"You're not going down there." She shook her head within her helmet. *"I am. You're staying here."*

"No, you're not. This is my job. You're . . ."

"Jules . . ."

"We don't have time for this. One of us needs to stay behind to run the elevator. You're the cargo master, so that's you. End of discussion." I paused. "If I get into any trouble down there, I'll tell you . . . but I should be able to handle this by myself. Just do your job, and with any luck we'll be out of here before the engines cool down. All right?"

Before she had a chance to argue any further, I stepped into the cage. I suppose I should have been impressed by Rain's willingness to accept the risk, but the fact of the matter was that I was stronger than her, and it would take muscles to manhandle the crate from the elevator and haul it a safe distance from the shuttle. She pouted for another moment or so, but surrendered to the inevitable; once I'd grabbed hold of the handrails on either side of the cage, I gave her a nod, and Rain pushed the levers that raised the cage from its resting position and telescoped the T-bar through the hatch.

The breeze was a little stiffer than I'd expected. The cage gently rocked back and forth on its cables, and I held on tight and planted my boots firmly against the pallet. Once the crane was extended to its full length, I told Rain to lower away. The cage shuddered and jerked a bit on the way down, but I didn't worry much about it; the elevator had a load capacity of one and a half tons. It was just the wind giving me a hassle.

It took only a couple of minutes to reach the ground. As soon as the cage touched down, I untied the crate and, taking hold of its handles, picked it up and carried it off the elevator. Even in the lesser gravity, the crate was just heavy enough to make it hard work; if I hadn't been burdened with it, I might have been able to bunny-hop across the desert floor. As it was, though, I found it was just as easy to put the crate down, then pick up one end by its handle and drag it behind me.

"What's it like down there?" Rain asked.

I stopped to look up at her. She was standing in the open hatch, watching me from above. "Like Kansas," I replied, "only without cornfields. Ever been there?"

A short laugh. *"You kidding? I've never even been to Earth."*

I'd forgotten that. "I'll take you sometime. To Earth, I mean . . . believe me, you can skip Kansas." I started to pick up the case again, then paused. "Hey, if you're not doing anything, patch into the long-range com and see if you can reach the *Pride*. They might be back in range by now."

"Wilco." There was a click as she switched from one band to another. I didn't wait for a response, but instead went back to work.

The terrain was rough, its coarse sand strewn with rocks the size of baseballs. Every so often I'd have to veer around boulders or haul the crate through small pits formed by micrometeorite impacts. Through my helmet, I could hear the faint moan of the wind; the atmosphere wasn't dense enough to hold up a kite, but still, I had to use my free hand to clear silt from my faceplate.

It took about fifteen minutes for me to drag the crate about a hundred yards from the shuttle; I figured that was far enough to keep the probe from being damaged by *Lucy*'s exhaust flare once we lifted off again. I checked the chronometer on my heads-up display; we'd been on Kha-Zann for a little more than a half hour, so time was getting short. I opened the crate and tossed away the lid, then reached inside. The probe wasn't hard to remove; a couple of hard tugs at its rungs, and it came straight out of its packing material.

"No word from the Pride *yet,"* Rain said, *"but that's probably because I'm getting a lot of static. How are you doing out there?"*

"Almost done." I grunted as I carried the sphere a few feet from the crate, then gently placed it on the ground. It rolled a couple of inches, forcing me to roll it back so that its top hexagon was positioned right side up. Once I was satisfied that it wasn't going anywhere, I pressed the blue button on the control hex.

The button lit up, but nothing happened. I waited a second, uncertain whether or not the thing was working, then I pushed the red button. This time, the reaction was immediate; the panels surrounding the lower hemisphere sprang open, and small multijointed legs unfolded from within the sphere, their horseshoe-like pads firmly anchoring the probe against the ground.

I pushed the white button, and had to jump back quick to avoid the rest of the panels as they peeled apart to reveal a smaller sphere hidden inside. From the probe's core, a narrow cylinder raised itself upon a stalk, then unfurled to become a dish antenna. The hyperlink transmitter, no doubt. As it swiveled around to point toward the sun, two more cylinders rose into view; judging from the lenses at their ends, I figured they were multispectrum cameras. One of them rotated toward me, and I took another step back. Realizing that it was looking straight at me, I restrained an impulse to wave at whoever might be watching. Or perhaps give them an obscene gesture.

A slender wand shot out from the core, then buried itself in the sand; that must be the seismometer. And meanwhile, valves opened and fluttered, wands were elevated, lights began to flash. Like some weird toy that belonged to an equally weird kid.

"*Jules . . .*"

"Wow." I stared at the probe in amazement. "You should see this thing. It's like some kind of . . ."

"*Jules . . . look up.*"

Something in Rain's voice gave me a chill. Turning around, I raised my eyes toward the sky and immediately forgot about the probe.

While I'd been busy hauling the crate out into the desert and deploying the probe, the sun had begun to set. Aerik had fully risen into view, yet that wasn't what got my attention, but Kasimasta instead.

I couldn't see all of the Annihilator, but what I could was enough to freeze my blood. The edge of its accretion belt was coming up over the horizon, with the nimbus of its ergosphere just behind it. The damn thing was four or five times larger than when we'd first seen it, and no longer looked like an eye but rather the storm front of a hurricane mightier than the wrath of God.

And it was heading straight toward us.

"Hell with this." I forced myself to breathe. "We're outta here." And then I turned and began to hightail it back to *Lucy*.

VI

No longer encumbered by the crate, there was nothing to prevent me from bunny-hopping. The gravity and atmospheric pressure were just low enough for me to make broad jumps that covered five or six feet at a time, just as I learned to do in Academy basic training on the Moon. Yet I hadn't covered half the distance between the probe and the shuttle when I went sprawling face-first across the ground.

Under other circumstances, it might have been funny. Spacer fall down, go boom. And my reflexes were good; I managed to raise my arms and cover my helmet faceplate before it was cracked open by a rock. But nonetheless, I knew at once that this was no mere accident; I hadn't tripped over anything, nor had my last jump been misguided.

The ground had moved beneath my feet.

I was picking myself up when I felt it again, a mild tremor that caused the sand beneath my hands and knees to shift ever so slightly. At that instant, Rain's voice came to me through my headset: *"Jules, get back here! We're getting . . . !"*

"Earthquakes. I know." I struggled erect, continued running toward the shuttle. Fortunately, it had remained stable, its landing gear still firmly resting upon the ground. I knew, though, that if the tremors became much more violent, there was a good chance that the craft would be rocked so hard that one of its legs might snap . . . in which case, we wouldn't be leaving Kha-Zann.

Rain remained at her post until I reached the elevator; I'd barely climbed aboard before she put the crane in reverse and began to haul

270

me back upstairs. The wind had picked up as well; I had to hold on tight as the cage swung back and forth, and I didn't feel safe until it reached the top and she'd retracted the T-bar into the hold. Yet that safety was little more than temporary; we had to get off Kha-Zann PDQ.

While Rain stayed below to shut the hatch and lock everything down, I scrambled up to the cockpit and got *Lucy* ready to fly. I'd just powered up the engine when she joined me on the flight deck. No time for a prelaunch checklist; I did my best to make sure that I hadn't neglected anything, but even as we were strapping ourselves in, another tremor passed through the hull, this one violent enough to scare me into thinking that the ship was about to topple over.

Rain felt it, too. Her eyes were wide on the other side of her faceplate. *"Jules . . ."*

"Hang on, sweetie. We're gone." And then I fired the engine.

Launch was more difficult than landing. By then the wind had picked up sufficient speed that, if I had been attempting to lift off from Mars, the ground controller would've probably called a scrub. But I didn't have the luxury of waiting for optimal weather conditions; no choice, in fact, but to root hog or die. So I kept the engine at full throttle all the way up and gripped the yoke with both hands as *Lucy* clawed her way into the sky, her hull plates creaking ominously with every bump and jolt she took.

In less than a minute, though, it was all over. The sky darkened, purple turning jet-black; the rattle faded away, and everything smoothed out. On the screens, the aft cams captured a brief glimpse of Kha-Zann falling away, our landing site no longer visible. Then the moon disappeared somewhere behind us, and we were back in space.

Rain let out her breath. *"Nice flying, pilot,"* she murmured. *"If I wasn't wearing this thing, I'd give you a kiss."*

"Save it for later." I was still on manual, but since we were through the rough patch, I throttled down the engines and engaged the autopilot. "See if you can raise the *Pride*. We should be able to get her by now."

"*Right.*" She reached over to the com panel, patched us into the long-range relay. "Loose Lucy *to* Pride of Cucamonga, *do you copy?*"

A moment of static, then Emily's voice came over: "*We copy,* Lucy. *What took you so long?*"

I almost laughed out loud. "Sorry 'bout that, *Pride*. Had a bit of a . . ." I stopped myself. "Never mind. Mission accomplished, and we're off the ground. That's all that counts. What's your position?"

A brief pause, then Ted came online. "*We're on course for the rendezvous point, same coordinates as before. ETA in forty-seven minutes. Think you can make it?*"

"Hold on." I finished reloading the program, then checked the comp display. Everything was copacetic; we'd arrive with just enough time and fuel to spare. "Roger that. We're on the beam and on our way for pickup."

"*Very good. We'll see you there.*" Another pause. "*Good work, guys. And, by the way . . . Mr. Goldstein has asked me to extend his compliments.*"

"Oh, how lovely," Rain muttered. "*Be still, my beating heart.*"

"*Repeat, please? I'm afraid we have some interference.*"

"Negatory, *Pride*. Just some static. *Lucy* over and out." I made the kill sign and grinned at Rain once she'd switched it off. "What do you want to bet Morgan gives you the pink slip for that?"

"*Ask me if I . . .*" Her voice trailed off as she gazed toward the starboard side. "*Oh, god . . .*"

I looked past her and was suddenly grateful for having had the foresight to wear diapers. Kasimasta filled the windows, its accretion belt now resembling a whirlpool of colored dyes, its ergosphere as bright as a star. Now that it had entered Aerik's orbit, the Annihilator's gravity well was beginning to affect the planet itself. Aerik's night side was turned toward the rogue, and even from this distance we could see brilliant flashes of lightning within its darkened skies, like the death throes of a swarm of fireflies, while the blue clouds of its daylight side seemed to writhe and roil in agony.

But that wasn't all. Aerik was no longer a perfect sphere; its equator was showing a pronounced bulge, as if it was a massive balloon that was being squeezed at its poles. As I watched, a wispy stream of blue-white haze slowly began to move outward from the planet's upper atmosphere. Kasimasta wasn't just a killer; it was also a vampire, the vast mouth of its singularity drawing blood from its latest victim in the form of hydrogen and helium. Kha-Zann would be little more than an appetizer for such a voracious appetite.

It was hard to be sure, but I guessed that Kasimasta was about a half million miles away. Way too close for comfort. I fought the impulse to throttle up the engine. Our rendezvous window had been calculated with precious little margin for error; if we arrived too early, we would miss the *Pride* just as surely as if we'd been marooned on Kha-Zann. I couldn't afford to take that chance; like it or not, I'd have to place my faith in Ali's calculations.

The next forty minutes were the longest in my life. There was nothing for us to do except wait for *Lucy* to intercept the *Pride*. If I'd brought a deck of cards, I might have broken them out and had a few hands of poker with Rain; as things stood, though, we could only stay on the lookout for our ship.

I was just beginning to regret not having written my last will and testament—not that I had much to bequeath anyone—when the lidar beeped; something was coming within range. A minute later, a tiny cruciform appeared through the starboard windows, its shape outlined by red and green flashes of its formation lights. Rain and I were still whooping it up when Emily's voice came over the radio.

"Pride to Lucy, *do you copy?"*

Rain toggled the com, then nodded to me. "Affirmative, *Pride,*" I said. "Great to see you again." A quick glance at the nav panel. "On course for rendezvous and docking."

"Roger that." Now we heard from Ted. *"Ready to match course and velocity."*

"Copy." I disengaged the autopilot one last time, then put my hands back on the yoke. Next was the tricky part. Although the *Pride* had cut its thrust, its momentum was still such that *Lucy* would have to run hard to catch up with it. I'd have to expend the last of our fuel in order to do so. But if all went well, it wouldn't matter. And if it didn't go so well . . .

I pushed that out of my mind. Keeping my eyes fixed on the instrument panels, I kicked up the engine, coaxing the shuttle closer to the rendezvous point. The next few minutes were as harrowing as any in my life, but the next time I looked up, it seemed as if the *Pride* was hanging motionless directly before us, its docking collar a big, fat bull's-eye that a rookie couldn't have missed.

I was just about to let out a sigh of relief when Doc's voice came over the com. *"Jules, is your cabin still depressurized?"*

"Roger that." I'd been too busy to think about that. "Want us to pressurize?"

"Affirmative. I'll be waiting for you at the airlock. Over."

"Copy. Over." I glanced at Rain. "What do you think that's all about?"

"Guess he wants to save time by not having us cycle through." She reached up to the environmental control panel. *"I'll handle this. Just keep your eyes on the road."*

She needn't have worried. A few final squirts of the thrusters, and a couple of minutes later there was the welcome jolt of the docking flanges connecting. I shut down the engine and major systems, then reached forward to pat the instrument panel.

"Thank you, sweetheart," I whispered. "You're a good girl."

I didn't know it then, but those were my last words to *Lucy*. Doc was waiting for us at the airlock, just as he said he'd be. As soon as we were aboard, he slammed the hatch shut behind us.

"Sorry, Jules," he said, unable to look me in the eye, "but we're going to have to ditch her."

"What?" Rain and I had already removed our helmets; I gaped at him, not believing what I'd just heard. "Why do you . . . ?"

"Skipper's orders. We can't spare the extra mass, so . . ."

I was about to argue with him when Ted's voice came over my headset. *"Jules! Get up here now! We've got an emergency!"*

(EIGHTEEN)

Never piss off a turtle . . .

faster than dirt . . .

doomsday . . .

what's harder than flying a spaceship?

VII

I headed straight for the bridge, leaving Rain behind to help Doc jettison *Lucy*. There wasn't enough time to pay last respects; I'd grieve for the loss of my ride later, if and when we survived. Ted hadn't told me what happened, and he didn't need to: when the captain says jump, everyone makes like a frog.

I was halfway up the access shaft before I realized that I was still using the handrails. If we were in zero g, that meant the ship was still coasting. Now that Rain and I were safely back aboard, though, the main engine should have been fired and the *Pride* would have been at full thrust. I was trying to figure this out when the bridge hatch slammed open and Emily came through, her left arm curled around something that, at first glance, looked like a bundle of clothes upon which someone had spilled ketchup.

"Make a hole!" she yelled. "Coming through!"

I flattened myself against the shaft as much as possible; hard to do, since I was still wearing my EVA gear. When she got closer, I saw that the object in tow was a person: Ali Youssef, unconscious, with a bloodstained shirt wrapped around his chest as a makeshift bandage.

"What the hell . . . ?"

"Jas attacked him." Emily squeezed past me, using her free hand to grasp the rails. "No time to explain. Get up top . . . Ted needs you to take the helm." Before I could get anything more out of her, she continued to haul Ali down to Deck Three, no doubt taking him to the med bay. She glanced back at me, saw that I'd frozen. "Move!"

That snapped me out of it. Hand over hand, I scrambled the rest of the way up the shaft. The hatch was open; I sailed headfirst through the manhole, nearly spraining my wrist as I grabbed a ceiling rail to brake myself. Ted was on the other side of the console, floating next to the helm station. He was bare-chested, and I realized that it was his shirt that Ali was wearing as a chest bandage.

"Come here and take over." He didn't raise his voice, nor did he need to. "Course is already laid in . . . you just need to take the stick."

I was wondering why he hadn't done so himself when I saw the stun gun in his right hand, and that he was using it to cover Mahamatasja Jas Sa-Fhadda. The Prime Emissary was backed against hisher couch; heshe was still wearing hisher weapon around hisher wrist. Behind himher, Morgan Goldstein cowered against the bulkhead; for once he was speechless, apparently terrified by whatever had just happened.

"Skipper, what . . . ?"

"Just do it." Ted grabbed a ceiling rail and pulled himself toward the engineering station, carefully keeping his distance from Jas. "I'll watch Jas. Just . . ."

"I assure you, Captain, I mean you no harm." The voice that emerged from Jas's environment suit was pitched higher than I'd heard before. "I was only defending myself. Mr. Youssef . . ."

"Shut up." Ted didn't take his eyes from himher. "Jules . . ."

"I'm on it." Suspended within the holotank was an image of Kasimasta; one glance told me that the Annihilator was way too close to our own position. Pushing myself off the bulkhead, I sailed straight through the miniature black hole, an irony that might have been poetic if I'd been in the mood for any such thing. Just then, though, my main concern was taking control of the helm and getting us away from the Annihilator.

I grabbed hold of Ali's seat and shoved it back as far as I could. Since I was still wearing my suit, there was no way I could sit down, so instead I anchored myself by shoving the toes of my boots within the foot rail below the console. Bending over it, I quickly studied the comp readouts. They confirmed what Ted had told me; our course was set, and all I needed to do was bring the ship around, point it in the right direction, and fire the main engine.

Silently thanking Ali for having shown me how to operate the helm, I pulled off my gloves, tossed them aside, and rested my right hand on the trackball. A faint tremor passed through the ship as I carefully rotated the ball, firing the maneuvering thrusters until the *Pride* was brought back into proper trim. Once the x, y, and z axes were aligned, I locked in the heading, then flipped back the cover of the ignition key. No time to sound general quarters; I'd just have to hope that everyone below was holding on to something.

"Main engine ignition, on your mark," I said, glancing up at Ted.

"Mark." He didn't take his eyes from Jas.

A deep breath, and then I turned the key. Green lights flashed across console as the hull gently shuddered. I took hold of the thrust control bar and pushed it forward, and the shudder became a smooth, steady vibration. An invisible hand tried to push me over; nothing I could do about that, though, except adjust my stance, hang on to the edge of console, and not let the g-force make me fall down.

For the moment, it seemed as if everything was fine. Then there was a sudden jolt, as if something had hit the ship from behind. An instant later, there was a gentle rattle against the outer hull, almost as if we'd run into sleet. I glanced up at the overhead screen where the view from the aft cam was displayed, and what I saw nearly gave me a heart attack. Kasimasta completely filled the screen, the vast band of its accretion belt rushing toward us. What we'd just felt was its bow shock; the rattle was the sound of sand and dust hitting the ship.

"Ted!" I snapped. "The deflector . . . !"

"Got it." He reached down to adjust the forward deflector, turning it up to full intensity. The rattle subsided as the field expanded to clear a path for us, but it didn't do anything for Kasimasta's gravity well. The *Pride* was shaking like a tree limb caught in the wind; all around us, I could hear deck plates groaning. If only the main engine had been fired sooner . . .

No time to worry about that now. The ship was only a few seconds away from being pulled into the accretion belt. Whatever we were going to do, we needed to do it fast.

I prodded my headset. "Rain, are you and Doc ready to detach *Lucy*?"

"*Roger that. Inner hatch sealed, outer hatch still open, cradle and docking collar disengaged.*"

I looked at Ted again. He nodded, then snapped a pair of switches, and an instant later there was a hard kick from the port side as *Loose Lucy* was jettisoned. Now I understood why Doc had insisted that we repressurize the cabin; the blowout helped knock the shuttle away from the ship.

"Sorry, *Lucy*," I muttered. "You were a good old bird."

Ted glanced at me. He said nothing, but his face was grim. We'd lightened our load by a couple of hundred tons, but even that wouldn't be enough to save us. One way or another, we had to find a way to outrun Kasimasta.

All at once, I figured out how to do it . . . and found myself grinning. Raising my eyes from the controls, I looked across the compartment at Morgan. "Say, Mr. Goldstein . . . how much would you give me to save your life?"

He stared back at me. "What?"

"You heard what I said. How much would you give me to . . . ?"

"Anything!" He couldn't believe that this was a matter open to discussion. "Whatever you want . . . just do it!"

"Thank you." I looked at Ted again. "How about you, skipper? Anything you'd like from Mr. Goldstein in exchange for his life?"

For a second, Ted gaped at me as if I'd just lost my mind. Then he caught on. "Sure," he said, his right hand creeping across the engineering console. "I can think of one or two . . ."

"For God's sake!" Morgan glanced at the nearest window. "Whatever you want, you can have it. Just hurry . . . !"

"Very well, then." Ted rested his fingertips on a pair of switches, then snapped them. "Jettisoning cargo modules."

If Morgan had any objections—and I had no doubt that he did—they were lost in the warning alarm of the emergency pyros being fired. Two hard thumps, and Cargo One and Cargo Two were decoupled from the hub. I glanced up at the screens in time to see two massive cylinders tumble away from the ship, taking with them forty crates of alien knickknacks.

Morgan stared in horror as his payload fell toward Kasimasta. For something that he'd once derided as being all but worthless, he certainly seemed upset at their sacrifice. He didn't seem to notice the abrupt change of velocity as the *Pride*, now having shed nearly one-fourth of its mass, surged forward. Leave it to a businessman to put a higher value on his merchandise than his own life.

I held my breath as I watched my instruments. The delta-V was steadily increasing, just as I thought it would. Another brief tremor as the *Pride* crossed the bow shock once more, and then we were racing away from Kasimasta, accelerating beyond the reach of its accretion belt.

The ship stopped shaking, and I slowly let out my breath. "I think we're going to make it," I murmured, then I looked over at Ted. "Now . . . would someone mind telling me why I'm here?"

Ted wiped sweat from his forehead. "Ali lost his temper and attacked Jas, and Jas shot him. That's pretty much it, in a nutshell."

"For the love of . . ." I'd seen this coming, sure, but nonetheless I couldn't believe it. "Why?"

"Heshe said that we should have left you behind, made a run for it to save ourselves." Ted glared at Jas. "Perhaps that's something the *hjadd* do, Prime Emissary," he added, his voice rising in anger, "but we humans have a slightly higher standard."

"It was only an observation, Captain." Jas settled into hisher couch. "Nothing more. I did not expect your pilot to react so violently."

"Yes, well . . . your own reaction left something to be desired." Ted looked at Morgan. "Mr. Goldstein . . . Morgan . . . if you're through crying over spilled milk, you can make yourself useful and disarm your friend."

Morgan's eyes widened. "I can't . . ."

"Yes, you will . . . or I'll be tempted to lessen our load by a few more kilos." Ted hefted the stunner. "Glad I had this squirreled away. Never thought I'd actually have to use it, though."

I nodded, but said nothing. Although it wasn't standard operating procedure, ship captains often concealed a sidearm somewhere aboard the bridge, in the event of mutiny or that someone might make a hijack attempt. Such occurrences were so rare, most spacers considered them unlikely. This time, though, I was glad my CO had erred on the side of caution.

Morgan hesitated, then turned to Jas. The Prime Emissary had already removed hisher bracelet; heshe pushed something on its side that might have been a safety catch, then surrendered the weapon to Morgan. "My most profound apologies, Captain. It was never my intent to put this ship in danger."

"Right." Ted stood up and walked over to Morgan, who reluctantly gave the bracelet to him. "Now go below to your cabin. I'll summon you once we rendezvous with the starbridge." The Prime Emissary rose from hisher seat, started toward the manhole. "And, Jas . . . next time we jump, no tricks."

Jas said nothing, but hisher head briefly moved back and forth in the *hjadd* affirmative. Then heshe disappeared down the access shaft, with Morgan behind him. Ted watched them go, then sighed as he dropped the bracelet on the seat behind him.

"God, what a nightmare." He shoved the stunner into his belt, then massaged his eyes with his fingertips. "If I ever let an alien aboard this ship again . . ."

"You and me both." Then I chuckled. "Hey . . . trade you a spacesuit for a shirt."

Ted looked at me, and a wry grin slowly appeared on his face. "Go on, get out of here." Going over to the helm, he pulled up the seat and sat down. "I'll stand watch . . . but just do me one favor."

"What's that?"

He rubbed at the goose pimples on his arms. "Fetch me another shirt. I'm freezing."

VIII

I went below to the ready room and got out of my suit, then went up to Deck Three and dropped by the med bay to check on Ali. Emily was still with him; she'd managed to carry our pilot to the autodoc, where she'd placed him on the table and activated the system. When I found her, she was standing outside the surgical cell, gazing through the window as the 'bot's insectile hands stitched the wounds in Ali's chest. He was being kept sedated, with a gas mask over his face and IV lines feeding fluids into his veins.

"He caught four darts," Emily said, motioning to a small kidney tray on the table next to the autodoc. "Lucky they didn't have enough forward velocity to pierce the rib cage, or he'd be dead by now."

I peered at the tray. Within it were four bloodstained flechettes, each no larger than a fingernail yet razor-sharp. Apparently human bones were a little tougher than a *hjadd's*, because a couple of them looked as if they had fractured upon impact. Still, it was enough to make my blood turn cold. "And Jas shot him because . . . ?"

"Ali wigged out when Jas said that you and Rain should've been left behind. Happened right after you docked." Emily sighed, shook her head. "I know, I know. It's stupid, but . . . guess the pressure finally got to him." I nodded, regretting the fact that I'd neglected to mention Ash's warning to anyone. Stupid of me not to have taken him more seriously. "At any rate," she went on, "I'm just glad you made it back in time to take over the helm."

"Yeah, well . . . so am I." I looked around the med bay. "Where's Rain?"

"Don't know. Maybe in her cabin. She looked pretty beat." She glanced at me. "How did it go down there?"

"Piece of cake." I was too tired to talk about it; just then, all I really wanted to do was get a shirt for Ted, then have something to eat and maybe catch a few winks. I looked at Ali again. "How long do you think it'll be until he's up and about?"

"Not soon enough for him to do his job again, if that's what you're asking." Emily smiled, patted my shoulder. "Don't fret about it. Ted and I will take turns at the helm until you've had a chance to recuperate."

I thanked her, then left the med bay and went up to Deck Two. A quick stop by Ted's cabin to grab a shirt from his bag, then I headed for the access shaft again . . . but not before I stopped at Rain's quarters. The cabin door was shut. I lingered outside for a moment, considering whether or not I should knock, before deciding that I owed her a nap. I hadn't seen Ash since we'd returned, but his cabin was quiet as well. I figured that he'd probably passed out again.

Ted was still at the helm when I returned to the bridge. He was grateful for the shirt, but he said that he didn't need to have me take over again. So I went back down to Deck Two, where I went about making myself some lunch in the wardroom. I was about halfway through a tomato and cheese sandwich when the door slammed open and Morgan barged in.

"Who do you think you are, jettisoning those modules without my permission?"

I took my time swallowing what was in my mouth before answering him, "You're welcome."

That brought him up short. "What?"

"Oh, I'm sorry . . . I thought you'd come to thank me." I pushed aside the rest of my sandwich. "I asked what you'd give for me to save your life. You said anything, and I assumed that would include the cargo." I picked up a napkin and wiped my mouth. "Silly me. Didn't know you thought *gnoshes* were more important than your skin."

Morgan scowled at me. "That was completely unnecessary. We could've gotten away without . . ."

"Probably not. Once we shed the extra mass, the ship was able to reach escape velocity . . . but not before then." I wadded up the napkin and pitched it at the disposal chute, and got two points for a perfect shot. "Ask the skipper if you don't believe me. It was his decision, not mine."

Ted couldn't have picked a better moment to call. Morgan was still mustering a retort when my headset chirped. *"Jules, where are you right now?"*

"Wardroom," I replied. "Need me back up there?"

"Negatory. Stay where you are but turn on the monitors. I'm going to patch you into the aft cams . . . there's something you really ought to see."

Standing up from my chair, I reached up to switch on the flatscreens above the table . . . and promptly forgot how to breathe. Displayed on the screens was a departure-angle view. With the cargo modules gone, the ship's stern was clearly visible, yet it wasn't that Ted wanted me to see.

Now that we'd put some distance between ourselves and Kasimasta, it once again resembled a cyclopean eye. Kha-Zann had disappeared, and a chill trickled down my back as I realized that the small world upon which I'd walked only a few hours earlier had been reduced to little more than dust and rubble. And now the Annihilator's angry glare was fixed upon Aerik.

The superjovian was no longer a distinct sphere, but rather a bauble at the end of an immense rope. Captured by the intense attraction of the rogue black hole, the planet was being pulled apart; a vast blue-white stream of gas flowed outward from what had once been its equator, curling across space to become part of Kasimasta's ever-expanding accretion belt. It was impossible to tell with the naked eye, but I didn't need the ship's sensors to know that Aerik's mass had already been reduced by half.

"Oh, my . . ." Morgan stared at the screens as if not quite believing the vast forces on display. "It's . . . it's . . ."

"Yup. Ain't it, though?" I pointed to the accretion belt. "See that? There's where you and I would be right now if we hadn't dumped the modules. Want to go back and look for them?"

Morgan didn't say a word, but the look in his eyes told me that he finally comprehended the fate that we'd barely avoided. "Have a sandwich," I added, then I left the wardroom and headed for my cabin.

IX

I slept like a stone for the next twelve hours or so, stirring only when I felt the shudder of the maneuvering thrusters being fired to correct our course back to Nordash. When I finally woke up, it was to the sound of Ash's guitar coming through the air vent. I listened for a little while, letting my mind replay the events of the previous day, before deciding that I really should report back to the command center. With Ali down for the count, I'd become the *Pride*'s de facto pilot; time to go back topside and take over the helm again.

So I fell out of the sack and put on a fresh change of clothes. Ash was still noodling at his guitar when I left my cabin. I thought about dropping in, but then changed my mind and instead went down the corridor to visit Rain. I hadn't seen or heard from her since we'd gotten back from Kha-Zann; she might want to talk about what we'd been through.

Her door was still shut, and there was no answer when I knocked. At first I thought she wasn't in, but when I tried the door, I found that it was locked from the inside. I knocked again, this time calling her name, but there was no reply. I was beginning to get worried, so I headed back down the corridor, intending to inform Ted that Rain . . . well, I'm not sure what I would've told the captain, other than express vague misgivings about one of my crewmates . . . when Ash abruptly stopped playing his guitar.

"She doesn't want to talk to you," he said from behind the door of his cabin.

I started to say something, but he beat me to it. "Seriously. She doesn't want to see you right now. If I were you, I'd leave her alone."

He already knew I was there, so I didn't bother to knock, but instead slid open his door. Ash was in his hammock, guitar lying across his chest. There were dark circles under his eyes, and I could tell from the absence of booze on his breath that he was sober.

"Been dry since yesterday," he said, in response to my unasked question. "That little party we had the other night pretty much pissed away the last of my supply." Ash idly strummed at his guitar. "That's why I'm staying away from you guys. Too many strong emotions right now . . . especially from you and her."

"What do you mean?"

"Oh, c'mon." He looked at me askance. "Maybe you can hide from each other, or even from yourselves, but you can't hide from me. A lot has changed between the two of you, and . . ." He shook his head. "Go on, get out of here. Please. It hurts too damn much to be around you."

Perhaps I should've left him alone, but his comfort was the least of my concerns. "Sorry, Gordon," I said, closing the door behind me. "Can't do that. Not until you tell me what's going on."

Ash said nothing for a moment, then he let out his breath as a long sigh. "Y'know, it almost would've been easier if you guys had failed." Propping his guitar against the bulkhead, he sat up in his hammock, slinging his legs over the side until his bare feet almost touched the floor. "In fact, I kinda thought that was what would happen. The shuttle would crash, or you'd miss making the rendezvous . . . and that would've been it."

I stared at him, not quite believing I'd heard what he'd just said. "Is that what you wanted?"

"Oh, no, no . . . not at all." He winced, perhaps from the second-hand impact of my emotions. "I'm happy you made it back, really I am. But"—he hesitated—"do you remember what she told you? When you suggested that she spend the night with you, I mean."

My face felt warm. "Ummm . . ."

"Right. And so does she . . . but the truth is, deep down inside, she really didn't think she'd have to make good on that promise." He forced a smile. "And then you had to screw things up and . . ."

"Yeah, okay, I get the picture." Then I shook my head. "No, I don't. I mean, that was something I did when I was drunk. She doesn't have to . . ."

"You know something, Jules? You talk too much. Just shut up and listen." Ash waited until he was sure that I wouldn't interrupt him again, then went on. "If you think you're confused . . . well, so is she, and even more so. If it was just about sex, that would be easy. You guys hop in the sack and bang each other's brains out. Problem solved. But the fact of the matter is that you're in love with her, and she's falling for you, too, and neither of you know what to do about it."

Bending forward, he clutched at his head. "God, I need a drink. Just get out of here, okay? Leave me alone."

There was little else for me to say, so I eased out of his cabin, shutting the door behind me. For a few moments, I stood in the corridor, uncertain of what to do next, until I finally decided to head up to the bridge.

Sure, I knew how to handle a spaceship. But I didn't have a clue how to handle a woman.

(NINETEEN)

The deserted world . . .
return to Talus qua'spah . . .
another point of view . . .
a line in the sand.

X

Half a day later, the *Pride* returned to Nordash. I was back in the pilot's seat again by then, and had initiated the braking maneuver that would slow the ship down and put it on course for rendezvous with the *nord* starbridge. Through the bridge windows, Kasimasta was a distant blur a little less than half an AU away; at that distance, it looked no more threatening than a cloud of interstellar dust and gas.

Yet even if the Annihilator wasn't going to collide with Nordash, the planet was doomed. Once Kasimasta passed close enough to HD 70642 for its intense gravity to have an effect upon the star, solar flares would be kicked up that would bake the planet's surface. As the *Pride* made its primary approach to the starbridge, we saw that the vast armada that had greeted us only a couple of days earlier had disappeared. Apparently the *nord* had completed the evacuation of their world; if any of their kind had been left behind, they were helpless against the monster rapidly closing in upon them. In any event, there was no traffic around the alien starbridge, nor did we receive any radio transmissions. Nordash was an abandoned house, its former residents long gone.

Once more, I performed a one-eighty that turned the *Pride* around, then fired the maneuvering thrusters that would put us on a proper heading for the ring. Everyone was in the command center except for Ali; although he'd regained consciousness, Ted had relieved him from duty and confined him to the med bay until we returned to Coyote. So the ship was mine, and I'd be lying if I said that I minded having the stick. Perhaps I'd lost *Loose Lucy*, but being able to fly the *Pride of Cucamonga*, at least for a little while, more than made up for it.

As we closed in upon the starbridge, Jas left hisher seat and used the ceiling rails to pull himherself over to my station. I was relieved to see that the Prime Emissary no longer wore hisher weapon; at Ted's insistence, Jas had left it in hisher quarters. Nonetheless, I couldn't help but feel nervous as Jas reached past me to insert hisher key into the *hjadd* navigation system. Nor was I the only one who was on edge. From the other side of the console, Ted kept an eye on Jas as heshe entered fresh coordinates into the keypad.

"You are taking us back to *Talus qua'spah*, aren't you?" he said at last. "No surprises, right?"

Jas's head rose slightly upon hisher long neck. "There is no deception, Captain Harker. Your ship has been programmed to return to Hjarr." The Prime Emissary turned to me. "You may now engage the control system, Mr. Truffaut."

I looked over at Ted. He gave me a nod, so I took a deep breath and switched to autopilot. Lights flashed across my panel, telling me that the *Pride*'s AI was slaved to the starbridge. Now I knew exactly how Ali felt when he'd done this; there's nothing worse than having to put your fate in someone else's hands.

The thrusters fired again, and the *Pride* began moving toward the ring. I checked my harness to make sure that it was tight, then settled back in my seat. But just before the ship crossed the event horizon, I looked across the bridge to where Rain was seated. She'd been continuing to avoid me, and although our eyes met for a moment, she hastily looked away. Once again, I wished I could talk things over with her, but for the time being that was out of the question. I was the pilot, and she was counting on me to get her home.

The wormhole opened. A blinding flash of light, and then we plunged into hyperspace.

XI

Jas kept his promise. When we came out the other side of the wormhole, we were back in the Rho Coronae Borealis system.

The second time around, though, there was nothing surprising. Jas got on the horn and spoke with someone in hisher own language, and a few minutes later the local traffic system took control of the ship and guided it the rest of the way to *Talus qua'spah*. I sat with my hands in my lap and watched while the *Pride* entered the same saucer where it had been berthed before. Once it glided to a rest within the docking cradle, the gangway arms telescoped out to mate with our airlock hatches. Ted and I shut down the main engine and put all systems on standby, then the captain turned to Jas.

"Right, then," he said. "We're back. Now what do you want us to do?"

Morgan was already unbuckling his harness. "For one, I'd like to speak with someone about replacing my cargo. I'm not responsible for . . ."

"Remain seated, Mr. Goldstein." Jas barely looked his way. "Our visit will be brief, but during this time, only one individual will be allowed to disembark." Then hisher helmet swiveled in my direction. "Jules, please come with me."

As startled as I was, I couldn't help but notice that the Prime Emissary had addressed me by my first name. Now that was a change; no longer was heshe calling me "Mr. Truffaut." I was about to respond when Ted shook his head. "I'm sorry, but no. As commanding officer, I'm the person who speaks for the ship and her crew. If the High Council wants to meet with anyone . . ."

"It's okay, skipper. I can take care of myself." Taking a deep breath, I unfastened my harness. "I think I know why."

Ted hesitated, then reluctantly nodded. It only made sense that the High Council would want to see me. After all, it was my screwup that had forced us to undertake the task we'd just completed, and it was also yours truly who'd delivered the *hjadd* probe to Kha-Zann. If anyone was going to answer to the Talus, it should be me. Yet I'd just pushed myself out of my chair when Rain spoke up.

"I'm going, too." She'd already risen from her seat and was pulling herself across the compartment. "I was with Jules, remember?" she added, looking at Jas. "If they've got a bone to pick with him, then they're going to have to pick it with me as well."

Jas's translator must have had trouble making sense out of Rain's colloquialisms—*pick a bone? whose bones?*—because a few moments went by before the Prime Emissary made a reply. "Yes, you may join us," heshe said at last, hisher head swinging back and forth in the *hjadd* affirmative. "However, you should be warned that, by doing so, the Council's judgment may be extended to you as well."

"Rain, don't . . ."

"Hush." Rain gave me a stubborn look, then turned to Jas. "I understand. So . . . let's go."

With Jas leading the way, we floated down the access shaft to the primary hatch, then cycled through the airlock. Jas told us that we didn't need to put on spacesuits, and artificial gravity was restored as soon as we entered the gangway. I was half-expecting to have to undergo decontamination again, but instead we went straight through the reception area without having to stop, take off our clothes, and get another dart in the ass. Yet when we found ourselves at the tram station, Jas stopped and stepped back from us.

"I am leaving you now," heshe said. "You may see me again later, but at this point you will travel in a different direction." Heshe motioned to the waiting tube car. "This will transport you to where you are supposed to go. May fortune be with you."

I didn't quite know how to take this; it sounded rather ominous. As heshe began to turn away, though, Rain spoke up. "Just one question . . . would you have really left us on Kha-Zann, if it had been your choice?'

The Prime Emissary halted, and hisher head swiveled around. "I was considering the safety of the ship. You were expendable."

There wasn't much to say to that, really, except perhaps that I strongly disagreed with hisher assessment of the value of our lives. I doubted that would've made much difference, though, so I simply nodded, and Rain reluctantly did the same, and then we climbed into the car. Jas watched as the canopy slid shut; one last glimpse of himher, standing at the platform, and then the car shot down the tube and out into space.

Hard to believe that we were back there, and so soon. Only a few days ago, I'd thought I'd seen the last of *Talus qua'spah*. Yet as the car hurtled through the immense habitat, I found myself wondering whether I should have stayed aboard ship. Sure, we'd kept our side of the bargain—the *Pride* had deployed the probe and survived to tell the tale—yet I couldn't shake the feeling that the Talus wasn't done with us quite yet. Only this time, I wouldn't have Ted or Emily or Ash or even Morgan to pull my bacon from the fire. Only Rain . . . and I couldn't figure out for the life of me why she'd insisted on sharing the risk.

I didn't get a chance to ask, though, before the car took an abrupt right turn and headed toward a cylinder that we hadn't visited during our previous trip. I'd just noticed that it didn't have any windows when the car began to decelerate. It entered a portal and coasted to a halt at another tram station, and then the canopy opened.

Rain and I climbed out onto the platform, looked around. As before, a sphincter door was recessed in the nearby wall. But this time, there was no friendly voice to tell us what to do; the door irised open, revealing another copper-paneled corridor. The message was clear: *this way, and don't forget to wipe your feet.*

"Y'know," I murmured, "this is a bad time to know me."

"Oh, hell, Jules . . . I've regretted knowing you from the moment we met." I glanced at her, and she softened the blow with a wink and a smile. "Just kidding. C'mon, let's get this over with."

The corridor took us to another door. Upon our approach, it swirled open, but beyond it lay only darkness. I stopped, reluctant to venture in. Rain was just as hesitant; her hand trembled as she took mine. Then a narrow beam of light came from a high ceiling, forming a circular spot upon a bare floor. Again, a message that was both unspoken and clear: *come in and stand here.*

Still holding hands, we entered the room. The door slid shut behind, and when I looked back, I found that I couldn't see where it was. The spotlighted circle was just large enough for the two of us. The room was cold; when we exhaled, the light caught the fog of our breaths. It was as if we'd entered limbo, some netherworld between one plane of reality and the next.

"Okay." Rain let go of my hand to rub her shoulders for warmth. "I guess this is the part where the trapdoor opens and . . ."

At that instant, the whole place lit up, and we were . . .

XII

Back on Kha-Zann.

Everything in the place was just as I had last seen it—same dark purple sky above a barren plain; same sun hanging low upon distant hills—yet somehow different. It took me a second to put my finger on it: utter silence, not even the wind. Yet it was unquestionably Kha-Zann: a ghost of a world that had recently been reduced to nothing more than debris. But how . . . ?

"Jules?" Rain said.

I thought she was talking to me. But when I looked around, I saw that we were no longer alone. A couple of feet away, a human figure wearing EVA gear was staring straight at us. His helmet faceplate was polarized, so I didn't recognize him at first. Then he took a step back. And that's when I realized who it was.

"Good grief," I murmured. "That's me."

It was as if I was watching old footage of myself, scanned two days ago and reproduced as a hologram. Behind me was the crate I'd dragged from the shuttle, its lid on the ground nearby, and now I could see that it was empty. But if that were so, then where was . . . ?

Rain laughed out loud. "Oh, now I get it," she said. "This is what the probe saw, right after you turned it on." She looked to the right, then pointed to the ground beside us. "See? There it is."

She was correct. Where our shadows should have been instead lay the elliptical shadow of the *hjadd* probe. I remembered the instruments that emerged from the probe's core right after it opened;

as I'd figured, one of them must have been a camera, which in turn captured ground-level images of Kha-Zann and transmitted them via hyperlink back to *Talus qua'spah*.

"And there's me." Rain pointed to the left; about a hundred yards away stood *Loose Lucy*. A tiny figure stood within the open hatch of its cargo bay, gazing in our direction. "If I'd known what was happening," she added, suppressing a laugh, "I would've waved."

I was still getting over the strangeness of seeing myself. As I watched, my doppelgänger turned its back to us, and I knew exactly what he . . . or rather, I . . . was looking at. To the east, Kasimasta was coming into view over the horizon, larger than when we had seen it from space.

"Oh, look . . . there you go." As Rain spoke, I saw myself begin to run away, heading for the shuttle. After the first few steps, I started to make bunny hops, trying to make up for lost time. "Okay, now," she said, "here it comes . . . one, two, three . . ."

Everything around us suddenly blurred and jiggled, as if reality itself had turned to gelatin. Apparently this was the moment when the first tremor hit. Right on cue, I went sprawling face-first against the ground. Rain laughed out loud, and I gave her a sour look.

"Not very funny," I muttered. She hadn't realized how close I'd come to smashing my helmet against a rock.

"No, it really isn't . . . sorry." But she was amused all the same. As we watched, I struggled back to my feet and continued running toward *Lucy*, no longer performing broad jumps but instead making an all-out dash for the shuttle. By then the image was in constant vibration; the wind had picked up, and *Lucy* was obscured by blowing sand. "Oh, c'mon," she said. "What's taking you so long?"

"You try . . ." My voice trailed off as, through the windborne silt, I saw myself climb aboard the elevator. As the cage began to make its ascent, I could see the shuttle rocking back and forth upon its landing gear. Even though I knew how this would turn out, my throat felt dry. Sure, it had been a close shave . . . but until then, I hadn't realized just how close.

The cage reached the top, then the crane's T-bar was withdrawn into the cargo hold. A couple of minutes passed, then the hatch shut. At this point, the image was shaking even more violently, but nonetheless there seemed to be a long, breathless pause to the entire scene. I waited, and waited, and waited . . . and then, all of a sudden, there was a billowing explosion of sand and grey smoke from beneath the shuttle.

Loose Lucy silently rose from the ground, riding atop a fiery column that scorched the place where it had once rested. Craning our necks, we watched the shuttle as it grew ever smaller, becoming little more than a tiny sliver that was soon swallowed by the dark sky. By then the tremors were continuous; the shuttle had barely disappeared when the dust storm obscured everything in sight. I caught a glimpse of the crate lid being picked up by the wind and hurtled away, followed a second later by the crate itself falling over on its side. And then . . .

Everything froze.

One instant, we were in the midst of a world's dying moments. The next, we found ourselves caught within a split second of suspended time, as if reality itself had come to a standstill. And at that instant, words appeared in the air, holographically superimposed upon the landscape.

Impressive. Quite impressive, indeed.

The words wrapped themselves around us, forming a semicircle of script. As we turned to read them, we discovered someone was with us.

The *chaaz'braan*.

XIII

The *askanta* holy man . . . well, holy frog . . . stood only a few feet away, unobscured by the dust that masked everything else in sight. Obviously another hologram: no breathing apparatus, but instead the same robes he'd worn the first time we'd met. His heavy-lidded eyes seemed to twinkle with amusement as he raised a four-fingered hand from beneath his robes, but when his thick lips moved, we saw his words instead of hearing them.

Allow me to make us a little more comfortable.

His fingers twitched slightly, and suddenly the scene around us reverted back to the way it had been a few minutes earlier. Once again, my doppelgänger stood nearby, caught in the act of backing away from the *hjadd* probe.

There. That's better.

The *chaaz'braan* sauntered toward my image, stopping to look at it more closely. When he spoke, his words curled around us, forming a ring.

This really was quite an act of courage. You could have simply thrown the probe from your spacecraft and launched again, but instead you chose to place it on the ground and make sure that it was properly activated.

"Thank you." Rain then shook her head. "Pardon me, but I don't understand why you're . . ." She gestured toward the holographic script, which was already fading from sight. "Communicating with us this way, I mean."

The *chaaz'braan* turned to us. Again, when his mouth moved, we heard nothing but silence.

It is the custom of Sa'Tong *that my voice remain unheard, save during formal ceremonies. Like other races of the Talus, I use a translator. Unlike them, though, what I say is transcribed. So this is my way of addressing visitors during informal occasions.*

As he spoke, other figures began to materialize, forming a broad circle that surrounded us: aliens whom we'd seen during the reception, apparently representatives of the High Council. They observed our conversation in silence; I assumed that they were also seeing what the *chaaz'braan* had to say, only translated into their own languages.

"But you didn't do that before." I did my best to ignore our audience. "I mean, when we were at the reception."

Saliva drooled from the *chaaz'braan's* fleshy mouth as it spread into a broad smile.

You didn't give me a chance. That's understandable, considering that you were not in a sober state of mind. Otherwise, we might have had a pleasant discussion.

Again, he turned toward my image. It seemed as if he was studying it with admiration.

This truly is amazing. Such courage is rare among intelligent races. Particularly the* hjadd, *who seldom take risks. At least not if they can get someone else to do it for them.

"So you're satisfied that we've done what you asked us to do?" Rain had noticed the other aliens as well, but she kept her attention on the *chaaz'braan*.

You've performed an immense service to the Talus. The probe didn't survive very long, but while it did, data was gathered that will be invaluable to our scientists. In time, it may eventually help us devise the means by which to destroy Kasimasta.

"Destroy a black hole?" I shook my head. "That's . . . I'm sorry, but that's impossible."

The *chaaz'braan* regarded me with what seemed to be condescension.

Nothing is impossible. Once your kind becomes more sophisti-

cated, you will learn this. Perhaps as you interact with other races of the galaxy.

"Then I take it that we've fulfilled our obligation." I let out my breath. "I didn't have a chance to say so myself, but I'm very sorry that I offended you. We will try not to do so again."

It was only a misunderstanding. You were not informed of the practices and customs of Sa'Tong. The god that is you will know better next time.

The god that is you? "What do you mean by that?"

Sa'Tong holds that there is no god except those that we create ourselves. Therefore, if you have created a god, then you yourself are a god, and therefore are responsible for your own actions.

I nodded. Made sense, although I imagined that a few theologians among my own kind would argue with it. Before I could say anything, though, my image faded away, and the *chaaz'braan* spoke again.

Be that as it may, you must know that, before your kind is allowed to join the Talus, there are other obligations we may wish for you to fulfill.

"Other obligations?" I stared at him. "What do you mean?"

As I said, you have demonstrated a certain fortitude that is rarely seen. This will be useful to us. So before your race is admitted into the Talus, you will be given other tasks that we wish to be performed on our behalf.

"No." I shook my head. "Sorry, but . . . no."

Rain looked around at me, her mouth falling open in astonishment. And indeed, I almost regretted my words even as I spoke them. After all, you don't tell the great galactic frog to go jump a lily pad.

But I knew where this was going to lead. One day, it was risking life and limb to place a probe in the path of a rogue black hole. The next . . . well, what then? Dive a ship into the heart of a supernova

301

to see if we'd get burned? Take on a race of killer tomatoes? Maybe Goldstein would assent to all this in hopes of getting a good deal for his next shipment of cannabis, but I wasn't about to let humankind become the crash-test dummies of the galaxy.

"Look," I went on, "we've kept our side of the bargain . . . and believe me when I tell you that we thought we were going to die doing it. But it's done, and that's it. No more."

The *chaaz'braan's* eyes narrowed.

You don't have a choice.

"Oh, yes, we do." Sucking up my courage, I took a step toward him. "We can go back to where we came from, and never have anything to do with you again. Nice to make your acquaintance, but . . . well, if you think we're going to be your cabana boys from now on, then think again."

From the corner of my eye, I could see the members of the High Council turning toward one another. We couldn't hear what they were saying, but I had little doubt that I'd ruffled fur, feathers, scales, or whatever else they had on them.

"Jules . . ." Rain whispered. "What are you . . . ?"

I ignored her. Too late to back down now. And damn it, it was time to take a stand.

"We are what we are," I went on. "Perhaps we're not as mature as you'd like us to be. Maybe we're going to make mistakes. I know I have, and my friends have had to pay for me being a fool. But you're just going to have to accept that, though, and cut us some slack."

I paused, then shook my head. "But no more conditions. No more jobs. Period."

The *chaaz'braan* said nothing. For several seconds, the air around us remained clear, vacant of floating words. He stared at me for a long time, the wattles of his thick neck trembling with what I assumed was irritation. Around us, the other aliens continued to talk among themselves. Hard not to figure out what they were saying: *who the hell does he think he is?*

I stole a glance at Rain. Her face had gone pale, but she nodded in quiet agreement. I'd just drawn a line in the sand; now we would have to see whether they would cross it. At last, the *chaaz'braan* spoke.

You may return to your world. We will be contacting you soon with our decision.

And then, without so much as a farewell, he faded from sight. An instant later, the other aliens vanished.

The room went dark, save for the shaft of light in which Rain and I once again found ourselves. The door through which we'd entered swirled open, revealing the corridor beyond. Neither of us said anything as we left the room, but as the door shut behind us, she let out her breath.

"So"—she hesitated—"what do we tell the others?"

I shrugged. "We tell 'em we can go home. After that . . . I don't know."

(TWENTY)

Home run . . .

a sudden Rain . . .

key to the galaxy . . .

the narrative ends.

XIV

Three days later, I was sitting in the bleachers of University Field, watching the Battling Boids thump the Fighting Swampers.

The Boids had gotten a little better since the last time I'd seen them . . . which seemed like a lifetime ago, although it had only been a week. Either that, or I'd become a little more forgiving; when the Boid pitcher allowed a Swamper to slide into first on a bunt, I wasn't cursing the way I once might have. Perhaps I'd grown up a bit. Or maybe it was simply because, once you've been halfway across the galaxy and back again, it's hard to take baseball seriously anymore.

Indeed, ever since my return from Rho Coronae Borealis, it had been hard for me to get back into the habits of my old life. Ash was right; now that I'd seen the Great Beyond, nothing was the same again. Oh, I still had my room at the Soldier's Joy, and the previous night I'd trooped over to Lew's Cantina and put away a few pints of ale . . . but when I had finally left the bar, I'd found myself standing in the middle of the street, staring up at the night sky. Somewhere out there were countless worlds whose inhabitants were waiting for humankind to join them. What are beer and baseball compared to that?

But it was more than that. I was alone.

Rain wasn't with me.

When the *Pride of Cucamonga* finally made the jump back to 47 Ursae Majoris, hardly anyone took notice of our return. I wasn't expecting a parade, mind you, but nonetheless it was disappointing to find that no one paid attention to the fact that we'd just completed a journey of more than four hundred and fourteen light-years. Indeed, we practically limped home; there was barely enough fuel left in the tank to get us from the starbridge, and a shuttle had to be sent up from New Brighton to meet us once the ship settled into orbit above Coyote. As the shuttle detached from the docking collar, I caught one last glimpse of the *Pride* through the window beside my seat. Before we'd left, she had merely been a beat-up old freighter. Now, with her cargo modules gone, her shuttle missing, and her hull plates pitted, warped, and scorched, she looked like a candidate for the junkyard.

Nonetheless, she'd brought us safely home. No one said anything as the shuttle peeled away, but I couldn't help but notice Emily rubbing the corners of her eyes, or the way Doc gnawed at his lower lip. I think everyone was saying farewell in their own silent way.

We touched down in New Brighton, and it was there that we saw the last of Morgan Goldstein and Mahamatasja Jas Sa-Fhadda. Once Rain and I had returned to the *Pride* after our meeting with the *chaaz'braan*, I was surprised to learn that Jas had already come back aboard and programmed the coordinates for 47 Uma into the nav system. After that, the Prime Emissary spent the rest of the trip in hisher cabin; when the shuttle landed, Morgan escorted himher to a waiting hovercoupe, and the two of them departed without so much as a good-bye, leaving the rest of us to catch the afternoon gyrobus to New Florida. Hell, we even had to pay the fare ourselves.

Not that our merry band had much left to say to one another. Perhaps it's uncharitable to say it, but the truth of the matter was that we were sick and tired of each other. It had been a long and exhausting journey, and I think all of us were just happy to get home alive. So the ride back to Liberty was made in near silence, and once we got there everyone pretty much went their separate ways. Ted and Emily caught a shag wagon to their house, Doc escorted Ali to the hospital for further treatment, Ash lurched off to the nearest watering hole, and Rain and I . . .

Ah, but that's a different story, isn't it?

Sure, we went back to the Soldier's Joy together. That's where we'd left our belongings; for me, it was the only home I knew, at least on Coyote. But if I had any notions that Rain and I would consummate our romance with a playful romp in bed, I was sadly mistaken. Once we retrieved our room keys from the front desk, Rain gave me a quick buss on the cheek and said that she'd see me later. Since the landlady was giving us the eye, I figured that it was a bad time to push the issue. Besides, I was dead tired; all I really wanted to do in bed just then was study the insides of my eyelids.

So I went up to my room and rediscovered the subtle charm of being able to sleep on a mattress. Eight hours in the hay, followed by a hot shower and a change of clothes, put me in a better frame of mind. The sun had risen on a new day, and I figured that the proper thing to do was find Rain and buy her breakfast. And while we were at it, perhaps we'd figure out what to do next.

Yes, well . . . maybe that's the way things should have gone. But it wasn't the way it went.

When I knocked on her door, there was no answer, and when

I checked the dining room, I saw only a handful of strangers. I was about to go back to her room and try again when the innkeeper spotted me crossing the lobby. Was I looking for my lady friend? Sorry, sir, but she'd checked out earlier that morning . . . and no, she hadn't left a forwarding address.

And that was it. She was gone.

XV

So there I was, watching a baseball game and trying not to feel like a guy whose heart had just been carved from his chest and handed to him, when someone sat down on the bench next to me. I looked around, and saw that it was Rain.

"Hi," she said. "Miss me?"

"Umm . . ." About a half dozen possible responses flashed through my mind, some more heated than others. I settled for the simplest and least angry. "Yeah, I did. Where have you been?"

"Away." She wore a homespun hemp sweater and a long cotton skirt, and it was the first time in a while that I'd seen her in anything that wasn't suitable for space travel; the change was nice. Aware that her reply didn't explain much, she went on. "I needed to get away for a bit, think things over. So I went to stay with my aunt and uncle, and now . . ."

A crack of a bat, and we looked up in time to see a Boid send a fly ball into center field. The Swamper outfielders, slow off the mark, scrambled to catch it, but they recovered too late to prevent the batter from making it safely to first or the guy on second from grabbing third. The crowd around us clapped and shouted, save for the handful of Swamper fans who scowled at another lousy defensive play by their team.

"So you're back," I said, once everyone had settled down again. "Did you . . . I mean, have you worked things out?"

Rain didn't say anything for a moment. She sat next to me, arms propped on her knees, a smile on her face that was both warm and cautious. "What about you? I see you've still got a room at the inn . . . or at least you did when I checked a little while ago."

That must have been how she found me; I'd mentioned to the landlady that I was planning to go to the ball game. "Yeah, I'm still there. Right after you left, Morgan sent over his man Kennedy with a check for what he owed me. Not much, but enough to pay the rent." I shrugged. "Or at least until the proctors haul me off to the stockade."

"They won't." She shook her head. "Whatever else happens, that's not something you have to worry about anymore."

She said this with such confidence that I forgot about the game. "How do you know?"

"Umm . . ." Rain hesitated. "I told you I went to stay with my aunt and uncle, right?" I nodded. "And you know, of course, that my family is pretty well connected?"

I recalled my argument with Ted, shortly before the *Pride* set out for Rho Coronae Borealis, during which he'd quietly let me know that Rain's family owned the Thompson Wood Company. I hadn't thought much about it since then, but now . . . "Yeah, I know that."

"But I bet you don't know just how well connected they are." Moving a little closer, she dropped her voice so that she wouldn't be overheard. "Ever heard of Carlos Montero? Or Wendy Gunther?"

I hadn't been on Coyote long enough to learn all of its history, but nevertheless, those were names that even people on Earth recognized. "Sure. Original colonists. Led the Revolution. Went on to become presidents of the Coyote Federation, one after the other. Why do you ... ?"

My voice trailed off as I suddenly realized what she was saying. Before I could do little more than turn my mouth into a bug trap, she gave me a solemn nod.

"Uh-huh. My mother is Carlos's younger sister. She married into the Thompson family, which makes Hawk and me ..." Realizing that she was about to mention her brother again, she stopped herself. "Anyway, they're my aunt and uncle. Surprised?"

"Yes." That was all I could manage at the moment.

"Thought you might be. At any rate ..." Rain folded her hands together in the lap of her skirt. "While I was staying with them, I told them all about you and how Morgan has tried to screw you out of the deal you guys made. Now, even though Uncle Carlos also happens to be one of Janus's major investors, he's also learned not to trust Morgan very much. And if there's anyone in Liberty with more clout than Morgan Goldstein, it's my uncle."

"So what does this ... ?"

"Mean?" A sly smile. "To make a long story short, this morning he met with the Chief Magistrate, and over coffee he managed to persuade her to drop all charges against you. Not only that, but your plea for political amnesty is being"—a sly wink—"considered. But since you've got him on your side, I'd say it's a safe bet."

I let out my breath, shut my eyes. For a few moments, I didn't know how to respond. Rain must have sensed this, because she took my hand. "It's okay," she murmured. "All you have to do is say, 'Thank you, Rain.'"

"Thank you, Rain." Then I looked at her again. "Do you know just how much I ... ?"

"I'm not done yet."

Down in the batter's box, a Boid finally struck out, ending the fifth inning. I wasn't paying much attention to the game anymore. "There's more?"

"Uh-huh." Rain gently removed her hand from mine. "Speaking of Morgan . . ."

"Oh, crap. Here it comes." I shook my head. "He's not very happy with me, y'know. Not after I dumped his cargo. And I can't imagine he's going to be very pleased about . . ."

"He's not, but that doesn't matter anymore." She hesitated. "He knows about what happened back there. On *Talus qua'spah*, I mean."

I stared at her. We'd been careful not to reveal the details of our encounter with the *chaaz'braan* and the Talus High Council, other than to tell the rest of the crew that we'd met our obligation and had been given permission to return to Coyote. "You didn't tell him . . . I mean, about what I said to . . . ?"

"I didn't, no . . . but he learned that for himself. From Jas." Another pause. "That's the other reason I'm here. Heshe called me last night and told me that heshe wants to see you."

"Jas?" I asked, and she nodded. "When? Now?"

"Uh-huh. Now." She glanced at the field. "Unless, of course, you'd rather wait until this is over."

It was the top of the sixth, with the Boids leading the Swampers 5–2. I figured that my team could get along without me, so I stood up. "No sense in keeping himher waiting," I said, offering her my hand. "Let's go."

XVI

We climbed down from the bleachers and left the field, then walked across the university campus until we reached the low hill overlooking the *hjadd* embassy. An ironic moment; it was at that very same spot Morgan had told me how he wanted to gain access to their technology. In only a week or so, I'd come full circle.

I thought Rain was going to take me the rest of the way to the compound; instead, she stopped and took a seat on the wooden bench beneath the trees. Puzzled, I was about to ask her why, when she looked past me and nodded. I looked around as two familiar figures emerged from the shadows behind a tree.

Jas, once again wearing hisher environment suit. And with himher, Ash.

I couldn't say which of them I was more surprised to see. The *hjadd* seldom left their embassy. Not only that, but judging from his steady gait, I could tell that Ash was stone-sober.

"No, I haven't been drinking." As usual, Ash was one thought ahead of me. "To tell the truth, I haven't touched a drop since . . ." A sheepish grin from within his hood. "Well, since the bender I had right after we got back."

Two days. For him, that was something of a record. "I've been wondering why I haven't heard from you . . . your guitar, that is. You're not at the inn anymore?"

"Checked out the next morning, after I spent the night in an alley." He reached up to pull back his hood. "Y'know, every now and then, an alcoholic receives a moment of clarity when you come to realize that, if you don't stop drinking, you're going to die. I think I had my moment while we were out there . . . just took a little while for it to sink in, that's all."

"So you're on the wagon?" I asked, and he nodded. "Good for you."

"Well . . ." Ash glanced at Jas. "I'm getting a little help from a friend."

"Mr. Ash is working for us now." Jas's voice purred from the grille of hisher suit. "The High Council has reached its decision, so we will need someone to act as an intermediary. I have offered him that position, on the stipulation that he discontinue his alcohol abuse."

"*Sa'Tong* is an interesting religion . . . well, it's not really a religion, or at least not as we know it. However you want to call it, though, it has some neat tricks for learning mental discipline." He paused. "I'm not over it yet, but I'm getting there."

"Well, that's . . ." I suddenly realized what Jas had just said. "Whoa, wait a second . . . what's that about the Talus?"

Jas moved a little closer, until I could see my reflection in the faceplate of hisher helmet. "Upon the recommendation of the *chaaz'braan*, the High Council has decided to invite humankind to join the Talus, provided that your race accepts and agrees to abide by its rules. Even as we speak, the *hjadd* embassy is sending a formal communiqué to the Coyote Federation, requesting a meeting in which we may negotiate trade and cultural exchanges."

For a moment, I was unable to speak. Feeling my knees giving way beneath me, I hobbled over to the bench. "Easy, now," Rain murmured, reaching up to help me find a seat. "Deep breaths . . . thataboy . . ."

"I thought . . . I thought . . ." For the second time in the last hour, I didn't know quite what to say. I took Rain's advice, and once my head stopped spinning, I tried again. "I thought the *chaaz'braan* . . . well, that I'd blown it."

"Blown it?" Jas's helmet cocked to one side. "I fail to understand."

"That I'd said too much. Or said the wrong thing."

"No. What you said to the *chaaz'braan* and the High Council was correct. Humankind has the right to exist on its own terms, without being subservient to others. Your race has met its obligations. There will be no others."

"In other words, they've decided to trust us." Rain smiled at me.

"She's right." Ash nodded. "I've heard about what you said to them. They didn't like hearing it, but it went a long way toward redeeming us." Another pause. "That took a lot of guts, man . . . but it paid off."

Now that was a lot to absorb. At the very least, it wasn't what I'd expected to hear. Another deep breath, then I sat up a little straighter. "So . . . well, that's great. Glad to hear that everything's going to work out for the . . ."

"I have not yet finished." Jas held up a hand. "Once the Talus has completed negotiations with your race, the *hjadd* will be able to resume trade with Coyote. Morgan Goldstein has already expressed his desire to continue transporting consumer goods to *Talus qua'spah*, although I understand that he wants a more equitable arrangement."

I couldn't help but grin. Couldn't blame Morgan for wanting something more useful than two thousand paperweights. And if I never saw another *gnosh* again, it would be too soon. "Sounds reasonable. Of course, he's going to have to get another ship."

Rain nodded. "Another ship, yeah . . . the *Pride* is pretty much shot. Doc's gone back up there to see what can be salvaged before she's scuttled."

I grimaced. That wouldn't be a pleasant task; the *Pride* was Doc's ship, and she'd brought us home alive. Maybe Morgan didn't consider it cost-effective to have her refitted again, but nonetheless it would be painful for Doc to let her go. "I hope he doesn't plan to retire after this," I said. "He's a good man."

"I hope not either. I'd like to work with him again." Rain hesitated. "I hope you will, too . . . once we get a new ship."

"Huh?" I gave her a sharp look. "But Morgan . . ."

"Morgan fired you, yes . . . and now he wants to rehire you." She shrugged. "Or maybe he just decided not to fire you in the first place. At any rate, I've been told to tell you that he'd like to offer you a permanent contract, once a new ship is delivered."

"Same job?"

"No." She smiled at me again. "This time, you've got the helm . . . unless, of course, you'd really rather be a shuttle jockey." She paused, then quietly added, "Don't say no. Please."

I wasn't about to refuse, even if it meant having Morgan as my boss again. "I take it that Ted and Emily still have their jobs, too," I asked, and she nodded. "And you?"

"The only person who isn't being offered a contract renewal is Ali," Ash said. "Or at least not until he learns to manage his temper a little better."

"Do I assume correctly that you are willing to accept this position?" Jas stepped toward me. "Or should I wait until you've made a final decision?"

I didn't reply at once. Instead, I looked at Rain. She said nothing, but something in her eyes told me that she'd make it worthwhile. And I still had a room at the inn . . .

"Sure. I'm in." I grinned. "Why not?"

She moved closer to me. Before I knew what was happening, she gave me a kiss. For someone whom I'd once considered to be a prude, she knew how to do that pretty damn well. I was about to put my arms around her when Ash cleared his throat. Damn telepath. I was about to tell him to get out of my head and go take a cold shower when I felt something prod my shoulder. Looking around, I saw what it was.

A *hjadd* navigation key. Jas held out hisher hand and offered it to me.

"You will need this," heshe said.

XVII

All this happened many years ago. I was a younger man then, immature and a little too full of myself. Looking back at it now, I realize that perhaps there were things that I should have done in a different way. On the other hand, if I hadn't been so young and stupid, would I have been so fortunate to be where I am now?

I don't know. Perhaps it's human nature to second-guess ourselves. What I do know is that I've got a woman who loves me, a ship to fly, and the key to the galaxy. We've been out here for quite a while, and there are still plenty of stars left for us to see.

And I also know Ash was right. If all you want is a normal life, then it takes nothing to stay home. But once you've been to the Great Beyond, nothing is ever the same again.

Trust me.

Trust yourself.

(TIMELINE: COYOTE HISTORY)

EARTH EVENTS:

July 5, 2070 – URSS *Alabama* departs from Earth for 47 Ursae Majoris and Coyote.

April–December 2096 – United Republic of America falls. Treaty of Havana cedes control of North America to the Western Hemisphere Union.

June 16, 2256 – WHSS *Seeking Glorious Destiny Among the Stars for Greater Good of Social Collectivism* leaves Earth for Coyote.

January 4, 2258 – WHSS *Traveling Forth to Spread Social Collectivism to New Frontiers* leaves Earth for Coyote.

December 10, 2258 – WHSS *Long Journey to the Galaxy in the Spirit of Social Collectivism* leaves Earth for Coyote.

August 23, 2259 – WHSS *Magnificent Voyage to the Stars in Search of Social Collectivism* leaves Earth for Coyote.

March 4, 2260 – WHSS *Spirit of Social Collectivism Carried to the Stars* leaves Earth for Coyote.

August 2270–July 2279 – The Savant Genocide; 30,000 on Earth

317

killed; mass extermination of savants, with the survivors fleeing the inner solar system.

April 2288 – First sighting of Spindrift by telescope array on the lunar farside.

June 1, 2288 – EASS *Galileo* leaves Earth for rendezvous with Spindrift; contact lost with Earth soon thereafter.

January 2291 – EASS *Galileo* reaches Spindrift. First contact.

September 18, 2291 – EASS *Columbus* leaves for Coyote.

February 1, 2344 – CFSS *Robert E. Lee* returns to Earth, transporting survivors of the *Galileo* expedition.

COYOTE EVENTS:

August 5, 2300 – URSS *Alabama* arrives at 47 Ursae Majoris system.

September 7, 2300 / Uriel 47, C.Y. 01 – Colonists arrive on Coyote; later known as "First Landing Day."

Uriel 52, C.Y. 02 – First child born on Coyote: Susan Gunther Montero.

Gabriel 18, C.Y. 03 – WHSS *Glorious Destiny* arrives. Original colonists flee Liberty; Western Hemisphere Union occupation of Coyote begins.

Ambriel 32, C.Y. 03 – WHSS *New Frontiers* arrives.

Hamaliel 2, C.Y. 04 – WHSS *Long Journey* arrives.

Barachiel 6, C.Y. 05 – WHSS *Magnificent Voyage* arrives.

Barbiel 30, C.Y. 05 – Thompson's Ferry Massacre; beginning of the Revolution.

Gabriel 75, C.Y. 06 – WHSS *Spirit* arrives.

Asmodel 5, C.Y. 06 – Liberty retaken by colonial rebels, Union forces evicted from Coyote; later known as "Liberation Day."

Hamaliel C.Y. 13 – EASS *Columbus* arrives; construction of starbridge begins.

November 2340 / Hanael C.Y. 13 – *Columbus* shuttle EAS *Isabella* returns to Earth via Starbridge Coyote; United Nations recognition of Coyote Federation.

Muriel 45, C.Y. 15 – *Galileo* shuttle EAS *Maria Celeste* returns to Coyote via alien starbridge.

Hamaliel 25, C.Y. 16 – CFS *Pride of Cucamonga* departs for Rho Coronae Borealis via *hjadd* starbridge.

(ACKNOWLEDGMENTS)

The author wishes to express his gratitude to his editor, Ginjer Buchanan, and his agent, Martha Millard, for their tireless support; to Sheila Williams and Brian Bieniowski, for serializing the novel in *Asimov's Science Fiction*; to Dr. Horace "Ace" Marchant and Bob and Sara Schwager, for reviewing the manuscript and offering suggestions; to Terry Kepner, for astronomical advice; to Patrick O'Connor, for the baseball team ("Beak 'Em, Boids!"); to Chris Offutt, for a phone call when it was needed the most; and to Rob Caswell, for acting as a sounding board during the genesis of this novel.

In addition to the books and articles cited in previous volumes of the Coyote series, works consulted for this novel include: *Infinite Worlds: An Illustrated Guide to Planets Beyond Our Sun*, by Ray Villard and Lynette R. Cook (University of California Press, 2005); *Extrasolar Planets*, by Terry L. Kepner (McFarland & Company, 2005); *Black Holes: A Traveler's Guide*, by Clifford Pickover (Wiley & Sons, 1996); *Black Holes, Quasars, and the Universe*, by Harry L. Shipman (Houghton Mifflin, 1976); and *Black Holes, Wormholes, and Time Machines*, by Jim Al-Khalili (Institute of Physics Publishing, 1999).

—Whately, Massachusetts
August 2006–March 2007